TERROR TALES OF THE MEDITERRANEAN

TERROR TALES OF THE MEDITERRANEAN

Edited by

PAUL FINCH

First published in 2023 by Telos Publishing,
139 Whitstable Road, Canterbury, Kent CT2 8EQ,
United Kingdom.

www.telos.co.uk

ISBN: 978-1-84583-227-8

Telos Publishing Ltd values feedback. Please e-mail any
comments you might have about this book to:
feedback@telos.co.uk

British Library Cataloguing in Publication Data.
A catalogue record for this book is available from the British
Library.

This book is dedicated to the memory of Don Tumasonis

TABLE OF CONTENTS

COPYRIGHT INFORMATION

THE CATACOMB
Peter Shilston

I am retelling this story as it was told to me. Imagine if you can, a coach making a tour of the island of Sicily in the middle of August, carrying a couple of dozen English package holiday-makers on the usual lightning inspection of places of interest – Palermo in two days, Agrigento in another two, Syracuse meriting only one, a trip by chairlift up Mount Etna, and then home. The sort of people one finds on such tours are invariably the same: a number of schoolteachers, earnest retired couples, parents who have inappropriately brought children and are beginning to wonder why they didn't save themselves trouble by going to the beach instead, and a handful of single unattached people. Furthermore, their behaviour is always the same: some spend all their time grumbling at the quality of the hotels and food, the young men wonder why there are no available attractive young ladies on the tour, the children get bored, and the schoolteachers carry guidebooks and maps around everywhere and take enormous numbers of photographs. Others seem to show no interest in the historical sites at all, and spend all their time either sitting in the nearest café or buying various unpleasant souvenirs.

This particular coach party was a typical one, I think. Among its members was a certain Mr Pearsall: a quiet, solitary, middle-aged man of vaguely scholarly appearance. He had enjoyed the tour, and had been duly impressed by the Greek temples of Agrigento and the mosaics in the great cathedral at Monreale, but he had not managed to make close friends of any other passengers, and now that the holiday had only a couple of days left to run, he was looking forward to getting back home again. Consequently he was mildly irritated when old Mrs

Tavistock in the back of the coach started to complain of stomach pains. She had been something of a moaner throughout the tour, but now she was looking genuinely ill, with the result that Giuliano the courier had to ask the driver to stop in the next town, so that a doctor could be brought.

The next town turned out to be a nondescript settlement nestling beneath an enormous cliff, with little apart from this huge overshadowing presence to distinguish it from any one of fifty other small towns that they had already passed through on their tour. Here Giuliano went in search of a medical man, leaving his charges dozing, idly reading their books or making desultory conversation. It was mid-afternoon and the sun was blazing fiercely. All sensible Sicilians were indoors having a siesta. Shutters were down on every window, and not a soul was visible in the street.

After a while, Giuliano returned, and regretted to inform them that they would have to wait at least an hour for Mrs Tavistock to receive attention before they could proceed. In the meantime they could get out and stretch their legs, though it was unlikely that they would find anywhere open. The coach would sound its horn to call them back when it was time to go. Here he engaged in an animated conversation in Italian with Umberto, the driver, who made many emphatic gestures, the upshot of which was some more unencouraging information. The local people, said Giuliano, kept themselves very much to themselves, and there were really no facilities for tourists at all. No coaches normally stopped there, and there was little point in trying to explore the town; really it had nothing to offer. He expressed his regret again and had a few more words with Umberto. Mr Pearsall's command of Italian was not great, but he seemed to detect the phrase, 'can't come to much harm if they're all together.'

Mr Pearsall, however, did not intend to stay with the others as they stood around on the pavement in a pointless fashion. He had glimpsed a church down a sides street as they drove into the town. It had looked old and surprisingly large for such an insignificant place, and he thought it might just be worth an exploratory visit. The 'harm' Giuliano had mentioned (assuming he had understood him right), he took to mean thieves. They had been warned to beware of bag-snatchers in the major cities, but it was hardly likely that gangs of muggers would bother to patrol a town where no tourists ever stopped. The streets seemed absolutely deserted. Besides, Mr Pearsall was still quite fit, and imagined he could hold his own against the average thief; or at the very worst, run fast enough to get away. So, taking his camera, he imparted his intended destination to a fellow passenger (who showed not the slightest inclination to accompany him) and set out at a brisk pace.

The side streets of the town were very narrow and ran steeply up the hill toward the great beetling overhand of the cliff. Some of them had steps in them. Mr Pearsall wondered how claustrophobic it would be to live beneath that great black shadow, and also speculated whether the town was ever damaged by rockfalls. After a couple of turns into dead ends, he found himself in a little grave-strew square, as devoid of people as the rest of the town, facing the church itself. A glance at the sun told him that he was approaching it from the west end; the southeastern corner of it almost touched the base of the cliff. Because it had exactly the same colour and texture as that towering mass, the church gave the slightly disturbing impression of having been carved by the hand of a giant in a single piece out of the living rock.

His first sensation, Mr Pearsall tells us, was of great age and general dilapidation. The church looked far older than the Doric temples at Agrigento which he had admired earlier in the week, though his intellect told him that this could not possibly be the case. He supposed it must be a Norman building, though possibly on an older foundation; Arabic or even Roman. The style was typical enough, though rather ill-proportioned. Two squat heavy towers, with hardly any windows (and those very small) flanked a portico of three large pointed arches. What little decoration there had ever been was now barely discernible. There seemed at one time to have been fresco paintings inside the portico, but now the plaster was badly cracked and in some places fallen away entirely. Only a few dim outlines of human figures – presumably saints – could be discovered. There was a large wooden door, decayed and worm-eaten, with panels carved in what had once been ornate abstract patterns. Moorish influence, said Mr Pearsall to himself, and tried the door. It was locked.

This was predictable under the circumstances, but still annoying. Mr Pearsall retreated to the square to take a picture, and then looked at his watch. A mere fifteen minutes had passed since he left the coach, and he still had plenty of time to kill. The day was hotter than ever, and if there were any shops in this godforsaken place, they were resolutely shut. He decided to stroll around the outside of the church, for sheer lack of anything else to do. Besides, he would be in the shade for part of his walk, and it would be cooler. Without any great enthusiasm, he set out. He was a mild-tempered man, but if there was one thing that caused him irritation, it was suddenly finding himself with nothing whatsoever to do when he had expected to be occupied.

Along the south side of the church, the shuttered houses ran so close that the street was more like a tunnel. He had not gone far when he noticed a small side door. It should cause us no great surprise that he tried to open it, and much to his gratification, found that it was not locked. Surprised at his good fortune, and congratulating himself on his persistence, he went inside.

At first there was nothing to be seen, do dark was the interior after the savagery of the afternoon glare outside. But soon Mr Pearsall's eyes had grown accustomed to the gloom, and he was able to look around him. He knew at once that his walk had been worthwhile. In his tidy fashion, he began to classify what he could see. A long, high nave with aisles on either side: clearly another Norman church; with the pointed arches learned from the Arabs. But unlike some of the others he had seen on his visit, this church had not been revamped later on in the Baroque period. There was not a Corinthian plaster to be seen. The capitals of the columns seemed to be a mass of grotesque carvings, but were so thick with grime that he could not distinguish them clearly. Indeed, the whole interior was very dirty; the pews were thick with dust and the candles so discoloured that they looked as if they had not been lit in years. Clearly they were expecting no visitors, for there was not a guidebook or a postcard visible anywhere.

Then Mr Pearsall saw the mosaics. He had already been initiated into the marvels which the Normans had bequeathed to Sicily in this field, in such staggering compilations as the cathedral of Monreale and the Palatine Chapel in Palermo; but even so, the examples of the art on display at this out-of-the-way place quite took his breath away. Here some nameless craftsman of the twelfth century had taken the Byzantine style and interpreted it with a vigour and a liveliness that were all his own. A veritable poor man's bible of astonishing power covered the walls. Mr Pearsall quite forgot the passing of time as he followed the treasures on display. Here was the creation of the world in a sequence of seven pictures, and there were Adam and Eve tempted by the serpent and expelled from Paradise. More scenes followed; Cain murdering Abel, the building of the Ark, the drunkenness of Noah, the Tower of Babel, Abraham and the destruction of the Cities of the Plain, the sacrifice of Isaac; on and on, each one more startling than the last.

How odd, thought Mr Pearsall, as he moved from scene to scene full of wonder and admiration., that the inhabitants of this town should discourage tourists! Here they had some of the finest mosaics on the island, if not in the whole of Italy, and yet they were left to decay out of sight in a locked and dirty church. Why, with just a little initiative and energy from the town's authorities, visitors would surely come flocking to see such marvels. Did they object to the very idea of tourists? Surely there were enough prospective café owners and postcard dealers in the place to insist that something was done! And why was the church not mentioned in any of the guidebooks which he had read so assiduously before starting on his tour? Such were the musings that passed through Mr Pearsall's mind, but after a while he began to have doubts.

It became noticeable that, though the artist had great natural vigour, it was the portrayal of evil which called forth his finest efforts. The serpent in the Garden of Eden, for instance, was given a human face that bore a sinister and seductive leer. In the story of Cain and Abel, there was no doubt that it was Cain who was intended as the hero; for Abel, as he lay helpless on the ground was a mere hapless simpleton, whereas his murderer, standing over him with a spade raised to cleave his skull, was full of savage power. King Nimrod's soldiers at Babel looked like mindless automata. The picture of Saul and the Witch of Endor was situated in the darkest corner of the church, perhaps deliberately, and was covered with cobwebs. After examining it closely, Mr Pearsall was almost glad of this, for inside the witch's cave were certain unpleasant nonhuman shapes that were perhaps well left unseen.

'Perhaps the artist was a Manichaean,' mused Mr Pearsall. 'A Cathar or an Albigensian (or are they the same thing? Have I got the dates right?), more convinced of the existence of evil than of good. Perhaps his mistakes were condemned as heretical. But in that case, why weren't they destroyed, instead of just closing the church down? Now I wonder what he's made of the New Testament!'

These mosaics were even more unsettling. Mr Pearsall could not find an Annunciation, or even a Nativity, but there was a quite horribly realistic Massacre of the Innocents, in which a number of ingenious and disgusting means had been devised of slaughtering the children, while King Herod sat on his throne overlooking the carnage and laughed. The portrayal of Judas receiving his thirty pieces of silver from Caiaphas would have stood as one of the artistic masterpieces of all time, were it not so exceedingly unpleasant. And so it progressed; through various nasty portrayals of people possessed by devils; through the stories of Simon Magus and Ananias, both of whom once again were the most vivid characterisations in their particular scenes; right up to a terrifyingly powerful portrayal of the Four Horsemen of the Apocalypse.

By this time, not only was Mr Pearsall distinctly upset by the mosaics, but he was feeling increasingly ill at ease. At first, the church had been completely silent, but as time went on it seemed full of little noises he could not locate. His footsteps echoed round and round in a long diminuendo, but they seemed to be answered by odd rustlings and creakings. No doubt these were the normal sounds of rodent life, or of aged woodwork at the start of its death throes; but when, like Mr Pearsall, one is alone in an ancient church in the middle of a strange town where not a single human habitant has yet shown his face, and when furthermore one is surrounded by the most disturbing illustrations of Biblical evil, such rational explanations carry distinctly less force. Once or twice he held his breath and stood perfectly still, to see if the noises continued. Not only that, he also increasingly felt that he was being watched. Probably it was only the faces in the mosaic that caused this, but on more than one occasion he thought he saw movement right in the corner of his field of vision, and whirled around in alarm only to find nothing.

Finally he came to a Virgin Mary who was quite devoid of the usual serenity, but instead had the usual voluptuousness of a vampire. So appalling was her expression that he thought for a while she must be a portrayal of the Scarlet Whore of Babylon, but no, she had the posture and the usual clothing of the Virgin, and there in her arms was the Christ-child, a hideous infant with an oily and sanctimonious grin which put Mr Pearsall in mind of a satiated appetite for something perverse. He shuddered and was filled with a sensation of such acute distaste that for a moment he quite forgot the noises.

All this time, he had avoided looked at the east end, intending to keep till last his viewing what was always the glory of the Sicilian churches; the great figure of Christ in the apse above the altar. Now he could keep from it no longer, and turned his gaze in that direction.

It was indeed a masterpiece, in spite of the dirt and the cobwebs that encrusted it. As usual, Christ's head and shoulders were portrayed, robed in red and blue, the right arm extended in blessing, the left holding an open book lettered in

Greek. The treatment of the material by the unknown artist was marvellous, but the expression on Christ's face was uniquely horrible; a malignant sneer of contempt. The eyes were very piercing. Mr Pearsall could not read Greek, but he suspected that the words written on the open page of the book were hardly a normal scriptural text. And the right hand – was that the gesture of blessing? Or was it the first and last fingers held up – the gesture known as the devil's horns?

'This is a blasphemous church,' said Mr Pearsall to himself. 'The mosaics may be very fine, but they are also very horrible. Some bishop, perhaps even the Pope, condemned them and had the church closed down. Even the townspeople don't like to talk about them, because they are still very religious people, and they don't let tourists in. Just as well, those pictures are enough to give anyone nightmares! Well; I'm glad I've seen them, but it's not a pleasant place to visit on your own, and I can't say I'll be sorry to leave.' He glanced at his watch, and was almost relieved to find that his hour had practically expired; it gave him an excuse to leave without exploring the rest of the church. With a brisk walk that an unsympathetic observer might have though perilously close to a panic-stricken run, he turned away toward the south door, by which he had entered. But now it was locked.

For some time Mr Pearsall struggled in a quiet, futile fashion, shaking the door, twisting the iron ring this way and that, searching for a catch, but he was entirely unable to shift it. He thumped the door with the palm of his hand and kicked it, and a great ringing boom echoed round the church like a salvo of cannonfire, and to this day he swears that from somewhere there came a kind of sinister chuckle in answer.

With a considerable effort, he pulled himself together. 'This is stupid,' he told himself. 'There is probably some custodian who forgot to lock the church up before his siesta, and only realised his mistake when he woke up. But he must be a very careless or stupid man, or he would have checked to see if anyone had gone inside.' All the same, he did not want to knock again and risk that dreadful echo, so he decided to search for another door that might be open. Logic suggested there should be one on the north side, perhaps opening to a cloister or something similar. Crossing the nave with a certain trepidation (and carefully avoiding a glance at the blasphemous figure of Christ, though he imagined he could sense the cruel eyes bearing on him with an almost tangible force), he went in search.

Sure enough, there was a door in the corner of the north aisle, and it was not locked, though it seemed a long time since it had been opened. A strong thrust was needed to shift it, and it groaned horribly as it swung inward, dislodging a shower of dirt. A peculiar must smell seeped into the air. Mr Pearsall found himself peering at a flight of worn stone steps running downward into the darkness.

Now this did not look like the way out at all; indeed, the smell suggested that the lower that the lower chamber, whatever it was, was completely sealed from the open air, and had been so for a very long time. It was a most unpromising route for one wishing to leave the building, and to this day Mr Pearsall has never been able to give a satisfactory explanation of why he decided to descend those steps. He was already late, and after the unsettling effect of the mosaics, most of his exploratory zeal had evaporated, but nonetheless he could not resist the lure of the doorway. He wondered afterwards whether he was in full control of his movements anymore. The whole place bore a distinctly sinister air, but still he had to push the door fully open and take his first tentative steps into the darkness.

The stairs were long and curiously dank in spite of the dryness of the climate. Soon all trace of the light of the main body of the church (which had itself seemed so gloomy when he had first entered) had been lost, and he was obliged to take his cigarette lighter from his pocket and procced by its flickering illumination. He turned a corner beneath a glowering archway of uncut stone, descended a ramp and gasped at what he saw.

It was a catacomb. A long corridor opened before him, with

side passages running from it. Perhaps the whole area beneath the nave was covered. And it was inhabited. A long double line of human forms stood along each passage. All ages and classes had their representatives here; men and women and infants, monks and warriors, learned scholars and ladies of fashion. They were dressed in clothes that must once have been their finest, furs and silks and embroidered gowns, now sadly mouldering and decayed, but bearing still a glimmer of their former glories. And they had faces, for clearly much ingenuity had been expended to preserve the bodies, though with mixed degrees of success. There was a girl-child whose clothing looked at least two hundred years old, but who from her skin and hair might just have fallen asleep; but beyond her a man in priestly robes had lost his nose and his cheeks, and his eyes had decayed to blank milky globules; and further on the soldier in the chased steel breastplate, who was perhaps a mercenary from the Renaissance period, had lost his flesh entirely, and now grinned mindlessly with a naked skull.

Poor Mr Pearsall! The effect would have been quite nasty enough under bright electric lights and surrounded by his fellow tourists; but here, on his own, locked in, and after already being alarmed and upset by those hideous mosaics, and furthermore with just a single weak flame to protect him from the darkness, the shock was overwhelming. Quite why he did not turn and bolt he has never managed to explain. He takes refuge in mysterious talk of 'feeling a call' which dragged him onwards. Certainly it is irrefutable that he walked on down the passage, through the grisly ranks of the dead, horror mounting within him, but quite unable to save himself.

All the bodies had been there a very long time. Mr Pearsall's knowledge of the history of costume was not great, but he was fairly certain that none of the garments worn could be placed any later than the middle of the eighteenth century, and the majority seemed to be medieval. What was left of his rational mind told him that similar catacombs were not unknown elsewhere, but such a piece of information seemed extraordinarily useless. As he walked onward, he appeared to be moving back steadily in time toward the early Middle Ages. Very few of the faces had any flesh on them by this time; some were left almost naked, with their clothing in flimsy rags, and others had simply fallen and lay in heaps on the floor. But still he had to go onward until he reached the end.

He had lost all sense of direction by now, but suspected he was moving beneath the altar, beneath the Christ of the devil's horns blessing and the malevolent glance. And here was the centre of this labyrinth of death; a great throne of gilded wood, much rotted, where sat a body clad in the gorgeous robes and mitre of a bishop. This much Mr Pearsall took in at a distance; but as he drew near, he would not look at the figure directly. He tried to force his eyes to look only at the slippers; he was sure he would lose his reason if he looked higher, but he could not fight as a force stronger than his mind raised his head gradually higher; the gold-embroidered cope, the skeletal hands with the episcopal ring loosely enclosing a bony finger, the crozier propped up in the other hand, the bones of the face bare of all flesh, the ginning yellow teeth, the eyes … the eyes! Not decayed at all, but alive, piercing, glaring! My God! The same eyes as Christ in the mosaic!

The lighter fell from Mr Pearsall's nerveless grasp and he plunged into darkness. It was a lighter of cylindrical shape, and he heard it roll tinkling away out of his reach. For a few seconds he scrabbled uselessly on the floor for it, then realised how pointless such a search was. He would have to find his way out in total darkness. How far was it? How many turns had he taken? He waved his arms in front and to either side, walked a few paces, touched stone, turned, walked more until he met another obstacle, turned again … it was at this stage that he began to hear noises again; a horrible dry rustling, which he would have loved to think was a rat. It came from behind him. He moved quicker, and walked slap into one of the bodies. His face buried itself in the rotting fabric and he felt the lifeless arms slump across his shoulders. His nerve snapped entirely and he screamed; a muffled noise quickly extinguished. He ran at random, hit another body, and ran again, and struck again. Corpses were collapsing all around him, but still there was a rustling and a padding and a dry, gravelly crackling behind him, and it too was moving; not fast, but it soon would reach him if he could not find the stairs. He fell and cut his hands, and screamed again, but not from pain. He lost count of how many times he smashed into obstacles, until, bruised and bleeding, he could go no further, and cowered back against the stone wall. The rustling was quite close now. Light; he must have light! He had lost his cigarette lighter, he had no matches. Frantically his hands searched his pockets for a miracle. Of course! He had flash cubes for his camera! With trembling fingers he pulled one out and fiddled for what seemed like an eternity to fit into place. He pressed the shutter-button and nothing happened. A dud! He turned it around and tired once more. Still nothing. The rustling was only inches away. Think, man, think! He had forgotten to wind on the film, so of course nothing would happen. Pull round the winding lever and try again ... just time ...

In a blinding instantaneous moment he saw; not more than a yard from his face; the golden robe, the mitre, the skull and the eyes, the terrible eyes ...

He must have fainted. When he awoke, it was bright daylight and he was lying on the back seat of the coach. Giuliano was leaning over him. The courier had been told where Mr Pearsall had gone, and when he failed to return on time, Giuliano and Umberto had gone to the church to find him. Entering by the south door (which they emphatically denied was locked) they heard his screams from the crypt and saw the flash. They found him without much difficulty; he was within a few yards of the steps.

Giuliano was more relieved than annoyed, but he chided Mr Pearsall for disturbing the bodies in the catacomb. Banging into them in the dark was careless and destructive, but as for deliberately dragging one body all that way from its resting place ... and it being the body of a bishop too! ...

Mr Pearsall did not have the strength to argue.

DUO OF DARKNESS

As the cradle of western culture and the headwater of so many of the world's great mythologies, the Mediterranean region has spawned countless monstrous and fantastical beings, the majority so hostile to mankind, and so utterly terrifying in power that it took the intervention of the gods themselves, or demi-gods in the form of ancient heroes, to destroy them. However, there are two in particular who transcend all the others, a duo of darkness who are so immediately familiar to us that they haunt our nightmares to this day.

The first of these is probably the most instantly recognisable and yet most fear-inducing of all the antagonists in Greek mythology: Medusa, the Gorgon.

Medusa's most distinctive features are the nest of writhing snakes she has in place of hair, and her ability to irreversibly transform any living thing into stone by simply making eye-contact with it. As monsters go, Medusa is in such a league of her own that she continues to appear in popular culture 30 centuries after the world first came to know of her. Film special effects pioneer, Ray Harryhausen, recreated her unforgettably in his 1981 fantasy adventure, Clash of the Titans, *while even Hammer Films got in on the act, their 1964 movie,* The Gorgon, *casting the alluring Barbara Shelley as an even more evil member of that serpentine species, Megeara, who was related to Medusa even though she was somehow lurking in a Gothic castle in 19th century Bavaria.*

It may interest readers to learn that the story of Medusa is one of the earliest Greek myths ever committed to writing, or at least one of the earliest of which physical scraps still survive (some dated to 500 BC and beyond). The story itself is a horror epic.

Medusa was the youngest of three sisters, Stheno and Euryale her older siblings. They were known even then as 'the Gorgons', which in old Greek means 'dreadful ones,' though that in itself is a contradiction as Medusa, the only mortal member of the trio, was said to be a ravishing beauty. The daughter of two deities, Phorcys and Ceto, she was a devout woman as well as a figure of male desire, and worked as a priestess in the Temple of Athena in Sarpedon (modern day Ayvalik, on Turkey's Aegean coast). It was here, or so legends tell, where the sea god Poseidon was so smitten by her that he attempted to seduce her, and when that failed, raped her on the altar. Enraged by this desecration of her shrine, Athena, who obviously could not punish her Uncle Poseidon, unleashed all her wrath on Medusa, transforming her into a monster of such vileness that no living thing would ever dare go near her again. With snakes for hair and a face that was still beautiful but also terrible, Medusa was reduced to living a hermit-like existence in a remote corner of Libya. Even here, travellers chanced upon her, and all were petrified into stone, so many in fact that Medusa's habitation was soon filled with the statues of men and beasts cowering in terror.

When Perseus, a mortal son of Zeus, was charged by King Polydectes of Seriphos with bringing him the Gorgon's head, he travelled to Libya, convinced that he was facing certain death. However, favoured by the gods, he was furnished beforehand with divine weapons, including a shield (courtesy of Athena herself), which, when he polished it, was as bright and clear as a mirror. When he entered Medusa's cave complex home, he kept his eyes covered by the visor of his helmet and was able to track her among the tortured forms of her victims by the hissing of her snakes. When he confronted her, he established her position through her reflection in his shield, and then struck with his sword, severing her head in a single stroke.

If that seems a rather simple outcome, fear not: the monster had more victims yet to claim.

En route *home, Perseus, carrying his prize in a bloody sack, learned that an Ethiopian princess, Andromeda, was about to be sacrificed to a colossal sea-dragon called Cetus. Immediately falling in love with Andromeda, Zeus's son waited on the coastal rock where she was chained, and as the Leviathan-like horror bore down upon him, lifted Medusa's head from the sack. Cetus promptly turned to stone and fell back into the waves, where its great barnacle-covered remnants can still be seen to this day.*

If that wasn't sufficient as body-counts go, Perseus also later destroyed the entire court of the evil King Polydectes in the same manner.

The popular tale was told and retold throughout the Classical era, Medusa's likeness carved and painted on temple doors and pillars, on bas-reliefs and even pottery. It is these days likened to a parable, the saga of a woman defiled and betrayed by men, and when she finally has her revenge, condemned all the more, transformed into a demoness for the rest of time. Little wonder she is mostly depicted today as the embodiment of female rage.

However, if Medusa personifies femininity gone horribly wrong, the second member of our duo is the polar opposite, and the absolute epitome of male monstrousness. Technically speaking, his actual name was Prince Asterius of Crete, though he is better known to antiquity as the Minotaur.

According to tradition, the Minotaur, or the 'Bull of Minos', was possessed of a tall, powerful human physique, but with a bull's head, a bull's tail, hooves on its feet and claws for hands. Its strength and unfettered savagery meant that it could overpower any opponent, and its lust for human flesh was insatiable. But it is perhaps the circumstances around this monster's conception, and even more so, the manner with which it was used as a weapon of terror, that makes this legend unique among so many others.

The story holds that King Minos of Crete, whose huge navy gave him vast dominion in the Eastern Mediterranean, was a favourite of Poseidon, who one year required a beautiful white bull as a sacrifice. Such an animal was procured with the assistance of the sea god himself, but Minos was so fond of this fine creature that he determined to keep it and used a replacement animal for the ritual. In his wrath, Poseidon compelled Minos's wife, Pasiphaë, to be overcome with lust at the sight of the bull. Unable to resist her abnormal desire, the queen had Daedalus, the royal architect, construct the guise of a cow in which she could hide and which the white bull would mount. The obscene coupling took place, Queen Pasiphaë became pregnant, and when she gave birth, it was to Asterius, a monstrous and uncontrollable being, whom Minos knew would soon become the curse of his island.

Not wishing to slay the creature himself for fear of Poseidon, the king had it enclosed in a labyrinth under his palace at Knossos, a pitch-dark maze of enormous complexity, also constructed by Daedalus. There, it should by rights have starved, but this was only part of Minos's plan. As tribute from a subject nation, the Athenians, Minos was in receipt every seven years of seven virgin boys and seven virgin girls, whom he would offer to the gods by having them thrown into the labyrinth. There, the Minotaur would hunt them down, tearing them to pieces one by one and consuming everything: meat, blood, bone, organs.

This horror only ended when the Prince of Athens, a warrior called Theseus, tired of the bondage his people lived in, volunteered to travel with the seven-yearly sacrifices. Even then, he would not have been able to defeat the Minotaur and escape the labyrinth had Minos's daughter, Ariadne, the High Priestess of Knossos, not fallen in love with him, and provided him with weapons and a ball of yarn, which, if he tied one end of it at the entrance to the labyrinth, would ensure that he knew the correct route back.

From here, the story is well known. Theseus confronted the Minotaur, and after a ferocious battle, slew it, shattering its iron-hard skull with a club, then slicing its neck with his sword, though as so often happens in Greek legends, his triumph would be short-lived. He took Ariadne away with him, fleeing back to Athens on a fast ship, but the priestess sojourned on the isle of Naxos, where she partook in further human sacrifices, which so disgusted the young Athenian that he abandoned her. So distraught was he on sailing back into harbour on the mainland that he forgot to raise a white sail as he'd promised his father, King Aegeus, in the event of success. Seeing a black sail instead, his father threw himself from the cliffs into the sea, which from that point on was renamed the Aegean.

Back in Crete, Poseidon was so angered by Minos's failure to preserve the Minotaur that he sent vast tidal waves to destroy Knossos, Minos himself and much of his kingdom.

It's another of the great Greek 'hero versus monster' sagas, and it figures prominently in the earliest Greek literature, but unlike many other stories of its time, the tale of Theseus and the Minotaur has many traceable links to actual history.

First of all, we know for a fact that the Minoan civilisation, as we call it today, was immensely successful both in seaborne trade and seaborne warfare. Their heyday lay between 2000 BC and 1600 BC, a period of unbridled success, which only ended with some cataclysmic event. Many historians favour the eruption of Mount Thera, again *around 1600 BC, which destroyed countless thriving communities in that region, including many on the island of Crete. This ties neatly with the legend that Minoan glory ended with the death of the Minotaur. It also connects with the semi-factual story that Athens, nothing like the power it would become later, was at this stage subdued by the Minoans and, according to ancient documents, required to pay seven-yearly tribute in the form of human sacrifices. Whether these unfortunates were fed to a monster lurking under the royal palace is moot, but it's not impossible that they were trained for bull-leaping, a high-risk activity that appears in much Minoan art, and would surely have killed them all in due course.*

It is undeniable that when Knossos was thoroughly excavated by the archaeologist, Arthur Evans, in 1900, there was profuse evidence that bull-headed figures and bulls themselves had played a central role in the religion of that ancient place.

Some scholars have speculated that these are actually representations of the horned god, Baal-Moloch, also worshipped widely in the Eastern Mediterranean of the Bronze Age, and another devourer of innocent children, but for those who fear dark entities, the bestial violence of the Minotaur is quite horrific enough.

ON OUR WAY TO THE SHORE
Maxim Jakubowski

We'd just left Palermo when I saw her for the first time.

She was sitting towards the back of the Botanical Lounge sipping a pastel-coloured cocktail, wearing a white cotton top with her shoulders uncovered, her skin a magical shade of porcelain, her auburn hair cascading freely down her back. I couldn't see her face. She was reading a book. I wasn't the only man in the bar to notice her. Heads turned as people walked along the ship's long walkway which ran parallel to the lounge, peering inside through the glass wall at the spectacle of this beautiful young woman sitting there alone. I was equally curious, but I also wondered what book she was reading. I sometimes have a skewed sense of priorities.

We'd embarked in Genoa a few days before, and although I'd already roamed through the ship before I hadn't come across her in any of the bars or the vessel's assortment of restaurants yet. Accompanied or on her own. Neither had she made an appearance at the disappointing drinks reception I had attended for single passengers the previous afternoon.

Palermo had been surprisingly windy, the sirocco in full flow, as our excursion group explored the sea front, and I almost lost my Panama hat to the elements as we exited one of the ice cream parlours on the main Piazza. I had hoped we would stay on shore for longer and I would get the opportunity to visit a local restaurant, but the schedule was too tight. At least in Genoa, I'd had the opportunity to eat locally, sampling again the local pesto sauce with penne, a taste so different from the pesto flavour generally available in England, more subtle and delicate. As I was growing older, food was becoming a greater pleasure than others, which were falling by the wayside through disappointment, indifference, or just lack of practice!

I was on my way back to my cabin. Eager to shower and change clothes. The fierce wind blowing in from Africa while we had been on land had been dusty and stifling; but I slowed down as I passed the Botanical Lounge, intrigued by the woman's presence and curious to see her face. Then decided against fully retracing my steps to do so. Maybe she would still be in situ an hour later when I would have to make my way to the ship's Buckingham restaurant for the formal dinner? As I moved on, I sighed, remembering how in younger days I would seldom invoke a lack of energy or willpower and turn down the opportunity to admire a beautiful woman.

Several hours later, after I ventured into the lounge post-meal, she was still sitting in the same place, now in the shadows, her mane a mass of flames, although she now appeared to be reading a different book. I felt oddly sympathetic: so, I wasn't then the only passenger who went on cruises with the intention of catching up with his reading pile.

I ventured to a nearby armchair.

Peered at the volume she was holding. A well-reviewed South American novel I had heard about but not read.

She glanced up at me.

Her piercing green eyes took note of my presence, as if daring me to say something.

I hesitated.

She set her book down and sketched a smile.

'I'm Sirène ...'

I couldn't place the faint accent. Halfway through Canadian and New Orleans-ish.

'I don't want to bother you, but I'm just curious. You don't appear to have moved from here for hours ...'

'It's a nice bar. It's been pleasantly quiet until now. I was absorbed in my book.'

The place was beginning to fill up now that the first dinner sitting had come to an end. The twin sisters from Kazakhstan who played a classical set on piano and violin were making their way to the back of the lounge, dressed in matching evening attire.

'You were reading something else earlier,' I noted.

'Highly observant of you.' She pointed to a small wicker basket by her feet, from which her previous paperback peered out. I couldn't help myself glancing at its broken spine. A book about mermaids …

I was about to remark that her name was actually French for mermaid, which surely she knew anyway, but the lounge was filling up fast. And any conversation would prove problematic. The Serbian drinks waitress walked over and I ordered a glass of bitter lemon. Sirène rose. 'It's getting too noisy for me,' she remarked. 'I'll be off. Might go for a swim. See you around the ship tomorrow, no doubt.' She was tall and rangy. Her green skirt, reaching down to her knees, was as green as her eyes. Colour-coordinated. I wanted to keep on talking, but my drink hadn't arrived and I was stuck until then. And my tongue was tied, as I searched for the right level of repartee. The music began. Vivaldi. I nodded as she sashayed away.

That night I slept badly. Personal memories assailed me, woven through with visions of Sirène's striking features and a circular dream I couldn't escape from with all sorts of crazy mythologies madly jumbled up as my panic rose, and finally waking up felt like a huge relief.

I arrived at the restaurant for breakfast late, and there was a strange atmosphere. I was guided to a table for six which still had a vacant place. The other passengers who had been placed there were chatting away. It wasn't the usual gossip about previous cruises they had liked or disliked. The rumour was flying through the ship that at dawn, a man had been found drowned in the pool on Deck 12 by early morning attendants. A married couple facing me believed it was a man who was a regular at their dinner table. 'A nice, quiet gentleman, but no one goes swimming after dark, surely,' they pointed out. 'I thought the pool was off-limits after dark,' another breakfaster pointed out.

It was a day at sea and, throughout, the ship's staff carried on their business, albeit with a worried look. Stories about the dead body kept on circulating, a macabre series of speculations and improvisations. That he had been found floating, face-down and stark naked. That his eyes were wide open in death and struck by an air of terror. That there had actually been two sets of towels found by the side of the small pool, indicating he might not have been alone. Travellers were whispering amongst themselves, rumours travelling freely and out of control.

Deaths do occur on cruise ships; they even have to have morgues onboard. It's the demographics of cruising, particularly long-haul journeys, that make this obligatory.

I took the lift to Deck 12 and saw that part of the area had been cordoned off and the pool emptied. The open-air bar, usually a hive of activity at all hours, was unmanned. I was retracing my steps towards the central bank of lifts when I noticed a paperback book abandoned on a deckchair. I walked over and picked it up. It was Sirène's book about mermaids. With a shudder, I then recalled her parting remark, the previous evening, about wanting to go for a swim.

I bent over and took the book and returned to my cabin with it.

I spent a few hours leafing through the well-read and annotated volume. It was a compendium of lore about the mythical creatures and their presence in legends and literature. Sirène (or a previous owner of the book) certainly had strong views on the subject as the pages had hundreds of particular lines and paragraphs highlighted, underlined or peppered with raging exclamation marks. Mermaids were not a subject I had previously given much, if any, thought to, and there was tons of information I had never come across before. All I had known were stories of mermaids on ocean rocks weaving spells and songs to draw sailors and boats to their destruction on reefs and other hidden abysses, or sentimental Disney adaptations. Of course, I didn't believe in them.

There were a couple of pages in a particular chapter about mermaids of the southern seas in local folklore which had been not only highlighted with a purple felt pen but where someone (Sirène?) had drawn a small smiley face! About a group of wild, terrifying mermaids who not only lured sailors to their fate, but also severed their genitalia and wore them as necklaces ... An image that rendered me somewhat breathless as I pruriently pictured it in my mind.

As I wandered aimlessly around the ship during the course of the day, I failed to come across her again. I hadn't yet decided, should I do so, whether I might return the book.

'Can I join you?' The voice was familiar.

I had given the Buckingham restaurant a miss and gone to Borough Market, the ship's more relaxed eatery, with its varied buffet and totally informal seating.

She towered over me, as I took a sip of my mushroom soup. She wore skinny jeans and a tight-fitting T-shirt. She visibly wasn't wearing a bra, the hillocks of her nipples straining against the white fabric of her top. To moderate her height, she had thin-soled ballet flats. Her green nail varnish matched her eyes.

'You're welcome.'

She set down her plate and faced me across the table.

Meat from the grill section. Looked like lamb.

'I didn't know mermaids ate meat. Thought you were on an obligatory diet of fish ...' I remarked.

She grinned. 'I've heard that joke before,' she said.

'Excuse my lack of imagination, then.'

'You're pardoned.'

She cut into her meat, took a bite then looked up at me.

'Have you found the book educational?'

I gulped. 'What book?'

'The one I left by the pool.'

How was she aware of the fact I had found it?

'Well ... I've learned a lot. I'll return it to you next time we cross paths. It's a relatively small ship.'

'No need. You can hold on to it. It's all old news to me.'

There was that grin again. She was toying with me, but did I want to play the game?

We sat in silence, both eating. I finished my bowl of soup and went to the service area to get myself a main course. By the time I had returned to the table, she had gone. Her plate had been cleared by one of the busy waiters, but the only trace of her earlier presence was a half-full glass of sparkling water.

Yet another febrile night of troubled dreams.

The ship docked, as planned, in Bastia on the island of Corsica. Passengers were not initially allowed off and the excursions were postponed. Murmurs began circulating that the ship had been boarded on arrival by the local police, because of the body in the swimming pool. Technically, the accident – or was it a crime – had taken place in international waters so there was little that French jurisdiction could actually do about it. And wasn't the cruise vessel registered, like so many are, in the Bahamas? Was every single passenger and crew member a possible suspect? How could they humanly interview over two and a half thousand people still onboard even if it came under their legal remit?

As we hung on for a further announcement, rumours continued to spread. Someone had spoken to a member of the security team, or the cleaner who had chanced upon the body, or someone who knew someone else in a position of knowledge, and word was circulating that the body had apparently been mutilated. Whispered conversations became increasingly bizarre and speculative.

Around midday, we were given the all-clear to disembark for what was left of the day and explore the town. I was sitting on the lower deck watching people travel down the gangway below, but never caught sight of Sirène. Like me, she must have decided to remain on the ship. I was inclined to look for her but had no idea what deck her cabin might be on and for all I knew she could be anywhere. I couldn't see myself asking about her at reception, describing her to one of the morose Ukrainian staff on duty, not even knowing her actual name. I'd present the appearance of a dirty old man perversely enquiring about what must be the most beautiful younger woman onboard!

I retreated to a quiet corner of the Botanical Lounge and began leafing through the book she had abandoned. On purpose? Reading about the differences between mermaids and sirens, sorting the legends from the rare facts on hand. There was a reproduction of the 1837 William Etty painting of *The Sirens and Ulysses*, depicting the scene from Homer's *Odyssey* in which Ulysses (Odysseus) resists the bewitching song of the sirens by having his ship's crew tie him up, while they are ordered to block their own ears to prevent themselves from hearing the song. While traditionally the sirens had been depicted as human-animal chimeras, Etty portrayed them as naked young women, on an island strewn with corpses in varying states of decay. The central siren had remarkable red hair, which couldn't help but remind me of Sirène. She actually looked like the creature in the painting in all her pre-Raphaelite splendour.

I felt a wave of dread wash over me, as I realised that Ulysses had actually roamed through the Mediterranean on his journeys following the Trojan War. Somehow, in my ignorant mind, I had until now assumed that sirens and mermaids came from farther, more exotic climes and weren't so close to home.

'Playing detective or just research?'

I looked up.

She stood by my chair, lips curled, a mischievous smile dawning across her face.

I was stuck for words.

Then realised she was not alone. Another guy was standing by her side, observing us. He was in his late forties, sporting a brightly-coloured and patterned Hawaiian shirt and cargo pants, almost as tall as she was. I thought I'd noticed him before; he was placed a few tables away from mine in the Buckingham restaurant early sitting.

Sirène turned towards him, reassuring him of her attention. 'Just a fellow passenger I've loaned a book to. We actually don't know each other well.' Then, pivoting round, she took his arm and they headed away. 'If the pool has been re-opened, we were hoping to have a swim, or failing that, a dip in the Jacuzzi …' They walked on.

It felt as if this was all a game to her. I might on occasion write mystery stories, but I was no sleuth, and I was confused by the situation. I set the volume aside. Enough. I'd come on this cruise to relax. And escape the bleak winter at home and the surging heating bills. She was just a pretty woman who enjoyed teasing me badly, and I had no intention of getting caught up in her mind games. But all the bad sleep was catching up with me and I felt bone tired. I returned to my cabin for a doze.

That evening, during the meal, I glanced across at the table where the man Sirène had been with earlier normally sat. His chair was empty.

'Did you hear there was someone who fell overboard earlier this afternoon?' The Scottish widow who had been outrageously flirting with me all week and was my immediate neighbour on our ten-person table was whispering in my ear.

'Really? Tell me more …'

'A few people thought they saw someone falling into the sea from Deck 12 but by the time they raised the alert, there was nothing to be seen in the waters. Apparently there is no way of knowing if it happened without doing a complete census of passengers and crew if no one is reported missing. They will only know for certain once we all disembark as we have to put our electronic cards through the reader.'

'And no one has been reported?'

'Seems not, and those who thought they caught sight of something had been at the deck bar for ages, so who knows?'

'Not quite Agatha Christie, eh?'

She giggled and stuck into her sirloin steak. And ordered yet an extra glass of wine.

Throughout the meal, I kept on glancing back at the empty chair on the nearby table.

Surely not?

We sailed away from Corsica.

Again that night I found sleep difficult, waking repeatedly

with my mind in a tizzy. At three in the morning, and unable to concentrate on anything in particular, I stepped out of bed, slipped on my trainers and jogging pants and made my way out of the cabin. The endless corridors were eerily empty, but then I wasn't expecting crowds. I took the lift to Deck 12. It was not quite a full moon, and the dark skies were utterly cloudless and full of stars. I felt like an intruder in a strange land. I circled the pool and the elevated jacuzzi, not quite sure what I was hoping to find.

But what I did come across confirmed all my suspicions.

Bunched up between two folded deckchairs: a Hawaiian shirt. One I recognised immediately. Same colour, some floral pattern repeated *ad infinitum* across the silken fabric. I actually owned a fairly similar one I'd acquired some years earlier in Aruba. I pulled it out, held it aloft, noticed a red stain at waist level on it, still slightly humid. I brought the garment to my nose, a metallic underscore, definitely blood.

There were now too many damn coincidences for me to dismiss my suspect thoughts.

She must be involved.

But had she no fear of consequences, leaving clues, evidence right out in the open where even an amateur like me could put two and two together? Not that I could fathom her motivations. But then do mermaids or sirens need a reason to kill? Isn't it part of their basic nature, built in, the reason for their existence?

There were only a couple of days left to the cruise. A stop in Gibraltar and then we would dock and disembark in Barcelona. Should I confront her at some stage or just ignore the whole farrago and return to my own life, however imperfect it was? I was neither a detective nor an adventurer. Just a coward, then?

I didn't fall asleep until dawn rose, as the ship arrived in Gibraltar, navigating along the seashore until it reached the terminal, the tall hill overlooking the waters and the docked ship.

I couldn't have slept long, but it was a lullaby of quirky nightmares in which I repeatedly ran out of breath and suffocated, only to open my eyes and find myself back in the cabin, where I would bury my head under the pillow to seek succour again, only to collapse straight into another waking dream, in which I found myself hanging from a cruise ship's funnel – which, like all dreams, made no sense – stripped naked and in excruciating pain. I only understood the pain when I looked down at my pitiful body and saw that I had been fully emasculated, a red, sharp-edged scar pulsing where once I had a penis.

I'm sure I was about to scream in my sleep but then I, blessedly, awoke, in sweat, crumpled white sheets sticking to my body, in a sheer state of terror.

I didn't leave the ship. I'd been to Gibraltar once before and congregated at the top of the rock with the pesky monkeys, and had no desire to play tourist and repeat the experience.

There was no sign of Sirène aboard.

I'm not one for premonitions but felt it wise to keep clear of her should we find ourselves on the same deck, in a bar or along one of the many corridors.

I became a ghost during the final forty-eight hours of the cruise, just eager for it to come to an end.

I snatched food from the buffet and ate in my room, avoiding company. I didn't wish to chance upon her and be attracted to her silent song of attraction and potential horror, as I knew I inevitably would, should we bump into each other, or, more likely, if she supernaturally chased me down with her magical powers.

I had opted to stay in Barcelona for a couple of days following the cruise. It had been several years since I had visited the city last, on a memorable occasion coinciding with San Jordi which Giulia had introduced me to; the local equivalent to Valentine's Day where men offer women flowers and they gift the man with a book in return. I still yearned for Giulia and had booked myself, for sentimental reasons, into the same hotel on Calle Condal in the Ciudad Vieja, where we had stayed.

I fled the ship, looking nervously over my shoulder repeatedly, seeking out that dangerous mane of flame-red hair, but nothing caught my attention amongst the milling crowd of disembarking passengers. There was a long queue for taxis but I arrived at the hotel on Carrer de la Boqueria three quarters of an hour later.

With a tightness in my throat as I approached the reception desk, I recalled how the erstwhile receptionist all those years back had given me a dirty look, noting the marked difference in age between Giulia and myself. No such cursory judgment today for the solo traveller I had become …

The door opened. I breathed a sigh of relief. I was now on dry land and no longer at sea. Possibly no longer at the mercy of mermaids and their murderous, siren calls.

I wasn't of course …

Sirène was sitting on the edge of the bed, her pale legs endless, with a quiet smile on her lips, calmly awaiting my arrival. She wore no lipstick; had no need for it, her coloration natural and discreet.

Why wasn't I surprised?

'You expected me?' she asked, noting my lack of surprise.

'Somehow I did,' I said.

'Good.'

'I'm sure you've been asked many times before, but do you truly have a tail? How do you conceal it? Or is it all a lie cleverly devised through the ages to deceive sailors, the men you wish to seduce? It's always men, isn't it?'

'Don't tell me you believe in all that nonsense? Legends, tall tales and all that?'

'I suppose not.' I'd become resigned to my fate.

She knew my name. Everything about me. The journey that had carried me along to this day, this hotel room, this crossroads in my life, why I had been travelling so much.

'I guess you have a final wish?' the mermaid asked me.

I had.

Not much of a surprise.

'Of course.'

She undressed. I did too. We made love. I tried not to think of Giulia who had shared the same bed, maybe even the same room, with me.

Her body was heavenly beautiful, her flowing red hair falling like sea waves across her pale flanks, her skin the texture of silk, her halting breath like music as I thrust inside her in a vain attempt to mine the depths of her pleasure. And all the while her green eyes bore into mine, drilling a road of kindness to my heart and guts.

When it was over she asked me if I wanted a cigarette.

Like an executioner asking for a condemned man's last request before having him kneel on the scaffold.

'I've never smoked,' I said.

'I see,' she remarked, and there was a devastating kindness in her voice. Outside, night was falling on Barcelona.

'Just one question?'

'Yes.'

'The other men, on the cruise, did you ...?'

'I did.'

'Can I see the necklace?'

'Of course.'

Sirène bent over her side of the bed and pulled out the small wicker basket she had left by the side of the nearby armchair. And pulled the dreaded necklace out.

'Will you wear it for me?' I asked her.

'If you want me to.'

'I do.'

She stepped out of bed and tiptoed to the bathroom where she carefully placed and adjusted the necklace around her neck.

She returned. Stood facing me.

She was damn beautiful, skin with the gloss of porcelain, small, high breasts with nipples almost the same shade of muted red as her lips, not a blemish in sight, tall, regal, the perfect woman of all the dreams, wet and otherwise, I had ever experienced.

The necklace was also beautiful. And, simultaneously, a spectacle of horror.

Six men's cocks severed at the root, in varying shades and girths and lengths, hung from a thin leather strap.

The display was hypnotic.

I found it ironic that seven had long been my favourite number. And that my own penis would become the seventh adornment of the necklace.

'Yes, that's the way the story goes,' she said. 'Now close your eyes.'

I obeyed. And, in darkness, heard her take the scalpel from her basket.

BELMEZ

It is a common misconception that our modern era is the best time there has ever been for forgers of paranormal events. The average person may point at the vast range of resources paranormal hoaxers now have at their disposal. Everything from advanced Artificial Intelligence, which can create ultra-realistic photographs of things that have never existed, to the astonishingly simple PhotoShop app, which enables amateurs to patch together images from various different photographs, again creating vivid depictions of things that have never been, to vast online reservoirs of horror sounds and visuals, allowing the production of scary home movies for a fraction of the previous cost.

But I'd draw your attention to one other important development of the modern age.

As the means by which the faking of paranormal events has improved exponentially, so has the means by which these fakes can be detected.

Which brings us to the perplexing case of the Faces of Belmez.

This is certainly one of the world's eeriest, most famous and yet most photographed incidents of supposed paranormal activity. It commenced in the year 1971, in the prosaic surroundings of Belmez, a provincial town in Andalusia, in southern Spain, but it centres around a woman, Maria Gómez Cámara, who was rumoured locally to be a psychic, though this wasn't her profession; in fact, by all accounts, she rarely indulged in any medium-type activity, which perhaps explains why she was so bewildered one morning that August to come downstairs and find an ugly stain in the middle of the concrete floor of her kitchen.

A stain, which over the next few days transformed into a crude human face.

Maria repeatedly tried to wash it away, with no success, and in fact became so disturbed that she persuaded her husband and eldest son to dig up the floor, which they duly did with pickaxes. What the husband and son thought about this is unclear, but they laid down a *new concrete floor, and life in the household returned to normal. But only for a handful of days, before more faces appeared, all displaying malformed, misaligned features.*

Before the end of the year, word had spread across Belmez, and a constant stream of visitors attended the house. Maria was reportedly unhappy about this, especially when out-of-towners began to arrive as well. Soon, there were huge queues extending down the street. Again, she demanded that her husband and son remove the offending floor, but people clamoured for her to keep it in place, as they were convinced this was some form of message from beyond, though a significant number of these were local shopkeepers, who'd suddenly found themselves doing a roaring trade. Meanwhile, the Mayor of Belmez, suspecting trickery, and concerned that it might make a mockery of his town, instructed workmen to remove the portion of floor on which the main face had appeared, so that it could be subjected to chemical testing. All of this happened, but scientists at the nearby university were unable to detect the use of any known paint or dye, concluding that the curious colour patterns in the concrete had formed naturally.

Those encouraging the new tourist trade were adamant that it was a ghostly occurrence. And indeed, more and more faces appeared, some half-formed, others more like the portraits of real people. Convinced the family were fabricating this whole thing, the authorities ordered them out of the building for several days and put people in place to watch the property. However, when that time had elapsed and it was seen that yet more faces had appeared and that some of the others had even changed, previously scowling visages now grinning, a supernatural cause was deemed the only explanation. Maria agreed to have the ground under her kitchen excavated, but before this happened, local planning papers revealed that the building had been erected on a long-deconsecrated graveyard. That might have been frightening enough, but when the workmen dug down several feet, they found something worse: the scattered relics of several unknown adults, none of whom appeared to have died peacefully or been buried with any kind of reverence.

Investigators suggested that Maria, as an unwilling psychic, might have channelled spirit messages from these forgotten unfortunates, burning the images of their faces onto the floor of her home through use of so-called 'thoughtography', a parapsychic method by which mental images are supposedly superimposed onto solid objects. (In what appears to have been an astonishing testimony to this, when Maria's husband died unexpectedly, the floor in her kitchen, normally a pale grey, was reported to have turned black for the duration of her mourning, though no photographic evidence of this exists).

The scattered bones were removed and buried properly, with Catholic masses said over the graves, but faces continually appeared, and to the incredulity of observers and the many photographers who were determined to keep a full pictorial record of the event (many of their images still viewable online), some seemed to have aged, whereas others, formerly bland of expression, were now twisted in horror or agony. The most inexplicable of all was the serene face of an unknown woman with a number of smaller, childlike faces around her.

The family were again asked to vacate the home, and this time a tape-recording device was left there overnight. In the morning, the tape contained a range of distant, bone-chilling cries and screams. What was more, investigations as to what might have been happening around the exterior of the house on the night in question found nothing untoward.

But even after this, in due course, the sensation waned. Not because the faces faded, but because they continued to appear (and disappear ... of their own accord) until they became a routine part of life in Belmez. Only when Maria, a woman who had never really courted the limelight, died in 2004, was there a revival of interest. By now, many of the images had indeed diminished until they were unrecognisable, only for a second crop of faces to emerge seemingly all at once. However, this latter crop was also subjected to detailed analysis, and this time the results were different, clear evidence indicating that they'd been created by the subtle use of chemicals, the finger of accusation finally pointing at Maria's younger son.

The argument has been made that, as the more recent faces were a hoax, the previous ones probably were too, and that this only remained unproved because, 30 years earlier, testing methods were more primitive. Of course, that can only ever be a theory.

The case of the Faces of Belmez is one of the great mysteries of parapsychology, and it is never likely to be explained.

MEET IN THE MIDDLE
Aliya Whiteley

It had been the last group of the day. From the window of the hut, Peter had spent the afternoon watching the sun getting lower, the side of the hill slipping into darkness. There was no place down in the tunnel to get lost, was there? The whole thing was ridiculous. It made no sense.

It didn't change the fact that two people had to be found.

'We go down there,' said Alexandra.

Peter said, 'We?'

Alexandra, his boss, was wearing the hi-vis jacket and hard hat required for the job – a long day, shepherding tourists, he didn't envy her. He preferred his own unimportant job in the ticket office. She stood in the doorway of the hut and looked him up and down. 'You need to do this now, Peter. There's no time.'

It had sounded, in Peter's head, like the plan of a very young man. Or perhaps a very old man. The ages with less to lose.

That's what he said to his friends on their regular meet up with a half-smile on his face, inviting them to find it funny. He laughed along with them, over their pints – this crazy idea, to sell up, travel, just when the business was going so well and he'd even joined a dating app after the divorce. It would involve renting out the house, too, in such a good position by the park and within walking distance of the gym and the pub. Who knows what kind of tenants he'd get? What state it would be in by the time he got back? So much could change in a single year. They all stopped laughing, and he said out loud what he'd been telling himself. This, the midpoint of life in which he had the most invested, was the perfect time to take a year off. It would mean something, be a profound experience, precisely because of what he left hanging in the balance.

'What if you decide you don't want to come back at all?' said Kyle, as he raised his pint to his lips. Kyle was an architect, serious and deliberate in his slow movements, working to an idea of permanence. Structures that don't disintegrate. It surprised Peter to be thought of as capable of a disappearing act.

'Then I won't have to hang out with you lot anymore,' said Peter. Kyle frowned at the table, but the others laughed and wished him well, and he wondered how much truth there had been in his joke. He didn't think he'd miss them much.

A few months later, in the spring, he left on the Eurostar, with an interrail ticket lined up, and a direction in mind.

South-east. From Paris to Florence, and the vineyards. He wore loose trousers and a collarless shirt, determined not to try to fit in with the gap year students and the fruit pickers still in their teens – no jeans and T-shirts for him. Still, he felt athletic, energised. He wanted to work and eat and live like a young man, and that meant travelling light, pretending he had no reserves: no back-up thousands in the bank, no credit card tucked into his washbag at the bottom of his rucksack.

Employers were amused by him, but happy enough to let him work, and claim a spot in the cheap accommodation blocks and barns, along with the young. It was hard work. He relied on caffeine and extra-strength ibuprofen to get through the first days, but then his body got used to the exercise and he kept pace, and was proud of himself.

The other workers, killing time until the start of university in September, didn't seem to mind the life advice he took to dispensing in the evenings, after they'd all had too much of the local red wine. He talked to them of grabbing opportunities and seeking out adventures, words he would have laughed at when he was young, and they would nod along with his words and fetch him glasses of water. 'You're not used to work like this,' they'd say, sometimes, as if they were.

At the end of the harvest they all went their separate ways and Peter continued south, certain he was both learning and teaching. To Greece. To the small island of Samos.

The southern mouth of the tunnel of Eupalinos was a few miles out from the town of Pythagorio, emerging from halfway up one of the hills that clustered around the harbour. Alexandra's family had been its caretakers for generations. They had built a rough road, cleared a car park, placed a fence around it and set up a hut for ticketed access. The tours into the first part of the tunnel made money.

Peter had only been inside once, when he'd first arrived on the island and had asked around for winter season work. Alexandra had sized him up with that way she had, a sharp unforgiving gaze, and told him he could sell tickets six days a week and live in the hotel complex her brother ran for twenty per cent of his wages. She never asked him questions, or expected to answer any. The most he'd ever heard her speak was during that guided tour he'd taken after accepting the job, when her voice took on an animated, youthful echo about this nearly forgotten wonder of the world.

The Tunnel of Eupalinos was built in the sixth century BC. It stretches for a thousand metres, from one side of the island of Samos to the other, dug out from the rock of Mount Kastro in order to safeguard the water supply to the main town, now known as Pythagorio, in case of siege. Eupalinos was an extraordinary mathematician and engineer. He calculated the route the tunnel should take, then split his digging team into two. He set them to work on either side of the mountain, relying on his mathematical ability to make them meet in the middle. It was the first time scientific calculation had been used to that end.

The teams dug by torchlight, two at a time, managing maybe twelve centimetres a day. Both teams had to trust in calculations they could not understand. They were full of fear and doubt, working in darkness, wondering if the tunnel might collapse, might swallow them, or lead to their gods or monsters.

In the final weeks, each team could hear the tapping of the other approaching, the hammers chipping away, such small amounts each day.

It took eight years for the two sides to meet.

Samos was once a playground for the ancient Romans – one of the most desirable tourist destinations. It had held marvels of religion, logic, science, and faith. How could all those things come together in such a small space?

This was not meant to happen.

He was meant to be free from responsibility, from stress, for a whole year. He wasn't being paid enough for this.

How could two people get lost in a perfectly straight tunnel? There were no diversions, no possibilities for a detour. Only a portion of it was open to the public, a comfortably wide area at the mouth on the south side, with mats and grating placed over the floor so nobody got their feet wet. The trip took twenty minutes – ten minutes in, ten minutes back. Floor-level strip lighting meant nobody had to even strain to see the work of Eupalinos' men.

Further in, the tunnel narrowed and was passable by only one person at a time, reliant on torchlight. Most of that central stretch had silted up in the past, and then had been dug out by archaeologists hundreds of years later. Once he'd heard that, from Alexandra's lips, Peter had pictured it often – that moment of finding it, excavating it, realising what it was: a perfect example of progress. Something about that had frightened him.

'Alexandra?' he called.

His voice was flat, caught between the pointed slabs of the roof. They only lasted for a short length; as the tunnel went lower, the slabs stopped and there was only rough rock above. She was nowhere in sight. She was a short woman, stocky, and he was never sure whether she liked him or not, was older than him or younger. Some people were very hard to read. She seemed committed to adulthood in a way he'd never managed. She had three kids. She'd shown him a picture, once, in a quiet moment. The three of them had been lined up against the mouth of the tunnel in order of height, like miniature versions of her, unsmiling. Maybe he'd said the wrong thing in response to their image, because she'd put it away and never mentioned them again.

He called her name a few more times, thought he heard her answer, further down. He started walking.

The slopes of the Tuscan vineyards had been beyond beautiful, all sweat and curling leaves, swollen grapes, busy days and drunken nights, no time to picture the past or future; he had much preferred it to Samos. He'd slept well every night. In the hotel complex on Samos he lay awake often, thinking about what lay over and under him, behind and ahead. There was a vast old temple not far from the tunnel – well, the remains of it. It had been one of the greatest of all Roman places of worship, according to the tourist signs dotted about the site. He'd visited it on his day off and walked its perimeter, marked by old stones that had fallen. It was a vast site, but impenetrable in meaning. Pieces of figures had sunken into the yellow grass without order; he'd put his hand on a disconnected foot and felt the residual heat of so many summers.

Peter reached the metal bars across the first section of the tunnel, and stopped walking.

VISIT IS ALLOWED TO
THIS POINT ONLY ACCORDING
TO THE MINISTRY OF CULTURE

Beyond the sign, the strip lighting ceased. The tunnel began to narrow.

The idiots must have climbed over.

'Hello?' he called. Strange, his voice, squeezed down the long tube, reverberating back and forth.

'Hello,' said Alexandra, so close to his ear that he flinched, and his torchlight skittered over the rough curve of the ceiling.

She was behind him; how did she get there? He must have passed her, walked right by at one of the wider points, somehow not seeing her.

'Gone over, you think?' she said. She gestured, and the light of her torch swung into the space beyond the railings, outlining it, making it real.

'We should get help,' Peter said. Beyond, it was barely big enough for one person in places, and pitch black, running deep under the mountain until it emerged on the other side.

Could they make it that far? But there, on the other slope, they'd find a small locked gate barring the way. He pictured them emerging into dawn after their long walk, only to find there was no exit. Their hands on the bars, their faces pressed to the light, so tired, so thirsty.

'I go back up and wait for the police,' Alexandra said. 'I get somebody to unlock at the far gate. You go on. Not far. Just to check. Don't go far.'

'I – I don't feel good about ...'

'Peter,' she said, as if she was ashamed of him, as if he was not acting like a grown man. Then she swung the beam of her torch around and jogged away, her footsteps loud. It made the silence seem worse when it came, and he was alone.

This stupid job, he thought. This fucking stupid job. The light and air of the vineyards, the green curling fronds, the heavy fruit.

There was nothing else to do but climb the railings.

He caught his foot on the sign, landed awkwardly. If anyone had seen it, they would have laughed.

There's nobody here, he told himself.

It was difficult to start walking, his ankle twinging, but he finally found some momentum. The sides of the tunnel began to taper straight away – or was it an illusion caused by the beam of the torch, narrowing his vision? No, the roof was closer, and the floor rougher. Loose bits of pebble pinged off his canvas shoes, making a new set of sounds, unnerving.

He walked for what he estimated to be five minutes, although maybe it was less, and the torchlight caught a flash of high-vis orange up ahead: thank God, he thought, as it picked up the dome of the hard hat, too, but it was low, on the floor. One figure, lying down. Hurt. Worse. He broke into a run, couldn't find his voice to call out. The beam shuddered with his steps. He'd had cursory training at school, in first aid and CPR – one afternoon, in the sports hall, and he'd paid no attention – why hadn't he paid attention? But it became more obvious as he got closer that he was not looking at a person. Only a vest, and a hat, placed in a neat pile.

He reached them and ran his light over them, not wanting to touch them. The vest was neatly folded. He thought again of the fallen stones at the temple, deliberately marking territory.

He found his voice. 'I'm here,' he said. It was a stupid thing to say. The wall snatched up the sound, took it along its length.

A different voice returned to him.

It was high, and surprisingly loud. A child. He couldn't make out what was being said, but once it started talking there was no break in the words, repeating, repeating, it had a rhythm, its own language.

'I'm coming,' he called, and moved forward, trotting. The feeling of dampness in the musty air grew stronger. There was another sound – trickling water, underneath. The child stopped talking.

The beam picked out a smooth stone ahead, an obstruction in the tunnel. It uncurled, and straightened to become the back of the child, who stood, facing away from him. The line of the shoulders was very still. The hair was dark, quite long.

'Here,' Peter said.

The child turned.

It was a boy, maybe nine or ten, in shorts and a dirty T-shirt bearing a cartoon drawing of the sun.

'You okay?'

The boy said nothing.

'Okay? Not hurt?' He had learned a few words of Greek, for emergencies, but none of them came to him now. Besides, as the boy began to speak again, Peter became certain he wasn't speaking Greek. It was an odd language, with a phrasing he hadn't come across before. The boy paused at random moments, then spoke again, his eyes latched on to Peter's, the pupils very wide in the torchlight.

The boy pointed further up the tunnel. There was urgency in his strange voice. He took Peter's hand, pulled him further along.

'I should get you back.'

But the boy was adamant. His hand was very cold, and delicate; Peter could feel the bones. Was the child underfed, possibly uncared-for? He let himself be steered along. In no time at all they reached a part of the tunnel that narrowed, and the boy let go of his hand and ran on. Peter bent his head, squeezed in, tried to keep up, but the boy was too fast for him. He couldn't remember how long the tunnel was. His torchlight bobbed on the back of the boy, and the closing curves of the walls.

The boy cried out, and stopped running.

There was a man.

The torchlight picked out a beard, a mass of white hair, an open mouth.

The voice reached Peter: it was a low rumble, like an earthquake; he felt it through the walls. The boy had his hands out as if reaching to be picked up, and the man's eyes were very wide and bright with emotion. Maybe fear, or anger. He hit the boy. It happened very fast. It was a slap, with an open palm, across the boy's ear, and the boy's whole body moved, was carried into the wall, his head colliding with the stone. The force of it was as if the tunnel was shaking, collapsing.

Peter couldn't take his torch away. The man took a handful of the boy's T-shirt and lifted him, very easily. The shirt ripped and the boy's knees gave out, he crumpled, and the man still did not stop. He hunched over, arranged the boy, stretching out his arms and legs, then reached into the boy's stomach. His hand was in the boy's stomach, material was pulled out, something wet, it separated into strands. The man put the strands into his mouth and chewed, he put more into his mouth, he kept chewing. The boy's own hands fluttered up to the face, to the beard, and Peter ran.

He ran back, very fast, shoulders banging on the walls, pebbles clattering. He dropped the torch and did not stop and still he ran, blind, arms held out before him, ran and ran while something, only luck, kept him upright, kept him moving. There was no time. No end. No breath. Nothing hurt. No part of his body felt even a moment of pain even though he knew he could not sustain this, his lungs would give out, his heart would stop. He ran.

Light ahead, blinding. He headed into it, the tunnel widening, and he heard Alexandra calling his name. Relief overtook him, carried him the last stretch of the distance to her, and to two others, in uniform. Police. All energy left him. He collapsed, and they came to him, and asked him, 'What's wrong? What's wrong?' until he had breath to speak.

'I don't get it,' said Kyle.

'It's not a joke.'

He'd chosen Kyle for precisely this reason – the architect, who looked as if no time had passed at all, would not even attempt to see the funny side of it. Not even the bit where the police showed him the person they retrieved from the north end of the tunnel. They'd taken him to the local hospital, and pointed out the shrivelled old man at the far end of an empty ward, sipping water, waiting for his family to arrive and claim him. The policewoman had raised her eyebrows, as if to say: *See? Harmless.*

When Peter had kept insisting on the presence of the boy, on the event he'd seen, he'd been told firmly that only one person had ever gone missing from the tour. Alexandra had agreed. Just one. She'd never said two.

They had offered to take him back down the tunnel to show him, and at that point he had collected his belongings from the hotel complex and flown home.

'Why did you think there were two people down there?'

'That's what she told me. I'm sure.'

'Could you have misheard?' Kyle asked him.

'I mean …' There was no answer to that, but yes. Obviously, yes. But to say it would be the start of travelling down a route with no turns, until he reached a day when he told it as an anecdote. That strange thing that happened to him on his ridiculous gap year. The culmination of his mid-life crisis.

'But you saw him. The boy.'

'I saw him.'

Kyle finished the final mouthful of his pint. Always measured, calm. 'It was real, then. To you.'

Peter thought over the words. He felt a profound wash of gratitude to his friend. Yes, Kyle was his friend. He could return to the world of his house, his job, his dates found by swiping right. This wasn't a bad life, and it was safe. He would stay home. He wouldn't travel, looking for answers, again. Sometimes there weren't answers.

'Another?' Peter asked.

'Great.'

Peter stood, walked across to the bar, and placed the order. The pints were pulled methodically. Behind the bar, above the row of optics and the orange glow of a string of fairy lights, the man from the tunnel was staring at him.

No beard, no white hair, this time. The eyes. The eyes were the same. Held the same emotion.

He jumped back.

'You okay?' said the barman.

'I –'

It was a mirror. Just a mirror. He'd seen his own reflection, met it halfway.

Peter took a breath, let it go.

'You all right, mate?'

'Fine,' he said. 'How much do I owe you?'

He paid, and took the pints back to the table. Kyle was watching him.

'It's okay,' he said. 'I just spooked myself. But I'm fine, really. Anyway. Tell me about you. How's work going?'

He listened to his friend talk about life, commitments, plans for retirement even though that was a long way away. There was plenty of time for it all, but it didn't hurt, Kyle said, to plan ahead. To be a grown-up about these things.

ISLAND OF THE DAMNED

There is so much history and folklore attached to the city of Venice that it could occupy an anthology entirely on its own. And indeed, it has done several times. Once a major maritime trading power and in the modern era a hotbed of tourism, Venice is famous the world over for its grand canals and baroque architecture, for its carnivals and masquerades, and for its overarching atmosphere of faded grandeur and ancient mystery.

But like most romantic Italian cities, it's a place where passions run deep. Many a love affair has been kindled here, but dark deeds have been done too.

Perhaps it's no surprise that ghost stories in Venice are widespread. Daphne de Maurier's bone-chilling 1971 novella, **Don't Look Now***, is a work of fiction, but draws strongly on the city's esoteric past. The Bridge of Sighs is supposedly haunted by the spirits of the many condemned prisoners who were once led across it to their place of execution, while the shadow of Giordano Bruno, an occultist burned at the stake in 1600, is said to wander the Doge's Palace. Though perhaps there is nowhere on the entire Venetian map more disturbingly haunted than Poveglia Island. Located midway between Venice itself and Lido, in the very centre of the Lagoon, Poveglia is no more now than a forlorn relic on the periphery of this wonderfully atmospheric city. A completely abandoned plot of land, it hosts a labyrinthine snarl of ruined, gutted buildings, all deeply overgrown and possessing an air of horror and despair. It's the kind of place you'd rather wasn't there. And with good reason.*

Poveglia first entered the Italian consciousness as long ago as 421 AD, when a horde of refugees arrived there, having fled not just Venice, but other towns on the mainland, in an effort to escape the barbarian tribes forcing their way into what was then the declining Roman Empire. The island was ill-prepared for such overnight inundation, conditions quickly becoming hard. There was overcrowding, hunger, thirst. Disease spread and soon there were deaths. Despite this, a permanent residency resulted, though this ended in 1379 when the small population was evacuated thanks to an advance warning that Genoan pirates intended to attack. Despite all this, Poveglia had not yet made itself a byword for human suffering. But all that would change in the centuries ahead.

The Black Death, a virulent combination of the bubonic plague and various other lethal ailments, visited Europe continuously from the Middle Ages onward, usually killing around one in every three of those it infected. At the time, there were no medical means with which to fight the scourge, and when the plague came to Venice again in 1793, courtesy of two ships that had docked on Poveglia, the citizens felt they had no option but to deport those afflicted over to the island, turning it into a plague colony or lazaretto, a status made permanent in 1805 by Napoleon Bonaparte. Once again, there was mass-overcrowding, and at the same time minimal care. The victims died in droves, the grave-pits quickly overwhelmed. The dead soon lay where they fell, turning slowly to carrion, the stench of which wafted across the Lagoon to the main city. Eventually, corpses were piled into human bonfires, but all this really did was transform Poveglia into a smoky, soot-blackened hell, the charred grease of its tragic victims smeared on everything.

If this wasn't bad enough, the Venetians, who, to be fair to them, were rightly terrified of the plague, ensured that anyone who demonstrated even mild symptoms of illness, any illness apparently, were shipped over there. More humanely, a rule was passed that any sent over who were still alive within 40 days could return, but unsurprisingly, there is no record that anyone did. So terrible was this time on Poveglia that an estimated 160,000 died there, while over 50 percent of its soil is still said to comprise the ashes of incinerated humanity.

It is even claimed that bones still scatter the island, only thinly covered by soil or vegetation, and that Venetian fishermen avoid casting their nets in the vicinity for fear of what they might bring to the surface.

Astonishingly though, worse than the plague was still to follow.

In 1922, the whole of the island was converted into an asylum for the mentally ill. It's difficult to be certain how severely disturbed those sent there were, but once again, it's tempting to assume that Poveglia had become a dumping ground for those whom nobody wanted. Because the inmates here had mostly been forgotten, appalling things were allowed to happen. The staff were often untrained, uninterested and underpaid. Abuse and neglect were therefore rife, while the old plague-era buildings, which were at best functional, were soon crammed again with filthy, uncared-for wretches. As if that wasn't bad enough, doctors arrived who were possibly influenced by the new pseudoscience of eugenics (which would take root most fiendishly of all in Nazi Germany) and who saw their patients as an opportunity for experimentation.

One doctor in particular, a real person though his name seems to have been expunged from the record, spent at least ten years on Poveglia, lobotomising one patient after another, procedures that were often carried out without anaesthetic or antiseptic, the tools used including hammers, chisels and bone-spikes. Many of these so-called operations were supposedly performed in the island's belltower, from the top tier of which the screams of the tortured would often echo across the encircling sapphire-blue waters.

However, perhaps deservedly, this deranged surgeon is the first person we're aware of who fell victim to the supernatural forces now encompassing the island. Driven mad by a cohort of ghosts that he now insisted kept full-time attendance on him, the shades of all those he had butchered, he climbed to the top of the belltower and threw himself off, though he didn't die immediately, suffering multiple injuries and lingering for days, all the time raving that the dead were gathered round him, rejoicing in his pain.

It would later be claimed that this same doctor then joined that legion of the damned, the bell, which no longer existed, now tolled by unseen hands on each anniversary of his death.

The other hauntings on Poveglia are less specific, but they are nonetheless legion. After the mental hospital ceased to function – incredibly, as recently as 1968 – the island passed into private hands, though a succession of owners found themselves unable to inhabit it. Even those with grand plans for hotels, casinos and private villas were dissuaded from proceeding by forces and events they would never give name to in public.

A wide range of poltergeist activity has been reported, while spectral figures are regularly sighted. But Poveglia's brooding *atmosphere is itself terrible, with every roof now fallen in, all rooms cluttered with rubble and inundated by rank vegetation, and many walls defaced by satanic graffiti, implying that Italy's supposedly numerous devil cults can still gain access. Almost no one is allowed to land here. Those who gain permits tend to belong to two groups: they are either seasonal fruit pickers, rich vineyards having sprouted amid the ruins, which suggests that human remains provide good nourishment for certain types of grape; or they are psychics and ghost hunters, many of whom go once and never return.*

A noted Italian medium said on a television programme in the early 1990s: 'There are dark forces on Poveglia that are very hostile to the living. It belongs to the dead now, and that is how it should remain.'

THE LOVERS
Steve Duffy

Though Corbin had visited Marseille on many occasions, he'd never before been to the Turkish baths in the little alley off the Canebière. That evening, feeling grimy and exhausted on his arrival, he decided on the spur of the moment to sweat out the day's exertions, and the porter at his hotel gave him directions to the nearest *bains turcs*. 'There's a Judas,' he said, and Corbin stared at him. 'A Judas,' he said; 'you knock on the door, they look at you, then they let you in. A hole, a spy-hole,' he clarified. Corbin nodded, and turned away abruptly. He disliked pointlessly involved conversations.

He found the address, and knocked as per instructions. There was indeed a Judas, and he must have passed muster, for after a second or two the door unlocked itself with a buzz and he stepped in from the bustling street. Inside the reception area was absolutely silent, with none of the piped muzak with which such establishments often soothe their clients. The place had quite probably remained unchanged since the 1930s: the tiled floors, the dark wood panelling, the green art deco shades that diffused the light from the dim electric bulbs. The combination of the fusty décor and the absence of windows gave the place a claustrophobic feel, to Corbin's way of thinking. It was an unpleasant reminder of his childhood of thirty years ago, all those wasted years of Sunday afternoons pent up in rooms like this where nothing ever happened, dead days evaporating between the fear of God and the threat of school tomorrow.

He paid the nondescript man at the desk, who directed him down a stairwell to the changing rooms. These too were old-fashioned and rather cramped, and again the lighting was barely adequate. A heavy swing door gave access to the baths, and Corbin stepped through into the hissing humidity.

The walls of the main room were tiled in anaemic sea-green, and there was old scuffed marble underfoot. Recessed arches around a central pool held wooden benches for the clients. Three or four men were sitting together in one of the alcoves, towels cast aside; Corbin saw one of them place a hand on another's knee, and noted the smile with which this overture was received. He took care not to show the flicker of irritation he felt. To left and right were entrances to further rooms: he chose the archway on the left, which led to a succession of smaller, more intimate chambers with multiple connecting corridors.

Wanting to get a plan of the place in his head, Corbin passed from room to room, but there must have been an unforeseen complexity in the layout, or the baths were much larger than he'd thought, because keeping to the right did not bring him back to where he'd started. By the fourth or fifth chamber he abandoned the idea and sat in a corner, pushing his damp hair back from his forehead. In the opposite corner lay two other clients, stretched out on adjoining benches, head to head at the corner, within whispering distance of each other. Both wore white towels at their waists, and their heads were covered with white washcloths, moulded by the humidity to the shapes of their faces.

Corbin could feel the heat opening his pores, leaching the toxins from his muscles. He arched his back, hearing the bones crackle, and stretched out his joints pleasurably. With a little grunt of satisfaction, he leaned back and allowed his eyes to close as the steam went about its work.

He'd crossed the border by road from Ventimiglia late the night before, the yawning customs officers glancing perfunctorily at his passport and waving him through. The passport was in the name of Corbin, and bore the stamps of several previous crossings. From there he took the A8 autoroute, *La Provençale*, to the outskirts of Hyères, where he parked his open-top DB Le

Mans on a quiet suburban street, put up the folding roof and dozed for a few hours. Awake before dawn, he strolled into town, taking breakfast in an unpretentious café among unsmiling workmen and slow-moving pensioners who scarcely looked up from their bowls.

Returning to the car, he drove through town to the Presqu'ile de Giens, the peninsula shaped like an upside-down hammerhead that extends south into the Mediterranean. He left the coupé at one of the scenic beaches near the head of the hammer, and proceeded by foot up a rough path that led to the high ground above the Pointe des Chevaliers. Over his shoulder was a khaki knapsack, and Polaroid shades shielded his eyes from the bright summer sun. In his shirtsleeves and chinos, binoculars strapped around his neck, he might have been a hiker or a birdwatcher, or just an everyday tourist.

Cicadas chirped steadily from the gnarled shrubs on the hillside as Corbin followed the track along the top of the limestone bluffs. Below, the sea was a dazzling dreamlike blue as it lapped around the inlets and steep-sided *calanques* cut into the cliffs. In a hollow between two high places on the trail, he stopped and consulted the IGN walkers' map of the Hyères region. So far as he could tell, he was in exactly the right place.

Looking up and down the deserted path, he stepped down into the *garrigue*, a rough mix of thistle and vanilla-scented broom. He tried not to disturb the undergrowth, pushing it aside rather than kicking it flat as he proceeded downhill. A rough stone wall topped with glass shards ran parallel to the path, some twenty metres below it. Nearby stood a Jerusalem pine, dry and lightning-struck. Its roots had forced a crack in the stonework, and one bare limb extended over the top of the wall. With another glance up at the empty path, Corbin nimbly scaled the tree and edged out along the leafless branch before dropping to the ground on the other side.

Before him lay a pleasantly wild garden, with winding brick steps that led down past cypress trees trimmed to teardrops and clumps of high wild lavender. At its foot, the roof of a villa rose amidst the greenery. Past the red pantiles, further down the hillside, the calm cobalt sea twinkled between high cliffs. Corbin studied the vista through his binoculars for a minute or two, then stepped lightly and silently down the mossy path.

The villa was neat and unpretentious, its rustic walls freshly limewashed, the wraparound patio busy with pots and shrubs and garden furniture. Corbin paused under cover of the cypresses and assessed the rear-facing windows. He could see no movement at any of them. Satisfied that nobody was watching, he crossed the black-and-red tiles of the patio, making a knight's move around the white painted tables and chairs towards a pair of folding French doors that stood partly open. Another quick glance inside, and he was in.

In the summertime, this room would soon get stuffy without a regular airing; Corbin supposed that was why the windows had been left open. Facing him across a long polished table were concertina room dividers which would, he guessed, convert the rooms at front and back of the villa into one long space when opened. At the moment they were closed. The formal dining table stood empty, high-back chairs pushed in around its length with a more elaborate seat at the head for the host. The floor was of polished parquet, and the cork soles of Corbin's dusty chukka boots made hardly any sound as he investigated the first of two doorways on the left. One led to a simply appointed farmhouse kitchen, where the smell of freshly brewed coffee hung pleasantly in the air. There were unwashed breakfast crocks in a pile alongside the sink, two of everything. From this, Corbin deduced that there wasn't a *femme de ménage* or cook on the premises. The other door led into the body of the house, and this was where he headed for next.

The hallway was dark, with closed doors on left and right and the only light coming from the narrow windows that flanked the front entrance. A worn *tapis arabe* ran the length of the hall, and the walls were hung with amateur watercolours of sailboats on the sea. All at once there was music playing somewhere in the house, a radio or a record player, a soft dreamy male voice floating over saccharine chords. An unwary person might have flinched at the sound, exclaimed in surprise, but Corbin did not. Instead, treading softly down the hall, he determined that the song was coming from the room on the right, the door to which was slightly ajar.

Listening from the hallway, he could identify the tune: it was Tino Rossi's *J'attendrai*, a song of which his mother had been inordinately fond, and which he consequently found exasperating. He stood near the foot of the stairs and listened carefully, but besides the music he could hear nothing else in the house, nothing moving, neither speech nor sound. Outside, only the soughing stillness of noon. Following the music, Corbin approached the door.

Through the crack he could see open French doors, just like the ones at the back of the house. Net curtains were blowing softly in the breeze from off the sea, towards which a mounted telescope was angled on its stand. The room was furnished as a study: there was a wall of bookshelves, an old-fashioned record player – not a radio, then – from which the music came, and a low leather armchair with drinks holder and ashtray set into the arms, tilted in the direction of the view through the window.

He moved a few inches closer, and one end of a desk came into view. On it was a green shaded lamp, a small geographer's globe with the nations picked out in faded autumn shades on a plain parchment sea, and – again he showed no reaction – two crossed feet in sandals resting on the surface of the desk. The toes of the wearer were twitching slightly in time with the music, he noted.

Corbin tiptoed back to the dining room and removed the knapsack from his shoulder. He set it down on the dining table with extreme care, lest its contents jostle together and make a noise. Each of the items it contained was wrapped and padded against this eventuality, but the essence of his work lay in not taking chances. Lifting back the canvas flap, he reached inside.

He retrieved an item wrapped in a small white towel. Pulling back the corners of the cloth, he closed his hand around the grip of a Walther Model 4 automatic. It was all of forty years old, but it was a reliable, unfussy weapon that was easy to maintain, and it held eight rounds of 7.65mm Browning ammunition. The only modification it had required was the fitting of an adapter to take a modern suppressor. The safety was well-oiled, and made no sound as he pushed it back.

On the radio, the last few bars of *J'attendrai* faded out on Rossi's plaintive high note, and the needle bumped into a crackling loop around the playout groove. By now, Corbin was watching outside the door of the front room again, on the balls of his feet and ready to move. One after another, the sandaled feet were withdrawn from the desk, and the sound of creaking leather suggested that the listener was getting up from his chair. And there he was: through the gap in the doorway a man came into view, bending over the record player and picking up the needle from the disc. His hair was iron grey, thinning a little on top: he was dressed in khaki shorts and a blue striped cotton shirt, and his wiry arms and legs were tanned a deep brown. He might have been a holidaymaker on one of the beaches. Corbin waited till the man straightened up again, then took aim with both hands on the grip and shot him in the back. The suppressor flattened the sound of the shot: someone standing outside the French windows would hardly have realised what he was hearing.

The man stumbled forward, crashing into the record player. The tone arm jolted back on to the record, and a harsh zipping noise was followed by a second or two of music, horribly incongruous, before the man collapsed backwards on to the floor, bringing the table and its contents down as he did so. Corbin stepped up to the body to check if one shot had been enough.

The man was lying face up: one look at him was all it took to see that he was dead. A gaping exit wound at the base of his neck had sprayed a hail of blood against the wall, and the man's open eyes did not flinch when Corbin tapped the corneas with a fingertip. The face, which seemed to show surprise more than anything else, was the one Corbin had seen and memorized in a set of photographs back in Ajaccio. Corbin straightened up and stepped across the body and the overturned table to the wall. Putting the gun on the desk, he took out a hunting knife. With the tip of the blade he gouged the flattened slug out of the plaster and pocketed it along with the knife, wiping both items clean with the towel in which the gun had been wrapped.

On the desk, a mug of coffee was steaming incongruously, losing its heat to the room like the body of the man who had brewed it. Corbin used a clean corner of the towel to pick up the mug without leaving his fingerprints on it. The coffee was not piping hot, but the blend was good, rich and nutty with a floral accent. He drained the mug, replaced it on the desk and considered his next step. There was the towel still in his hand: almost without thinking, he dropped it across the face of the dead man. What now?

There was the telescope: something he should check. Bending to look through the eyepiece he saw a clear sharp image of the beach at the foot of the hill. On a white beach towel a young man lay tanning, flat on his back with his naked body exposed to the sun. Corbin watched him for a minute without expression. Straightening, he glanced at the older man sprawled on the floor, who had been enjoying the same view only minutes before. The landscaped terraces and the fresh salt smell of the sea were pleasant, and Corbin lowered himself into the leather armchair facing the window. To anyone watching, it might have seemed as if he was making himself at home, but the concept was not one that held any real meaning for Corbin.

The man lying on the floor must have spent many hours in this chair drinking in this vista, feeling himself safely removed from the world and its concerns. For the first time in his life, Corbin considered the prospect of retirement, at some point in the indefinable future. It was what people did at the end of their labours. An out-of-the-way place, no neighbours, tucked away on a hillside with a view of the Mediterranean, furnished to suit a tidy bachelor with modest yet well-defined tastes. Idly he toyed with the thought of putting in a bid for this property when it came on the market: the idea was impractical, but he found it diverting nonetheless.

Outside the cicadas sang steadily, *ri-ri-ri*. Many years ago his mother had told him the story of the cicada and the ant, how the careless *cigale* had chirped all summer long while the diligent *fourmi* laid in his store for winter. He had never wanted to be that ant. '*Il ne fait pas bon de travailler quand la cigale chante,*' he quoted softly; 'it's not good to work when the cicada is singing.' Well, there was a little more work still to do. He wasn't retiring just yet.

Someone was whistling on the path up from the beach, still a way off but coming closer. Corbin rose unhurriedly from the chair, took the gun from the desk and pocketed it. He braced himself against the angle of the walls in a corner of the room near the windows, where the billowing net curtains would conceal him at first glance. Anyone entering the room from outside would find it took time for their vision to adjust to the dim interior, more than enough time for Corbin. Imaginative types might glance that way and think they'd seen a revenant lurking in the corner, all ghostly in its shroud, the spectre of the dead man, perhaps, haunting the room. This notion did not occur to Corbin. For a moment, though, he thought of a statue draped in white …

The tune was *Volare*, a liquid trilling whistle, perfectly pitched. Corbin listened to it coming closer, heard the slap of bare feet on the stone slabs of the patio. With a little skip across the threshold, the sunbathing youth entered the room, still unclothed, towel slung over his shoulder. The whistling died away as the verse resolved into the chorus, and the young man saw what was lying on the floor of the room.

A single word, involuntary, his voice catching on the second syllable: 'Alain.' Reflexively the younger man knelt by the body, and Corbin stepped out from behind the curtain. Taking the other completely by surprise, he put his knee hard in the man's upper back, hooked an arm around his head, then yanked it back, all in one brutal jerk. The sound of the snapping spine seemed almost as loud as the shot had been, and no less decisive.

The sunbather gave one convulsive whole-body shudder then lay still, collapsed across the older man. There was no need to check that he was dead: the angle at which his head had come to rest told its own story. Rising to his feet, wincing slightly as the muscles in his shoulder protested at the sudden strain he'd put them under, Corbin contemplated his handiwork. No need to dig around for another bullet, he thought with satisfaction. With an eye to symmetry he pulled the towel from around the young man's neck, arranged it so that it covered his head.

This business of covering the faces: where had it come from? It was a reflex by now, the one part of his routine that had no grounding whatsoever in forensic necessity. And yet he'd been doing the same thing since his very first kill, a man whose name he couldn't even remember, it was so long ago, in a cold room in the nineteenth arrondissement. The man had turned away at the moment Corbin pulled the trigger, and the result had been messy. He was not scared of blood or bone, but the ruin of the man's face had offended his sense of orderliness. It seemed to cast an unfavourable reflection on his ability; hence the cloth across the face. There must have been something that appealed to him in the symbolism, though, since he'd repeated the action on every job since then. Being not in the least imaginative, it had never occurred to him to ask himself what exactly, until now. He rummaged in his memory for correlations.

There was the dank-smelling parish church from his youth, how in Holy Week the bone-white statues would be covered up with starched linen palls. He much preferred them that way; their blank and righteous stares no longer seemed to be fixed so accusingly on him, as if they could read his mind, or tell his future.

There was the family doctor, old Auclair, checking his mother one last time for a pulse and then pulling the sheet over her head. How he'd waited at the bedside for something to change, for emotion to overtake him, and yet in the end it just never happened. In death, as in life, he felt nothing as he looked at her. What lay beneath the lace-trimmed sheet would never move again, and that was an end to it. Had there been cicadas singing through the open window that day? No, that wasn't it: it had been the ticking of the clock on the mantelpiece. Why did he remember that? After a moment, it came to him: the clock had stopped while he was sitting there with the body, no one left now to wind it on a Sunday.

At the graveside, Corbin had wondered whether her face was covered still as she lay in the coffin. It seemed proper, somehow. Before the first wet clod of earth had fallen on the polished wood, the idea had vanished from his mind.

Was that all? There was something else, something at the very edge of his memory: a painting, a reproduction he'd seen in a book maybe, or more likely an illustrated magazine, lying open on a lounge table in one of the hundreds of hotels through which he'd passed. What had that to do with it? He tried to summon up an image. A couple of lovers embracing, their heads swathed in cloth, their identities erased, a kiss that would never be joined lip to lip, skin on skin, the ultimate denial of intimacy and desire. Strange, that he should remember it. Could that be it? What did it matter anyway? It was all in the past, like the statues in the church and his mother in the graveyard, and the two fresh corpses that kept each other company on the floor at his feet. With one last glance he slipped back down the corridor and retrieved his knapsack, wiping the surface of the table clean of any prints with his sleeve.

Retracing his path through the house and up the garden path, he kicked a few stones loose from their crumbling mortar and scaled the wall with the help of the overhanging branch. From the path, everything seemed calm and changeless under the blue skies of summer, and the tranquil cicadas sang him back to the car.

There had been an accident on the autoroute, and the traffic had backed up in a long hot hydrocarbon crawl for miles outside Marseille, leaving Corbin tapping the steering wheel in irritation. Between that and the lingering soreness in his shoulder, a Turkish bath had seemed the ideal preparation for bed and an early start in the morning. And the treatment had succeeded almost immediately, lulling him in a haze of steam and perspiration, the long day's labours trickling away like the condensation that ran down the pale green tiles. Using a technique he'd read about in a magazine, he tried to think of nothing: he gave himself over to sensation, his body being drained limb by limb of aches and pains, a thick anaesthetic numbness creeping up his spine until it filled his empty head. No dreams; he never dreamed. Each night the long dive into nothing, surfacing in the blue bay beneath the villa with the sun shining –

How long had he been asleep? Corbin awoke with an unpleasant chill at his back. The tiles against which he was resting were cold; the steam still rising from the vents seemed thicker if anything, thick enough to lose oneself inside it, but the room was no longer humid. Was there a problem with the heating system? Had the place closed down for the night, and the attendants neglected to tell him? What sort of establishment was this?

The other two bathers were still laying on their benches, exactly as they had been when he entered the chamber. They reminded him of something – the cloths across their faces – but his head was still foggy from sleep, and it took him long seconds to make the obvious connection. Precious seconds.

Corbin tried to stand up, but his limbs wouldn't react. He pushed feebly against the bench with both hands, flexed his knees but the hinges stayed bent, the quadriceps weren't working. Subsiding against the tiles, he tried to collect his thoughts. Loss of control had always been at the heart of his infrequent nightmares: the brakes locking, the car spinning out across the tarmac, the face of the driver in the onrushing vehicle. No time to react, no time … and yet he had lots of time now, enough time to grasp the nature of his predicament, if not its absolute reality, not yet. Enough time to realise that it would be useless to cry out, that no help would be forthcoming in this unfathomable state of affairs. More than enough time for panic, that most unfamiliar of emotions, to set in, if he let it. He fought against it as best he could. Why couldn't he move?

The bathers were moving, those bodies across the room.

Stirring from their repose, bending from the waist, raising themselves ever so slightly from the bench. A man whose nickname was Le Fossoyeur had told him once that this sometimes happened to dead bodies in the morgue, as the muscles stiffened and contracted on the cold marble slab. Sometimes, the man had said, air was expelled from their lungs and they gave a little sigh, a groan. Imagine that, he'd said, with a greasy chuckle. How was he to have known that Corbin had seen enough bodies not to have to imagine anything?

But were these corpses? Had he fallen asleep in the *bains turcs* and woken up in a mortuary? For the first time in a very long time, Corbin knew the torment of uncertainty, and the sensation of fear that came with it. The first death was the final death, and there was nothing beyond. Mother had not moved. The statues were white marble and blank-eyed beneath their shrouds. The lovers …

Now the figures were upright, and perhaps they did groan a little, or perhaps it was him. He was too far gone in brain-fog and panic to tell. The most terrifying thing to him at that moment, he thought distractedly, wasn't even the movement of the blank and faceless men, not yet at any rate. It was the concept of him having shown weakness, however involuntary, an emotion outside his control.

The bathers turned to face him, and now he knew beyond a doubt that it was he who had groaned, for he did it again. Now there was no question as to what terrified him the most. The white cloths still clung to the planes of their faces: the material was taut, the hollows deep, the angles sharp and distinct, as if what lay beneath had very little of flesh about it. Slowly, deliberately, the figures rose to their feet and began to walk towards him. With every last scrap of his willpower, he forced himself upright against the tiles at his back, crabwalking along the wall and through the archway into the next room, away from the bathers.

The next room was the same as the first, only smaller – was that an illusion, a trick of the labyrinth? Or was it that the two bathers sitting on the benches there were taller, larger than the two who were pursuing him? They too got to their feet, faces veiled and unreadable.

Helpless, Corbin tottered through to the next room, and the next, each room seeming smaller than the last, and in each new room the faceless bathers that rose to meet him seemed larger, more threatening. He felt his legs giving way, the muscles no longer responding. Falling to his knees, he crawled on from room to room, scrabbling at the smooth glazed surfaces, too terrified to look behind him.

On he went, until his forehead collided painfully with a blank wall, and he slumped over, moaning, twisting away from the grip of many hands, the silent figures that loomed over him in the thick and clammy steam. Even as the damp cloth wound around his face, he was unable to scream.

WHEN MADMEN RULED THE EARTH

'First among cities and home of the gods is golden Rome,' wrote the poet Ausonius, circa 390 AD.

It is easy to understand what he meant. The world of the Roman Empire captures our imagination with its power and grandeur. Its culture underpins modern western civilisation, and its achievements in an age of chaos beggar belief. Driven by a messianic conviction in their innate superiority, the occupants of a small city-state conquered over a quarter of the known world in an effort to 'civilise' it in their own image, and in the process turned the whole of the Mediterranean Sea into their personal lake. If one complied with the rules of the Roman Empire, life could certainly be good, but as always there were winners and losers in such a story. The Romans were never less than cruel conquerors. Enslavement and exploitation were the standard fate for those who fell into their clutches. For anyone who resisted, it could mean annihilation and even worse – complete erasure from history.

All the rulers of Ancient Rome were ruthless. Nearly all of them considered non-Romans to be vermin. But two of them in particular were far worse than the rest, a demonic duo who would have been regarded as monsters and maniacs in any society in human history. So heinous were their deeds that even toadying Roman writers would find little good to say about them.

The first of these was Gaius Julius Caesar Augustus Germanicus, better known to history as Caligula.

It is quite conceivable that Caligula was clinically insane, though there was no obvious sign of this at the time of his coronation in 37 AD. The son of a war-hero, Germanicus, and official heir to his uncle, Emperor Tiberius, whose reign had started well but gradually drifted into tyranny and debauchery, he was at first seen by the rest of the Empire as a breath of fresh air. Handsome and fond of the arts, he cut an immediately attractive figure, and having been raised in the *military camps of his late-father, was also regarded as a straight-talker and a man's man, someone you could easily do business with.*

But Caligula hadn't been on the throne long before oddities began to emerge.

He spent lavishly, putting on colossal gladiatorial shows even when there was no money for this, and building luxurious new dwellings for himself. In response to non-existent plots, he had his cousin, his brother-in-law and his father-in-law executed, none of whom were given a fair trial, and his grandmother poisoned. Rome was shocked, but this would soon become the new Emperor's normal method of dealing with anyone he considered a risk. In fact, so certain was he that these 'traitors' should die that he often partook personally in their despatch (he hammered one high priest's skull to pulp with a mallet, laughing 'like a hyena' as he did). And the plebs from the backstreets fared no better. On one occasion, Caligula had half the crowd in the arena thrown to the beasts because he felt they didn't appreciate the show he was putting on.

Having emptied the imperial coffers, he filled them again by stripping the temples and the homes of the wealthy, and fining and taxing the ordinary citizens. Even then money was wasted. An abortive mission to conquer Britain, which Caligula led himself, got no further than the shores of northern Gaul, when the emperor inexplicably had his forces gather shells from the beach so that he could proclaim he had defeated Neptune.

This combination of buffoonery and murder didn't just make a mockery of the Empire, it actively endangered it. When holding audience with foreign kings, Caligula insisted on being introduced to them as Jupiter and Lord of All Things, and as such would mock and belittle them as puny mortals who should worship the ground he trod upon. It took a full year for his advisers to talk him out of erecting a statue of himself as the Sun God in the Jewish temple in Jerusalem, which would likely have provoked the rebellion of all rebellions. Stories that he had his horse Incitatus made into a consul are untrue. However, he did grant Incitatus a priesthood. Meanwhile, other senior posts were granted to equally unsuitable applicants because Caligula auctioned them off. But this worst of all Roman rulers is probably best known for his sexual perversions. As a young man, he enjoyed intimate relations with his three sisters, and as Emperor he had them prostituted in a royal brothel, for which he charged astonishingly high entry fees. He was also known for turning up at weddings and blessing the bride by ravishing her in front of her husband and family. Anyone who objected was instantly condemned to death.

Unsurprisingly, Caligula didn't last long.

In AD 41, having cheerfully announced that Rome was no longer the capital of the Empire, and that he intended to move the entire administration to Alexandria in Egypt, he was hacked apart by his own bodyguards. It is perhaps a miracle that his reign had lasted as long as four years.

Second in the imperial hall of infamy is Nero Claudius Caesar Augustus Germanicus, or as history best remembers him, plain old Nero.

Nero was another whose arrival in 54 AD was initially welcomed, yet who in due course would become regarded as one of the worst tyrants in history. Nero's uncle, Claudius, had been a fine administrator and one of the era's more humane emperors, while his childhood tutor, Seneca, was Rome's wisest philosopher. It was felt that such influences in the young heir-apparent's life could only be positive, and hopes were high on his succession.

But in actual fact, Nero had suffered a very abusive childhood.

His mother, Agrippina, had learned about sex from her brother, Caligula, and by the time she'd reached adulthood was renowned for her own excesses, not just taking lovers from the patrician rank but from among servants and slaves as well, and also, apparently, embroiling her underage son in these adventures. In addition, Agrippina was suspected of having murdered a number of rivals, maybe even her own husband, Claudius, a habit that appears to have rubbed off on Nero, because after a promising start to his reign, during which he won a couple of minor wars and donated funds for the improvement of the Empire's cultural life, he suddenly began killing people.

At first, it was the usual rash of 'lawful' executions, his rivals eliminated on trumped-up charges. But then, seemingly bored by the lengthy judicial process, Nero turned to murder. The first victim was his mother, whose domineering ways he had finally tired of. Initially, he tried to have her drowned in a collapsible boat in the Bay of Naples, and when that failed, he sent an assassin to bash in her skull with a club. His wife Octavia had become an irritation too, mainly because he now wanted to marry his new mistress, Poppaea, so in 62 AD, Nero had her immersed in a scalding hot bath and then beheaded. Poppaea, whom historians also implicate in Octavia's death, was mistaken if she'd thought that she at least was safe. It wasn't much later when Nero kicked her to death in a fit of rage, even though she was pregnant at the time. Two years later he got married again, this time to a young manservant, Sporus, whose similarity to Poppaea had attracted the emperor. But just to make Sporus even more suitable, Nero first had him castrated and then changed his name to Poppaea.

After this, it should come as no surprise that sexual deviance was another aspect of Nero's life. He enjoyed seducing other men's wives, usually in the presence of their husbands, and had a penchant for very young slaves, both girls and boys, whom he would leap upon and rape while wearing only a lion-skin. Such a costume might itself have been prophetic as his most infamous atrocities were yet to come.

Unjustly blamed for the Great Fire of Rome in 64 AD, Nero didn't help his position by immediately clearing the burned ruins of the houses so that he could build an extravagant new palace and a colossal gold statue of himself. But once he heard the Roman mob was turning against him, he sought a scapegoat, and so blamed the fire on an obscure but innocent religious sect, the Christians.

In the first instance, Nero had two very practical reasons for being suspicious of the Christians. Firstly, they were associated with the Jews, who in their own country lived in a state of near continuous revolt against Rome. And secondly because they were monotheistic, refusing to accept the existence of any God but their own, which meant they denied the divinity of the emperor. Couple this with Nero's sadistic nature, and you had an unfolding tragedy quite literally of epic proportions – as Hollywood movies like The Sign of the Cross *and* Quo Vadis *would go on to illustrate.*

Scholastic arguments still rage as to how uniquely cruel Nero was to the Christians, some modernists claiming that he was equally murderous with all enemies of the state. But it wasn't just Christian historians who would demonise him for these crimes. Roman authors like Tacitus and Suetonius also recount lurid tales of men, women and children being herded into the arena, having first been clad in sheepskins and daubed with blood so that lions would attack them, or being smeared with pitch and used as human torches with which to light the imperial gardens. So violent was Nero's persecution of the Christians that they would later nominate him the world's first Anti-Christ, making his very name into a coded Greek reference for evil that is still familiar today – 666.

But like Caligula, the hatred Nero spewed out would soon be visited back on him. In 68 AD he was forced to commit suicide by stabbing himself in the throat rather than face the rebel forces of General Galba, who, not content with the label 'Anti-Christ', had also pronounced him the official 'Enemy of Mankind'.

THE WRETCHED THICKET OF THORN
Don Tumasonis

The little island harbour below, so enclosed from the winds by cliffs, was sickeningly hot and humid. Here above, where they had their small hotel, a breeze played constantly across the hilltop and made life bearable. Anticipating the plunge into the furnace, Charles, still acclimatising to the bright Greek sun after a cold and rainy summer at home, stopped for a moment, wiped the accumulated sweat from his forehead, and looked about him.

His gaze wandered to a nearby building under construction. He had stopped here the day before, in an effort to find out whether a luminous rectangle on a wall in the roofless second floor was sky through a real window or light so intense that it pierced the solidity of concrete, dissolving it, turning matter to light and light to substance. In the end he took out his binoculars and, focusing on the spot, saw it resolve into the granulated surface of thrown plaster.

Looking down, he caught sight of Elizabeth's tanned bare legs; she was already well along on the way down to the docks and the restaurants lining the quay. He sighed, and then began to pick his way along the zigzag path, shaded by a plane tree and tamarisks, hoping his body would soon adjust to the heat.

But entering the basin where what life there was on this outlier to the bigger, more heavily trafficked tourist islands had concentrated was equivalent to entering a steam bath. A few beadlets had already re-formed on his brow in the short while since he had started down.

One supposed that the clammy humidity, unusual this far

north in Greek waters, was a result of the place being so heavily wooded. It was green, even greener than Thassos. Most Aegean isles were sun-scorched rocks with rare, if any, natural shade; Charles and Elizabeth had chosen this place just because it promised change from the eternal sun-bleached landscapes that had begun to form the habit of their travel each year.

Before reaching the asphalted bit connecting the path to the main shore road, Charles saw that Elizabeth was, in her impatience to get out of the sticky pre-noon haze, entering post-haste the air-conditioned office of Poseidon Travel. Across the street from that agency, on the narrow town beach, its little flotilla of rental boats was neatly lined up, waiting for the next customer to make a choice for the day's excursion.

Today was the first of September, Elizabeth's birthday, and the climate was still molten in these parts, as Charles had found out to his extreme discomfort the day before. The two had separated: Charles determined to reach the island's highest point, his variant on Munro-bashing developed over repeated visits to the Aegean, whilst his spouse had settled for relaxation on the strand, Sybaris ahead of the local Olympus.

His walk had started well, but the lack of shade had left him exposed to the sun and broiling before too long. Later, alone, with metalled road turned to track, local resin-collectors and any traffic far behind, he had left the cutting for the peak. The place was silent but for the wind.

Charles had never seen brush so dense as on those lower slopes, a thick, barely penetrable maquis. Treelike bushes, plants whose baking in the sun erupted forth with aromatic, pungent odours. And bushlike trees bent by the wind, with thick exposed roots, so rocklike themselves that the stones between their twistings appeared to have grown there, organic intrusions studding and enveloped by the worn mineral bark.

The only way was along animal trails, literal tunnels through the steamy, thorny mass, that made passage a travail of clothing and hair caught in spiky and desiccated vegetation. When he saw his progress to be a few tens of metres that hour, he had given up, disgusted.

Resting on a block of stone in a rare clearing, he had sat facing the nearby island to the east. Gulping water from his plastic canteen, he had regarded the place between swallows. It was greener even than Tiflos.

With half the bottle finished, he had taken out his map, matching names to the prospect in front of him, a favourite private game. The island was Aghios Mikhailis, Saint Michael. The chart showed it to be about half the length of the main island and divided into two distinct sections, each with its own pronounced summit, separated by a narrow saddle-like neck of land in the middle.

The peak on the left was called Frangòberga – something to do with the Franks, a presence here in the Middle Ages? – and the one on the right was called Stefáni, which he vaguely remembered from Greek classes to mean 'bridal wealth' or 'crown'. Through the binoculars, he had explored the visible parts of the opposite shore, four or five kilometres out. There was a white spot high up that hill, probably some herd of sheep eking it out in the sparse shade of the afternoon.

On the long return to town, Charles had suffered near-heat stroke, and took an icy shower to recover. Stretched out nude on the sheet, he had sip of their duty-free Scotch, and read a few pages of Symonds's *Michelangelo*. He had then put the book down and broached the idea of taking a boat out to Aghios Mikhailis, suggesting the outing as the perfect day-trip for a birthday.

By habit, Charles avoided the area of the harbour promenade that he knew was covered with what looked to be a permanent oil slick. As he came up to the spot, he saw a weathered old man, face gnarled and darker than tanned, forcefully throwing something like the head of a wet mop on to the pavement. A rusty three-pronged harpoon, shaft like a weathered broom handle, lay at his feet.

Charles stopped to see, and then realised that the object being thrown was an octopus. The man repeatedly dashed it against the concrete, the hard slaps resonating throughout the seaside neighbourhood. That was the explanation: no motor oil wilfully dumped here, but a slick that was the sudsy juice of cephalopods.

Why did the people do it? The claim was that the animal was only edible if made tender in this fashion. Charles thought, however, that there was more to it than that: some form of revenge, or beating out of a devil, or the liberation of a form forced unwillingly to leave its mortal habitat for a new round on the wheel of all existence.

Unable to say why, he abhorred the practice. There was something nasty and unpleasant about it, connecting at some illogical level in his thoughts with fantasies of furtiveness, and impotence.

When he entered the agency, he saw his wife already seated, chatting and joking with the proprietor, who was related to the owners of their hotel.

'Panagiotis,' she said with a small smile on her face, 'has been telling me how his boats are the best in the Sporades.'

'It's true,' the Greek interjected, standing up to move to the other side of his desk, where Elizabeth sat. He was bearded, bulky and dark, with a gold chain that swung from his neck, like some *faux* crack dealer.

Leaning over her shoulder, the man placed a thick, hairy hand on her bare arm, ostensibly for balance, as he reached with his other for a folder that lay in front of her. He opened it to a section showing coloured photographs of boats, calling Charles over to see. Charles thought that they could just as easily have gone to the window, from which the boats could be seen perfectly well.

While Panagiotis pointed to the various models, extolling their individual virtues, Charles saw that he had not removed his hand from Elizabeth's upper arm. Voluble and vociferous, the words rolled out of him in a friendly bass boom. However, there was a look of stealthy challenge in his eyes each time he glanced at Charles, a look like that of a pickpocket caught in the act, daring a bystander who has discovered him to blow the whistle; a sort of smirk, full of arrogance blended with contempt.

All the while he kept his grip on Elizabeth, while Charles, too polite to react while still unsure about what after all might only have been effusive Greek friendliness, though the saw the man's thumb stroke his wife's bronzed skin lightly, as she imperceptibly leaned in to the Greek.

'Now this boat, it's the one you should have. Only ten thousand drachmas for the day, until sunset, with gas in the tank. A special price for you, my friends, on this, your wife's name-day.' So she had told him of her birthday.

The boat indicated was a quasi-inflatable, a Zodiac-type raft, with rubber pontoon sides and a plywood floor, that took a heavy outboard motor.

'What about that one?' queried Charles, intruding his pointing arm between the two in such a way that Panagiotis was forced to relinquish his grip on Elizabeth. A pout formed on his face like that of a child denied extra sweets.

'Which one?'

'That one, there.' Charles had placed his finger on the picture of a small cabinless in board with a sunshade, made of plastic or fibreglass. He had a vague notion of touring the sea rocks a few miles out in the water, visible beyond the office window, that the large-scale map showed strung out in a line, like beads on a chain from here to Syros. *Perhaps,* he thought, *we could even get to Syros and back, and dive for fish at each of the uninhabited islands along the way.*

'My friend, how much time have you spent in boats? Have you ever driven one before, huh?'

Charles was forced to admit to little knowledge of things nautical; his maritime experience was limited to a few pulls of the oar in rowboats, and a turn or two at the rudder of pleasure craft owned by friends.

'Well, then, don't think about a big boat like that. It will only get you into trouble, my friend. Besides, it costs too much for you.'

It grated to realise how much the islander had sized up their economic status, as did his contempt for their boat-handling abilities, and his constant use of the word *friend* when his relation to them was that of a shopkeeper. Charles nonetheless acquiesced on the choice of vessel, noticing at the same time that Panagiotis had again insinuated his hand on to Elizabeth's upper arm, now massing it openly between this thumb and fingers as if it were a piece of cloth he were testing before deciding on purchase. Was she luxuriating under the attention, or was it his imagination? If she were a cat, would she be purring now?

A contract in Greek and French was signed, something about insurance; money changed hands; and suddenly the man was all business, the cloying attention turned off like a tap. He yelled through the door to a colleague or employee, or, most likely, a family member, 'Dimitri, take these nice people over to number four, and show them how the boat works.' He turned back to the couple. 'Dimitri will take care of you. Where are you thinking of going today?'

Before Charles could frame his answer, Panagiotis continued. 'Maybe you stay away from Aghios Mikhailis. 'There's rocks along the shore you can't see. They can tear the bottom off the boat. Especially around the middle of the island. And the police don't want anyone around the south of the place – the archaeologists are working on a wreck there. *Byzantine.* Too many people going over to watch them, someone might get hurt. Much nicer beaches here, on Tiflos. Stay here.' That last almost coming out as a grunt, he turned on his heel and ambled back to his desk.

And the devil to you, sir, thought Charles. He had already had enough of the Greek's thinly veiled sneering and half-disguised fondling of his wife. They would go where they pleased, now that payment had been made.

Dimitri, a somewhat sullen young man of twenty or so, got up from lubricating a motor he had taken apart, and led the couple down to the inflatable, which was drawn on to the browning sand. In English more broken than that of his chief, he gave them running instructions for the operation of the motor and its refuelling. He drilled them through starting and stopping the motor a couple of times, until he was satisfied they could handle the job. He was more serious than Panagiotis, more concerned with doing his work, and more distant.

With Dimitri gone back to his motor, the two loaded their picnic and gear, and Elizabeth shoved off, nimbly jumping in just after the boat left shore. When the water was deep enough, Charles lowered the motor and started it according to the instructions he had received moments before. He was pleasantly surprised when it took life just as easily as it had during Dimitri's demonstration, although there was no reason why it should have behaved otherwise.

He opened the throttle and, going slowly, they exited the harbour in a few minutes, entering the chop, before swinging to port to follow the coastline northwards. They had discussed their intended route over breakfast at the hotel, and had decided to visit the several bays strung out along the shore of Tiflos, where beaches were promised by the parasol symbols on their crude map. With confidence built by several landfalls, stops and starts, and the boat holding up, they would cross the channel between the two islands at its narrowest point, and visit what was perhaps a settlement that Charles had seen with his binoculars the day before, at the middle of Aghios Mikhailis.

Rounding the point, their cruise along the coast continued uneventfully; that was to say, it went well, and they each handled their end of the routine of landfall and launch in a way that made them begin to feel that they were well suited to the sea. Putting in at the small yacht basin at Steni Vála, way from the bigger boats, they were not displeased with the lack of attention paid to them, since it meant that they had handled themselves in a passably honourable nautical fashion, which was what they had hoped. Beaching the craft, they went ashore and had an iced drink on the verandah of the small marina café before starting out again.

The next stretch was longer, past the middle of the island to Aghios Dimitros. Its umbrella on the map called forth undue optimism; the triangular cape was loose shingle of large rounded stones. A pair he recognised as French, from having exchanged a few words with them in town, occupied one end of the enormous strand. Elizabeth and Charles so no reason to linger; at the narrowest point between Aghios Mikhailis and Tiflos, they were eager to get on with their odyssey of one day and cross the strait to *terra incognita.*

The sun was out as they crossed over but, with the breeze, the air was cool. Elizabeth removed her top and let her naked breasts catch the sun and spray. Charles, hand on the throttle, watched her with a mixture of admiration and exasperation. He did not share the typical sunseeker's disdain for local custom, and was afraid that even on this deserted stretch of sea someone might see them and try his hand at pestering them afterwards, justifying the unwanted attention with the excuse that Elizabeth was a loose woman.

She, for her part, did not care a bit what the locals might think. They were only here for a week, and the chances they would be remembered when they came back – *if* they came back – were minimal. Charles was a prude in any case, and she would do as she pleased, Greek sensibility be damned. Besides, she thought the local men nice, and was not averse to the idea that more attention might be paid to her if she was, in her desert innocence, reported back to Panagiotis by some rumour-monger shepherd hidden in the hills, watching through binoculars.

The northern part of the island loomed before them; the water seemed deep enough to manoeuvre in close to the cliffs. Charles, without a hat, was feeling the effects of the sun and wanted the few yards of shade that the steep slope could provide. They entered the narrow shadow and Elizabeth, sighing, drew her top back on, and watched the depth as they sped on. Hugging the coast for a quarter of an hour, they burst into sunshine again when the cliffs turned to low hills. The middle of the island broadened to contain the sheltered bay of Vassiliko, where Charles had seen some traces of habitation from his perch the day before.

They eased around the northern point of the opening and he

cut the boat's speed, seeing numerous low-lying jagged rocks that broke the surface on the approach to shore. Carefully navigating past these, they saw an arm of the bay appear and grow to port; a small homestead or summer farm lay at its head. Because of the rocks, and also on account of his unwillingness to expose their craft and selves to the curious pokings and proddings of local adults and children bound to assemble if they landed nearby, Charles pointed the prow at a sandy flat a hundred yards or more away from the buildings.

There was only one main whitewashed house, meaning that no more than a single family lived here. Some olive-oil cans, tops removed, sported wilting geraniums; a few unpainted rails and drystone walls topped with dried-out thorns were corrals for sheep or goats. The area immediately around the structure, long grassless, was dusty and bare.

'It would be nice if there was a *kafenion* there,' Elizabeth commented forlornly, having already given up hope.

'Mmm. It looks deserted to me,' Charles answered. 'But I agree – help me pull this thing up on the shore and let's have a look.'

What they had taken from a distance to be sand was mostly rotting seaweed and dried-out mud, cracked tan plates curling at their edges. Its breakage as they walked on it, evidently the first to do so in months, made a crisp noise, like flatbread broken at the breakfast board.

'No chapel,' he commented, half to himself.

'It's probably on the other side of the island; there's likely ten of them about.'

They had visited Greece often enough to have developed an amateur passion for the place, even having studied the language at local evening courses; both were aware that the smallest of rocks in the sea would have its little *ecclesia*, or at least a ruin thereof, built by mariners in grateful devotion, as thanks for rescue from the sea's travails or for some favour granted by a saint.

Here, obviously, there was no little church, the expected adjunct to any such lonely house, protection against the terrors of isolation and night, and the demon that walks at noon. It must be, as Elizabeth had said, invisible from where they were; there was certainly enough bush about to hide one in, or ten of them, for that matter.

'If there's anyone around here, we can enquire,' she said, watching the place for signs of life as they approached. A few ducks and geese waddled towards, and then around them, hoping to be fed. Charles thought he heard a dog bark, from not so far away, but was not sure and so said nothing to his wife. A faint smell of smoke, as from a fire burned out the day before, would now and then waft their way. Of people they saw no trace.

'Clearly there's no one here, and I think we can forget the café, let alone human contact,' he ventured, stating the obvious.

'They're all back on Tiflos, and probably come out here every other day to water the goats and feed the birds,' Elizabeth replied. They stopped, nearly on top of the house, realising that to go any further would be a violation of the owner's private space, even with the hospitality of the local countryside and the relaxed Greek attitude to invasion of the blurred division between public space and private property taken into account.

The geese and mallards, giving up on the couple, went back with honks and quacks of disappointment to the shade from whence they had come. Motionless for a while, the two regarded a dovecote behind the house, and then without speaking, turned to their boat.

'I think if we continued around the bay, to the south, we might find a picnic spot.'

'Yes, I thought I saw something that way when we came in.'

The two of them shoved the boat off the shelf of decaying plants, Charles boarding first and Elizabeth hopping on board with the mooring line afterwards. When the water was deep enough, Charles dropped the motor to its upright position and started up. Cutting across the rough half-moon of the bight, they found, as they had hoped, a small beach at its further end. The map gave the place's name as *xilo* – wood. It was backed by an open grove of olives that climbed the steep surrounding hillside.

Behind the silvery-bladed trees was a thicket that seemed to cover the hill right up to the ridge line, and to the summit somewhere at their right. It stretched in both directions, seemingly impenetrable, swinging across the narrow neck of land back towards the distant house, now barely visible. No paths ran from or along the shore; the olive harvest would necessarily be taken to its pressing by boat, on account of the difficult and broken ground on both sides of the solitary cultivation.

With no one about, they landed and took the craft up on the shore. Spreading a large towel as a picnic blanket, they laid out the bread, tomatoes, and cheese that they had brought from town. Elizabeth washed the tomatoes in the salt water of the sea, and Charles got busy with the bottle and two metal cups from home. They were out in the open, away from any shade, and the sun beat down violently upon their little feast.

'I saw that bit, with Panagiotis, in the shop.'

'What bit?'

'Don't be naïve: the way he was pawing you under the pretence of showing us that brochure.'

'What? Oh, he was just trying to impress himself. You don't think for a second …?'

Charles, surly from his sense of unavenged wrong, the sun and the wine, which was acting quickly, said nothing. Instead, he locked his hand around Elizabeth's ankle, pulling her slowly across the rucking towel towards him.

'Come off it, now; you don't think I'm about to do it out here in broad daylight, do you? Don't you have a book to read?' she teased lazily, with a half-suppressed giggle, making no effort to defend herself.

They awoke, sated and indolent, in the shade of the enormous fig tree to which they had removed an hour before. The figs, overly ripe with no one to collect them, lay half-burst and rotting under the branches. Wavelets were coming in slightly higher, a sign of shifting breeze. The sun still rode high in the heavens, and a profound stillness infused the air about them.

'Come on, get a move on,' Charles yawned, throwing Elizabeth's tank top at her ruddy head as she stretched, arching her back. She flicked off the corner of the towel that had covered her in her sleep. Something about sleeping under a fig tree, Elizabeth thought, but she could not remember the bit of folklore associated with it; only that for Greeks, it portended something or other.

Nude, she lifted herself to her feet and stretched out a leg, bending it, to put on her shorts. She left her shirt off, tucking it partly into a pocket, so it trailed her from behind. They packed up the remains of their picnic for loading on the boat.

Everything aboard, they went through the drill of setting off: Charles after, shirtless himself now, ready to lower and set the motor, only the nose of the raft remaining on the strand, waiting for Elizabeth's push. She shoved and jumped in, and they drifted out into clear water, which deepened quickly. The parti-coloured stony bottom was exquisitely visible, like pebbles in the bottom of a fish tank, and the boat rocked slightly as Charles commenced his routine. A few pulls to clear the vapour, and short rest, and try again. Only this time, instead of faithfully catching, the outboard refused to start.

'It's been out in the sun, unprotected so long, it'll need a few more turns before it starts up; it's vapour lock,' he told Elizabeth unconcernedly. A few more turns, and the result was the same. Charles rested a moment, and motioned for her to move forward, in case he fell backward pulling the cord. He clenched his fist around the curved plastic handle, and yanked powerfully, almost viciously, at the line, but the only sound was the spin of the disengaged motor in the quiet air. Sweat was beading on his face as the boat began to drift out slowly.

'If I open the tank cover, it'll get some air,' he said, screwing off the top for a moment before replacing it. With the beach near one corner of the bay, they would soon drift out of it, into water that was becoming more disturbed by the rising puffs of wind. He pulled once more, and almost fell over backwards, as the cord spun freely in the direction of his pull.

'Christ, we've got to get it back to shore, and hold it steady while I work on it.'

Elizabeth did not reply. She was the superior rower of the two; without saying anything, she took up the plastic oars provided and began the task of pulling them back into the shallows. Beads of perspiration rolled down her freckled breasts, while Charles, in black anger, cursed Greek maintenance.

When they had re-entered their picnic cove, Elizabeth, taking off her shorts and donning her plastic sandals, entered the water to hold the raft steady while Charles repeatedly tried to start the engine. Once or twice, during the next half-hour, it gave a weak cough, in promise of something more substantial; but after that the machine's cooperation stopped. He tried the various knobs and buttons, without any effect. Tugs on the cord became more infrequent; finally, nearing exhaustion, he sat down in disgust, Elizabeth regarding him curiously, her eyebrows raising in her question-mark expression.

'What next?'

'I don't know. It's impossible to go along the shore in either direction – perhaps go up and look about, try to get up on the ridge. There must be a trail or path through it, it can't be as bad as it looked from here. Maybe I can get the attention of the archaeologists diving at the wreck: I'm sure that once they finish, they'd help out and tow us back. Might be a path along the top, where I could get back to the house we saw, and see if anyone is there now. They might have a way of signalling back to Tiflos. Then again, perhaps someone is anchored around here. The main thing is to go up, where I can see.'

'Well, one thing's sure, I'll never be able to row us across; it must be two kilometres back and I'd never outdo the current. You go up, if you're so keen on it, and I'll stay here and swim and watch our things.'

'At worst, if we have to overnight here, I'm sure Panagiotis will come out looking in the morning,' Charles said; then, seeing, the hint of contempt forming in Elizabeth's eyes, hastily decided then and there to do as much as possible to get help from anyone who happened to be on or near the island. Anything but have his own incompetence put on display for the leering boat-concession owner.

So they pulled the boat in, and Charles started up the hill towards the encompassing bush. He had put on a shirt and long pants to protect against the snagging burrs and thorns. Elizabeth tied the inflatable firmly to a solid onshore stump with the boat's long mooring line; still nude, she swam out to the craft and climbed into it, to use I as a diving platform-cum-floating sun deck.

In fifteen minutes, Charles had nearly reached the wave of greenery and its precursor, an almost tangible wall of humid heat. The route through the olive grove had steepened quickly, the pebbly orange-brown soil changing to gravel except where, beneath each tree, the small stones had been cleared. Footing was difficult because of the slope; he would have to watch it on the way down, or he would be in for a nasty slide and tumble. He stopped for a couple of minutes in the shadow of a tree, catching his breath, and viewed his wife far below, a small brown figure diving yet again from the useless boat. Her plunge into the water carried no sound at this height. Wiping the sweat, which was quickly condensing on his face now that he was out of the sun, he struggled to his feet and dusting the seat of his pants, trudged up towards the thicket.

He saw then that he was following the faintest of narrow tracks, with fewer pebbles to roll on, the only route where he could be reasonably sure of his balance. Had he not been forced on to it by the nature of the terrain, he doubted he would have spotted it.

Almost the lower end of the enormous thicket, which was twice his height and unbelievably dense, he saw with relief an opening in the thorny barrier. Even more than the maquis on Tiflos, this was almost solid – so grown together that the tangled bush would tear to shreds anyone daring the leafy mess. He was all the more thankful then that this path continued into some sort of tunnel pointing uphill into the heart of the jungly vegetation.

He turned once more, looking back at the raft, and could only vaguely make out the sprawled form his resting wife basting in the sun, limbs spread out. Swinging around, he bent his head and entered the dark tube that ran through the plants.

Almost immediately, his nostrils were struck by a rank smell, confirming his suspicion that this was an animal track which, although it lacked the distinctive sweet smell of their excreta, might have been made by goats. The reek was stronger when he went a few yards further in. A few long hairs of different colours were twisted among the nearest branches; these he could not identify as belonging to this beast or that. The light was largely filtered out by the intermingled boughs that formed a solid roof above, although here and there a clear beam shone through, showing innumerable dust motes dancing in the pillars of light.

Only a little bit further on, Charles hesitated; once into this maze, he was on his own. If something happened, it would be impossible for rescuers to spot him from the air, assuming that the passage through the thicket was totally enclosed, as it seemed to be.

Beyond that thought, there was a deeper reluctance – he did not like the word 'fear', it was too unmanly – that held him from immediately continuing. Something that was not quite right, probably only an impulse in the limbic stem, the reptilian brain, Aristotle's dragon, warning against a place where he might suddenly come up against – what?

This is the physical world, he thought to himself, *and there is no reason to be frightened.*

It was only natural to react to dark, enclosed spaces smelling of animals; it probably had something to do with deep-based instinct. The point of it was to suppress the irrational notion that something other than a goat was lurking in the tangle of greenery: worrying would do no good. The main thing was to attain the summit of Stefáni, perhaps three to four hundred feet above him now. He seemed to remember it as being clear of shrubbery from his distant survey of the day before. Once up, he could orient himself, spot any trails, and conceivably even get help. In spite of any nagging doubt, he would have to carry on.

Charles went up, suddenly feeling damp and clammy. Sometimes her had to duck low as the path twisted along, even to the point of moving on all fours now and then. The height of the passage allowed only an inconvenient crouch that left his back aching after a few minutes. He kept lower than was necessary, after having scraped his uncovered scalp on some thorns and losing a few hairs that way.

Not long after, that which he had hoped against happened: the game trail split. Charles reached down at the junction, plucked up three flattish stones, and piled them on each other, marking the path by which he had come. It was most unlikely they would be disturbed: from the look of the many spider webs hanging down, it had been days, or longer, since any beast had wandered through.

Not much further on, he saw the turds of some largish animal. No sheep, goat or dog had left the pile. From its size, it must have been something bigger, but Charles was baffled when he tried to match it up to any animal he knew. Whatever it was, it ate meat: bits of white bone, undigested, poked through the fecal mess, which from its dryness must have been there weeks, if not months.

Beyond that, still plodding uphill, the going often like climbing up a narrow staircase, he came to another junction in the trail. He did not mark it, since the spoor he had seen would be sufficient for that purpose. Not far from there, no more than a few yards, was a place where the dusty tunnel divided into three; again, he did not blaze it – with only the one way down, he was sure that was unnecessary.

From there, things were a bit more straightforward, although the dust, thick on the ground between the exposed roots and long undisturbed, irritated his lungs. He stopped at least twice, his sides heaving from coughing fits. Once, while hawking, he heard a sharp crack deep in the brush, as if a large object or animal had moved through it; but that was impossible. Nothing bigger than a cat could manage, he was certain. Whatever it had been, it was impossible to judge its distance. He had frozen at the noise, and feeling foolish at that, went on.

With stones piled on one another, Charles marked three or four more turn-offs before the proverbial light at the end appeared and he popped out of the labyrinth of thorn and brush. He emerged on to a slightly rounded top, open and clear to all sides – Stefáni, without question. A trig-point marker, a concrete column about three feet high, set up by the mapping authorities, stood at the highest point, a few yards in front of him. He wobbled over to it, straining to straighten out his sore and stiffened spine.

Finally upright, he stretched a foot onto the bronze medallion implanted on the top, and with both hands flat on either side of it, he carefully lifted himself up. There was just enough room to balance on both feet. With the extra height, he could just see in all directions, establishing by sight what was already known in the mind: that all land is surrounded by sea.

To the south, the *Byzantine* diving operation was clearly visible, and he could make out two black dots in the water, the divers, no doubt, now heaving themselves on to the floating dock that must have been the excavation headquarters. He thought of taking off his shirt to wave at them to attract their attention, but knew that he was too far off to see, unless they were looking directly at him. Even then, it was unlikely they would interpret any such action from that distance as a plea for help.

Pivoting slowly, he looked back to the main axis of the island. The ridge spanning the waist of the island to the north was absolutely bare of paths. This half of Aghios Mikhailis showed no trace of trails or roads. Except for the tiny cove where they had landed, and the olive grove and one or two others like it, the entire southern part was covered by the same thicket in which he stood. Nor was there any sign of the predicted chapel. There was nothing to do but turn back, and wait it out until rescued.

It was at that instant that Charles, looking back the way he had come, realised that there was something decidedly wrong. Focusing for a moment after hopping down from his perch, it slowly came to him. There were three openings in front of him, each more or less identical in appearance to the others. He simply had not thought of this possibility when, tired and half-blinded, by sweat, he had entered the clearing, and so had not bothered to note his exit. And now he had no way of telling which path would lead him back below, where Elizabeth waited.

One thing was certain: he had no desire at all, none whatsoever, to remain at the top until someone came to fetch him. The bareness of the place, the isolation, and the solitude, were beginning to weigh on him, even after the short while had had spent on the hilltop. It was evident that the trails were interconnected: as unpleasant as getting lost might be, the paths were sure to rejoin as long as he kept following the trend of the slope downward.

Hesitating in front of the three openings for only a second longer than a moment, and with the distinct feeling that something was watching, Charles chose the middle way on impulse, and began his descent.

Elizabeth, by this time, was getting bored. She hauled herself on shore using the line, and with a bit of a struggle, beached the boat. The light was getting longer now, and she wrapped a thin rectangle of cloth around herself, sarong-style, the way lightly packed young Antipodeans did on their rites-of-passage pilgrimages around the world's seasides.

Squatting on her heels, and wondering what was taking Charles so long, she idly contemplated the flowers that grew from the edge of the eroded low cliff backing the shore. Something in form like a hummingbird was feeding from a bloom, and interest aroused, she went over to look at it more closely. Its movements were so rapid, together with the motion of its wings, that she could not say at first whether it was insect or bird. Then, vaguely remembering that *Trochilidae* were restricted to the New World, she opted for the first, and moved up slowly to inspect it more closely.

It was then, only a foot or two away, Elizabeth noticed the large thin sherd. Its inner concavity projecting out of the red dry soil. Forgetting the creature in front of her, she tugged at the piece of pottery, freeing it with some difficulty. When she turned it over in her hand, she saw to her surprise that it was decorated.

The glazed fragment showed a black limb upon a red background, with its muscles, defined by white line, straining against something pulling at it. Part of whatever that was was just visible where the break fan across the figure's ankle. She looked up to the place where she had found it, but there was no other sherd protruding. Glancing down the vertical face towards her feet, she discovered among the stones a few more bits of fired clay, which she picked up. One or two were worn smooth by the sea, and had obviously been washed up from there. But another, sharp and unworn, was decorated. Turning it in her hand, she matched it perfectly to the first piece. Sun-dazzled retinas slowly adjusting to the dull glaze of the pottery, Elizabeth tried to make sense of the story it depicted. Black skin, she knew, was a convention used by ancient Greek artisans to indicate the male. All the skill of the artist had gone to convince the viewer of a great struggle: a dark moulded leg, tendons straining through the flesh in a futile effort to escape that which was wrapped around the man's ankle.

Whatever was holding him, was horrific, and matched no noble proportions that she had seen through all their Greek museum wanderings. Of course, she knew the old Greeks had their darker side: many a little hybrid monsters or grotesque was hidden away in smaller local collections, unknown to any sanitised mythology smoothed out by a Bulfinch of a Hamilton.

The powerful hand, or paw, or appendage – it was hard to say, really, what it was, although it was depicted with clear sharp lines – was decidedly huge, grotesque and malformed. The painter had, with a few hints of the brush, perfectly suggested a pale, mottled skin, covered with welts and half-burst blisters, bubbled as if diseased. It had its victim in its unbreakable hold, and was dragging him towards the unseen owner of the monstrous limb. She shuddered, glad that there were no more fragments to show what the ugly thing was attached to.

Studying her find a bit more, Elizabeth saw that the painter had even tried to give a hint of depth, by clearly indicating, with only a few economical strokes, a background of thornbush. Perhaps it had something to do with a mystery religion; the Greek world was so full of those in the olden times. She put her find into the boat.

Charles was thoroughly lost. That is to say, having taken the wrong way, he had no clear sense of where he was in the thicket, other than a vague impression that he was approaching its edge somewhere in the general direction of the beach where Elizabeth waited. It was hard to tell – the light was gradually weakening, and if he was not to spend the night amid the thorny jungle, he would have to leave it soon.

As he crouched, stumbling over rocks in the waxing dimness, he found growing within himself a faint perception of someone walking parallel with him. The illusion took the form of a faint echo of his own footsteps, and was so strong that he stopped at one point to see if it would continue on its own. But there was nothing save the humid stillness, and the choking clouds of dust that he had kicked up on his progress down.

He came to an intersection of tunnels that he took to contain a subtle hint, triggering a weak memory of having been there before. Perhaps, unknowing, he had rejoined his original trail. One thing was certain, though: there was something tracking alongside him, in the seemingly impossible snarl to his left, the uphill side. From the time he had started again, the faint echo had grown louder; he was convinced that some curious beast was following him, although he could not imagine what it might be. But from the sound it made, it was large. How anything could manage in the impenetrable brush, so thickly grown together, was beyond his comprehension. The uncomfortable feeling that he was being herded glimmered through his mind, and lingered faintly. He found himself feeling faint, and on the edge of panic, wishing more than anything else that he was through the thicket jungle and out on the hillside on the way down to Elizabeth and the boat, which they could row out, if they had to.

Just then, Charles suddenly saw the tunnel widen ahead of him, and, seeing the light beyond, hoped that it was the end of his trials, the end of the impenetrable brush.

The narrow throat of greenery opened to a wide mouth, and he tumbled into the open, having to climb up a metre or more over a solid tangle of bleached small branches. Dazed by the heat, salt in his eyes, he dully registered that there were broken into bits, perhaps the result of coppicing or cutting, covering entirely what he now saw was only a large clearing, about as wide as a football pitch, with no other exit. His despair at not having broken out was mixed with relief on realising that whatever had been following him was now silent, perhaps having given up its stalking.

Out of the dark interior of the thorns, he could see that there was still a surprising amount of light, making for good visibility, even though twilight was not too far off. There was still a glare from the sun, which had not yet departed the ridge of Tiflos, now visible across the strait to his left. Although light and colour were here in sufficiency, his impression of the clearing was shades of black and grey.

Looking about, Charles saw in the middle of the open space a thin blackish stone, upright and flat, a little taller than the height of a full-grown man, standing on position on some kind of platform, loosely supported in its vertical position by a couple of small rude boulders at its base. He walked towards it, the cracking twigs and branches under his feet making an odd sound, something like the wind-chime noise that comes when walking on beaches made of broken coral branch.

Going around the object, he saw that it was roughly anthropomorphic. What could have been wide shoulders now came into view, along with a narrowing at the top that perhaps was meant to represent a head. The whole plan of it suggested the smoothy polished Cycladic figures he had seen with his wife two years before in Athens. But when he came to the base of the menhir-like object, he saw that where the museum figures had folded arms and breasts and genitals incised, this figure was more rough, and whatever was meant to be represented by the crude hacking of the basaltic rock departed from the canonical in a suggestive, frightening and ugly fashion. He was not sure what was being shown, but he did not like it at all.

Looking on from the base of the platform, he could see that a long section of the hedge on the far side of the clearing was full of openings, through which the light showed. Perhaps only a bush thick, it was woven into a meshlike net: he had reached the edge of the tangle after all. The gaps between the twisted interlocking vines were too small to crawl through without enlargement. The glint of the sea below was beckoning; if need be, he could use the saw on his pocket tool to cut through the few tough branches and wriggle through. He would not, under any circumstance, consider some further maze-wandering with the daylight diminishing so quickly.

Just then, starting towards the thin remaining barrier and freedom, Charles kicked something, and looked down. By the tip of his right toe, amidst the carpet of broken wood, rested a round object, looking somewhat like a blanched fragment of rubber beach ball that had sat too long out in the sun. Reaching down and picking it up, he was stunned to see that it was a piece of human cranium.

This focused his thinking sharply for the first time since he had entered the clearing. Looking around him, seeing details he had ignored, he felt sick to realise that what he had thought was stripped wood was, in fact, bone. The entire open area was covered with cracked splinters of it, and the pit of his stomach dropped when this simple fact sank in.

Nauseated, he stumbled, and his hand reached out for support towards the primitive statue behind him. He leaned on it, only to have it move under the pressure. Charles jumped back, and saw it crash and crack across its middle on the rim of the platform.

At which moment, from the edge of the clearing by the single entrance, a clatter arose. Something big had somehow forced its way *under* the blanket of bones, and was moving smoothly and rapidly along, like a shark on land, throwing out a visible ripple along the axis of its movement, which was towards Charles. The clacking was more resonant than the chimelike sound he had made crossing to the sculpture. Something was rising through the loose whitened mass as it approached, with a small bow-wave of skeletal remains and pieces being tossed out to either side.

As the white bulk beneath the bony sea neared him, Charles broke, screaming, and ran for the far tangle.

Elizabeth shivered with the sudden coolness as the sun disappeared behind the ridge, at a loss for what to do. Going up into the thicket in the darkness would be no good whatsoever. She was better off waiting below, in case Charles made it out soon. Nothing would be worse than his coming down, finding her gone, and then running up into the impossible bushes again in an effort to find her.

While rationalising this choice, the sound of a motor behind her intruded into her thought. Full of unease, she wheeled around, and saw a boat similar to their approaching. Splashing into the shallows, she saw at the throttle a single figure that resolved into Panagiotis as the inflatable craft neared the strand. She stumbled backwards as he ran the craft up on to shore, cutting the motor and lifting and locking it into an angled position in one near motion, to protect the propellor from the bottom rocks. A young goat, a kid, was trussed up in the bow, bleating poignantly.

With the man's appearance, Elizabeth's reserve broke down. She grabbed his thick hairy arm by the wrist even before he set foot on land. 'Thank God you're here! Charles has wandered up on to the hillside, and I'm afraid he's lost. Is there anything you've got that we can use to signal him, to help him find his way down?'

The Greek, who had been smiling slightly, was suddenly grim. 'Where on the hillside did he go? Up by the olives?'

'No, higher. He was trying to get up on top, to see if he could find a path or help. You see, our motor stopped and we couldn't get it started again, so –' her breathy explanation was interrupted by some loud but distant sound from above, at the edge of the green wall nearest them.

A tear ran down Elizabeth's cheek. Panagiotis peered into the gloom, and then more noise came to them, something like a loud ripping of leaves intermingled with a splintering sound. He turned his gaze to Elizabeth, and she saw that he had begun to sweat. A look was in his eyes that she had never seen in anybody's before. It was extreme fear, with undertones of greed and awe commingled, and a hint of undisguised lust. She could not, in her building panic, interpret its import.

He turned as the intensity of the racket from the distant thicket increased, and dragged the kid roughly from the boat, tossing it on the pebbles, where it rested, supine, tongue hanging from its mouth, slitted eyes bulging with fear. The sound from high up now changed, both like and unlike the roar of a lion.

'Get in the boat.'

'We – I can't. Charles is up there, he's in some kind of trouble. We can't leave him!'

Panagiotis said noting more while she protested, but took the line of the disabled vessel and knotted it to a cleat on his boat. About to shove the couple's disabled transport out not the water, something caught his attention, and he reached down into the craft, taking something out. Stepping briskly up to her, he shoved the ancient pottery into her face, demanding loudly, 'What is this? What is *this*?'

'It's nothing, nothing, it's only pottery I found here by the shore! What does it matter? Can't you *help* Charles?' By now she was nearly screaming, while the sounds above them increased.

Between clenched teeth, anger having got the better of fear momentarily, the Greek muttered, 'I told you not to come here! What *fools!*' and flung the two shards from him.

Elizabeth started away, going up, inland, when something totally unexpected happened. Panagiotis took her by the shoulder, swung her round and slapped her across the face so hard that she saw stars.

She was stunned, and stood motionless while he shoved the boats into the shallows. Without any preamble, he walked back, grabbed Elizabeth by the wrist, and dragged her out to the bobbing Zodiac. She tried to dig in her heels, but his bulk and strength made her efforts futile, and he effortlessly threw her into the vessel before jumping aboard himself. He started the motor and two craft began to draw away swiftly, their prows swinging around towards the darkening channel that separated them from Tiflos.

Limp, drained of all resistance, all thinking gone from her mind, Elizabeth slowly lifted her gaze to where the sounds still came from, and saw, for the first time, something very large, and white, tearing uselessly at the barrier of thorn from inside. It threw itself again and yet again at the shaking net of roots and branches, but could not penetrate it. The barrier yielded, sagging beneath the impact, but did not give. It was as if the massive thing was trapped, and was raging inside, casting itself against the wall of vines that held it in. Something wet was being slapped against the thicket, and then being picked up and dashed against it again. Now and then, she thought she saw a splotch or two of red against the huge paleness, but she was not sure. Half in shock, she remained passive when she felt Panagiotis's grip high up her thigh, kneading it in his oversized paw, stroking the inside of her leg.

She knew that whatever it was saw them in the boat, and that its rage was somehow connected with this. At that knowledge, she broke down and finally began to weep, collapsing onto the gunwale, as the pulsing motor unwaveringly pushed them across the channel, into the night.

THE BLUE ROOM

One of the most interesting hauntings in the whole of the Mediterranean region comes to us from Zarautz in northern Spain and is connected to the famous Blue Room in the Palacio de Narros, which dominates the coastline there.

In purely historical terms, the Palacio has no huge significance. First constructed in the 16th century and occupied by the local nobility, it also served as the occasional summertime residence of two queens, Isabella II of Spain and Fabiola of the Belgians. However, the main incident of note is the one most connected with the alleged supernatural events for which the Palacio would in due course become famous.

In 1575, a man was washed up on the shore nearby. There was no trace of the vessel he might have come from, but he'd been half-drowned and was suffering multiple injuries. Taken indoors, he claimed to be French, though he was fluent in both French and English, and understood enough Spanish to communicate with his rescuers. He explained that he was an ordinary sailor whose ship had gone down in a storm and that he'd been in the water for days. The story was believable, because the fellow was in a very poor state. He was thus installed in the Blue Room, which was one of several variously coloured rooms – there was believed to have been a green one at the time, as well as a red one, a yellow one, and so forth – but his condition deteriorated steadily.

While all this was happening, rumours spread that, in performing this generous act, the local marquis had inadvertently rescued one of the Huguenots, a French Protestant group widely regarded as undesirables and seditionists in their staunchly Catholic homeland. The Huguenots of Paris (and sundry other towns) were subjected to a terrifying ordeal on St Bartholomew's Day, 1572, when, on the orders of Queen Catherine de Medici, the mother of the French king, a military force attacked those of them who had gathered in the city for a royal wedding. True horror followed as hundreds of unarmed civilians were butchered in the street with swords, axes and pikes. It was a sectarian bloodbath lasting several weeks, in which as many as 30,000 men, women and children were slaughtered.

An atrocity in modern eyes, at the time it was regarded across France as a well-deserved punishment for a band of heretical scoundrels. And now back in Zarautz, the word spread that one such Protestant malefactor, in fact one of the very Huguenots believed to have escaped 'justice' in Paris, was lying low in the Palacio de Narros. The Spanish locals, as zealous Catholics themselves, formed a lynch-mob and would have marched on the premises had the authority of the marquis not held them back. For his part, the patient, though he was questioned repeatedly, denied that he was a Protestant until he eventually ceased to communicate because he was too weak.

It was only when he finally expired in the Blue Room, an event probably hastened by the stressful interrogations he'd been subjected to, that strangeness comes into the tale.

On the very point of death, he was said to have loudly condemned his carers for having poisoned him, which they hadn't done, but then declared himself an opponent of both the Pope and Roman Catholicism in general. At the same moment, many by his bedside were witness to a mysterious flash of flame, which emerged from one wall of the room and streaked straight across to the other. No damage was done, but there was a strong smell of burning. Startled and frightened, many worrying about whose displeasure they had just been witness to – God's or the Devil's – the onlookers withdrew. Only with great trepidation was the Frenchman removed and secretly buried.

Diverse hauntings are said to have resulted, everything from groans and cries to a strange, mad babbling sound, which was nearly always accompanied by a recurrent stench of burning. Several times over the next few centuries, this suggestion of smoke and flames caused the Palacio to be evacuated while the staff searched for a real fire, even though none was ever discovered. This implied to some that a demonic entity was in their midst. Seeing as the Blue Room was often the epicentre of these events, and though by this time no one lived who remembered the incident with the shipwrecked mariner, many now wondered who or what he'd actually been. The proclamation he'd made with his last breath had only been interpreted as an anti-Catholic statement because the Wars of Religion were at their height. But had he conceivably meant that he was an enemy of Christianity in general?

Had he been a warlock or diabolist?

In 1912, a certain Jesuit, a Father Coloma, became determined to clear the premises of its unclean spirit, though according to the record, he was actually sceptical of these things and mainly interested in experiencing the Blue Room for himself.

During his first night there, he beheld what he considered to be a remarkable apparition: a glowing ball of light in the middle of the room, which descended to the floor and proceeded to burn its way through the floorboards and their underpinnings into the chamber below. Other members of the household saw this damage for themselves and were able to confirm the priest's story. Once again, the smell of burning was so intense that the occupants were forced to vacate the property, allowing it to linger for some considerable time.

Father Coloma clearly got nowhere with his proposed clearance, but was so impressed by the things he saw, heard and felt that he later wrote a novel, The Blue Chamber, *describing the incident and the events leading up to it.*

In the years after World War One, when ghost-hunting had become a more technical occupation, another priest, Father Pilon, installed himself in the Blue Room, equipped with various apparatus: reel-to-reel tape recorders, thermographic gauges and the like. Though he beheld no physical manifestations, he went on to produce evidence we would these days refer to as an EVP, or electronic voice phenomenon. It comprised a tape-recording of an eerie voice, seemingly female, yet babbling in French in furious, incoherent fashion. No copy of the recording exists today, but many who heard it were said to have been both mystified and terrified at the same time.

The Palacio de Narros is now kept as a stately home. Other ghost stories have attached themselves over the years, recent visitors reporting a tall, thin, sombre-faced woman in fine raiment walking in the gardens or along the upstairs corridors. Believers consider this to be the spirit of Comtesse de Bureta, a French expatriate, who lived in the Palacio during the early 19th century and was one of the resistance leaders during the invasion of Spain by Napoleon. Whether she provided the voice on the tape is unknown.

THIS HAUNTED HEAVEN
Reggie Oliver

It is almost fifty years since I was last on Skliros. Has it changed? Have I? We have both changed drastically; we have also remained the same.

The tourist industry has colonised the island, but the sun still shines brilliantly on its silver olive groves, its white villages tumbling down yellow crags and dark green valleys; the Mediterranean Sea surrounding it is still an intense, inky Royal Blue. ('Wine-dark,' the romantics will tell you, imagining they are quoting Homer, but wine was never this wonderful colour.) Though the little fishing port which is Skliros's one principal town is now bloated with hotels, bars, and holiday apartments, the rest of the island remains almost untouched. That is because the coastline is mainly rocky. There are some sandy beaches around the port of Skliros, but nowhere else. You can visit the site of the temple of Cybele on the other side of the island but few tourists do. There is, to be honest, not much now to see. Off the beaten track, the island's stark, hot beauty remains as untouched as when I first visited it in the 1970s. Then it was for me a kind of heaven but it became, in the words of Ludwig Krull, a 'haunted heaven.'

It is not nostalgia that has brought me back. In fact, I would much rather not have come, but I felt I had to. My book *Middle Eastern Cults and Greco-Roman Culture* is nearing completion, and so a visit to the place that first inspired my study was necessary. Photographs need to be taken; resident experts consulted.

I know that *Middle Eastern Cults and Greco-Roman Culture* is hardly the most thrilling of titles, but it is not intended to be. I am a university don, but not the kind who has sold his soul to

BBC4 for a documentary series, and my book is a work of scholarship. It will be published by the Oxbridge University Press and bought almost exclusively by the university libraries that can afford its exorbitant price. It will be the standard work on the subject for, I hope, decades to come, because otherwise my life has been wasted. That is why I feel compelled to set down how it all began. How it all ends, I have yet to find out.

In 1972 I won a scholarship to read Classics – or *Literae Humaniores*, to be pedantically accurate – at St Saviour's College Oxford and I had almost a year before going up. 'Gap year,' I believe they call it now, and it was a gap I needed to fill. I wanted to travel round Greece, but my parents were poor, and the travel grant I had applied for would not cover all I wanted to do. Then, a schoolfriend, Hutton, also a classicist, suggested I write to his uncle Dr Frith. Frith was starting up an archaeological dig on Skliros and was looking for young assistants with a knowledge of Ancient Greek. It sounded ideal. I was to have my flight out and back paid for and be given board and lodging for a couple of months on the island. After that I could use what money I had to go travelling on my own.

The result was that my application to join the dig was successful and in the first week of April I found myself flying to Heraklion in Crete with Hutton who had also volunteered. From the airport we took a bus to the harbour, and, from there, an island-hopping ferry called the *Ariadne* brought us towards evening to Skliros. On the way I saw my first dolphins which accompanied the ship for a while, their polished pewter backs curving joyously in and out of the azure waves.

I shall never forget my first sight of the island, its yellow rocks, made golden by the evening sun, rising out of the sea, high, mountainous pine-clad crags, and a gathering of whitewashed houses around the harbour of Skliros. And there on the jetty Dr Frith was standing, ready to meet us. Hutton pointed him out to me from a distance, and, as we approached the harbour, he slowly came into focus.

He must have been in his forties, but to me he looked older. He was thin, his face was tanned and lined, and his hair, sparse and a little wild, was beginning to turn grey. He stood awkwardly, head tilted to one side, fidgeting restlessly with a bunch of keys, a habit of his, I was to discover. When Hutton and I were finally off the boat with our knapsacks, he shook hands with us and ushered us towards a Landrover which was parked carelessly in the middle of the town square.

He was genial and seemed pleased to see us, but I thought I detected in him something of the professional deformity of the academic. His talk was fragmentary and intermittent, he was abstracted some of the time; he drove erratically. Admittedly, the roads on Skliros in those days were poor, often little more than dirt tracks, but this, I thought, did not excuse his lack of caution. He once nearly ran over a goat which had strayed into the road.

'You'll be staying with me and a few other chaps in the villa I've hired,' he said. 'I hope you and Hutton won't mind sharing a room.' I had been rather expecting this, but I was a little surprised at his addressing his own nephew by a surname.

It was all an adventure then. The villa, or The Dig House as it was called, because it was close to our archaeological site, was spartan. There was a tap for running water in the kitchen, but no electricity. Cooking was done on a primitive stove fuelled by gas bottles. Oil lamps and candles were used in the evenings. Our room consisted of two camp beds, a table, a chair, and an old-fashioned washstand.

After we had deposited our bags, Frith took us over to the site. We were the first assistants to arrive from England, but Frith had made a start, digging trenches with some hired local labour.

It was situated on a plateau amidst the rocky hills in the north of the island. Several stands of pine trees surrounded the few foundations that stood above ground. There were a couple of half-buried segments of Doric tufa columns lying around, but most of the building materials for the temple and its surrounding precinct had been raided long ago for incorporation into houses and chapels on the island. The site was known to be dedicated to the goddess Cybele from tradition, backed up by Pausanias who wrote a famous travel guide to Greece in the second century AD.

From one edge of the plateau a vertiginous slope of rocky scrub plunged down towards the sea a couple of hundred feet below.

It was a strange place. I am not myself a great believer in 'atmosphere', but I must admit I was conscious of something a little oppressive about it. Perhaps it was the tall pines which hung over the scene. They gave us some shade in the heat of the day, but the scent given off by the fronds when the sun shone through them was heavy and musky, like the perfume on a woman's body.

My memory of those first few days on the island is hazy. I know we worked hard and slept heavily. In the evenings, after a rudimentary meal at the villa cooked by a taciturn local woman, we would walk to a taverna at a nearby village called Chora and drink bottles of the local 'retsina' which had a curious orange colour. It was probably vile stuff which I wouldn't think of touching these days, but it eased us and made us laugh. Frith, who always joined us on these expeditions, was as enthusiastic a drinker as either Hutton or I. It seemed to do him good, at least temporarily, as he became notably less fidgety and nervous when he had had one or two.

It was on the third or fourth night that we noticed at another table outside the taverna a group of people who were not the usual dour local men who would sit in huddles, clicking their worry beads, playing dominos, and downing Turkish coffee and ouzo.

There were some young females, scantily clad with brightly coloured bandanas round their heads: 'hippy' types, as we would have called them in those days. One of them, a startlingly beautiful girl in very short denim shorts, was strumming a guitar, rather to the disgust of the old and gnarled ouzo drinkers. Among this group were two older people, one, a huge and immensely fat man with a long straggly beard.

He wore a loose sky-blue caftan. Then there was a woman with white hair and piercing dark eyes who wore black. She seemed detached from the rest, but somehow in charge. I asked Frith who they were.

'I think they're from the Villa Attis,' he said and began to fidget with his keys. I asked him about the Villa Attis but got no further information other than that it was a large house on a nearby mountainside which was owned by a Madame Dimitriou. Was she the lady in black, I asked? Frith could not be sure, but he thought it possible. I saw that the fat man and the older woman had noticed us and were casting glances in our direction, but when I waved at them, they looked away. Frith became restless and said we should be getting back to the Dig House.

The following day several others joined us, undergraduates in their second or third years at Oxford, and, Hutton and I thought, very sophisticated and knowledgeable. The local Greek workers at the site left, to give way to them, seemingly without complaint. Though they deferred to Dr Frith, the new arrivals were also prepared on occasion to tease him mildly about his driving skills and other weaknesses. When in the evening we went down to Chora I wondered if we would see the hippies from Villa Attis again, but they were not there.

The plan that Frith had for the excavations was firstly to dig along the line of the foundations of the main building (believed to be the temple of Cybele, as mentioned in Pausanias) and determine its exact proportions, and then to go inside the precinct and make a few trial diggings there. Now that the undergraduates had arrived and the local labour dismissed, we became a very lively and companionable group.

It was on our second or third day together that we began to find a few objects of note. They were mostly coins of various denominations, dating from the fourth century BC up to the third of our common era, and there were some pottery shards, but the items that excited most interest from Dr Frith were what he described as 'votive offerings.' They appeared to have been deliberately buried around the foundations. They were human figurines, mostly of baked clay, though some were of marble. Their faces were blank apart from a simply delineated nose; no eyes or mouth were depicted. Their bodies were sexless and neither breasts nor genitalia were in evidence, so that they could not be described even as hermaphrodites in the normal sense of the term. They were lay figures, stripped of all gender. Why such sexless images should have been offered to Cybele, a mother goddess, an icon of fertility, was a question which interested some of us, but not, apparently Frith, who merely shrugged his shoulders when we asked him. All the finds, however, were meticulously recorded and photographed.

One particularly hot afternoon I was labouring alone in a trench under the partial shade of a stand of pine trees. It had been dug along one side of the foundations of the temple, so that one wall of the trench had masonry embedded in it and the other was composed of the orange clay soil of Skliros. I was hot and stopped frequently to sieve the earth that I had dug meticulously for coins or artefacts, but also to rest in the shade that sitting in the trench gave me. My hands would search for cooling moisture at the bottom of the trench but found little.

Quite suddenly I became aware of a new shadow above me. I looked up, anxious that I should not be caught idling, and saw a sweep of blonde hair and a pair of perfectly shaped legs, tanned by the sun. A girl of about my age stood gazing down at me in my trench.

'Hi,' said a voice. I screwed my eyes against the sunlight which danced behind her and saw a face of perfect, young beauty smiling at me. She came to the edge of my trench and sat down, dangling her legs into it. Her feet were bare; but my eyes were drawn irresistibly to the frayed ends of her denim shorts which lay like pale blue hair on her beautiful golden thighs. I recognised her as the guitar strumming girl from the taverna the night before.

'Hello,' I said. 'Didn't I see you last night at the taverna in the village. Aren't you from the Villa Attis?'

'Yeah! Cool!' She seemed delighted by my recognition. Speaking in an American accent which I later identified as Californian, she told me that her name was 'Perse' – short, apparently, for Persephone – and that she was living with her grandmother, Madame Dimitriou, at the Villa Attis. She was here because her parents 'back in the States' had separated 'which really sucks,' but 'living with Grandma' was 'like really cool.' 'Cool' appeared to be her favourite adjective and she applied it liberally to the information I gave her about myself and the dig we were doing. If there was something routine and formulaic about the enthusiasm with which she greeted almost everything I said, I did not notice it at the time. I was captivated.

She was, I think, the most beautiful creature I had ever seen, and this was what cast the initial spell. But she was also fresh, seemingly uninhibited, and deliciously strange to this product of an English vicarage and a single-sex minor public school. Even the rather whining strain of her Californian 'wood-notes wild' enchanted me, even the endlessly repeated 'cool.' Perse had become, instantly, the romantic heroine of my Mediterranean adventure.

I saw her look round in agitation. The look reminded me somehow of an animal in a forest, a deer perhaps, that hears a hostile sound. And, as she turned, I noticed for the first time, a strange sickle shaped scar on her neck below the left ear. Its silvery surface was faintly opalescent. It was hard to tell whether it was the product of a birth defect or a later accident; whatever the cause, I found the blemish perversely alluring. She turned back to look down at me.

'Hey, look, let's meet up again and hang out. Why don't you come up to the Villa some time?'

'When?'

'Like tonight? Like after you've had your chow, or whatever?'

'Where is it?'

Perse pointed inland in a westerly direction and spoke in sentences with that interrogatory inflection at the end, more common now than it was them. 'Like up there? There's like this dirt track that goes up and round the mountain? It's not far. You can't miss it. Like it's the only road round here?'

'Tonight then, after dinner. It's a date.'

'Cool!' Then she added: 'Hey, don't tell anyone else where

you're going.'

I nodded.

'Cool!' she said again and was gone.

I remained sitting at the bottom of my trench, dazed, and wondering stupidly why I had used the word 'dinner' to describe our evening meal at the Dig House. Presently another shadow loomed over me. It was Frith.

'Who was that talking to you?' he asked.

'Oh. Just someone from the Villa Attis. American.'

'Mm. Pretty girl.' I was surprised he had noticed her beauty, my teenage presumption being that no-one over forty ever thought about sex. 'Anything interesting? Here, I mean,' he said, indicating the trench.

'Nothing found. Oh …' Then I remembered something I had noticed earlier in the day while scraping one side of the trench to expose the stonework around the base of the temple. It had briefly intrigued me, but not enough to make me call anyone's attention to it. 'There *was* something odd. An anomaly.' I pointed to a part of the foundations where a heavy stone slab had been placed over two uprights, still partially buried. Between them was what looked like bare earth. 'Looks a bit like – '

Frith jumped into the trench. 'Yes! Well spotted. Looks like an entrance with a stone lintel on top of the two uprights.' He picked up a trowel and started to jab at the earth between them. It was soft and yielding. I took a pick and hacked at it. The soil fell away and a small dark hole was revealed. 'It *is* an entrance! To an underground chamber perhaps!' Frith had become wild-eyed with excitement. I had never seen him like this before.

Suddenly he seemed to check himself. 'No! No! We must do this properly. Too late now. Cover it up! Cover it up!' I looked at him enquiringly. 'Cover it up for the moment! And don't mention this to anyone. We'll tackle it in the morning.'

Frith was in an unusually febrile mood that night during our evening meal which he seemed anxious to finish so as to get to the taverna for a drink. He was mildly irritated when I declined the expedition, pleading exhaustion from the heat.

As soon as Frith and the others had left for Chora, I set out to find the Villa Attis.

It was not difficult. Taking a torch with me to guide me on my return journey, I walked down the path from the Dig House till I hit what passed for a main road, turned right, instead of left towards Chora, and went on until I came to a crossroads. There, a handmade sign with the words VILLA ATTIS painted on it in psychedelic colours pointed me up a winding track.

Up ahead on a hill and surrounded by pine trees I saw the villa which stood on a little rise. There were two floors and the architecture was of no great distinction, but the ground floor had plate glass sliding French windows which opened onto a wide terrace, on which I saw figures moving. Presently I could identify one of them, her long golden legs astride the stone balustrade that bordered the terrace. She was looking towards me, shading her eyes against the setting sun. My heart began to beat faster; other senses were aroused. There are moments when the body dictates to the mind, all too often I sometimes think. I waved; Perse waved back.

'Hi. Glad you could make it!' she said when I came closer. She was joined on the terrace by the fat man with the beard whom I had seen at the taverna. He wore his long, blue embroidered caftan and carried a tambourine. As I approached, he laid his hand on her thigh in a proprietary way which I disliked intensely. In those days I had a prejudice against ugliness. Perse ignored the intrusion.

I climbed some rough stone steps to the terrace. And was introduced to the fat man by Perse who told me his name was Ludwig Krull, as if I should know it. His hand was soft and damp and his voice was a high falsetto. These two factors only enhanced the unfavourable feelings I already had for him. Disgust was mingled with a faint hint of fear; though why I should be afraid of this creature I could not conceive.

'Ludwig was in Vietnam. Now he's like this cool poet,' said Perse. 'Come and say hi to the gang.'

She led me through the French windows into a large well-shaped room which ran almost the whole length of the villa.

There on gigantic sofas and well-embroidered cushions lounged a selection of the girls I had seen at the taverna. Perse told them that I was 'one of the boys digging down at the temple.'

They looked at me with mild interest and said things like: 'Hey, cool!'

Their hair was elaborately braided and their eyes were heavily made up, and outlined with kohl which gave them a hungry, predatory look. My unease grew. It was as if they were waiting the arrival of someone.

Ludwig piled several cushions on top of one another and sat down heavily on them, producing a huge exhalation of air, like a discontented sigh. All attention was suddenly concentrated on him. Perse picked up a guitar and began to strum it.

'Ludwig, give us your poem,' she said and played a few chords to encourage him. Ludwig gave her a petulant look, but I thought he was pleased to be put on display. He began to recite in his shrill, wailing voice, accompanied by the odd guitar chord from Perse. Once or twice to emphasise a point he would bang and shake his tambourine. I can remember little of the words except for a repeated refrain:

A million planets rage
Over this haunted heaven
I heard my mama Earth cry out
Down in her nuclear shade:
Why is my flesh drained of its joy
Why are my ores afraid?

It seemed to be a general complaint about the world: wars, bombs, hierarchies, pollution, a counter-cultural rant. I felt some sympathy for its themes even then, but there was something about the tone in which it was expressed – whining, self-indulgent – that I did not care for. Worse still for me, I am afraid to confess, was the shrill voice in which it was chanted. The more I heard him speak, the more I was baffled and alarmed by its utter sexlessness. It was not feminine; it was alien and neuter. He ended on a howl of anguished pleading:

My mama Earth, my goddess dark,
When I go to my tomb
Under the world of men,
Take me to your womb,
I wanna go to my tomb!
I wanna go to my womb!

Just as he finished, a pair of double doors at the end of the room opened and a woman in dark red flowing robes entered. Her entrance was timed and performed with a theatrical precision, almost too exact to be entirely effective, but it was still impressive. I recognised her as the woman identified by Dr Frith as Madame Dimitriou, Perse's 'grandma'.

The scattered applause which had greeted Ludwig's finale died away when the company saw her. She looked round the room, searching for our reactions. She seemed satisfied by what she saw and finally her eyes rested on me. My heart beat faster. Was this a kind of fear? Determined to conquer it I stared back at her boldly.

'Who is our stranger?' She spoke in a deep, resonant voice which, like Ludwig's seemed androgynous, yet unlike his in every other way.

'This is John from the dig, Grandma,' said Perse. 'You remember, I told you.' There was apology in her tone.

Madame Dimitriou nodded dismissively and continued to stare at me. The very fact that I knew she wanted somehow to intimidate me, gave me confidence. I continued to stare back.

'That's right,' I said.

'You are digging in the shrine of the Great Mother?'

'The Temple of Cybele, yes.'

'We call her Cybe*be*, the Great Goddess.'

'That is the alternative spelling. The one Catullus uses in his poem, I think.'

'Ah! Catullus! He knew nothing. He just wanted to create sensation!' She spoke as if she knew the first century Latin poet personally and disapproved of him. I could not quite place her accent. There were traces of American, Greek, even Italian. Her eyes, encircled with a hard line of kohl, burned me.

'So! Tell me. What have your little diggings found so far?'

'Nothing much to date. A few coins, pottery shards, a number of votive offerings –'

'What do you mean by "votive offerings"?' Before I could speak, she held up her hand. 'Yes, I know what your academic jargon thinks it means. Do not waste your time explaining to me. I want to know what kind of things it is you call "votive offerings".'

I told her about the figurines.

'Ah, yes! These are images of Attis. He whom the Great Mother made into a god because he mutilated himself in her service –'

'And regretted it, according to Catullus.'

'Catullus! A Roman pig! He knew nothing! I should like to see these images.'

'I'm sure Dr Frith would be delighted to show them to you, if you come down to the site.'

'You will ask him to bring them to me here.'

'Dr Frith is rather busy. I don't know if …'

'You will tell him I wish to see. Let us have some wine.' She clapped her hands. One of the girls who had been stretched on a sofa smoking looked at her. Madame Dimitriou clapped again, and the girl, dragging another with her reluctantly, left the room to fetch wine. Ludwig stared vacantly into space crooning to himself in his shrill voice. I sat myself close to Perse who was cross-legged on one of the sofas, still strumming her guitar. We talked. I have no recollection of what we said only that the experience was strange and full of delight.

The wine came in great earthenware jars decorated with stylised snakes and flowers in black. It was poured into shallow terracotta bowls which were not easy to drink from without spilling but, I suppose, authentically Greek. I was expecting the taste of it to be crude and resinous, like the retsina one drank at the taverna, but this was soft, dark red like Madame Dimitriou's robes, and perfumed with some indefinable scent, herbal and of the earth. The wine excited me almost as much as Perse and her golden legs, and my senses were heightened not dulled by long draughts of the nectar. I felt as if I were caught up in a vivid dream.

Madame Dimitriou clapped her hands. 'Now Ludwig will dance for us,' she said.

Ludwig who had collapsed onto his pile of cushions opened his eyes and looked around fearfully. My callow revulsion towards him was beginning to be tinged with sympathy, or pity at least.

'Ludwig will perform the dance of Attis,' said Madame Dimitriou, turning to me. 'It is to celebrate the gifts of the Great Mother and the vital energy he receives from her.'

Ludwig had by now got to his feet wearily; his eyes pleaded with Madame Dimitriou.

'Now pick up your timbral,' she said. He bent down and picked up the tambourine which he proceeded to shake listlessly.

'Good,' said Madame Dimitriou. 'Now dance!'

For such a large, indeed obese man, Ludwig, once he had got going, showed extraordinary energy. The rest of us watched transfixed.

The effect on me, perhaps enhanced by the wine, was powerful. Anything about his performance which might have been comic was wiped out by the sheer grotesqueness of his antics, as he turned this way and that, shimmering the tambourine high above his head and letting out plaintive falsetto cries from time to time. I had the distinct feeling that he was in the grip of some force that was manipulating him. His twists and leaps reminded me of a string puppet being jerked about by an enthusiastic but clumsy puppeteer. His sweating, terrified face told me that he wanted to stop but somehow could not. At one point, when he seemed on the brink of sheer exhaustion and was beginning to droop, Madame Dimitriou started to clap her hands rhythmically. This clapping was taken up by others, even, eventually, by me I am ashamed to say, and this drove him on.

Madame Dimitriou still clapping, slid over to the sofa where I was seated next to Perse and whispered in my ear:

'Ludwig was badly wounded in Vietnam. He was cruelly maimed.' She spoke with a relish that made me uneasy. I looked at Perse, but she, absorbed in the spectacle, seemed not to have heard.

The sky-blue caftan Ludwig wore was made of cotton so that it swayed as he danced and emphasized the erratic frenzy of his movements. He was by now sweating profusely and I could smell a cloying, faintly fishy odour coming from him. Parts of his garment were beginning to stick to his body and show his gross corpulence even more pitilessly. I noticed a stain, pinkish in colour, beginning to form between his thighs. Ludwig now looked as if he was in pain. His sweat-slicked skin had assumed a greyish colour, but still he danced on, if anything with more frenzy, shaking his tambourine above his head from time to time in a kind of defiance against the forces that were goading him towards catastrophe.

Then quite suddenly, without any premonitory slackening of his fury, he collapsed onto the tiled floor. Everyone was now concerned and rushed forward to pick him up and restore him. Everyone, that is, except Madame Dimitriou who merely ceased her clapping and sat watching the drama with a faint smile on her face, as if even this debacle was an entertainment of sorts, put on for her pleasure.

Some of the girls helped him from the room, Perse following with a suitably concerned look on her face. I turned to look at Madame Dimitriou who had remained seated. She fixed me with her basilisk stare.

'You will ask Dr Frith to meet with me. We need to talk. You will persuade him.'

'I don't know if ...'

'You want to see my granddaughter again? You will persuade him.'

Perse came back into the room and said: 'Ludwig's okay. We put him in his bed. He's cool. He'll be just fine.'

Madame Dimitriou nodded. 'You had better see this young

man out. It is getting late,' she said.

Perse nodded, took my hand, and led me out onto the terrace.

'I'll see you again soon,' I said.

'Cool!'

I took her in my arms and kissed her. Everything that had happened that night faded into this one moment. My hand reached inside her shorts and felt the exquisitely smooth and firm curve of her buttocks. At the same time her hand reached for my genitals and she began to squeeze them. She continued until the pain overwhelmed the thrill and I shook myself free. I could not think what to say except: 'Right! See you!'

'Cool!'

I switched on my torch and plunged into the night. I think I found my way back by a kind of instinct because my mind was in confusion. The next thing I remember was passing the excavations of the Temple of Cybele. How I found myself there I don't know because it was not on my most direct route to the Dig House. There I stopped, bewildered. A breeze made the pine trees whisper and dissipated their heavy scent through the hot night air. I shone my torch around.

The light found its way into the trench where I had been digging that afternoon. Somehow the opening in the foundations which Frith and I had blocked up had unblocked itself. A doorway into darkness had appeared. When my torch shone into it there was nothing but black – or was there? Just for a moment I thought I saw something shift and move beyond the entrance. Something white and shiny, like pale sweaty skin. Could Dr Frith have gone in there? It seemed unlikely. I chose not to investigate.

There were what looked like columns of white mist between the pines that surrounded the temple. They swayed slightly in the warm night breeze. I thought they were almost human in shape. The effect was not pleasant so I hurried towards the Dig House.

It must have been later than I thought because there were no lights on. I went to my room and saw Hutton asleep in bed. I undressed quietly but he woke up.

'Christ! Where have you been? We were worried about you.'

I explained briefly.

'So *that's* where you were! You don't want to have anything to do with the Dimitriou woman.'

'Why not?'

'Frith can't stand her. She tried to stop the dig. Said it was on her land or something. It was all bollocks, of course, but she has some quite influential friends in Heraklion. Took the whole of the Greek Archaeological Institute, with help from the British School at Athens to face her down.'

'I see. Well, now she wants to meet Frith. She's interested in the finds.'

'I bet she is. Fat chance of making it with Frithy, though. So, you fancy her granddaughter, do you?'

'I'd rather not discuss it.'

Hutton snorted with laughter and I felt very superior to him. Soon we were both asleep.

The next morning Frith, Hutton and I went down into the trench. Frith seemed genuinely baffled by the fact that the entrance had been opened up in the night. He looked at me suspiciously, but I shook my head.

'No harm done anyway,' he muttered as we cleared the last earth from the entrance which was four foot high and three wide. Frith shone his torch inside.

It revealed a barrel-vaulted chamber made of dressed stone. The floor was covered with detritus, but the roof was high enough, once the entrance had been crawled through, for one to stand up in.

Frith looked back at us, his eyes shining with excitement: 'Hutton, go and get the camera. I'm going in.'

The other diggers were summoned and the rest of the day was spent photographing the chamber we had unearthed, and cataloguing the items we found on its dirt floor. There were miscellaneous fragments of rusty metal which could have been knives; there were pot sherds, some of them inscribed with brief dedications in Ancient Greek.

One of them was in the form of a hexameter, and read:

ἔνθαδ ᾿Αττιs Καλαου Φρυγοs ὄργια ἔτελει Μητροs

Here Attis, son of Kalaos the Phrygian, celebrated the orgies [or, *rites*]
of the Mother.

'So, Attis was a real person?' I said, excited by my discovery,
and elated at having translated my first inscription.

'Not necessarily,' said Frith. 'He's recorded as the son of
Kalaos in Pausanias. Obviously a semi-mythological figure. The
pottery only looks third or fourth century BC to me. It was
probably written by a devotee who identified themselves with
the demi-god Attis, probably after going through some sort of –
erm – initiation.'

He jangled his keys in his pocket, always a sign that he was
nervous and agitated. I noted the awkward use of the word
'themselves', and wondered if by 'initiation' he meant the ritual
self-castration recorded in Catullus's poem.

We discovered more votive figurines of the kind we had
previously found in our excavations. These were of finer quality
than those we had hitherto discovered. Some were made of
marble and bore faint traces of paint, even gold leaf, but our
principal discovery was found leaning slightly drunkenly
against the back wall of the chamber its lower half buried up to
the calves of its legs in the earthen floor.

It was a life-sized statue of a naked boy in pure white
marble. The style was that of the 'archaic' Greek *Kouroi* of the
late seventh and early sixth century BC, erect, facing forward,
clearly influenced by Egyptian statuary. The face was bland and
smiling, the long, braided hair fringed his wide forehead and
extended down his back: the effect was quietly epicene. It might
have been a thing of serene beauty, as many Greek statues of
the archaic period are, but for one detail. The penis was small,
almost non-existent and the scrotal sac was missing. It had not
been knocked off or worn away by an accident of time, it was
deliberately absent and in its place was a stylised scroll of

wrinkled skin. We were looking at the statue of an emasculated man.

'Attis,' I said, almost involuntarily.

Frith nodded and jingled his keys. 'I think we'll leave it in here for the moment,' he said. 'Obviously, it's an important find. I will inform the Institute of Archaeology at Heraklion as soon as possible. Meanwhile, I think we should keep this under our hats. We don't want gawpers and rubberneckers hanging around and getting in our way.' He did not sound as elated as I thought he should have been about making such a major discovery.

I thought this might be the moment to tackle him on the subject of, as I put it, 'meeting with' Madame Dimitriou.

'*Meeting with?* Terrible transatlantic expression. Don't you mean just 'meet'? Certainly not. Ghastly woman.'

I felt suddenly ashamed of my Americanism; it was as if I had been involuntarily infected. As we emerged from the underground chamber into the trench, we saw standing above us against the sun two figures, one in shorts, the other in flowing crimson robes.

'Professor Frith?'

'It's Doctor actually, Madame Dimitriou.'

'I wish to meet with you.'

'Yes, well … Just at the moment …'

Madame Dimitriou bent down and beckoned, fixing him with her kohl-framed eyes. Frith hesitated a moment, jangling his keys, then climbed out of the trench to join her. She put her arm around his shoulders and drew him away from the rest of us towards a grove of pine trees. I came out of the trench to greet Perse who was staring after them with a puzzled expression.

I said: 'Hello again!'

'Oh! Hi there!' She smiled brightly, but it was almost as if she were seeing me for the first time.

'Can we meet again tonight?'

'Oh, yeah, cool, that would be great. But … My grandma has something on tonight. Maybe soon? Okay?'

'Soon then? Maybe …'

'Soon! That would be great.'

I saw that it would be no use pressing the point; or rather, I lacked the courage to do so and risk a stronger rebuff. She seemed distracted. Besides, it was almost enough just to look at her. She had a beauty that was like a Greek statue in its perfection; and yet, in so many ways how unlike a Greek statue she was.

Presently Madame Demetriou and Frith returned. They were walking some distance apart but seemed on reasonably cordial terms. Then they shook hands. I could not hear what they said, but their manner was formal. Madame Demetriou beckoned to Perse.

'Come, we go!' she said and her granddaughter obeyed without glancing back at me.

When they were gone Frith jangled his keys and said: 'Right! I must go into the village and phone Heraklion.' There was no telephone at the Dig House. 'No need for anyone else to come with me.'

The following day, as a result presumably of his phone call, Frith took the ferry to Heraklion. He returned that night, but he did not tell us what had resulted from the mission. When we went into the Taverna at Chora after supper, he got more than usually drunk, but fended off all enquiries, and seemed reluctant even to discuss archaeology. Hutton and I felt particularly left out because all he would talk about with the others was Oxford gossip which mainly consisted of determining whether some figure in its academic world had 'a first-class mind.' Amid much laughter, second, and even third classes were more liberally awarded than firsts.

Tiring of this, and, in an attempt to join in, I said: 'I'm beginning to think that Oxford must be the most class-ridden city in England.' The remark was not well received.

In the days following we continued with our excavations, but saw less of Frith, though he was always with us in the evenings. I waited, hoping that Perse would come to the diggings or that I might see her in Chora, but she never did.

Even then, wholly unexperienced as I was, I sensed she was unlikely to respond, so one night after supper I walked up the road to the Villa Attis. If only I could just see her, I was thinking, that would be enough. I might laugh at it all now; I couldn't then.

A bright unclouded moon was approaching its fullness. I stood, half hidden in a belt of fir trees looking up at the Villa Attis and the long terrace at the front of the house. The windows had white muslin curtains so that I could see lights on and the vague movement of figures behind them. Music was playing, whether live or recorded I could not tell. I heard the shrill wail of a pipe and the bang of a tambourine. Several people appeared to be dancing. Then the music stopped abruptly, and one of the French windows slid open, presumably to let in air. What I had been waiting for – stupidly longing for – happened. Perse came onto the terrace.

I could see her quite clearly under the moon. She leaned rather wearily on the balcony and stared into the night. I moved out of the shadow of the trees and she saw me. She showed surprise, then she looked away, distracted by a voice from within. Without looking at me again she put out her hand as if to warn or prevent me in some way. I retreated into the trees. Two people came through the French windows to join Perse. One was Madame Dimitriou, the other, to my amazement, was Dr Frith. He was on Madame Dimitriou's arm and looked more than usually distracted and dishevelled. Perse made another, smaller gesture with her hand, again without looking at me. She seemed to be shooing me away. I obeyed her because I had seen more than enough.

I did not tell Hutton or any of the others of my escapade, but when I was in bed, lying awake when all others had fallen asleep, I heard Frith stumbling into the Dig House and banging shut the door of his room.

The following morning Frith appeared briefly at breakfast, drank nothing but coffee and then returned to his room. The rest of us continued rather listlessly mostly in clearing away and cataloguing.

Hutton and I went into the chamber under the temple to see if there were any fragments or artefacts that had been missed. I asked him if he had noticed anything strange about his uncle, but he seemed defensive. When we broke for lunch, Frith had made no appearance, and no-one seemed eager to discuss the fact. The mood was subdued. After lunch Hutton and I returned to the chamber for one last look before it was sealed.

The wall against which the statue of Attis leant was of dressed stone. We had scraped away most of the earth that covered the wall, but I decided to finish the task. I had an idea that there must be another entrance to this temple crypt, but it was not a feeling that I cared to share with the others. Hutton was beginning to grow rather impatient with my tappings and knockings against the wall until quite unexpectedly a portion of it gave way revealing an irregular black entrance.

'Now you've done it,' said Hutton. 'You've made the place unsafe.'

'No, I haven't. I'm going to investigate.'

'You can't do that. You're not supposed to. Anyway, it isn't safe.'

'*Life* isn't safe,' I said. I was young, and I believed it. In a way I still do, but what I would do today in consequence of that belief might be different. I shone the torch into the hole. 'There's what looks like a passage and some steps. Coming?'

'God, no! And you shouldn't ...'

I didn't properly hear the rest of what he said which no doubt was sensible. I had cleared the hole enough to crawl through.

I found myself in a narrow, vaulted passage, the shape of a lancet window in a Gothic cathedral. There was just room enough to stand up. The masonry looked older than what I had seen in the chamber; it was made up of great irregular blocks of cyclopean masonry, like the passages at Tiryns in the Argolid from the fourteenth century BC.

Hutton was shouting something at me at my back, but I shone my torch forward and pressed on. The passage began to slope downwards in a series of shallow steps, then the steps became narrower and I was descending more vertiginously but always in the same direction. At any moment I expected the way to come to an end, but it did not. I began to worry that the battery of my torch would expire, so that I would be left in the dark and would have to crawl back. Often I thought of turning round, but I did not. I was probably the first person to make this voyage in over two thousand years. The masonry did not vary, nor the architecture. I think I had made my descent for an hour when I began to hear a noise. It sounded at first like a hoarse whisper. By this time I felt entombed in another world, almost another time and this, to some degree, inoculated me against fear. The experience of travelling down through this narrow, dark, vaulted tunnel, so monotonously strange that it seemed not so much another world as another state of mind.

Hitherto the sides of the tunnel had been dry; now their dark grey sides began to glisten in the torchlight with little trickles of water, and the hoarse whisper began to swell into a stertorous roar, like the ragged breathing of a giant. Still, I could not identify it. I went on. I could not now even think of stopping to rest; I had to go on because to go back now would render this whole journey futile. It must be endured for the sake of its unknown end.

There was a sudden explosion of sound like a gigantic sneeze, and I guessed at last what I had been listening to. It gave me hope because it was the sound of the sea. It was the sea breaking into a rocky cavern, now not too far distant and funnelling the sound up the passage into the womb of the earth. I switched off the torch and saw, tiny specks of light like stars reflected from the monstrous, wet slabs of stone that lined the tunnel like upright crazy paving. I switched the torch on again and pressed on.

In addition to the specks of light on the wall, I could now see, some meters below me, a splinter of brightness, the shape of a lancet window stretching from floor to roof. It was still far in the distance and for a while did not seem to get appreciably larger. I switched off the torch and fixed my eyes on the end. In doing so, I slipped and nearly fell on the stone floor which was now slicked with shallow patches of water.

By now the tunnel's bright end was rapidly increasing in size. Then I could see blue sky and, beneath it, sunlit rocks, and the deep, inky azure of a sunlit sea. At last, my confined man-made passage debouched into a huge cavern through which the sea came flashing and roaring, flanked on each side by narrow platforms of rock a mere matter of inches from the water's surface.

At this sight I felt an elation that I had never had before, and rarely since. The sight of the sea and the rocks, commonplace perhaps in other circumstances, was invested with a hitherto unrealised sense of beauty and meaning. I had come from a dead world into a living one, albeit one devoid of human or animal presence.

Taking care, not to slip on the wet surface of the rocky platform, I walked out of the cavern's shelter into the blinding glare of day. I found myself standing on the rocky shore of Skliros, about a mile or so to the east of, and several hundred feet below, the remains of the Great Mother's temple. I was alone at her entrance. To my left and right black cliffs rose almost vertically towards unseen earth and trees. Not far from me in the sea, like an erect phallus, stood a tall bare column of rock against which the sea flung shafts of brilliant sunlit foam. I found a place to sit and watch. My thoughts slowed to a standstill until the present moment stretched out into the infinite.

I cannot tell how long I was there, but I know that the sun had westered and long shadows were beginning to stretch from the rocks into the sea when I felt I had to come away. I dreaded the journey back into the Mother, but I had to make it. There was no way that I could climb the cliffs and come back to the Dig House overland.

The walk back up the tunnel was wearisome and more filled with fear and anxiety than the way down. The stimulus of adventure was missing, and the diminishing roar of the sea was like a threat at my back.

I was leaving the light and walking up through darkness

and my torch was fading. My beatific vision of the sea and its phallic rock was beginning to give way to an unspecified dread as I mounted up into the earth's core again and made my way back into the shrine of Cybele, the Earth Mother.

The words of Ludwig Krull insisted on running in my head:

My mama Earth, my goddess dark,
When I go to my tomb
Under the world of men,
Take me to your womb,

As the roar of the sea faded, I began to hear other sounds, little tappings and scrapings, as if there were animals alive in the ancient masonry: Paracelsan dwarfs perhaps mining the earth for their ransom, or the salamanders who dwell in subterranean fire. Vicious, mad thoughts they were, assaulting my mind, driving out true memories. The tramp upwards and away from the sea became an exhausting forced march. I imagined that I was being followed by a swarm of little unsexed men. Then another sound, sharp, real and decisive forced me out of my delirium: a foot stumbling on stone.

I swung my torchlight up the steps and let out a gasp as I saw a figure standing above me on the stairway. It looked down at me and gave a shrill unnatural shriek, like the cry of a fox in pain. It wore a long print dress of floral design and its mouth had been smeared with a gash of bright red lipstick. There seemed to be blood on his hands. I was so startled that it took me a full ten seconds to make sense of what I saw.

'Dr Frith!'

He shrieked again and turned to escape up the steps, but slipped and fell. As he scrambled upright he began to whimper.

'Stay where you are,' I said. 'I'll help. I've got a torch.' That would have been obvious, but I felt the need of something to reassure him that I meant no harm. He paid no attention, and finally managed to right himself, whereupon he scuttled upwards away from me as fast as he could. I heard a cry again as he banged against a rock protruding from the tunnel wall, then he was gone.

I followed on upwards as fast as my exhausted limbs would carry me. At last I came to the top of the passage and, without stopping, I passed through the barrel vaulted chamber under the temple and into the open air. It was almost dark.

At the Dig House Hutton and the others were standing outside, looking bewildered.

'Where the hell have you been?' asked Hutton.

'Never mind that,' I said. 'Where's Dr Frith?'

'We don't know. We thought you might know.'

'Why should I know?'

'The Landrover's gone.'

'He might have gone into Chora. You go and look for him there.'

'Where are you going?'

'Villa Attis. He might be there.'

'Want any of us to come with you?'

'Best not. I know them up there. They might be of help.'

So, exhausted as I was, I took the road up to the Villa Attis. My torch had failed but the moon in a cloudless sky was at its fullest and brightest. The Villa was waiting me, or so, in my troubled mental state, I thought.

The lights were on and the curtains only half drawn over the windows that opened onto the terrace. I looked in and saw two people in the room. Ludwig was sprawled on a pile of cushions, his eyes shut, mouth open, stertorously sleeping. Sitting cross-legged on a sofa was Perse, strumming her guitar. I tapped on the window. She looked up and saw me. A complex of expressions passed across her beautiful face. She came to the window and slid it open.

'Hi there! What are you doing here?' by this time complexity had vanished to be replaced by a smile.

'Can we talk? Have you seen Dr Frith?'

'No. Why?' There had been a hesitation before the 'no' which I did not notice at the time, but remembered later.

'He's gone missing. I think he took the Landrover.' Perse looked round anxiously, as if in search of the missing vehicle.

'Well, he's not been here ...' Again, that momentary hesitation.

'Can we talk?'

'Yeah, sure ... Cool ... But not here. Ludwig's kind of ... Look there's a garden at the back of the house. You'll find it. Go there. Now. I'll come to you in a minute. Wait for me. I just got to ...'

I tried to grab her arm, but she was too quick for me. She slid shut the window and gestured to me to walk round the building to a garden I had never seen.

The Villa Attis seemed to be in two halves. The side which I had seen was modern, apart from the terrace itself with its stone balustrade; the other side was antique in style, with a Palladian pedimented porch and steps leading down to a formal garden with cypress trees and statuary. Under the moon, it looked more like a mausoleum than a house; the formality of it was strangely daunting.

The garden itself was laid out as if it were an outdoor temple with cypress trees as columns, and a raised portion at the end in stone like an altar but with a marble basin on it. Formal parterres were flanked by stone benches on one of which I sat. Behind me was the house, ahead the raised marble basin. Between the cypress trees on either side of me were statues in white marble, clearly modern in design but resembling in shape and form the votive figurines that we had found, the sexless icons of the cult of Cybele.

At the site, ancient provenance had robbed the images of offence for me, but I found their modern imitations abominable. It was quite irrational, I know, and yet ... The place did not seem right. Behind the 'altar', as I called it, was a tall pine tree whose base was bound with white cloth for what reason I did not know, but the cloth appeared to be stained with blood. I could have confirmed this by looking closer, but I did not want to; in fact I was beginning to consider leaving the garden altogether when a voice close behind me said: 'Hi!'

I turned and saw her.

It was Perse. She was naked, her smooth, faultless skin

silvered by moonlight. Violets were entwined in her blonde hair. I reached out to touch her but she gently grasped my wrists and held them away from her.

Smiling, she said: 'Well, aren't you going to get naked too?'

You have to remember that I was little more than a schoolboy, and the son of a vicar. I was not so much innocent as painfully inexperienced. The concept of 'getting naked' with anyone was terrible and, with the sight of Perse in front of me, also thrilling. I began to undo my trousers, turning my back on her, absurdly, as I did so, knowing that such modesty was ridiculous under the circumstances, but still obeying my instincts. It was an instinct, I believe, which saved my life, or perhaps more than my life.

As I turned to disrobe, I saw a fluttering in the bushes behind the altar. Someone was moving quickly to conceal themselves. It was only the red robe which had caught in the undergrowth that betrayed her identity: Madame Dimitriou. Quickly I fastened my belt and turned to face Perse.

'What the hell – ?'

She was naked still, but now holding a knife in her right hand. It was long and bright and curved like a crescent moon. The shape reminded me of the scar on her neck.

'Don't be afraid,' she said. 'Come on! Get naked.' Her smile was beatific but her eyes were not focussed on me. They looked through me and beyond.

'You must become one with the Great Mother,' said the voice of Madame Dimitriou behind me, alarmingly close. 'Only then will you become blessed.'

'What the hell have you done to Dr Frith?'

'He became one with us, but then he changed his mind. He betrayed the Goddess.'

I half turned to face Madame Dimitriou, but in doing so saw Perse lunge forward with the knife. I seized her wrist and made her drop it, then twisted round to face Madame Dimitriou who had picked up a stone. She threw it at my face, but I dodged and it only grazed my cheek. I pushed her aside, knocking her to the ground in the process; then, pausing briefly – and oh, so absurdly! – to apologise to her, I ran from the Grove of the Great Mother. I had not been to a public school for nothing, it would seem.

I had only the moon to guide me but I got back to the Dig House safely. There the others were still up, discussing the situation. There was no sign of Dr Frith or his Landrover in Chora or elsewhere. I told them that I had not seen him up at the Villa Attis.

'Why would he be there?'

I did not answer and said no more. We decided to go to bed and renew the search in the morning.

The following day Professor Volonakis from the Heraklion Institute of Archaeology arrived, hoping to inspect our new finds. He was dismayed by the disappearance of Dr Frith and was able, far more effectively than we ever could, to alert the police and organise a search. That day the Landrover was found on some land above a cliff on the eastern shore. The following day the body of Dr Amyas Frith was found by some Skliros fisherman floating in the sea. He was naked and the rocks had mutilated his body so that his penis was half severed and his testicles were missing. Suicide was suspected, but I never knew if that became the official verdict. I had left the island as soon as I decently could.

And so, fifty years on, I have come again to Skliros, 'this haunted heaven,' as Ludwig Krull put it. I was met on the quayside by Professor Volonakis of the Heraklion Institute of Archaeology. My initial astonishment at his youthful appearance was modified when he told me that he was the grandson of the one who had come to the island all those years ago. He took me to the site of the Temple of Cybele. The place had been tidied up, the oppression of the pine trees mitigated by judicious felling, but there was surprisingly little that was new to see. I asked about the underground chamber beneath the temple and the Professor told me that it had been blocked up, having been deemed unsafe. The great statue of Attis that we had found was in the Heraklion Museum, but not on display.

'I understand you were yourself here when it was found,' said Professor Volonakis.

'Yes. With Dr Frith.'

'Of course. Doctor *Firrit.*' His otherwise faultless English stumbled over the name. 'There was a tragic accident, I believe?'

I nodded.

'I remember my grandfather telling me.' I wondered whether he would question me further, but he seemed uninterested in doing so, or perhaps unwilling. 'And now, I take you back to Skliros Port. I believe we have a room for you at the Hotel Ariadne.'

When I expressed a wish, before returning to my hotel, to see the village of Chora and buy the Professor a drink at the taverna there, he looked puzzled but consented. His manner was extremely deferential towards me and I had to remind myself that it was only the respect due to a senior academic; I was no longer a boy.

Chora has barely changed at all. There is the taverna, with its toothless nut-brown old men clacking their worry beads and playing dominos. There is the faint but pungent smell of thick, strong Turkish coffee. And there – !

There is a group of young people sitting at a table outside. They surround one older person who has her back to me. I cannot see her face, but know her at once from the faintly opalescent sickle-shaped scar on the back of her neck. The young people around her are girls mostly, but there are two adolescent boys with long hair. One wears what looks like a long floral cotton dress – possibly a caftan – and carries a tambourine. The woman knocks back a glass of ouzo and laughs raucously.

I begin to tremble, so that Professor Volonakis looks at me with concern. Persephone – Perse – is old, but so am I. She appears to be drunk, but that isn't a crime; nor is the fact that she had once been the most beautiful creature I have ever seen.

I stand there paralysed, waiting for her to turn. She does so, and I see her full face. Time has ravaged her, as it has me, but the worst of it is this: I have been recognised. The look she gives me with her watery drink-sodden eyes, now outlined heavily with kohl, is one of hatred and terror. The spell of fifty years is broken.

Fifty years ago, I left Skliros, still her slave; now I am free, but too late.

Dea magna, dea Cybebe, dea domina Dindymi
Procul a mea tuus sit furor omnis, era, domo
Alios age incitatos, alios age rabidos.
Catullus LXIII ll 91-93

Great goddess! Goddess Cybele! Queen Goddess of Dindymus!
Far from my house be all your fury, mistress!
Drive *others* demented, you demon! Make *others* mad!

BORN OF BLOOD AND MYSTERY

The great port city of Thessaloniki is the second largest city in Greece, and the current capital of the northern Greek state of Macedonia. Most of us will know that it was Macedonia, formerly a small independent mountain kingdom, from out of which emerged Alexander the Great, and indeed, the city of Thessaloniki indirectly celebrates this because, though it was named after Alexander's half-sister, Thessalonike, her name means 'Thessalian victory', and is a direct reference to the incredibly bloody battle of the Crocus Field, fought in 352 BC, which saw the annihilation of Macedonia's old enemy, the Phocians, by Alexander's father, Phillip II of Macedon, and the founding of the city by Cassander of Macedon in 315 BC.

Another ferocious but less factually based battle was also fought in the vicinity, just over the border in Thessaly itself, when Zeus took on the monster of monsters, Typhon.

Typhon, son of Cronos, king of the Titans, was said to be half human and half reptile in form, but so vast that he brushed the stars, and that he had many heads and claws, representing all kinds of different, hellish creatures. It is also said that he was winged and breathed out fire and poisonous gas, and that he was bent on the destruction of all mankind, though his ambition didn't end there. So terrible was this monumental beast that he even posed a threat to the gods and in fact was lumbering towards Olympus, causing indescribable devastation on Earth as he travelled, when Zeus confronted him, only winning victory by striking the monster over and over with his trusty thunderbolts.

But whether the savage battles that cleared the way for the creation of Thessaloniki were fanciful or factual, there is little evidence of either in the thriving modern metropolis that it is today, though intriguingly, of all the great Mediterranean cities, with the possible exceptions of Rome and Venice, it is this one that has the most famous reputation for urban mythology.

Probably its most oft-told tale concerns the so-called Bleeding Stone.

This remarkable artefact harks back to 390 AD, when a dreadful event occurred in the city's great Hippodrome (a vast sports arena mainly used for chariot racing). At this time, all of Greece was under Roman control, the Empire not yet having permanently split (though that great sundering of imperial power was imminent). Its ruler at this stage was Theodosius I, a devout Christian, generally held to have been an approachable and even-tempered ruler, so perhaps what happened that terrible day is all the more shocking because it is so out-of-character. Theodosius responded to the lynching of a public official by unleashing the Roman Army against a huge crowd gathered in the Hippodrome. The orgy of violence lasted three hours and turned into a wholesale slaughter, the stadium soon swimming with blood.

At the end of it, 18,000 citizens lay dead.

As major incidents go, almost no contemporary written reference to this event can be found anywhere, which is very odd given what meticulous record-keepers the Byzantines were, but we know that it genuinely happened, because what was recorded was a reprimand issued to the emperor by Bishop Ambrose of Milan for the killings in the Hippodrome, and a threat that he'd be denied the Eucharist until adequate repentance had been shown. Also recorded was Theodosius's acceptance of this. So, in other words, this was a real atrocity and the man responsible acknowledged his part in it.

Shortly afterwards, in response to the bishop's rebuke and as an act of commemoration, Theodosius erected a marble pillar outside the stadium, and had it carved with the names of all those who'd been murdered. And here is where the strangeness commences, because according to the many eyewitnesses, every year on the anniversary, the pillar was seen to be streaming with fresh blood. It became an annual reminder of the ruling power's guilt, and before the end of his reign, Theodosius was so tormented by it that he had it removed.

However, the story continues into relatively modern times. Because even now, in Hippodrome Square, which stands on the site of the raceway that became an abattoir, a curse is said to afflict any person who doesn't show sufficient reverence for the incident. So, for example, in 1978, when Thessaloniki was struck by an earthquake, a block of flats collapsed on Hippodrome Square, killing 37 people, rumours soon circling that it had been built on the exact spot where the memorial column had once stood. Of course, no one knows whether this was true or not, though reports had been made even before the earthquake that several tenants of the flats had reported a reddish, blood-like substance oozing from the walls of their apartments. Either way, the authorities took no chances with the building they raised in its place, for it now houses the Archive of the History of Thessaloniki, which contains many historical documents lamenting the slaughter in the Hippodrome.

But the city possesses other, equally frightening myths.

The first of these concerns Black Rock Street in the heart of Ano Poli, one of Thessaloniki's oldest neighbourhoods, which is reputedly a passage to unknown realms.

In Greece, there is more than one route by which mortals can literally walk into 'the other world'. The most famous location was probably Delphi, which the ancients considered 'the navel of the world', and which was once a great religious site: the Temple of Apollo stood there, dating to at least four centuries BC, which was also home to Pythia, the High Priestess and a famous Oracle who, according to multiple written sources, would descend through unknown vaults to commune with the gods directly on behalf of her supplicants. Modern archaeology has never yet located the route she would take, most scholars believing that she would simply head down to a volcanic cavern, where narcotic fumes would put her into a dream-state.

A perhaps eerier tale concerns the River Acheron in Epirus, or the 'River of Pain', as it was better known, though it looks tranquil enough today. Both Virgil and Dante and later John Milton described this as the waterway along which Charon would ferry the dead rather than the River Styx. The legend no doubt sprung from the route it took in ancient times, when it plunged beneath the terrifying Necromanteion. This great temple of necromancy, dedicated to the goddess Persephone, Queen of the Underworld, was believed to provide a doorway into Hades. It was here, according to Homer, where Odysseus asked questions of the dead. Various archaeological sites claim to be the remnants of the Necromanteion, but all are disputed.

Which brings us back to our original tale, Black Rock Street in Thessaloniki, which is widely believed to be Greece's current entrance *to the Kingdom of Shadows.*

With its real name of *Odos Mavris Petras*, this narrow thoroughfare, which ultimately leads to a dead-end, seems harmless enough superficially, but many visitors have reported feeling queasy and disoriented there, and following it on and on until they found themselves lost in a network of narrow lanes, lined with very archaic buildings, which seemed limitless, and which they never remembered entering. Others have told even more fantastical tales, of meeting dead relatives down there, or characters from Greek mythology. Sci-fi writer Pantelis Giannoulakis, also described it as a passage to alternative dimensions, while urban myths tell how a heavy black stone once fell from the sky here, not just giving the street its name, but tearing open the fabric of reality. Nearby meanwhile can be found Pasha's Gardens, a lush green oasis, but a site filled with ruins so old and peculiar that no one knows who built them or why.

More traditional ghost stories of Thessaloniki concern curious red buildings.

The Red House is a handsome city centre mansion dating to the 1920s, which supposedly afflicts all those who live in it with a malediction meaning they will never do well. The numerous ghosts of its former residents are now said to roam its empty rooms and corridors, and often to gaze out, pale and seemingly lost, from its many windows. Meanwhile, an inexplicable Red Tower supposedly appears here and there around the city, usually catching both sightseers and residents by surprise – because no such building exists. Rumour mongers will tell you that it was once part of a prison used by the Ottoman Turks, who controlled Thessaloniki from 1430 to 1913, and was the section wherein tortures and executions occurred (though others claim that this was in fact the White Tower, which still stands, and which may simply have been whitewashed from its original red once the Greeks regained control of the city).

It is no wonder that Thessaloniki is considered the natural home to Greece's poets, intellectuals and bohemians. Mystery and esotericism are written into its very stones.

THE QUIET WOMAN
Sean Hogan

At 7.34am on an unquiet September morning, Mira Russell awoke believing herself a murderer.

It was just a nightmare, of course; a vision of guilt and incarceration conjured up from the murk of her subconscious. That didn't prevent it from feeling horribly, viscerally real. In the dream, she had set off a bomb as an act of political protest, leading to the deaths of several innocent bystanders. As the authorities closed in on her and the nightmare built to its climax, Mira had been seized by the awful knowledge that her whole life was about to end, that she would now spend the rest of her days rotting helplessly in prison. All at once, it had seemed as though she was drowning in quicksand; her limbs held fast, the air bleeding from her lungs.

Even after she'd finally escaped the dream, the sickening feeling had pursued her into wakefulness. Lying there in her motel room bed, Mira found she could barely move, such was the sensation of shame and dread pushing down on her chest, squatting on her ribcage like a malevolent goblin. It took her several seconds to convince herself that she was not in fact a killer.

Lifting her head to gaze around at her motel room, as featureless and utilitarian as a jail cell, Mira thought, *I'm on holiday. I haven't done anything wrong.*

Even then, her dreamsick mind struggled to believe it. But it was true. She wasn't on the run from the law. The very idea of it was laughable, Mira being the sort of woman who broke out in a cold sweat if she so much as got on a train without first having purchased the right ticket. No, she was in Italy, travelling alone, entirely free to do as she pleased.

It was all still quite unfamiliar to her, this newfound sense of liberty. Not needing to check in with anyone, being able to change her plans at will, on the flightiest, most ridiculous whim, without having to fear the slightest criticism or disapproval. She might have been a zoo animal released back into the wild, torn between an instinctive yearning to be free and an equally primal fear of the unknown. When the iron bars of a cage are all you know, to suddenly be confronted with nothing but wide open space can be terrifying. But here she was, completely free to run in whatever direction she chose, as fast and as far as she liked.

Still, that much freedom could be dangerous. In a cage, you were protected. Kept safe from predators, your every need provided for. But out here in the world, anything might happen.

Mira forced herself to sit up. To let such fear dominate her now was unthinkable. It was just the after-effects of the nightmare, seeping into her thoughts like an infection. And she had waited so very long to be her own person again. It was okay to be afraid, but you couldn't let it rule your life. Because that would make her weak and helpless, just like Rob always said she was. *You just can't look after yourself, Mira,* he would always tell her with a weary sigh. *But it's okay, that's why you have me.*

She craved a long hot shower, to wash away the stain of the dream. But when Mira tried to stand, she found her legs could barely support her weight. The lingering dread still coursed through her system, sapping her strength. It would be so much easier just to stay in bed and hide under the covers for another hour, two hours, a whole day.

But what sort of person can't even stand up straight after a stupid nightmare? A weak one, that's who. And she would not be that person, not anymore.

Clutching onto the bed's headboard, Mira heaved herself upright. The sudden effort made the room lurch queasily around her, but she closed her eyes and took deep breaths until the dizziness passed. Weakness could be overcome. It was like anything, you just had to wait it out. Like a stomach bug, or a bad marriage.

Stumbling to the bathroom, Mira turned on the shower, adjusting the temperature dial to full heat. In a cheap motel like this, she was in little danger of scalding herself. Once again, she found herself thinking that she could have stayed in more comfortable lodgings, closer to Ravenna's town centre, maybe even the same hotel she and Rob had visited on their honeymoon tour here all those years ago. But something had warned her away. If she was going to reclaim her memories, her life, she needed to keep the past at arm's length. At least until she had made it her own.

The shower was at least hot enough to help drive away the last nagging twinges of ill-feeling, and by the time Mira had brushed her teeth and dressed, she felt restored enough to go and fetch coffee. Exiting her room, she walked across the motel forecourt towards the neighbouring building, a large entertainment complex. In truth, the whole area was something of a brutalist eyesore, and it was obvious why the town planners had kept it so far away from the historical centre. But its grey anonymity suited Mira. The complex housed a small cafe which opened first thing in the morning, and after her breakfast needs were met, Ravenna was only a couple of miles away. Easily walkable, and just a short hop in her rental car if the weather proved unfavourable.

The sky this morning matched Mira's mood: stormily overcast and claustrophobic, pressing down on her like a sodden blanket. She could see lightning flashes in the distance, edging closer to the town. Normally Mira enjoyed a thunderstorm, but for some reason, she found the sight unsettling. She had been toying with the idea of visiting the coast today, but had no wish to get caught in a sudden downpour. Very well, she would just spend the day sightseeing instead.

Quickly downing two espressos in the cafe, Mira returned to her motel room to grab her things. Finding the door open, she discovered that the maid, a sour-faced middle-aged woman, was already stripping her bed. As Mira entered the room, the woman glanced over at her, fixing her with an annoyed glare.

'*Scusi*,' Mira mumbled.

The maid grunted and returned to her task. Not wishing to attract any further ire, Mira hurriedly gathered her belongings and shrugged on her jacket, then made a speedy exit. Outside, she debated whether to take her car into Ravenna, then decided against it. The storm did not appear to have crept any closer, lingering in the middle distance as though it were laying siege to the town. And the exercise would do her good. With a few miles' walking under her belt, hopefully she would sleep easier tonight.

Once in town, she spent an absorbing couple of hours wandering between the sites of Ravenna's various Byzantine mosaics. She was particularly taken with the mosaic depicting Theodora, wife to Emperor Justinian. A guide leaflet informed her that Theodora had started life as a showgirl and courtesan, but by virtue of her beauty and cunning, had succeeded in catching the emperor's eye. After their marriage, she had used her newfound status to enact laws helping women and the poor. Still, she could be merciless too, famously ordering the executions of some thirty thousand insurgents.

Mira tried to envision herself up on the wall, imagining the weeks of painstaking work it would take to assemble her image out of hundreds of tiny constituent tiles. The very thought of it brought a wry smile to her lips. People like her didn't end up on the walls of chapels, still drawing admiring crowds thousands of years after their passing. Theodora had been a strong, wilful woman, who had escaped her lowly beginnings and won the heart of an emperor. Mira had practically married the first man who came along and then spent the next several years trying to escape the disaster that her life had rapidly become. She and the imperious-looking woman pictured in the mosaic could hardly be any more different.

But we do have one thing in common, Mira thought. *We're both impossibly fragile, pieced together out of countless fragments. And one blow could send us flying apart into tiny pieces, never to be made whole again.*

She could once again feel herself growing dizzy, her vision blurring around the edges, and Mira decided it was high time she ate something. After buying a sandwich from a vendor, she retreated to a nearby park to eat her lunch. The sky overhead remained grey and foreboding, but the threatened storm had still not materialised, and the day was temperate enough otherwise. Devouring her sandwich, Mira consulted her tourist map, wondering where she should visit next.

Scanning the illustration, her eyes fell upon the symbol marking Dante Alighieri's tomb, just a few streets away from where she currently sat. Visiting the tomb was one of the most vivid memories of the trip she'd taken here with Rob: turning down the innocuous little side street, such an unlikely place for one of history's most famous poets to be buried; the solemn hush that surrounded the monument itself, enforced by a so-called *Zona Dantesca,* demanding that visitors stay silent and respectful at all times; standing before the shadowed marble tomb, feeling Rob's lips brush her earlobe, his voice murmuring, *Wishing to speak I know not what to say / And lose myself in amorous wanderings.*

She had never felt so loved before that moment. As they exited the tomb, Rob had pulled her close and murmured, *You're my Beatrice.*

Mira hadn't thought much of the comment at the time. She'd known very little about Dante; only that he'd loved a woman named Beatrice, writing several poems about her. Now, all these years later, after everything that had happened between her and Rob, the irony of it was at last clear to her: Dante had never really known Beatrice, and had certainly never come close to consummating his passion for her; the poet had only ever admired the woman from afar. The Beatrice he loved existed only in his imagination, forever silent and idealised.

Finishing her snack, she decided to revisit the tomb. Her

memories of it were so bound up with Rob that the prospect filled her with some trepidation, but going there would only take a few minutes, and besides, the entire point of this holiday was to have some fresh recollections of Italy to take away with her.

Navigating her way through the town's streets, Mira soon arrived at the tomb, seemingly unchanged from her memory of it. *Of course it is, you idiot,* she chided herself. *That's the whole point of a monument.* Still, as she moved inside the *zona dantesca* and made to enter the tomb itself, Mira could not escape the uncanny feeling that she was about to step back in time.

The shadows parted to admit her, the funereal hush of the small building enveloping Mira like the cool waters of a shaded pond. It felt safe here, a peaceful refuge from the nagging fears of her everyday life. Approaching the tomb, Mira started to feel rather stupid, a little disrespectful. She knew next to nothing about Dante, really, and here she was, barging in and interrupting his rest. 'I'm sorry,' she whispered, immediately feeling even more foolish for saying it aloud.

Closing her eyes, Mira let the immaculate silence wash over her. She stood there for several seconds, taking long slow breaths. *If anyone came in and saw me, they'd probably think I was bonkers,* she thought with a small smile. *If Rob could see me, he'd ...*

The unprompted thought of her husband caused her skin to suddenly prickle. Mira shivered and opened her eyes, then froze. She still had her back to the tomb's entrance, but now, out of nowhere, she felt as though she were being watched, observed from behind; as if a dark figure was standing unseen at her shoulder, studying her, trespassing on her solitude and relishing the secret power it gave them.

At any moment, they might step forward and place a resolute hand on her shoulder, reclaiming her, pulling her back into the past ...

Wishing to speak I know not what to say ...

Mira span around on her heels, only to find herself quite

alone in the tomb.

The uneasy sensation of being watched still persisted, however, and Mira decided to beat a hasty retreat outside. Her moment of blissful peace had been rudely shattered, no matter that it had been her own disordered mind to blame. She now craved the safety of a crowd, the reassurance of hearing laughter and conversation around her.

Pushing the heavy door open, she stepped out into the daylight, the sudden shift away from the interior gloom causing her eyes to blink furiously. Momentarily disorientated, Mira found herself colliding with another visitor to the tomb, a dark-haired Italian man.

'*Mi scusi,*' the man said politely, no matter that the collision had not been his fault.

'I'm sorry, I'm so sorry,' Mira gabbled.

'No, it is fine,' he replied, looking at her with sudden interest. 'You are English?'

'Yes, but I really have to go,' Mira said hurriedly. Being drawn into polite conversation with a complete stranger was the very last thing she wanted right now. 'Sorry again!'

Without waiting for a reply, she hurried away down the street. No doubt the man thought her extremely rude, probably she was, but Mira reminded herself that one of the things she had vowed to work on was the necessity to stand up for herself, to learn to be forceful when the situation required. If that meant people occasionally thinking her rude, then so be it.

She sought refuge in the town's main piazza, losing herself amongst the throngs of people eating and drinking outside the several open air cafes situated there. The storm she had glimpsed earlier seemed to have now passed harmlessly by, and the afternoon sun was playing a mischievous game of hide and seek behind the last few remaining clouds. Finding an empty table, Mira slumped down into a chair and quickly ordered a beer from a passing waiter.

Gazing around, she luxuriated in the warm pastel beauty of the surrounding Venetian architecture. This is what being on holiday was really about, Mira decided. Taking time to allow the atmosphere of an unfamiliar country to seep into your bones, not continually rushing to get to the next landmark or monument, fastidiously mapping and scheduling every last free minute of every remaining day. The way Rob always had done on their trips away together.

I wish I could just disappear here, she thought, imagining herself as a chameleon, slyly vanishing amongst a tree's foliage. How wonderful it would be to at last feel safe, to rest easy in the knowledge that no one could ever find her unless she wished it so.

Mira tried to recall the last time she'd felt safe, truly safe. Probably not since she was a child. Certainly not during the long years of her marriage to Rob, and not even since she'd finally summoned the courage to leave him, after that dreadful final argument where he'd seized her by the arms and held her fast, poised and helpless, at the top of their home's staircase, coldly telling her, *I could just throw you down the stairs now. I could do that, and who would even care, Mira?*

The next morning, she'd pretended to be asleep when he left for work. Mira had kept her eyes tightly closed even when her husband bent over her, flooding her nostrils with the cloying scent of the expensive aftershave he favoured.

He'd kissed her forehead and whispered, *I'm sorry.* And then, moments later: *I know you're awake, Mira. You can't hide from me, ever. Remember that.*

She'd waited until she was sure Rob was gone, waiting an additional couple of minutes after he'd exited the house, in case he unexpectedly returned under the pretence of having forgotten something, then leapt out of bed and called her friend Poppy, who she'd not even spoken to in a year because Rob despised her so much, praying that Poppy didn't hate her for it, that she still cared about Mira enough to answer her call.

And when she did answer, immediately telling Poppy, without even saying 'Hello' or 'I'm sorry,' *I'm leaving him, can you please come and get me?*

She'd moved into Poppy's spare bedroom, hardly any

bigger than a closet, really, but it didn't matter, it was her space, a place where she could exist without being watched or grabbed or incessantly hectored. *Stay as long as you want,* Poppy had told her, and although Mira didn't want to take advantage of her friend's kindness, a few days had quickly become a few weeks, and then a few months.

Of course, it hadn't taken long for the calls and texts to start. Mira never answered the phone when Rob rang, but she saw all his texts, alternately patronising and pleading and outright abusive. Eventually, after much coaxing from Poppy, Mira had simply discarded the SIM – the phone contract was under Rob's name anyway – and fitted a new pay-as-you-go card.

Shortly after that, Rob had started waiting outside the house.

One evening, Mira had glanced out of her bedroom window to see Rob's car parked across the street. The vehicle interior was in complete shadow, but she could make out the faint glow of a cigarette tip burning in the darkness.

He's started smoking again, Mira thought. *He'll blame me for that.*

She sat watching the car for an hour or so, steadily working her way through a bottle of wine, anticipating the moment Rob would finally climb out of the car and storm over to their front door, angrily demanding that Mira face him, that she stop all this childishness and return home, but he never did. He merely sat there in the darkness, silently observing her from the shadows, a revenant of the old life Mira had tried so desperately to bury and forget.

Eventually, the car engine snarled into life and he drove away, vanishing into the night like a half-remembered dream. But he was there again the next night, and the night after that. When he didn't appear on the fourth night, or the fifth, Mira became hopeful that Rob had perhaps tired of this sinister game, but then he reappeared again the following week, and she finally broke down and confessed to her friend that rather than escaping her troubles, she had merely succeeded in bringing them to Poppy's door.

That creepy fucking prick, Poppy said. *I'll teach him.*

Grabbing a large shillelagh she kept on her mantelpiece, she'd stormed outside to confront Rob, but he merely started the engine and drove away as soon as he saw Poppy emerge from the house.

Satisfied, Poppy returned inside. *You've just got to stand up to the bastard*, she told Mira. She placed the shillelagh on a small table adjacent to the door. *If he comes back, I want you to take this and give him what for.*

Managing to summon an uneasy laugh, Mira promised her friend that she would. But when she awoke at 3am later that night and peered out of her window to discover that Rob had returned, she did no such thing. Instead, she tossed and turned all night, drifting in and out of anxious dreams in which she would awake to find that the house had been broken into, only for the dream to start all over again. Each time it recommenced, the nightmare seemed more and more real, turning her sleep into a series of Chinese boxes; each one containing ever increasing amounts of worry and alarm.

The next morning, sharing a pot of coffee with Poppy, Mira told her friend she had decided to go away on a long holiday.

How long? Poppy asked, her face etched with concern. It wasn't like Mira to be this impulsive.

Until the money runs out, Mira told her simply.

And so here she was, drifting aimlessly across northern Italy, staying in budget hotels and subsisting on sandwiches and cheap pasta meals in a bid to make her dwindling funds last as long as possible. Still, while the constant infusion of carbs probably wasn't great for her, the trip had otherwise proven wonderfully restorative so far. Mira felt as though she was rediscovering herself anew, as though she were stripping away layers of faded wallpaper from the brickwork of an old house to reveal the original décor underneath.

At least, she'd felt that way until today, when the vertiginous feeling of being watched had overtaken her, sending her plummeting helplessly back to those nights at

Poppy's where she would stare out of her bedroom window at Rob's waiting car. All at once, she'd been the old Mira again, the frightened, defenceless Mira without a voice or a will of her own.

I'm not like that anymore, Mira told herself. Wasn't this trip proof of it?

Suddenly thirsty, she drained her beer. As long as she was sitting here, lost in the anonymity of the crowd, Mira could convince herself she was anything she wanted to be. So she ordered another beer, and then another, along with a plate of ragu. By the time the cafe had begun to close up for the evening, she was feeling pleasantly tipsy. Leaving a large tip for the waiter, she got to her feet and tottered unsteadily out of the piazza.

But as soon as she was alone again, that same sensation of creeping disquiet slowly re-asserted itself. The sun was dipping in the sky, its gradual descent displacing a tide of shadow that was quickly spilling through the town's streets. Before this moment, Mira had conveniently managed to disregard the fact that she still had a two-mile walk back to her hotel ahead of her, but now, with the gathering shadows greedily poised to ensnare a lonely inebriated woman, the looming prospect of the journey was no longer possible to ignore.

Mira knew she should try and catch a taxi back to her motel, but first she had to actually locate one. Ravenna's tangled streets could be confusing at the best of times, let alone after several drinks. If her Italian weren't so non-existent, she could attempt to ask someone, but Mira's inherent self-consciousness, now pushed to even greater levels by her mounting anxiety, precluded it.

So instead, she blindly wandered through the town, praying that she would eventually stumble across a taxi rank. Left and right and left she turned, with no success. Gazing hopelessly around her, Mira noticed that the surrounding buildings seemed to be growing older and older, as though she was moving inexorably back in time. *If I go far enough back,* she thought crazily, *I might bump into Rob and me, when we first came here together.*

As irrational as it was, the thought horrified her all the same, and Mira immediately quickened her pace. But hastening her speed only served to get her lost at an even faster rate, and she was soon forced to admit her situation was hopeless. Slumping down onto a nearby wall, she fought a rising urge to burst into tears. It suddenly occurred to her just how much Rob would relish her predicament, if he only could see her now.

'*Senora?*'

Initially, Mira paid the call little heed, but when it was repeated again moments later, she glanced up and looked around. Across the street from her, sitting outside a little neighbourhood bar, was the same dark-haired man she'd bumped into outside Dante's tomb. He motioned to Mira, inviting her over to his table.

For all her perpetual shyness, Mira very much did not want to be alone right now. Getting to her feet, she crossed the street to join him.

He stood up and gestured for her to sit. 'I am Alberto. Please.'

Accepting the invitation, Mira introduced herself, then realised she had absolutely no idea what to say next.

Alberto smiled at her, then pointed at the open bottle of wine sitting in front of him. 'You like?'

'Er, yes.'

Signalling to the waitress, Alberto asked her to bring them another wine glass. Once the glass was delivered and the wine poured, Mira took a tentative sip. Drinking any more alcohol was probably inadvisable, but on the other hand, she could hardly get any more lost than she was already.

Alberto studied her. 'You seem … troubled.'

'Do I?' Mira's face flushed. 'Well, yes. I suppose I am. I've gone and got myself completely lost. I feel like such a stupid bloody tourist.'

'Where do you stay?'

She was about to tell him the name of the motel, and then immediately thought better of it. 'Outside of town,' she said.

He nodded vaguely. 'You like Ravenna?'

'Oh yes. It isn't my first time here, though. I visited with my husband years ago.'

Alberto looked around, as though expecting her husband to materialise from the shadows. 'You are married?'

'Oh, not anymore.'

'*Bene*,' he said with a small smile.

Was he trying to pick her up, Mira wondered? Alberto seemed gentlemanly enough, but perhaps it might be a good idea to change the subject.

'Anyway, I was thinking that it would be nice to see something different this time,' Mira said hurriedly. 'Ravenna is lovely, but I wondered what else there might be to visit in the area.'

Alberto's eyes lit up. 'I know a good place.'

'Oh really? Where?'

He looked at her closely. 'You might not like, perhaps. I go there to take photographs. Maybe you think is …' He paused. '*Spaventoso*. Scary.'

Mira was intrigued. 'What is it?'

'In Italian, the word is *manicomio*. I think you say, "madhouse", maybe?'

'An asylum?'

'*Si.*'

Mira tried not to look as appalled as she felt. Did they really still do that here, let people visit mental institutions to gawk at the patients? Like London's Bedlam, something ripped out of the eighteenth century.

Alberto must have glimpsed something in her eyes, because he immediately let out a laugh. 'Is not open! Was closed many years ago. Abandoned now.'

'*Oh*. I see.' Mira felt like an idiot.

'There are many such places in Italy. I like to go there, take photographs.' He seemed to be searching for a word. 'There is a phrase in English, I believe.'

Mira thought. 'Oh, urban exploration, you mean?'

'*Si!* Anyway, perhaps you not like so much.' Producing his phone, Alberto pulled up some pictures of the derelict asylum to show to Mira. A succession of desolate, empty rooms that still had the sense of being somehow occupied. They were very striking, she had to admit. Unsettling, but possessing an eerie beauty.

'It's close to here?' she asked him.

'Yes. Only a short drive on the autostrade. You will go?' He seemed genuinely excited by the prospect.

Mira shrugged, not wanting to seem too keen. 'I might do, if I have time. It looks quite interesting.'

'Here.' Picking up a napkin, Alberto jotted down some directions. 'Take the exit for Imola. Is easy to find.' Smiling, he handed Mira the napkin, which she carefully folded up and put into her purse.

'Many women were sent to such places,' he added abruptly. 'The quiet women, they called them. *Tamburini.* Later, under Mussolini, they would send women there for … resisting their husbands. Even Mussolini's own wife.'

The alcohol suddenly tasted bitter in Mira's mouth. She pushed away her glass. 'That's horrible,' she murmured.

'Is life, yes?' Alberto said off-handedly.

Picking up the wine bottle, he made to top up Mira's glass. Hurriedly, she placed her hand over the rim. 'No, I really mustn't. It's been very nice talking to you, but I have to get back to my hotel.'

He considered this, then quickly drained the remainder of his wine and announced, 'I take you.'

Mira sat in silence for a moment, her mind racing. A part of her wondered whether to simply accept the offer. It was entirely possible Alberto was only being chivalrous in his desire to see her home safely.

But if he wasn't?

Mira studied him as he settled the bill with the waitress. He wasn't unattractive. And charming enough, for all that she couldn't quite read his intentions. The idea of having some kind of holiday fling had never even occurred to her before she came here, but now? Hadn't the whole point of the trip been to start over? What better way to do that than by meeting someone new, even if she never saw Alberto again after tonight?

For a fleeting instant, Mira found herself seriously considering the possibility, and even growing excited by it. But then, her inherent sense of caution quickly reasserted itself. *You're just drunk*, she told herself. *Don't be that person.*

Her mind leapt back to a terrible film she'd watched on late night TV as a teenager, in which a supposedly straightlaced schoolteacher went out at night to pick up men in bars. At the film's conclusion, one of the men had brutally stabbed the woman to death, a scene so nightmarish it had reduced teenaged Mira to tears.

She got to her feet. 'Thank you, no. I can get myself home.'

Alberto looked at her, a little surprised. 'Is okay.'

Mira shook her head firmly. 'Is not okay. But I appreciate the offer.'

He shrugged casually. 'Then I show you where to get taxi, yes?'

It seemed a harmless enough suggestion. Nodding her acceptance, Mira allowed Alberto to lead her away from the table and guide her through the town's darkened streets, listening politely as he chattered on about points of local interest. He would occasionally touch Mira's elbow to emphasise a particular point, but made no overt advances on her otherwise.

When they finally reached the taxi rank, Alberto opened the passenger door for her, then kissed her on both cheeks. '*Ciao*, Mira,' he said. 'Maybe we will see each other again.'

'You never know,' she said, climbing into the taxi. Telling the driver the name of her motel, she watched Alberto as the vehicle pulled away from the kerb. He gave her an enthusiastic wave goodbye, then turned and disappeared into the night.

The darkness rushed in to fill his absence. Gazing into the

empty space he'd left behind him, Mira felt a momentary pang of disappointment, which ached all the more for the fact that things might have been so very different, had she not chosen as she did.

Like everything, she thought, suddenly hating herself.

Ten minutes later, they pulled up outside the motel. Mira overpaid the driver, then climbed awkwardly out of the cab. By now, her head had started throbbing, and she sternly reminded herself to down a glass of water and some ibuprofen before attempting sleep. But all thoughts of rest were quickly banished the moment Mira unlocked the door to her room and stepped inside.

The first thing she noticed was the unmistakeable reek of urine. Recoiling, Mira quickly hit the light switch, at which point the second wrong thing presented itself: her suitcase lying open on the bed, the neatly-packed clothes inside now disordered and strewn messily about, their extremities hanging over the sides of the case like panting tongues.

Reaching down into the case, Mira plucked out her favourite blouse, gingerly holding the collar between two fingers. She lifted it up to the light, revealing a damp yellowish stain discolouring the breast of the garment.

Shuddering with revulsion, Mira flung the ruined blouse across the room. She fought the urge to vomit. Who could possibly have done this? Who would even have *wanted* to? Nothing appeared to have been stolen – her iPad still lay untouched on the nightstand – so it wasn't some random burglary.

Mira's thoughts flashed back to the sour-faced maid. Had she offended the woman somehow? But even if she had, surely nothing warranted this grotesque level of retaliation.

She would have to report it to the management, she knew. But the motel office would now be closed for the night. Mira supposed she could go to the local police station, but tired and inebriated as she was, the prospect of spending the rest of the night attempting to explain her situation to a bunch of foreign policemen filled her with dread.

Regardless, she could not possibly stay here. Some unknown intruder had broken into her private space, *violated* her, and might easily return at any moment. Were it not so late, were she not quite so exhausted, Mira could attempt to find another hotel, but mustering the necessary equilibrium to do anything other but flee was entirely beyond her right now. So, pausing only to grab a spare blanket from the wardrobe, she simply turned on her heels and ran.

Once outside, Mira once again found herself seized by the insidious sense that she was being watched. Looking around, she frantically scanned the forecourt. It appeared deserted, the only audible sound the unsettling hum of a nearby vending machine. Mira supposed she might just be letting paranoia get the better of her – after the grim discovery she'd just made, she could hardly be blamed for that – but if ever there was a moment to trust her most primal instincts, it was undoubtedly now.

Hurrying over to her hire car, Mira leapt inside and started the engine. No matter that she was drunk, no matter that she had absolutely no conception of where else she might go, she could not remain here a second longer.

Reversing out of the motel car park, she turned out onto the main road and drove off into the night, heedless of whatever monsters might be awaiting her there.

Mira awoke to the distant sound of crashing waves, whispering in her ear like an attentive lover. Curled up on the backseat of her vehicle, she threw off her blanket and eased herself upright, doing her best to ignore the creaking stiffness that had settled into her limbs while she slept. Wiping the car window clean, Mira peered out at the new day, silently praying that it appeared brighter than the one before.

A few feet beyond the glass, an empty expanse of clean white sand stretched down towards the nearby ocean. The vista lying before her might have been a hasty monochrome sketch; a smudged pencil sky hanging over the charcoal swirl of the sea. But the stark loneliness of it soothed Mira; if she was alone, then she could not be watched, could not be followed, could not be hurt. Not knowing where else to go, she had driven here seeking the perfect solitude of an off-season beach, the soft lullaby of the rolling tide.

Opening the car door, she inhaled a lungful of briny air, the teasing sting of salt on her tongue luring her down to the water's edge. Although overcast, the day was mild enough, and Mira contemplated taking a short swim. It would undoubtedly help soothe the torpor caused by spending the night nestled in the cramped interior of the car; more than that, she hoped, she might be able to wash away the lingering dread of the last twenty-four hours, casting it down to the bottom of the ocean like a ship's ballast.

Mira looked up and down the beach, which looked to be deserted in both directions. Perhaps she was still too tired to think straight, perhaps it was just due to the dawning realisation that her habitual vigilance had so far failed to protect her from the unseen threats that seemed to lurk wherever she went, but Mira suddenly decided that she'd had quite enough of being cautious. Stripping down to her underwear, she splashed into the oncoming waves, delighting in the sharp nip of the water against her bare skin.

She did not consider herself a particularly strong swimmer, but the Mediterranean was calm enough that morning for her to feel secure enough to venture out some distance from dry land. Mira could already sense the vitality sparking back into her limbs, the cloud of doubt and disquiet lifting from her mind. She had left all of her worries abandoned back on the beach, piled alongside her clothes, and while they would certainly still be waiting for her there once she returned, for this short time at least, she was free of them.

Turning onto her back, Mira allowed herself to drift contentedly on the current, gazing up into the overcast heavens, a fine mist of falling drizzle bathing her upturned face.

After a few more minutes, she at last became conscious of

the ocean's chill, and decided to swim back to the shore. Rolling back onto her front, Mira's gaze fell upon the distant beach, and she immediately felt the gathering cold in her limbs harden to ice.

There, waiting right next to her discarded clothes, stood a motionless figure. In the grey half-light of the dawn, her eyes stinging with salt, Mira could discern none of the figure's identifying characteristics; it might have been another hasty addition to the crudely-sketched landscape, a frantic, featureless scribble.

Her mouth opened in mute shock, allowing a swell of seawater to flood inside. As the sour brine cascaded into her throat, Mira immediately began to cough and struggle for air, panic quickly overwhelming her. All at once, she could not breathe, could not see, could not keep her head above the passing waves, which now seemed to grow in size and intensity, suddenly hungry to claim her for their own.

She went under.

Mira found herself suspended in a lightless netherworld. Emptiness stretched away under her desperately kicking feet; her hands reached for a distant heaven they could never hope to grasp. The surface of the ocean, mere inches away from her outstretched fingers, seemed impossibly remote. It would be far easier simply to allow herself to fall, to descend into the insensate black oblivion lying below.

If I die here, she thought, *everyone will think I drowned myself. Rob will think it was all because of him, that I couldn't cope without him.*

The very notion appalled her so much that a wave of anger coursed throughout her body, giving her an unexpected burst of strength. Mira's feet kicked again, forcing her upwards, and she felt her fingertips break the surface. Moments later, her head emerged from the water, and she finally managed to snatch a few ragged mouthfuls of air. Realising that it had lost its claim on her, the ocean begrudgingly allowed Mira to struggle slowly back to shore, depositing her limp body upon the sands like a jumble of wet kelp.

In her desperation to survive, Mira had forgotten all about the distant figure, but as her awareness gradually returned, her mind flashed back to the image of it watching her from afar. Her head jerked upright, panic blossoming within her skull all over again, but she quickly saw that she was quite alone on the beach.

Had she imagined it, then? Her discarded clothes still lay a few feet away from her, and as she crawled weakly over to reclaim them, Mira noticed a line of footprints leading over towards the piled garments, then retreating back towards the nearby road.

So, whoever the figure had actually been, it had at least been real, just as tangibly real as Mira herself. Did this therefore mean that the persistent feeling of being watched was also not a mere product of her imagination? Mira stared mutely down at the sandy footprints, torn between a feeling of relief that she was not after all delusional, and a sense of mounting horror at the possible implications of having her worst fears confirmed.

Forcing herself to her feet, she hurriedly gathered up her clothes, then ran back to her waiting vehicle as fast as she was able. She did not even bother to dress herself before speeding away, and had been driving for more than ten minutes before the leering glance of a passing driver convinced Mira to finally pull over and throw some clothes back on. It was only then that she permitted herself to at last dissolve into tears.

This whole trip had been a terrible mistake, she could see that now. The very notion of trying to reclaim her past, the many years she had lost to a bad marriage, was nothing but a fool's errand. She should return home to England as soon as possible, in the hope that Poppy would allow her to continue to stay long enough for Mira to figure out a more sensible plan. She wasn't yet sure what that would be, but it would probably involve her leaving London for good, trying to put some distance behind her and the miseries of her past, the past that threatened to drown her just as surely as the ocean had only a short time ago.

Wiping her eyes, Mira restarted the car and pulled back out onto the road. Within thirty minutes, she was back at the motel, where she set about packing what few belongings she had left. Her ruined clothes she simply took outside and deposited in the nearest rubbish bin. The motel receptionist looked at her quizzically when Mira told him she was cutting short her stay. She did not attempt to explain the reason why, and when the man apologetically informed her that he could not refund the extra nights she had already paid for, Mira simply waved him away.

The airport in Bologna was only about an hour's drive from Ravenna. She would head there in the hope that she could get a flight out today; failing that, she could find a room somewhere in the city and leave tomorrow.

Navigating her way to the autostrade, Mira set out for the airport. She tried to concentrate only on the road ahead, emptying her mind of all other concerns. She told herself that it was unlikely she would ever know the truth of what had just happened, and chose to believe that was almost certainly for the best.

She drifted into a vacant lull, aware of little else but the speeding cars around her. Spotting an upcoming road sign, Mira's eyes flickered over to check the remaining distance, but when she noticed that the next junction was marked for Imola, her mind immediately flew back to the previous evening.

They would send women there … for resisting their husbands.

Without really being cognisant of it, Mira abruptly changed lanes and signalled her intention to turn off the autostrade. Taking the Imola exit, she followed the winding slip road around until she found a spot to safely pull over.

Breathing heavily, she applied the handbrake and collapsed back into her seat. Now that she had left the motorway, Mira realised that she had absolutely no idea what she was doing.

You're losing it, she thought.

Did she really intend to go and visit an abandoned mental asylum out in the middle of the Italian countryside, on the say-so of a complete stranger, a man who, as much as she'd tried not to consider the possibility, might even have been the one stalking her?

The quiet women, they called them. Tamburini.

For all that it made no sense to her, Mira suddenly found herself seized by a desperate desire to visit the building where these luckless women had been imprisoned. No, it was more than a desire; it was an outright compulsion. She understood that she could no more resist the summons than a moth could resist the deadly lure of a burning candle flame.

Trying to rationalise, Mira told herself that she wanted to go and pay tribute to the countless victims of such systemic brutality, that the gesture would somehow prove meaningful to her. *That could have been me,* she thought.

But truthfully, she understood that the sudden need to see the *manicomio* was an entirely nameless, irrational one, a need she could not hope to properly comprehend.

Reaching for her purse, Mira found the directions Alberto had written down for her. If she understood them correctly, the asylum should only be a short distance from where she was.

And if I think for one moment I'm going to get lost, Mira reasoned, *I'll just turn around and get straight back on the motorway.*

But Alberto's instructions were clear and concise, and ten minutes later she came upon the abandoned building, squatting behind a curtain of trees in a stretch of overgrown countryside. The whole area had been cordoned off behind a tall chain-link fence, and for a moment Mira found herself wondering whether the barrier was intended to keep trespassers out, or to keep something else safely locked up inside.

Pushing such outlandish notions from her mind, she set out on a slow drive around the circumference of the fence, searching for a way through. Alberto had already managed to gain access, so it stood to reason there must be an entry point somewhere.

The fact that she would normally balk at the very suggestion of trespassing on private property did not ever occur to Mira.

Eventually she found what she was looking for: a curled section of wire, torn loose from a fencepost. Parking her vehicle at the kerbside, Mira cautiously approached the fence, checking about her to make certain she was not being observed. Despite the persistent twitch of paranoia at the nape of her neck, the road looked to be quite deserted. Summoning her courage, she lifted the loose section of wire clear of the ground and hunkered down to scramble though the fence.

Inside, clusters of looming fir trees gathered protectively around the asylum, shielding it from prying eyes. The grounds were shrouded in a gentle verdant hush; one could easily walk here without ever suspecting the myriad horrors that had been perpetrated inside the walls of the nearby *manicomio*.

Mira made her way through the trees towards the main complex, an impressive-looking neoclassical structure with several orderly rows of buildings sprouting off from its sides, like the legs of some great insect. Quickly locating an open doorway, she stepped across the threshold, leaving the present behind and slipping back into the distant past.

The quietude of the asylum grounds extended inside the main building, but Mira was struck by how quickly the precise tenor of the silence had changed. The once-tranquil hush had been transformed to something aching and melancholic, suggesting a suffering so profound that it could not be expressed in mere words. Mira could feel herself starting to tremble with the dreadful weight of it, and debated whether she should step back out into the daylight.

But the exact same compulsion that had first called her here continued to summon her forth, and so she turned and plunged deeper into the building.

At first Mira could see obvious evidence of other trespassers – broken windows, cursive swirls of day-glo graffiti – but the further she walked, the more untouched the building seemed to become. Beyond the expected signs of age and neglect, the *manicomio* might have been inhabited only a short time ago. She passed one ward where the beds were still covered in tangles of blankets and yellowed bedsheets; in a nearby office room, she noticed several bottles of medication and a rusted syringe sitting untouched on a desk. Next to them lay a folded newspaper, dating back some twenty-plus years. To Mira's eyes, it did not appear at all as though the building had been properly vacated or closed down; instead, it seemed to have been simply abandoned in full flow.

It's just like the Marie Celeste, Mira thought. *One minute it was full of hospital staff and patients, only for them to vanish into thin air the next.*

The possibility struck her that if she tarried here for too long, then she might perhaps vanish too, and as illogical a fear as that was, it was nevertheless enough to prompt Mira to abandon her explorations and turn back the way she had come. Whatever urge had initially led her here seemed now to be fading, and Mira's desire to flee Italy and return home was gradually returning.

Still, there was one more thing she needed to do.

Mira closed her eyes. 'I'm sorry for what was done to you,' she whispered to the darkness. 'I know that doesn't mean much – God, I'm not even from here, I'm nobody to you – but I'm sorry all the same. Maybe that counts for something.'

The darkness listened to her for a moment, and then the darkness answered.

'Just who are you talking to, Mira?'

The sound of another human voice at her back caused a choked shriek to rise in her throat. Mira whirled around with such force that she thought she might faint, but what she saw waiting behind her was enough to instantly shock her back to her senses.

There, sitting awkwardly on a child's tricycle left discarded in the middle of the corridor, sat her husband. The image might have been surreal, even comical, had its implications not been so monstrous.

Mira stared at him in mute incomprehension. She could suddenly feel the awful silence of the *manicomio* seeping into her bones, like damp eating away at the walls of a house.

Rob gazed back at her for a moment, then abruptly looked away, taking in his surroundings like he was seeing them for the very first time. 'Look at this shithole,' he said. 'What the fuck are you doing in a place like this, Mira? Do you even know?'

'You,' she said numbly.

He climbed up off the tricycle, kicking it over to the side of the corridor. 'Of course it's me,' he replied. 'I've come to take you home. It's quite obvious you're having some sort of breakdown. You shouldn't be wandering around a strange country on your own, let alone in derelict buildings. I mean, what the fuck, Mira?'

She took a step backwards. 'How are you, how are you even *here?*'

Rob rolled his eyes. 'I knew you were coming to Italy the moment you booked. I still have access to your email account.'

'My *emails?*'

He continued to advance on her. 'I shouldn't have, I know, and I'm sorry. But Jesus, Mira, someone has to look out for you. Who else is going to take care of you but me?'

Mira shook her head violently. 'No. *No.* Rob, you have to go. Please, *go.* Get out of here and leave me alone.'

He looked incredulous. 'Are you completely mad? I'm not going to leave you alone in a place like this.'

Mira couldn't bear this an instant longer. 'Fuck off!' she screamed.

I'm going mad, she thought. *They should just lock me up here and be done with it.*

Rob rubbed wearily at his eyes. 'God, Mira, calm down. I'm doing my best to be reasonable here ...'

'*Reasonable?* You broke into my private room and, and ...'

Abruptly turning away, Rob moved across to the corridor window. 'I admit it, sometimes I lose control a bit,' he said quietly. 'But Christ, I'm only human, and you ... just ... keep

… on … PUSHING ME!'

His fist lashed out, violently smashing through the windowpane.

Mira flinched, recoiling yet further when Rob removed his bloody hand from the shattered window and extended it towards her. 'See what you've done now,' he said, resuming his remorseless advance.

Stumbling away, she found herself backing into a wall. She was trapped, Mira realised. No matter that she could just turn and run, try to hide herself in the cavernous shadows of the abandoned asylum, Rob would always follow her. And in the end, he would always find her.

'Please,' she whispered, pressing her cheek against the flaking plaster.

Rob leaned in, his face looming inches from Mira's own, his arms thrust square against the wall, encircling her. 'I think it's fairly clear what's going on here,' he murmured. 'It's obvious you're trying to reconnect with something, coming back to the same place we spent our honeymoon …'

'No, that's not it, it's not …'

'You made a mistake when you left, and that's okay, we all make them. You just have to be strong enough to admit when you're wrong, is all.'

Mira forced herself to meet his gaze. 'I *was* wrong, yes.'

'See? Now we're finally getting somewhere.'

'*We* were wrong.'

His eyes flared. 'You have no idea what you're saying.'

Something was happening, Mira could feel it. A vibration building within the bricks and mortar of the building. Something bound to the asylum's very foundations, a force that would not be denied any longer.

Implicitly, she knew she could either choose to resist it, or allow the force to use her as its willing vessel.

She opened herself to it. 'It's true.'

Mira could feel Rob's fingers clawing at the wall, digging into the plasterwork. 'Just shut up,' he hissed. 'Just shut the fuck up and *be quiet!*'

The *manicomio* erupted around them. Previously unbroken windows shattered, locked doors exploded off their hinges. It was as though the desperate desire for escape that had built up here over the long decades of the building's existence, the suppressed craving for freedom felt by every unfortunate wretch who passed through the asylum's gates, had been massing here all this time, absorbed into the same walls that that imprisoned them. It had been primed to explode for too many years to count; all that was needed was someone to at last light the fuse.

Rob's eyes widened in shock. He seized Mira by the wrist, trying to lead her to safety.

She had intended only to try and push him away, but Mira's flesh no longer belonged solely to her. Now, she had the strength of hundreds of women flowing through her, women who had been brutally cast into the darkness for the crime of speaking their minds, for the crime of being different, for the crime of loving the wrong person or not loving at all.

As she shoved at her husband's chest, she felt them pushing with her, sending him flying backwards with preternatural force. His body slammed to the ground, the strength of the impact winding him. Goggling, Rob looked up at his wife in stunned amazement, struggling to say something.

But his time to speak had passed forever. Mira stared down at him, her eyes growing empty. She could feel the women's cries building inside her, all those quiet women who would be silenced no more. Opening her mouth, she finally gave voice to their torment, a shriek of mingled pain and grief and unfettered rage that was almost beautiful in its terrible, wordless purity.

The moment the scream issued from her lips, Rob's hands flew to his ears, but he could not hope to drown out such a dreadful sound. As the shriek continued to build, flowing out of Mira as if it were molten lava spilling from the earth, she could see his flesh beginning to rupture and disintegrate.

And if the sight gave her the slightest pause, it hardly

mattered, because she could not possibly hope to stop what had now been unleashed.

The next instant, her husband's body came undone.

It was not quite accurate to say that he exploded; there was no physical residue to mark his passing from this world. To Mira's eyes, it appeared as though he had simply dissolved, like a handful of salt scattered across water, his constituent atoms becoming one with the fabric of the building around him.

I am a murderer, Mira thought, recalling her dream of the morning before.

But in the moments after he vanished, she quickly realised that she could discern traces of Rob wherever she looked: a network of cracks in a nearby wall seemed to outline the contours of his face; an overgrown spill of ivy through a broken window suggested his unkempt hair; the insistent grating of a door swinging drunkenly from a single hinge reminded her of the sound of his snoring.

Her husband still lived on in these walls, it seemed. And might do so forever, or at least until such time as the authorities decided to finally tear the *manicomio* down and consign its remaining ghosts to the four winds.

Hearing the chatter of excited voices inside her skull, Mira realised the building's other unquiet spirits were now agitating for their freedom. They desired to once again feel the sun's warmth on their flesh, no matter that the borrowed flesh was not their own.

With one final look back, she turned and made her way towards the light, consigning her past life, everything she had once been, to the shadows.

As for the question of what she might be now, even Mira could not properly answer that.

When the police found her silently wandering the hospital grounds later that afternoon, having been alerted to the presence of two vehicles sitting empty outside the perimeter fence, they attempted to question her, without success. This left them with little choice but to take Mira back to their station house, in the hope that she would, in time, tell them exactly what had happened to her. Subsequently, it did not take the policemen long to discover that the other abandoned rental car had been hired by Mira's husband, of whom no trace could be found. They persisted in their efforts to question the mute Englishwoman, whom they were quickly coming to regard as a person of interest in the matter of her husband's disappearance.

Yet for all their probing and badgering, Mira remained resolutely silent. There would be time enough to speak later, if she so chose.

But for the present, she had nothing more to say.

Nothing at all.

HOLY TERRORS

It almost seems blasphemous to consider the possibility that evil spirits might be found in the vicinity of Christianity's most holy citadel. And yet it was Father Gabriele Amorth himself, the Chief Exorcist of the Diocese of Rome, recently portrayed by Russell Crowe in the horror movie, **The Pope's Exorcist**, and a man who claims to have performed 50,000 exorcisms, who went on record as saying that darkness could indeed be found within the Vatican City, evil lurking there in the form both of devils and their disciples. He even referred to the infamous disappearance of Emanuela Orlandi, a 15-year-old schoolgirl abducted within the Vatican in 1983 and never seen since, implying that she was taken to become a plaything for an organised gang of sex-attackers.

Perhaps we shouldn't be too shocked. Like anywhere else on Earth where humans gather, sins and even crimes will be committed. But the Vatican also has its fair share of harder-to-explain mysteries.

Much gossip has often centred on the Vatican Archive, a tightly guarded underground repository of important documents and accounts relating to the governance of the Catholic Church, but also a vast library of books and papers collected by the Church over countless centuries, many of which are deemed too dangerous ever to be seen by the public. There are even stories about an ultra-secret vault, the Black Room, in which 'works of true evil' are held securely for the safety of mankind.

Such stories have grown with the telling, of course, but have largely been disproved since around 2008, when the Archive was finally opened to journalists. However, certain types of esoterica are never far from the Vatican rumour mill.

It's undeniably the case that a number of exorcisms of allegedly possessed people have taken place within its precincts. It wasn't widely known back in the 1970s, when Hollywood's publicity offices preferred to put out stories that the 1973 horror blockbuster, **The Exorcist**, had so offended the Catholic Church that it sent out priests and nuns to *protest at cinemas, but given that it was adapted from a novel written by a devout Catholic, William Peter Blatty, and from the outset featured a storyline in which the self-sacrificing heroes were themselves Catholic priests, it should be no surprise to anyone that the film was actually made with Vatican approval. Director William Friedkin claimed that he'd been allowed to witness and film a real exorcism inside the Vatican, which he said horrified and awe-struck him in equal measure.*

Later stories would emerge in which it was even claimed that some of the film's demonic moanings and groanings were the real thing, devilish voices recorded on tape during one such Vatican ceremony.

The Catholic Church itself doesn't deny that exorcism falls within its remit, but always insists that every other avenue – mental illness, alcoholism, drug-addiction and so forth – be investigated first. Two relatively recent popes, John-Paul II and Benedict XVI, are said to have personally performed exorcisms inside the Vatican, including one that supposedly took place in St Peter's Square itself, during which a woman began to fit and then screamed and shouted obscenities and drooled like an animal, before scaling a sheer wall like a spider. However, one of the most remarkable stories of all concerns Pope Pius XII, who at the height of World War Two, from the silent austerity of his private cell, supposedly attempted the long-range exorcism of Adolf Hitler. According to Vatican documents released in 2006, the papal authorities at that time were firmly convinced that Hitler was under the control of a demon, and that the astonishing outbreak of evil in Nazi Germany was diabolically inspired. That this attempted long-distance ritual failed was no surprise to Father Amorth, who later taught that for an effective exorcism to take place, the exorcist must be in close proximity to the possessed.

Of course, a succession of religiously themed horror novels set in and around the Catholic Church and the Vatican itself, such as The Exorcist *in 1971 and* The Da Vinci Code *in 2003, not to mention a whole range of Vatican-set horror movies –* Stigmata *(1999),* The Rite *(2011),* The Vatican Tapes *(2015) – have helped persuade the public that the heart of the Holy See is a hotbed of evil. But in fact, most of the paranormal occurrences reported there in real life appear to be of a more ambiguous nature.*

To begin with, there have been at least two occasions when the recorded apparitions might even have been celestial in origin. In 2007, a retired British police officer and his wife were in attendance at St Peter's Basilica while Pope Benedict was making an address from the pulpit. Fascinated by the ethereal patterns created by sunlight shimmering through the tall, stained-glass windows, the husband took several photographs, but when he checked them later, realised that in one he appeared to have captured a winged, white figure hovering above the crowd. No obvious explanation was available, and the image was seized on by the British press as a possible angelic visitation. In a second instance, one of that multitude of paranormal channels now proliferating on YouTube presented impressive looking footage, also supposedly shot in the main basilica of St Peter's, in which a human-like figure wearing archaic robes appears without explanation in the air above the altar.

Perhaps less obviously holy, but not necessarily connected to evil, are several other noteworthy supernatural events.

One of the most widely circulated snippets of footage, though its provenance is unknown, depicts a shadowy figure standing in an opening in the upper section of the basilica's belltower on what seems to be a normal day, because tourists are lining up outside to enter. Various explanations have been offered, from the usual demonic one, ie that this is one of those many evil spirits that Father Amorth fears are prowling the papal palace, to the sadder possibility that it's the soul of a past suicide unable to detach itself from the scene of its death. However, the two most famous ghosts reputed to walk the Vatican date far back into antiquity. One of these, a screaming woman in a spectral carriage frequently seen crossing the Sisto Bridge, is said to be all that remains of the Italian noblewoman, Donna Olimpia Pamphili, who, as sister-in-law to Pope Innocent X, sold many favours to enrich herself, but after his death in 1655, fled the sacred city with chest-loads of stolen Vatican gold, only to escape to a place where the plague was rife, and subsequently die. The other is probably the very last entity you'd expect to find roaming the halls of Christianity's HQ: the spirit of Julius Caesar, who was assassinated over four miles away, 44 years before Jesus Christ was even born, and 369 years before Constantine the Great consolidated Christ's teachings as the official State Church of the Roman Empire. Caesar has allegedly haunted the Vatican ever since the year 1580, when Pope Sixtus V unwisely opened the urn that contained his ashes.

It seems that multiple shades, both ancient and modern, are still attracted to Europe's most hallowed halls of all.

THE TEETH OF THE HESPERIDES
Jasper Bark

My misfortune started when I opened the email from Nils Lundberg.

I've put off writing this for a long while. I've wanted to write my whole life, but I never seem to settle on a single style. I move from genre to genre like I've moved home these past two years.

I've been afraid to tie myself to one literary category. Like I've been afraid to stay in one place for too long. I've good reason to fear settling in a single location.

The two things I never wanted to write were a ghost story, or a personal memoir, and here I am attempting both, because they're the same thing. I've never completed anything of consequence. And I regret that, because this is likely to be the last thing I ever write. I hope I get the chance to finish it.

I'm a botanist studying for a PhD I'll never complete. It was my PhD that led me to open the email from Nils Lundberg.

I suppose I should introduce myself. If you're the one who found this manuscript you may already know who I am, perhaps you even came looking for me. There may not be any trace of me by the time you find this.

In case you need to verify who wrote this, my name is Sarah Mágissa. And yes, if you're wondering, the renowned botanist Nicholas Mágissa *is* my great uncle. Like him, I also specialise in the study of carnivorous plants.

When I was eighteen, I was contacted by a solicitor on behalf of my uncle's son, Clarence. He was my first cousin, once removed. Clarence had just passed and made me his beneficiary. This meant I got all of Nicholas's papers and scientific samples.

The samples contained specimens so rare that selling them helped fund my education. In fact, I might well have clinched my place at Camford University by promising to donate his papers. It certainly got me a place on their PhD programme. Several tutors at Trinity College were keen to explore my great uncle's papers in relation to their own work. Like Dublin and Durham University, Camford has a college system, and my great uncle attended Trinity.

Along with the rare specimens, my cousin left me a curious artefact of my great uncle's. It was inside a shoebox, wrapped in old newspaper bearing the date – September 3rd, 1829. The artefact came in a cylindrical, earthenware container, with a separate lid that had a hairline crack down one side.

When I lifted the lid, I found a wad of sackcloth that crumbled as I unwrapped it. Inside was a small, silver sickle, around six inches long, with a sharp, curved blade and a polished wooden handle. The handle was severely worn, but in remarkably good shape considering its age. I was guessing it was over a thousand years old.

Strange symbols were etched into both sides of the blade and also the handle. It was harder to make out the symbols on the handle because it was so worn. The blade was sticky to the touch and had a faint resinous odour.

Professor Brown, my PhD supervisor at Camford, suggested I show the sickle and container to a colleague of his, a specialist in ancient artefacts. A couple of weeks later I got an email from a Dr Jonathan Van Clef, inviting me to visit.

His office was a cramped room in the Archaeology department. Books, boxes and papers spilled from shelves and lay in piles on his tiny desk and floor. He looked up from his laptop and smiled warmly when I knocked.

I wasn't sure if I was in the right place. 'Are you Dr Van Clef? I'm Sarah Mágissa, you sent me an email, about some artefacts.'

Dr Van Clef had receding, curly, black hair and a short

beard, flecked with grey. There were leather patches on the elbows of his jacket. He waved me inside and pointed to the only other chair. 'Yes, yes, come in, shut the door. A pleasure to meet you Ms Mágissa, I understand you've been very generous to the college, donating your great uncle's papers.'

I took off my coat and sat down. 'Call me Sarah. I'm sure my great uncle would have been delighted to have his papers at his old college. Do you have anything to tell me about his artefacts?'

Dr Van Clef pulled open several drawers in his desk. He located the old shoebox and moved a pile of papers so he had room to open it. He smiled at the newspaper. 'A novel way of preserving an ancient artefact, but your great uncle was known for his eccentricities.'

He placed the container on the desk in front of me. 'This is a pyxis, they were very popular in the classical world, especially in Greece and Rome, often given as wedding gifts.' He held it up and pointed to its sides. 'Normally there's a painting or a relief on the outside, showing either a marriage procession or a mythological scene. The only elaborate thing about it is the lid handle, which is customary for these items. If it was given as a gift, then I don't think it came from a wealthy family.'

He put on a pair of protective gloves and took the sickle out of the sackcloth. 'This is another matter altogether. It appears to be a ceremonial object, the design is Mycenaean, from about the second or first century BC. The blade is made of silver, most likely from the mines at Laurion which provided the Athenians with a lot of their wealth. The handle is applewood, I think, and remarkably well preserved.'

It was a lot older than I thought. 'What makes you think it's ceremonial?'

He turned it around in his fingers. 'Well, it's too small to have any practical use, it's not an agricultural tool, you wouldn't cut any crops with this. It's more likely to be used in a religious ceremony of some sort. A lot of the goddess cults that worshiped Hera or Demeter, used similar implements in their rituals.'

'Do you know what the tiny symbols mean?'

Dr Van Clef put on a pair of bifocals and peered closely at the blade. 'I haven't been able to identify them yet. They're not in any language I recognise, certainly not Greek. I think they might have some occult significance, but that's not my field. If they do, it would strengthen my hypothesis that it's a ceremonial object.'

He put the sickle back in the sackcloth and put the lid on the Pyxis. He looked at me with genuine excitement. 'You've done me a great service showing me these items. I'll get at least two papers out of them, maybe even three. Not to mention the conferences at which I plan to present my findings.'

He rummaged around in another desk drawer and produced a clipboard with some paperwork on it. 'Now, before I forget, I need you to sign these release forms for me.'

'Release forms?'

'Yes, relinquishing them to my custody on behalf of the college.'

I looked down at the pyxis and the sickle wrapped in sackcloth and felt a weight on my chest. The idea of leaving them with Dr Van Clef left me bereft, like a mother who's been asked to leave her children in the company of strangers. These artefacts had likely been in the Mágissa family for generations and that's where they belonged. I would not be the one to give them away.

I reached over his desk, put the lid on the pyxis and placed it back amongst the newspaper of the shoebox. 'I'm sorry, Dr Van Clef, the artefacts are not part of my donation to the university. I'm very grateful for the information you've given me.'

I gathered up the shoebox and put on my coat. Dr Van Clef stood up. He seemed most perturbed. 'Now let's not be too hasty about this. You'd be making a great contribution to the field of archaeology and I would give you an acknowledgement in at least one of those papers I mentioned.'

I raised a sardonic eyebrow. 'One of the papers? Weren't you going to write three?'

'All of the papers, I meant. Maybe leave them for a few more months. I could find out so much more for you.'

He was eyeing the shoebox like a bear eyes a honeycomb. This increased my proprietary feelings. 'Goodbye, Dr Van Clef, it's been a great pleasure talking to you, you've been very helpful.'

He sank back into his seat. He had the dejected air of someone who's confessed their love and been turned down flat. I left his office without another word.

There are six basic trap mechanisms that carnivorous plants use to capture their prey. Five of these are universally recognised by botanists. The sixth was discovered by my great uncle. It's unique to the plant he named *Dryadis Pygocentrus*, or the Teeth of the Hesperides.

Both the plant and the trap mechanism are unknown to botanical science and, when I'm gone, I hope it stays that way. From the sounds I hear at my window, I don't think it will be long until I'm gone.

The first trap mechanism is the *pitfall trap*. Pitcher plants employ this. They have a long, rolled leaf with a small pool of digestive enzymes at the base. They attract their prey with the bright, flower like patterns on the leaves and the nectar they secrete. The leaves are coated with waxy flakes which cause insects to slip and fall into the pitcher where they're broken down and absorbed by the plant.

I don't want to beat you over the head with symbolism, but this does sum up my search for the Teeth of the Hesperides. I was attracted by the idea of identifying this mysterious, carnivorous plant, but before I knew it, I'd slipped down the leaf of my investigation and was trapped.

My great uncle had a theory about the symbiotic relationship between plants and insects. Without getting too technical, he argued that what was normally a mutually beneficial relationship could be subverted by a harsh and unwelcoming environment. Normally plants provide nectar as food, and insects spreading pollen to help them reproduce. But the unwelcoming environment resulted in the evolution of carnivorous plants, which were forced by limited soil nutrients to find the sustenance they needed from the insects they would otherwise have helped.

He devoted half an unpublished paper to this theory. He claims that nowhere is his theory better exemplified than in the Teeth of the Hesperides, a unique carnivorous plant. He promises to detail every aspect of the plant in the second part of the paper, but sadly this has been lost.

I went through every one of his papers before I donated the bulk to Camford, and I couldn't find another mention of the Teeth of the Hesperides. The closest I came was a page of sketches, showing a small tree, whose branches were bare, with two words scrawled at the bottom – *Dryadis Pygocentrus*, the Latin name he gave the plant.

This unfinished paper was one of several items I held back from the university. Not least because I planned to make it the subject of my doctoral thesis. I became obsessed with finding and identifying the plant and completing my great uncle's work.

I was aware of the stir this would cause, and I knew if I held back the last of my great uncle's papers until I'd published my thesis, Trinity would be incentivised to pass me, for fear of not possessing the full collection.

There's an old joke among faculty members:

Q: Why is there so much politics in academia?

A: Because the stakes are so low!

I guess that's a lot funnier if you've worked at a university. Maybe I should feel more shame for this, but I wasn't above playing politics when it came to *my* academic career.

My problem was, I had no idea what sort of plant the Teeth of the Hesperides was, or where it could be found. After a year of searching, I had yet to turn up one plausible lead.

I had started a blog about my doctoral thesis. I liked to

drop hints about the direction I was taking. I knew my supervisor and several other Camford professors were following it. I soon found out they weren't the only people.

That's when I got the email from Nils Lundberg.

Nils lived in Norway, but he spoke and wrote perfect English. He was a specialist in locating rare and exotic plants for extremely rich collectors. He'd founded a company with his late brother, Lukas, and they'd made a lot of money applying geographical and botanical datasets to their searches. In this way they could map the location of even the rarest plant based on the soil and climate it needed to survive.

Nils had been following my blog and claimed he could help me find the Teeth of the Hesperides. I was interested in what he had to say, given his profession and expertise. My initial enthusiasm waned in the face of his evasion. He gave no direct answers to my questions, but he knew of my great uncle's investigations in North Africa, not an area known for carnivorous plants. Nils told me his brother, Lukas, had been commissioned to find the Teeth of the Hesperides by a wealthy client.

It was a commission Lukas took on alone, at the client's request. Nils wasn't party to Lukas's research or travel itinerary. For this reason, he wasn't alarmed when he didn't hear from his brother for a few weeks. It was only when Lukas didn't come home for their mother's birthday, something neither of them ever missed, that Nils became worried.

Another week went by and Nils was unable to reach Lukas by phone, email or text. That was when he began to contact anyone who might have information about his brother's whereabouts. When that failed, he reported Lukas as a missing person, but the authorities weren't able to do much. Lukas disappeared abroad and no one was entirely certain where he was last seen.

Try as he might, Nils couldn't locate Lukas's mysterious client. The only lead he had was the Teeth of the Hesperides.

Now he'd located it, he was fairly certain what had happened to his brother. But he couldn't prove it and he'd run out of funds. He'd spent over a year looking for his brother and had exhausted his savings.

He was aware of my generous trust fund and he made me an offer. If I was to fund the trip, pay him a generous fee and cover all his expenses, he would take me to the world's most unique carnivorous plant. After wrangling a little over the terms and costs, I agreed.

Nils refused to give me the exact location of the Teeth of the Hesperides. He claimed this was for my own protection and everything would become clear when he showed me the plant. Now, I know you're probably thinking this sounds like a text-book con, but he did know a lot about the Teeth of the Hesperides, in fact he seemed to be the only person who knew as much about it as my late, great uncle, and his credentials were impeccable. Don't think I didn't check him out. He was the real deal.

I think it's time to mention the second trap mechanism, known commonly as *flypaper traps*. The leaves of plants that use this technique are coated with mucilage, a sticky substance that attracts insects and glues them to the plant so they can't fly away. By this point in our negotiations, I was so fixated on finding the Teeth of the Hesperides I couldn't fly away myself.

I'd been exchanging emails for some months and had even agreed to fund the expedition, when, at the end of a tedious discussion about logistics, he asked me:

Can I enquire you about a small matter? Was there anything else among your great uncle's papers?

This question seemed to come out of the blue. But I was intrigued enough to reply:

There were a lot of papers, and botanical samples from all over the world. Too many to catalogue in an email like this. Was there something in particular you wanted to ask me about?

His next couple of emails avoided my question, almost as if he regretted asking. Then, out of the blue, at the end of an email exploring travel, he asked:

Picking up on your great uncle, I'm curious, were the botanical samples the only thing he left you? Humour me on this.

To be honest, Nils had been so evasive about the Teeth of the Hesperides, I enjoyed stringing *him* along.

Happy to humour you, happy to answer your questions, but you need to be less vague. If there's something you think he left me then you have to be specific. Maybe I can go and look for it if I know what it is.

His next email was more direct.

Hi Sarah,
Okay, since you need me to be more specific, I was wondering if you came across any artefacts amongst your great uncle's things?

I felt I'd played with him enough, so I opened up. There weren't many people I could discuss my great uncle's bequest with, and I was curious why he was asking.

Hi Nils,
In answer to your question, yes, there was one thing. According to one of the professors at Camford, it's from classical times. It's in the shape of a sickle, but too small to be used for anything practical. He thought it was some sort of ceremonial object. I still have it, even though it should probably be in a museum.

I didn't expect his next response to be so enthusiastic or insistent:

Oh, thank goodness. Listen, could you bring it along with you on the expedition. It's really important we have it when I take you to the plant. I can't say more now, I'll explain everything when we meet. I promise.

I wasn't very keen, I'm afraid.

It's an ancient and unique artefact. I'm not sure I could bring it in my hand luggage. The cost of insuring it would be astronomical.

He kept mentioning it in every email, insisting on its importance and hinting that he couldn't take me to the Teeth of the Hesperides if we didn't have it. Finally, I capitulated and agreed to bring it along.

We arranged to meet in Melilla, an autonomous Spanish city that sits on the eastern side of Cape Three Forks, bordering Morocco and looking out onto the Mediterranean Sea. I'd never heard of the city until Nils suggested we meet there and, to be honest, I wasn't aware that parts of North Africa were considered Spanish.

After a five-hour flight, with one stop over, I found myself in the back of a taxi, with no air-conditioning, crawling through traffic on my way to a beach bar. What the locals call a *chiringuito*. The bar had an open-air terrace with a view of the ocean and a motley collection of tables and sun loungers on the beach. Nils was sitting at a table on the terrace. He wasn't hard to spot, he was the only unaccompanied man in the place.

He stood up when he saw me, and it seemed like he kept standing up and up. At 5ft 4 I'm not the world's tallest person, but Nils seemed, to my eyes, to be about 6ft 7. He was wearing a black t-shirt and khaki cargo shorts. He had a long face with clear blue eyes and brown hair that was cut long at the back and shorter at the sides, like an ageing surfer.

He frowned as I approached his table. 'You're late.' He had the tiniest hint of a Scandinavian accent.

I made a dismissive sound and dropped my suitcase. 'Tell that to the baggage claim and the taxi driver who couldn't find the place.'

He seemed taken aback that I hadn't apologised. Then he remembered his own manners, as well as my trust fund, and indicated a chair. 'Won't you sit down? Can I get you a drink?'

'I'll have a vodka and cranberry juice.'

He called the waiter and ordered my drink. Without bothering with small talk, he proceeded to discuss payment and money transfers. When he'd concluded, he fixed me with those clear blue eyes. 'Did you bring the artefact, the sickle we spoke about?'

'It's in my suitcase, carefully wrapped. I couldn't hardly carry it in my hand luggage. I didn't bring the pyxis it came in.'

'That doesn't matter, we don't need that. Can I see it?'

I looked at my bulging suitcase and thought of how I'd had to sit on it just to zip it up. 'I'll show you later, after I've unpacked.'

'Can't I see it now? I've gone to a lot of trouble to organise this trip.'

'I can't get to it that easily and I don't want to unpack in the middle of a bar.'

Nils didn't say anything, but he continued to stare at me intently, willing me to do what he asked until I became uncomfortable.

I sighed and unzipped my suitcase with more than a little passive aggression. 'Fine, give me a minute.'

After rummaging through my carefully packed clothing, my fingers touched on the crumbling sackcloth. I pulled it out, and blushed as an item of red, lacy underwear fell at Nils' feet. He glanced at the underwear, but said nothing as I stuffed it back in my suitcase.

I put the sackcloth on the table between us, unwrapped it and revealed the sickle. Nils' eyes widened and I swear I saw tears in them. He picked up the sickle with great reverence, as though he were an ancient priest and the sickle was the ceremonial object Dr Van Clef suspected. He sniffed at the object and smiled, muttering something to himself. It sounded like: 'There might be hope, there might be hope after all.'

Maybe it was the way he turned the sickle over in his hands, squinting at the markings on the blade, but a sudden proprietary feeling stole over me again and I took it from his reverent fingers, wrapped it in what remained of the sackcloth and put it back in my suitcase.

Nils didn't resist, but his face fell. 'You *are* going to bring that tomorrow, aren't you?'

I frowned. 'It's a priceless artefact, why would I take it into the field? We're hunting plant specimens, not archaeological remains.'

He looked a bit confused. 'You did read my last couple of emails, right?'

About a day before my last-minute preparations, I got some strange emails from Nils. The first one was long and rambling and contained a lot of local folklore and the second had links to some arcane sites about esoteric topics, which are not my subject and don't generally interest me.

I sighed. 'To be honest, they were rather long and I only skimmed them.'

He frowned, sounding like a professor scolding an undergraduate. 'I told you that information was essential to this expedition. If you'd read them properly, you'd know exactly why you have to bring the sickle along.'

I just about managed to stop myself rolling my eyes. 'Okay, as your client, why don't you humour me and tell me what I missed.'

With a bit of huffing and puffing, Nils mansplained the folklore he'd sent me. He was very didactic and went on at great length. I ordered two more drinks during the course of his lecture and they didn't improve it any.

If I'm honest, I'm not sure I could accurately recreate what he said. But I need to give you the gist of it if I'm going to explain what happened next. So, I went and found the emails he sent and I've paraphrased it below. I've tried to make it as interesting as I can and hopefully you won't need three drinks to get through it.

The Garden of the Hesperides was an orchard belonging to the goddess Hera. Classical historians placed it in Morocco, near a town called Lixus. It was planted by the goddess Gaia as a wedding present for Hera's marriage to Zeus. The trees grew golden apples with magical properties. They were tended by seven dryads called the Hesperides and guarded by a dragon called Ladon. When Hercules slayed Ladon and stole the golden apples, the garden fell into disrepair.

All but one of the Hesperides deserted the garden. The seventh who stayed behind, inhabited the tree from which Eris, the goddess of strife, obtained the Golden Apple of Discord that started the Trojan War. When the tree she lived in died, the dryad took possession of its final apple, and when that withered, she lived in its seeds.

The withered apple was found by a farmer who lived on the other side of the Atlas Mountains. Not knowing its worth, he took the apple to the town of Aegle, on the Mediterranean coast of North Africa. The farmer used the seeds from the apple to grow first a tree and then an orchard. The trees of this orchard were possessed by the dryad. The harsh and unwelcoming environment of Aegle's rocky soil, and the loss of the garden she and her sisters tended, subverted the dryad's beneficent nature and the orchard became cursed. All who tasted the fruit of this orchard became maddened and were forced to spill blood.

Sibling turned against sibling, wives against husbands and children against their parents. The farmer was obliged to call in an old 'wise woman' to lift the curse. She began by drawing a circle around the orchard in a potion made of hemlock and mandrake that was poison to the dryad. This forced the dryad to hide in a tree in the very centre. Then she drew a circle of potion around the tree, forcing the dryad to hide in one of its boughs. The wise woman drew another circle around the bough and the dryad hid in a single apple. Finally, the wise woman picked the apple and drew a circle of potion on its skin. With nowhere left to run, the dryad moved into three of the apple's seeds.

The wise woman cut open the apple and trapped the dryad in the seeds with a magical song in a forgotten tongue. Then she removed the seeds and placed them in a tiny sack, bound with magical symbols. The curse was lifted and the wise woman kept the sack safe for the rest of her life.

Just before the wise woman died, she swallowed a dried apple from the cursed orchard. The seeds remained in her stomach and a strange tree grew on the spot where they buried her. The wise woman left instructions with her sons and daughters that, should the curse ever fall on the orchard again, they were to bathe a silver blade in the sap of the tree and use it to cut themselves. Then they should scatter their blood over the roots of the possessed tree.

The children did not take good care of the seeds, and a mouse nibbled a hole in the tiny sack where they were kept. The hole was just large enough for the dryad to sing through, late at night, and her song entered the dreams of an impoverished goat herder named Kataraménos.

The dryad told Kataraménos where the seeds were hidden and promised him great prosperity if he stole them. Kataraménos did as she asked and planted each of the seeds on his land. Within weeks the seeds had grown into three trees that were as unique as the tree on the wise woman's grave. The trees spoke to Kataraménos and promised him bounteous crops and good fortune in return for an annual human sacrifice. Kataraménos complied and grew very wealthy, buying all the land in Aegle.

When the wise woman's grandchildren learned of Kataraménos's theft, they took their grandmother's ceremonial sickle and bathed it in the sap of her tree. Then they made their way to his lands to banish the three trees from the stolen seeds.

Kataraménos learned of their plan in advance and waited in ambush with his men. He killed the grandchildren, seized their land and tore up the wise woman's tree. Only the youngest grandson escaped. He sailed across the Mediterranean taking his grandmother's sickle with him, vowing that he, or one of his descendants, would return one day to vanquish the trees that gave the Kataraménos family their wealth.

When he'd finished, Nils stared at me meaningfully, his gaze pregnant with implication. I ignored his insinuations and turned the conversation to the logistics of the next day's boat trip. Nils remained evasive about the details. We ate a rather greasy meal and he departed, leaving me to pick up the tab.

I didn't sleep well that night. I was nervous and anxious about the boat trip and though it was the end of autumn, there were parties on the beach outside my hotel that spilled into the corridor outside my room.

The third trapping mechanism of carnivorous plants is known as the *bladder trap*. Plants that use this mechanism create an internal vacuum that sucks their prey in so they can't escape. I didn't realise it when I set out the next morning, but that's a perfect metaphor for what had happened to Nils when he started to investigate his brother's disappearance.

I nearly slept through my wake-up call, and my taxi driver had to check the address on his sat nav. It wasn't any of the big marinas that lined the *Puerto de Melilla*, our final destination was a ramshackle jetty a few kilometres north of town, away from the main tourist spots.

Nils was waiting for me on the jetty. He got a little agitated when I asked him about our transport and destination. It wasn't until I threatened to cancel the whole expedition that he admitted he chartered a boat to sail round Cape Three Forks and dock in Morocco for the night, before making our way to Aegle, overlooking the Gulf of Hoceima.

I was furious that he hadn't told me this last night. 'That's in international waters. We're sailing to a different country. You should have let me know, I don't have my passport, or any overnight bag.'

'You won't need them, there are no border controls where we're going, and trust me, on clandestine trips like this, the accommodation and transport don't lend themselves to overnight bags.'

'This isn't clandestine, it's illegal on multiple fronts. You didn't tell me any of this before I got here.'

'Because I knew you'd make a fuss and ruin the whole operation, just like you're doing now. I promised to take you to the Teeth of the Hesperides and that's just what I'm going to do.'

Before I could say any more, a small fishing boat came into view and moored itself on the jetty. It had a four-man crew who Nils addressed in Arabic. It wasn't until they offered me a sandwich, hours into our trip, that I realised they spoke English. I didn't have a great journey, I'm not good on boats and the constant rocking of the waves left me nauseous. I spent a stifling night on a hillside, in a single person tent, unable to sleep from the heat. I kept to myself the whole time, but I imagine they thought I was sulking.

We rose before dawn and made the last leg of our sea journey. When the boat reached its destination, we rowed ashore in an inflatable dinghy. I was stiff, sore and in need of a shower. Nils hardly spoke, just reminded me to take the sickle.

The rocky beach where we landed led to a winding path up a steep bluff. I had no signal on my phone, but Nils had downloaded a map onto his. The long hike took us most of the day. The ground was barren and dusty apart from the odd patch of scrub grass. Nils kept making strange turns when a more accessible route was open to us. When I called him out, he told me he was avoiding security cameras.

That was the last straw. 'Security cameras?! We're in the middle of nowhere, why would anyone need security cameras? Just where exactly are you taking me.'

'It's just a few more kilometres, then everything will become clear.'

Maybe it was the heat, but I was done. I stamped my foot. 'No, I've had enough of your evasions. I'm paying for this whole trip. If you don't tell me exactly what we're doing out here, I am turning right around and going back to that boat and it's leaving without you.'

'We don't have time for this.'

I turned and walked away from him, back the way we came. I wasn't even sure I could find the boat. He called after me and when I didn't respond he ran to catch up and took hold of my arm. 'Okay, okay, I'm sorry, it really is easier to show you. We're nearly there, but we're going to an orchard just a couple of kilometres from here, that's where you'll find the Teeth of the Hesperides.'

'An orchard? Out here? There's nothing growing.'

'Yes, for real, an orchard. I'm sorry, please come with me.'

He was so worried by the thought of my departure that I couldn't say no. We trudged on in silence for another hour then the barren ground gave way to rich soil and rolling grass. We came to a chain link fence that seemed to run for miles in either direction and sure enough, there were apple trees beyond it.

Nils led us along the fence to a security gate. He checked his phone again and punched in a number on the keypad. The gate whirred and clicked and he pushed it open. I stayed where I was. He almost let the gate close in my face, before he saw I wasn't following.

'What are you doing? We have to move quickly.'

'I'm not going in there. It's private property, we're trespassing. We're here illegally without passports or anything. If they call the police, it's over for us.'

'We had to come this way, it's the only way to avoid detection. Please you have to come. You need to see this.'

'I'm not doing it, Nils.'

He looked at me imploringly. 'Please, you can save hundreds, maybe even thousands of lives.'

I saw the desperation in his eyes and I knew this was really about his brother. He'd been sucked into this and he couldn't get out. I intended to close the gate on him, walk away and never look back. That's what the part of me observing from a distance was screaming for me to do. But instead, I felt my feet move forward to join Nils and I heard the gate click shut behind me.

The fourth carnivorous plant trap mechanism is the *snap trap*. This is what people usually associate with carnivorous plants. The best-known example is the *Venus Flytrap*. That's what it felt like when I heard that gate shut behind me. Like I'd brushed a trigger hair and the jaws of a flytrap had closed around me. Now I couldn't escape.

Nils led me through the lush orchard. The grass at our feet was verdant and the fruit on the boughs was swollen and ripe, ready to be picked. The sage green leaves of the trees sheltered us from the sun's relentlessness and I felt the muscles in my shoulders unknot for the first time in days. A luscious, sweet scent hung in the air. It was heady and intoxicating.

We made our way to a small glade in the centre of the orchard. In the middle of the glade were three stunted trees. The grass around them was yellow and brittle as if from drought. The scent of apples gave way to something cloying and metallic.

The branches of the trees were gnarled and twisted. The trunks were knotted, and the bark was the pale grey of spent ashes or corpse skin. Two of the trees still had their leaves, they were golden and autumnal and looked ready to fall. When the sun caught them, they were iridescent when they caught the light, sparkling with many hues, as if they had scales. When the breeze stirred, they seemed to have a life of their own.

The middle tree was bare. Its leaves were lying at its base and there was something achingly familiar about its sinuous branches. At first, I couldn't place it, then it came to me. I had seen it before. My great uncle had sketched it in his papers.

I turned to Nils. 'Wait, are these …?'

He nodded. 'Welcome to the Teeth of the Hesperides.'

I stepped closer to get a better look. I was confused. Carnivorous plants don't tend to be trees or live in soil this rich.

I peered down at the leaves scattered around the base of the middle tree. They were steeped in a thick puddle of sap. It was dark, berry red, almost coagulating in places. The sap seemed to be oozing out of the leaves. Those at the bottom of the pile were thin, brittle and spent, while the leaves at the top were fat and swollen with the sap. As I bent to get a better look the metallic odour got stronger.

Nils was not so curious. He watched me from the edge of the glade. 'That one's just fed, it means we're in time to stop the other two.'

I wasn't paying attention. I reached into my knapsack and the first thing my fingers touched was the sickle. 'Do you think I could take some samples for study?'

'I wouldn't.'

A female voice rang out in the glade. 'What are you doing here? This is private property.' I looked up and saw a woman walking towards us. She moved and spoke with authority. I come from a wealthy background, so I know money when I see it. She was very well dressed and though she may have been in her fifties, she could easily pass for thirty something.

My mouth went dry and I found it hard to draw breath. A cool panic gripped my stomach. I'd blindly followed Nils into breaking and entering in a country I'd illegally entered. I felt like a schoolgirl caught by the housemistress trying to sneak out of school. I was surprised to find I was close to tears. All I could think to say was: 'I'm sorry.'

She ignored me and stared furiously at Nils. Her English was perfect with just the hint of a Moroccan accent. 'Nils Lundberg, I have a restraining order banning you from my property. I take it you bribed another member of my staff for the security codes?'

She turned to regard me haughtily. 'And who might you be?'

I took a ragged breath and tried to smile. 'I'm Sarah Mágissa.

I'm terribly sorry about trespassing, this is all a big misunderstanding.'

Her expression changed to one of warmth and surprise as soon as she heard my name. 'Mágissa, as in the English Mágissas, like Nicholas Mágissa?'

'Yes, he was my great uncle.'

She spread her arms in a gesture of welcome. 'Our families go way back. I'm surprised we've never met, we're practically related.'

I blushed at this and tucked a strand of hair behind my ear, relieved to be out of trouble. 'Well, I don't get to this part of the world very much.'

'I take it Mr Lundberg has roped you into another of his incursions? Told you all sorts of tales about us.'

Nils stepped forward at this point and spoke over the woman. 'Sarah, before she tells you any lies, this is Angeliki Kataraménos, a direct descendant of the farmer I told you about. The story that people call folklore is all truth, it really happened. The Kataraménos family is fabulously wealthy. All because of the Teeth of the Hesperides and the people they sacrifice to it every year.'

I looked to Angeliki who sighed in exasperation and pursed her lips. 'Ms Mágissa, I'm so sorry that Mr Lundberg has dragged you into his wretched campaign against my family. He's been harassing us for some time now with the most ridiculous claims.'

Nils became more agitated. 'Don't listen to her, she's lying because she's afraid of you. The wise woman's family that I told you about, their name is Mágissa, like yours. You and your great uncle are direct descendants. The mysterious client who commissioned Lukas to find the Teeth of the Hesperides, it was your cousin, the one who left you your great uncle's papers. The Kataraménos family killed him, and my brother, sacrificed them to the Teeth of the Hesperides so they wouldn't banish the trees. The sickle, the reason it smells so peculiar is because it's still impregnated with the sap of the tree from the wise woman's grave. *You* can banish them, Sarah. *You* can put a stop to all the deaths.'

Angeliki put a hand on my shoulder. 'You see the nonsense he speaks. We've had to put up with these outlandish accusations for over a year now. He needs help, he's delusional. Come with me up to the house and we can discuss this over coffee. I'll have my men escort Mr Lundberg from the property.'

I looked sheepishly at Nils and then Angeliki. 'I'm a bit dependent on Nils to get back to my hotel. I'm staying in Melilla, on the other side of the cape.'

'That's all right. I can get my driver to take you back.'

'That would mean crossing the border and I'm afraid I don't have my passport. We came by sea to avoid detection.'

She smiled wryly. 'You have been naughty, haven't you? No matter, I own a yacht. I'm quite an experienced sailor. We can make a trip of it, if you'd like to be my guest.'

I couldn't believe she was being so hospitable when I'd broken into her property. I thought at the time it must be our family connection, or that she felt sorry I'd been taken in by Nils.

Nils soon changed my mind. He called out as Angeliki led me from the grove. 'Wait, I can prove it. I can prove everything I've said. Just promise me you'll put a stop to all the murder, promise me you'll banish these evil trees.'

There was more than desperation in his eyes. There was the deep pain of loss and a sense of injustice. I realised it had always been there since I met him, but I'd chosen not to see it, too caught up in my thesis and my selfish needs.

Nils bent and put his fingers in the puddle of sap at the base of the middle tree. I was beginning to suspect it wasn't sap. He drew a strange symbol on his forehead, like a sigil, or a rune. 'This is how they mark the victims for death. It's how the Teeth of the Hesperides know who to attack.'

Angeliki called out a warning. 'Don't be an idiot!'

It did no good. He held out his arms like a martyr, sacrificing himself to avenge his brother's death. The Teeth of the Hesperides struck.

I screamed when I saw what the plant did to Nils. I became

hysterical. I ran to help him but Angeliki caught hold of me and held me back.

I fought her. I tried to pull free and when that didn't work, I lashed out and hit her. I was still holding the sickle I'd taken from my knapsack. It bounced off her cheekbone and cut her. Her head snapped backwards and she let go of me. I've never hit anyone so hard in my life. I was in shock from what I'd seen. Angeliki flew backwards and her head struck a tree trunk. She dropped to the ground, unconscious.

Nils was beyond saving. I walked to the three trees filled with cold fury and deadly resolution. I sliced open my palm with the blade of the sickle and made a fist, letting my blood drip onto the roots of all three plants.

The effect was instantaneous. Their boughs began to wilt and droop. Their bark peeled away and dropped from the trunk which rotted from within, turning into soft pulp.

For a second, I swear I felt the earth tremor as though something was being sucked out of the Teeth of the Hesperides and drawn deep into it. The tremor seemed to be a scream of rage.

I backed rapidly away and saw that Angeliki had come round. She glanced over at the trees and then back at me. She touched her cheek where I'd cut it and laughed bitterly, all the bonhomie gone from her voice. 'It won't work. You mingled my blood with your own when you cut me. You haven't banished her, you've only destroyed her vessels. She's angry and she has your scent now. She'll follow you wherever you run. She'll hunt you for the rest of your life, which won't be very long.'

Something about her words filled me with panic. I was nauseous from what had happened to Nils and the trees. I ran from the glade, stopped against a tree and threw up. Another wave of panic overcame me and I bolted for the back gate.

As I approached, I realised I didn't know the code to open it. I started to cry but I saw through my tears that they'd left the gate ajar. Probably because they knew the fate that lay in store for me.

I made it down the steep bluff in half the time it took to

climb, tripping and stumbling in my haste, sliding on my backside half of the time.

It was night when I got back to the shore. I was muddy, dishevelled and my clothing was torn. The wind had blown the dinghy down the rocky beach, and I could only find one oar.

I tried to reach the boat using only the oar like a paddle, but I got turned around and had to call out to the crew. Eventually they threw me a line and pulled me aboard. I told them we had to go straight away, but they were reluctant to leave without Nils.

I shouted. 'He's dead! They killed him and they'll kill us if we don't get out of here.' I took the wad of euros I had left and thrust it at them. This seemed to convince them and we were soon on our way.

I caught the next flight home and I've been running ever since.

The fifth trap mechanism is known as the *lobster-pot trap*. These are plant chambers that are easy to enter but impossible to leave, forcing their prey on, with slanting spikes, to their inevitable doom. That's what the last couple of years has felt like.

I've moved countless times, often before I'm able to sell my last property, exhausting my funds in the process. I've tried penthouses and high-rise apartments in the middle of urban wastelands. I've tried salting the earth for miles around or covering it in concrete. Nothing works.

Wherever I go the same gnarled branches, with the corpse grey bark, will always find me. They break through paving stones and asphalt. They take root in neighbour's roof gardens. No environment is too harsh or unsustainable for them and they grow to full maturity within weeks.

Even here, in an old prospector's house in the baking heat of the Negev desert, with only a generator for power and an old well for water, I'm not safe. There's no plant life for miles in any direction, but the Teeth of the Hesperides still broke through the barren sands.

It's late Autumn, I can hear the rustling and scratching at the window. I don't have much longer. Maybe not even to the end of this story. I'm trapped in here and I'm tired of running.

I suppose I should tell you about the sixth trap mechanism. The mechanism my great uncle identified and that I witnessed that day in Aegle. I don't have a name for this mechanism and I don't know what my great uncle called it. All I can do is describe what I saw.

When Nils painted the symbol on his forehead, and marked himself out as a victim, the leaves on the left-hand tree began to stir as if struck by a huge gust of wind. But the air in the orchard was still and the branches of the tree didn't move.

The leaves detached themselves from the branches and rushed into the air above the tree. At first I thought they were caught in a localised dust devil or whirlwind of some sort. But they weren't swirling, they were moving in some kind of formation.

They looked, for all the world, like a school of fish. The sun glinted off their golden blades and accentuated their scales as the leaves darted towards Nils like a shoal of piranhas. To this day I don't know how they did it, but the leaves were moving under their own volition.

They swarmed around Nils who tried to bat them away and cried out with fear and pain. Then I couldn't see him for the cloud of leaves that enveloped him.

The leaves spun as they touched Nils. Their edges must have been razor sharp because they tore his shoes and clothing to tatters in seconds. Tiny wisps of material flew from his body like a coloured mist.

When they reached his naked flesh, the leaves spun faster and Nils screamed louder. The leaves themselves got fatter and their veins swelled and turned red.

It took them a minute to strip Nils of all his skin and muscle tissue. They burrowed into his sockets, taking his eyes and his brain. They consumed all of his organs and even the connective tissue of his skeleton.

When they were done, all that remained was a pile of bones that looked like it came from a butcher's shop.

The leaves rose into the air and flew back to their tree. They dropped to the ground at the base of the trunk and fell lifeless. The blood and flesh they'd consumed began to leak from them and drained into the soil to be drunk by the tree's hungry roots.

This is how the Teeth of the Hesperides fed. This is their unique trap mechanism. And this is what I've been running from for the past two years.

It's late autumn. The leaves have left the trees. They're rustling and scratching at the window. Letting me know they're out there and they want to feed.

I have no water in the house, there's only the well outside. I need to leave the house to get to it. I've drunk nothing for two days and the generator is almost out of gas.

I'm going to die of thirst if I don't get water. And the leaves are waiting patiently outside.

CYCLOPS

Classical painter, JMW Turner's 1829 canvas, 'Ulysses Deriding Polyphemus', depicts a terrifying scene: the Ancient Greek hero, Odysseus (Ulysses, as the Romans knew him) on board his storm-battered ship with what remains of his crew, as they row away from a rugged island. Raging above them, but mostly concealed in a fog of low cloud and swirling dust, we sense a vast, primal something, an obscure but colossal horror descending on the escaping humans with elemental fury.

Everyone knows the story, of course. How Odysseus, one of the last survivors of the Trojan War, took refuge with his sole remaining ship on a rocky island, only to find it occupied by a race of gigantic, misshapen brutes, each with a single eye in his forehead, known as the cyclops (or, technically, the cyclopes). One in particular, Polyphemus, enclosed Odysseus and his men inside the cave where he lived by use of a giant rock, and there, one pair at a time, bound them to a spit, roasted them over a roaring fire, and devoured the cooked remains. Between meals, the monster would glut himself on wine, and sleep soundly, though his captives could never escape because they could not move the rock blocking the entrance.

When six of them had been eaten, Odysseus, a rarity among heroes in the Ancient World as he mostly utilised brain rather than brawn, hatched a clever scheme. By strengthening Polyphemus's wine, the Greeks ensured that, after his next meal, he would sleep particularly deeply, and while he did, they sharpened his great club and plunged it into his eye.

Driven mad with agony, but unable to lay hands on his assailants because he was blinded, Polyphemus moved the rock and sat in the opening, allowing only his flock of sheep to leave. But he was unaware that the Greeks, also on Odysseus's instruction, were clinging to the bellies of these innocent animals, and so passed under the monster's groping hands unnoticed. When they were outside, Odysseus couldn't resist calling scornfully that the cyclops had been tricked by 'Οὗτις', which in Greek means 'Nobody'.

The incapacitated Polyphemus blundered after them down to the shore, calling for help from his fellow cyclops. When some called back, asking what his trouble was, he replied that he'd been blinded by Nobody ... that he'd been destroyed by Nobody. Assuming that this meant he'd been stricken at the whim of the gods, his neighbours saw no purpose in assisting.

But even then, Polyphemus, a prodigious force, was almost successful, for as the Greek ship sailed out of the bay, he hurled huge rocks, several times missing it only narrowly.

The story appears repeatedly in early Greek literature, but was made most famous by Homer, who gave a lavish account in his epic adventure, 'The Odyssey'. Interestingly, many scholars who have sought to establish real-world locations for the various islands visited by Odysseus (Gozo as the domain of Calypso, Djerba as the home of the lotus-eaters), nominate Sicily as the land of the cyclops. And there is a logic to this because, Sicily, which hosts Stromboli, Vulcano and Mount Etna, sits at the heart of Europe's most volcanic region, and the cyclops, though they later ranged all across the Mediterranean, are associated from their earliest days with volcanoes, and that is not just because both shared the habit of flinging massive rocks out to sea.

In modern times, the cyclops are seen as straightforward monsters, fearsome adversaries who would kill and eat anyone they encountered, but when they first entered written mythology (possibly in the work of the poet, Hesiod, who was writing around 700 BC but referring to a distant, primordial past), they inhabited the realm of the immortals rather than men. The offspring of Uranus and Gaia, there were only three of them initially, Brontes, Steropes and Arges, and their main task was to fashion weapons for Zeus. This was an age of chaos, and the gods of Olympus were engaged in a life and death struggle with another race of monsters, the Titans, who were led by one of the most ferocious beings in the cosmos, Cronos. It was the cyclops who tipped this balance in the Olympians' favour by providing Zeus with thunderbolts, which even the Titans could not resist (in a later battle, he also used them to best Typhon, Cronos's vengeful son and probably the most terrifying monster in the history of the world). Most important for our purposes though, the cyclops' armouries and workshops were believed located inside the craters of 'fire-mountains', as the Greeks knew them, hence the smoke and constant rumbling.

However, at some point during the chronological lifespan of these mysterious one-eyed entities, they seem to have transitioned from industrious but servile demigods into savage Earthbound monstrosities. This was certainly the way Homer (also writing around 700 BC but referring to events of around 1200 BC) referred to them.

One theory holds that when Zeus appointed Hephaestus to be his blacksmith, the cyclops, by this time numerous, were left redundant, and so were either thrown into Tartarus, or abandoned to the Earth, where though they could sometimes be used to perform difficult tasks, such as building the immense walls of Mycenae, they would mostly just live out their rest of their lives in an angry and lawless state. Polyphemus himself embodies this strange transformation. In Homer, he was an opponent of civilisation, a murderer and cannibal, a bestial betrayer of the laws of hospitality. Yet at the same time he was of noble lineage, descended from Poseidon, and capable of love as well as hatred, as demonstrated in his courtly but unsuccessful pursuit of the nymph, Galatea.

The cyclops are now so iconic that they have become go-to monsters in the annals of mythology or mythology-inspired fantasy, yet it is unusual that their legend extends far beyond the boundaries of Graeco-Roman culture. Sinbad the Sailor, a fictional hero of Islamic myth, most commonly appearing in the 'One Thousand and One Nights' lexicon, encounters the cyclops during his Third Voyage, in this case a male and female pairing of the monsters, on an unnamed island in the Indian Ocean, and though he survives the resulting battle, most of his men are slain. However, similar monsters appear in Celtic, Germanic and Slavic myths and legends, including one particularly familiar folktale from the Caucasus, wherein a family of shepherds are captured by a one-eyed giant, and killed and eaten one by one, until the surviving two brothers blind it with a red-hot spit and then escape from its lair disguised under sheepskins.

It's been suggested that all these stories boast a common origin, namely the skulls of woolly mammoths, which were enormous to behold and each one possessed of a single monstrous aperture. We know now that this was to accommodate the mammoth's trunk. In the Ancient World, though, they might easily have assumed it was an eye socket.

Another explanation of course, perhaps marginally less plausible, but fun to ponder nevertheless, is that the cyclops were every bit as real as the mythmakers tell us.

REIGN OF HELL
Paul Finch

When Pavlos first saw the Security Battalion enter Messia, they were exactly the kind of military rabble he'd expected. Though remnants of the old khaki field uniform of the *Evzoni* were in evidence, most of the men wore furs or sheepskin doublets over the top and were wrapped in bandolier belts filled with cartridges. They were bearded and dirty, and smoked idly as they slouched along the village streets. They might lack for soap, water and shaving cream, but they had no shortage of firearms: rifles were slung over their shoulders, pistols and revolvers slotted into their belts; some carried heavyweight machine-guns, others bore stick-grenades on their webbing.

They had two vehicles with them: a dusty Alfa Romeo convertible, in which their officer rode, and an old Italian army truck, on the rear deck of which a pair of prisoners were held at gunpoint.

It was not yet eight o'clock in the morning, but the Battalion wasted no time in rousing the entire village, going house to house, banging on doors and shuttered windows. If shops were already open for business, they were summarily closed, and the shopkeepers and their families brought out and made to stand in the village square, in the shade of the big carob tree. The occasional yelp was heard as a barking dog was brutally dealt with. When the entire population was assembled, Pavlos and Thea included, the main event commenced.

The Security Battalion, which had formed a cordon around the square, parted on its west side, and the truck reversed into view. The two prisoners were young men, possibly natives of this district, though nobody recognised them for their swollen faces were blue and green with bruising and streaked with blood. Their clothes were ragged and filthy, their hands tied behind their backs, and wooden plaques bearing the word *prodotis* had been fixed to each of their chests. A burly sergeant unfolded a sheet of paper and read out a list of their heinous offences. Behind him, two of his underlings threw thin cords over one of the carob's lower branches. Nooses had already been prepared on the ends of these. Pavlos glanced towards the Security Battalion commandant, who sat alongside his driver in the open-topped Alfa Romeo in the northeast corner of the square, puffing impassively on the stub of a cigar.

'Long live the real Greece!' The feeble cry drew Pavlos's attention back to the truck, where the two nooses were being knotted around the prisoners' necks. 'Long live ...' the first one tried to shout again, but a punch in the gut silenced him, doubling him halfway over.

The sergeant stepped back and stamped hard on the truck-bed. With a rumble of exhaust, the vehicle lurched forward, and the two young men were left behind, dangling three feet above the square, kicking and jerking for neither had fallen far enough to snap his neck. It lasted for several torturous seconds, during which the villagers watched in numbed silence. By the time it had finished, the commandant had climbed from his car to straighten his back. He wore a smarter uniform than his men, complete with a black-tasselled cap, knee-high Italian boots, and leather gloves. His *Evzoni* overcoat was draped over his shoulders, and he carried a riding crop.

The people of Messia said nothing as he strode along the front of them. Despite his advancing years, he was well-built, with a lean, tanned face, a firm jaw and a waxed grey moustache. He touched his cap to the women. To the men he was indifferent, until he sighted Pavlos standing three rows back.

He halted and they regarded each other, a half-smile playing around the commandant's mouth. He flirted his cigar stub away, summoned his sergeant and ordered the assembly dispersed.

'Miserable wretches!' the sergeant bellowed, as his men used their rifle butts to send the villagers scurrying back to their shops and houses. 'Let that be a lesson to you! This is the fate all traitors to Greece will face!'

Thea clung to her father's side, frightened, but Pavlos sent her away sternly, so that now only he and the commandant remained. The rest of the Security Battalion were slouching again, standing around in groups; some even produced bottles of beer. The two bodies swung limply, the Carob branch creaking. The commandant pointed with his crop to the open door of the village taverna. Pavlos nodded and limped towards it.

There was nobody else in the dim interior except the proprietor, a short, stout man with a wide moustache and pointed beard, who stood rigid behind the counter. Pavlos greeted him wordlessly and chose a small table in a private corner. The commandant arrived and sat down facing him. He called for two glasses of Ouzo as he pulled off his gloves; his tone was sharp, curt – and yet he regarded Pavlos almost fondly.

'Satisfactory morning's work, Anton?' Pavlos asked.

'The culmination of several days' such work,' the commandant replied. 'Those fellows led us a merry dance. There are more of them, of course. But we obtained good information before we finished.'

Pavlos took off his spectacles and polished their lenses with a handkerchief. 'You must feel you've gone up in the world. Father would have been so proud.'

The commandant's smile hardened into an icy mask. 'Do me the honour of not confusing our father with someone he wasn't. He despised the communists, as well you know.'

'He was also a humanitarian.'

The commandant pondered this. He downed his Ouzo and called for another. Pavlos's glass still sat on the table, untouched.

'These harsh measures are only temporary,' the commandant said. 'In case you'd forgotten, we're fighting a war.' He raised an eyebrow. 'Though of course you *had* forgotten, hadn't you? Fuzzy old Pavlos, his head still stuffed with straw, living only for his studies and his pottery and his bits of fossilized bone. Well, I'm sorry, brother, but even you can't remain separate from this for much longer.'

Pavlos considered the two bodies swinging outside. Already the flies would be buzzing around them, yet no doubt they'd be left there until they putrefied. It had been two and a half years since Mussolini's forces had first invaded Greece, and two since General Tsolakoglou had been installed as the Axis puppet, and yet life had remained cosseted here in this remote northeast corner of the Peloponnese. Pavlos had heard of such atrocities occurring but had never seen any until now. Of course, at fifty years old, he was hardly a child; he'd known this horror would arrive at some point.

'You moved here, they say, because your researches led you to this region,' the commandant remarked, sipping from his replenished glass.

'And?' Pavlos said.

'I'd hate to think there was some other reason.'

'What other reason could there be?'

'The whole of this countryside is alive with partisans. That is commonly known.'

'Anton … Thea and I have lived here since Marisa's death. That was many years before this war started.'

Commandant Anton nodded but tapped his fingertips on the table as if something troubled him. 'And yet … every few days, or so I'm told, you make trips into the hills.'

'For my work. Anton … you *know* this.'

'Your work, yes … the documentation of ruined buildings.'

'It's called archaeology, Anton. It's a respected occupation.'

Anton filched another cheroot from his tunic pocket. 'And this pays you … how?'

'Father's estate provided for us both. I haven't needed to teach for over a decade. In addition to that, I've had several bursaries. But again, you know all this. I don't understand why you even ask the question.'

'Pavlos, you worry too much.' Anton put a match to the cigar and puffed on it. 'I don't suspect *you* of sedition. How could I? I know you too well. But then again … it may not be me you have to convince. And while you introduced Thea to the conversation, perhaps we should discuss *her* role in this.'

'*Thea's* role?

'There is a rumour she was romantically involved with Giorgos Konstantinos – one of those two felons outside.'

Pavlos's mouth slackened open. 'But … that's not true!'

'You're sure? Thea is not a child anymore. She is eighteen years old. You know every move she makes?'

Pavlos shook his head. 'Anton … why are you doing this?'

'You are my brother, Pavlos. It gives me no pleasure to implicate you and your family in dangerous activities.'

'But if you do, it makes you appear strong – is that it?'

'If I am to clamp down on the armed rebels who infest this region, I must be feared. I must be seen as a man of iron who, if necessary, will condemn his own flesh and blood.'

'Even though we've done nothing?'

'Sometimes doing nothing is itself the crime.'

'You know,' Pavlos said hesitantly, 'on that you may be right.'

Anton gathered his gloves and riding crop and stood up. 'My men and I will be in this area for the next week. During that time, I want your cooperation. First of all, find billets for us. Good ones.'

'I'm not the mayor of this town …'

'If you were, I'd already have had you shot for failing to bring these partisan vermin to justice under your own power. After you have arranged billets, you will report any subversion that has come to your attention.' Anton strode to the doorway, where he paused. 'You know, Pavlos … but of course you know, you're a historian … they say there have been settlements in this area since before the Bronze Age. Can you imagine? People have lived in Messia for so long, and yet in the blink of an eye it could all disappear.' Without awaiting a reply, he stepped out into the May sunshine.

Pavlos and Anton were the sons of Gino Xanthou, an eminent anthropologist at the University of Athens. They spent their formative days in a large, comfortable townhouse in the shadow of the Acropolis, and, as there was only two years between them, grew up the closest of friends, sharing their father's love of Greek history, literature, philosophy and folklore. Only in later days did their paths diverge, Anton entering university to study political science, Pavlos following the family tradition, and exploring the origins of Greece and the Greek nation.

Their paths crossed several times in those years of academe, and on each occasion, Anton was a colder presence. Only once did he visit Pavlos's rooms, which were more cluttered with books, scrolls and parchments than he could ever remember, their walls hung with all kinds of maps and incomprehensible scribblings. He turned his nose up in superior fashion, as if he'd caught his brother playing some childish game.

'No-one loves this country more than I do,' he said, 'but the glories of the past won't return just because we dream about them.'

'And how *will* they return?' Pavlos asked.

'We must assert our ownership of the future as well. We must embrace the modern world and all the new theories of social order.'

This had been in 1913. If Pavlos had ever visited his brother's own accommodation – a Spartan cell that would not have been out of place in a military barracks – he would have found among the few items of reading material on its single shelf: d'Annunzio, Barrés and Drumont. But he never went, some sixth sense advising against it.

At the end of their education, Anton enlisted in the Greek Army as a commissioned officer. He served in what became known as the Great War, fighting against the Bulgarians, and in 1919 on the expedition to the Ukraine. The next time he fired a shot in anger was in 1940, in Albania, at that stage in opposition to the Italians. By contrast, Pavlos never saw action in any of these turbulent years, as a severe leg injury incurred during a college caving expedition had rendered him unfit for military service. Instead, he became a teacher, and at the same time pursued his scholarly interests, to a point where, by his own admission, many events in the 'real world' simply passed him by.

Of course, Pavlos now reflected as he stood huddled inside his overcoat, it was a matter of opinion where the real world actually lay. Especially after the things he'd discovered at Lerna. But though he didn't love his brother anymore, blood was still thicker than water – he felt he owed it to Anton to at least give him a chance. So, he waited longer at the farmhouse door, even though the yawning Security Battalion sergeant had answered it some ten minutes earlier. Around him, the dawn was still; there wasn't the bleat of a sheep or goat, or the clank of a cowbell. Wisps of thin, milk-white mist lay unmoving on the rural landscape.

When Anton appeared in his shirtsleeves and braces, an oil-lamp in one hand, he was grumpy to have been disturbed. 'Good Christ, man, the first cock hasn't crowed yet!'

'You wanted information,' Pavlos said.

'You have names for me?'

'I have a location.'

'A hideout?'

'Of sorts.'

'I'll rouse the men …'

'Wait.' Pavlos held up a warning hand. 'Only bring a handful. There are no partisans there at present. But I promise you'll find things that will interest you.'

'Things that will interest me?' Anton sounded suspicious. 'That wasn't our agreement.'

'We made no agreement.'

Anton's eyes narrowed. 'Don't play silly games with me,

Pavlos.'

'Why would I be playing games? It's clearly in my interest to win your favour.'

A short time later, Pavlos and Anton were crammed into the cab of the truck, the sergeant, whose name was Mateus, seated next to them at the wheel, still yawning and rubbing at his face as they rumbled along a winding, rutted lane. In the rear, three Security Battalion troopers struggled to come around from their drunken sleep.

Beyond a range of high, boulder-strewn bluffs, they descended into a broad valley, where the lowland vapours thickened until they were almost like fog. Sergeant Mateus slowed down as the road was lost in shifting blankets of grey. After ten minutes, Pavlos indicated they should turn left. From here, they juddered along a route that was little more than a dirt track between twisted trees. The mist drifted, revealing bog pools and wild vines trailing from above. A warm dampness intruded through the open windows; they heard the loud croaking of frogs.

'Where are we?' Anton asked curiously.

'This was once Lake Lerna,' Pavlos replied.

'I remember that name from somewhere.'

'It's silted up now. Only these swamps remain.'

'How far do we have to go?'

'We round what was once the lake's southern shore. The thing I have to show you is on the eastern side.'

'After all this it had better be worthwhile.'

'By comparison with what you will experience today, every mission you've undertaken in this war will seem like a waste of time.'

Anton *harrumphed* as if *he* would be the judge on this matter, and initially his skepticism appeared well-founded. They had to stop the truck when a stream cut across the track from the surrounding hills, turning what remained of it into an impassable quagmire. They thus proceeded on foot, following a path that looped between tall, straight willows growing upright from the encircling morass, their roots exposed like slimy green bones. When they reached their destination, it was a gap in dense foliage, which led downward at a steeply tilting angle to a cave mouth. Much of the rock encompassing this had cracked and decayed and was braced with timbers. It resembled the entrance to an abandoned mine.

'We're going underground?' Anton asked, suddenly sounding uneasy.

'A little way.' Pavlos took a notebook from his coat pocket and flicked through it.

'What is that?'

'It contains maps, among other things. Homemade but they'll suffice.'

'You never mentioned that we'd be going underground.'

'The things I intend to show you could never be left lying in the open.'

'What are we talking about, treasure?'

'Valuable items, certainly.'

'I'm not here to get rich, Pavlos.'

Of course not, Pavlos thought. *That is why you brought only the four troopers billeted in the farmhouse with you and left no message as to your whereabouts for the others.* For all the zealotry of his youth, the middle-aged Anton, like so many officials in the totalitarian state, had quickly come to appreciate the privileges of unfettered power.

As if sensing his brother's cynicism, Anton added: 'My sole purpose is to serve the Prefecture of Argolis-Corinthia.'

'Who I'm sure will be most pleased with some of the items you will shortly present to them.' Pavlos started downward, his twisted leg giving him little trouble for he was experienced on this slope. At the bottom, he removed his cloth cap and stuffed it into a pocket as he stooped beneath the cave mouth's low, moss-covered lintel.

A few feet beyond this, he crouched and reached into a niche on the right, where he cranked a handle. There was a rattle and *clunk,* and then the loud, prolonged grumble of an engine. Electric bulbs, suspended at regular intervals down the tunnel from a loose network of overhead wiring, flickered to life.

'You have your own generator?' Anton called down, incredulous.

'Of course,' Pavlos replied.

'And who provided the fuel?'

'I provided it, myself. I bought it.'

'You must have paid a high price.'

'Some prices are worth paying.'

'Hmmm.' Now that his road into the subterranean realm was lit, Anton seemed surer of himself. He straightened up and turned to his men. One of them would be left to guard the entrance. The other three, Sergeant Mateus included, would accompany him.

Once inside, they ventured downslope in single file, Pavlos at the front, Anton directly behind him. Initially, they advanced bent forward, for the passage was low and narrow. However, it was laid with duckboards, which made the going easier, and soon enlarged so that they were able to walk upright. When the duckboards ran out, the floor was a hard, well-packed loam, but there were still difficult moments as the path would turn and twist steeply, sometimes switching back on itself. The electric lighting revealed walls and ceilings scraped over and over by the edges of tools.

'These burrows are not natural?' Anton enquired.

'No,' Pavlos replied.

'Who made them?'

'A very ancient people. Searching for flints, copper ore and such.'

They now entered a stretch of passage where additional timbers had been employed; the entire right-hand wall was a façade of heavy split logs, bound together with iron brackets and held in place by crossbeams and buttresses.

'These hoardings and supports are my own addition,' Pavlos said. 'Beyond this wall lies the old lakebed ... and a torrent of mud that could swallow this entire complex.'

'You dammed it by yourself?' Anton asked.

'There was an earlier bulwark here. I merely reinforced it.'

'Even so, it must have been a difficult task.'

Pavlos glanced back at him. 'And you consider that I've never worked in my life.'

'Whether you performed *useful* work down here remains to be seen.'

The man on guard at the cave mouth was called Dimitri, and he was a dullard.

Unlike many of his comrades, he'd never been a serving soldier, and in fact had only enlisted in the Security Battalion three months previously because he'd kidnapped an infant girl from a village and been hunted with dogs all the way back to the ramshackle farm he'd inherited from his late mother in the hills of Larissa. Brought to trial on charges of abduction, he'd faced a possible severe punishment, except that the magistrate, who had secretly been one of Dimitri's mother's former lovers, feared that the big, dishevelled young man standing in the dock, regarding the proceedings around him with bovine incomprehension, might be his own son, and so gave him the opportunity to serve his country rather than face prison.

Even though the morning mist had melted away and the sun lay in rosy stripes through the marshland glades, any normal Battalion man would have felt alone and nervous in partisan country like this. Most likely, he'd have crouched out of sight amid the foliage, his bolt-action Carcano rifle loaded and ready. But Dimitri simply stood there, his weapon slung at his shoulder, his eyes half-closed. It had been an early start even for a man who had formerly been a farmer, though in truth he hadn't been a very good farmer, as his overgrown fields and straying animals would often attest.

When he heard the music, his eyes snapped open.

It was an eerie piping lilt, at once strange but also beautiful. Dimitri pivoted around, puzzled rather than alarmed. It seemed vaguely familiar, perhaps some rural lullaby or folksong that he'd heard as a child. There was no sign of movement in the trees or bushes surrounding him, but the music continued.

An image came into his mind of a Gypsy encampment, and he felt his first tremor of excitement. A Gypsy camp would mean girls whom no law in Greece now protected. In truth, there was little protection from the Security Battalion for *any* girls or women. That was one huge advantage of having joined up, which Dimitri had never expected but had enjoyed to the full ever since. But the Gypsies were particularly reviled, almost as much as the Jews. He could do what he wanted and there'd be nothing anyone would say.

Deciding the music was coming from the north, Dimitri lurched off in that general direction. Of course, Gypsy men often carried knives, so he checked that his rifle was loaded. It was, and he even had a couple of grenades on his belt, should he decide to blow up their caravans when he'd finished. There were so many different ways to persecute undesirables. He licked his fat, blubbery lips as he ploughed through a blackberry thicket and into a cypress wood beyond, where traces of mist still lingered.

When they entered the main cavern, they descended by a timber ramp, but this was only part of a multi-levelled scaffold of walkways, platforms and ladders, which almost filled the airy, church-like interior. Far below, the cavern floor was a chaos of crates, boxes and tools. A central space had been cleared, where there was a table acting as a desk. Books, documents and writing materials were scattered across it.

'And how on Earth did you construct all this?' Anton demanded, his voice echoing.

'For ten years I had my students to help me,' Pavlos replied. 'It was a grand project.'

'And where are those young men now?'

'For the most part in uniform.'

Anton smiled approvingly. 'What a disappointment for you. Instead of building monuments to your vanity, they now build the new Greece.'

'Either that, or they are in the hills,' Pavlos added.

Anton's smile faded. 'Stop wasting my time and show me what you've found here.'

'Well ... look around.'

The ramp descended past a section of cavern wall in which niches had been scooped. Pavlos pointed into each one as they passed. Anton glimpsed fragments of pottery and crude, broken figurines embedded in dirt.

'Is this all?' he said. 'These esoteric oddments?'

'Oddments?' Pavlos sounded outraged. They'd now descended to the next platform, where he displayed a row of knee-high urns. They were thick with dust, though the illustrations with which they'd been covered were still partly visible, mostly comprising octopoid forms with swirling tentacles. 'These jars were securely sealed when I found them. They contained unfeasibly ancient manuscripts.'

'Falling to pieces no doubt.'

'Of course falling to pieces. I had to remove them to my study with the utmost care.'

Anton stuck a fresh cheroot between his lips and struck a match. 'I can picture them ... crumbling rags adding very nicely to the rodent-like mess you usually wallow in.'

'Are you mad? I've had to place them under glass. No-one may handle them but me. Anton, these are aeons old, written in some pre-Hellenic tongue I have only partly managed to translate. They're very likely priceless.'

Anton blew smoke as he pondered this. His dismissive attitude was partly false. He had some knowledge himself about the value of antediluvian artifacts. 'Priceless?'

'Priceless!' Pavlos insisted. 'Anton ... this is not old Greece that we've uncovered down here. This is the oldest Greece of all. Think how valuable that could be to your new society. The Italians have their Romans, the Germans have their ... well, their Teutonic Nirvana, which we both know never existed, but *us* ... look what *we* can bring to the table. Look how ancient and venerable *our* civilisation is. Even more so than we thought.'

'Well ... there may be some truth in what you say.' Anton

glanced around the cavern, at its high-rise scaffolding, at the many nooks and crannies where precious relics still waited to be uncovered. 'I suppose this is something of an achievement, though I'm loath to admit it. As an archaeologist, this will make your name, Pavlos. But that means you have even more to lose. For this reason alone, you should *ensure* you back the right horse.'

'Why do you think I'm showing you all this?'

'And I know you haven't brought me down here to see scraps of the past.' Anton tried not to let the greedy anticipation sound in his voice. 'There is something else, yes?'

'Yes.'

'Lead on.'

They descended to the cavern floor and threaded through the forest of joists and support pillars to another tunnel entrance. On entering, Anton saw that this passage only ran thirty yards or so before ending at the top of a stairway. He also noted that crucifixes had been set into its walls, three on either side, arranged in triangular formations. He looked more closely. They were ornate in the traditional Byzantine style, and apparently made from solid gold. A couple appeared to be inset with gemstones.

'What's this?' he asked, fascinated.

'An attempt was made some time in the more recent past to Christianise the lower vault,' Pavlos said. 'Or at least prevent whatever lurks down there from coming to the surface.'

Anton glanced round at him. 'What do you mean "whatever lurks down there"?'

'They're just old ghost stories, Anton. Tales of baleful, chthonic beings abound in our myths and legends.'

The commandant glanced at his three troopers. Two were rural oafs, and they seemed faintly unnerved by what they'd just heard. But the other, Mateus – a brute thief by nature – was more interested in the crucifixes. His eyes gleamed as he assessed them.

'How much further down do we have to go?' Anton asked.

'We are almost there,' Pavlos said.

'You are certain this will be worth my while?

'I promise you will never have seen anything like it.'

'Sergeant Mateus!' Anton said. 'As this narrow defile appears to be the only passage down to the next level, I don't want it closed behind us. Guard it with your life.'

Mateus snapped to attention. Whether he realised that his commandant didn't trust him and wanted him out of the way because a more valuable hoard was soon to be unearthed, was uncertain – but he was clearly delighted to have been left alone with the gold and jewel-encrusted crucifixes.

The rest of them proceeded down the stair.

'There's water here,' Anton said, noting for the first time that moisture glinted on the rocks overarching them. 'And what are these deposits?' He indicated the rocks themselves, which were curiously patterned: striated purple, green and yellow as though filmed with oil.

'All kinds of different minerals compose these formations,' Pavlos explained.

'I imagine we are now beneath the swamp?'

'That is true.'

'In that case, perhaps there should be more supports?'

The timber props so prevalent in the higher galleries were absent down here.

'Don't worry,' Pavlos said. 'This place has remained intact for several thousand years. You haven't noticed these steps?' He indicated the stair, the treads of which were cut from smooth marble rather than the primitive stone they had seen before. 'I date them to the Mycenaean era.'

'I thought you said this place was older than that?'

'It is … infinitely older, but clearly the Mycenaeans also felt it worthy of veneration.'

'There's no lighting either!' Anton gazed back along the sloped ceiling. The last bulb was suspended some forty yards to their rear. 'Is that because of the damp?'

'That's because it isn't needed,' Pavlos said.

Anton glanced down the stair. It was true; they were descending into a form of natural bluish light. 'What causes that?'

'Come.' Pavlos started down again. 'See for yourself.'

It was several minutes before they reached the bottom, but here the floor was levelled off and again paved with marble. It led twenty yards to a row of Doric pillars, their lintels carved with eldritch characters. The source of the blue light appeared to lie beyond these, for it cast columnar shadows to the foot of the stair.

'Through here,' Pavlos said.

The others followed, the troopers now with rifles at the ready. On the far side of the pillars there was another paved area, though this had the aura of a harbour dock, for it ran only ten yards before ending with a straight edge at a pool of still, clear water. Pavlos limped forward. Anton hesitated, throwing his cigar stub away. He bade his men hang back and watch. As a young soldier he had fought at Skra-di-Legen, where he'd developed a sixth sense about danger, which had not yet deserted him. There was something menacing about this seemingly tranquil grotto. Almost reluctantly, he joined his brother on the lip of the dock, from where he observed similar carvings to those on the lintels, though vastly cruder, covering the rugged stone walls that dropped into the pool; these too glimmered with iridescent colours as though smeared by oil. The water looked exceedingly deep, but at its farthest depth – maybe two hundred feet down – there was a blob of aqua-blue light so bright that even from that limit its luminosity filled the cavern.

'We must be far under the Earth now,' Anton said, confused. 'Yet a portion of sunlight somehow works its way down there?'

'Sunlight?' Pavlos replied, his attention divided between the pool and his pocket-watch.

'Isn't that natural light reflecting on sand?'

'It's natural, but there's no sun and no sand.'

'Pavlos, I warn you … I'm tiring of this cryptic nonsense.'

But Pavlos was barely listening. He'd noticed a single ripple pass across the surface of the water, and now turned to his brother in brisk, businesslike fashion. 'Anton, I am well aware that I can't change your political views. They are too deeply rooted. But I'm begging you to at least contemplate the sanity of the course you've chosen.'

Anton looked taken aback. 'My sanity is perfectly intact, thank you. As for yours, I'm not so sure ... why are you suddenly sweating?'

'Listen to me, Anton ... for once in your life.' Pavlos mopped the wetness from his brow and grabbed his brother's wrist. 'Has it never struck you that in swearing an oath of allegiance to Adolf Hitler you have made yourself a pariah to your countrymen?'

Anton yanked his arm free. 'Or alternatively, I've made myself a national hero.'

'A what?'

'It doesn't surprise me that you don't recognise the threat the Soviets pose to the civilised world, Pavlos, you having spent so much time grubbing in holes in the ground.'

'In Heaven's name, Anton, end this folly! By allying our country with Hitler, we are not just at war with Soviet Russia, but with the whole world. I'm making a final appeal to you ... throw off these ridiculous Nazi trappings and join the partisans.'

'Is this really why you've brought me here?' Anton whispered, his brow reddening. 'To talk God-damned treason!'

'I brought you here to educate you.'

'You disappoint me, Pavlos.' Anton stepped back, drew his Luger and cocked it. 'Clearly there is nothing here of value. No enemies of the state hide in these caves ...'

'Something hides here,' Pavlos warned, 'though maybe "hiding" is too strong a word. It sleeps rather than hides, but not for much longer,'

Anton said no more, merely pointed the Luger at his brother's sweat-soaked face.

Maybe he would have triggered it, maybe not. But he was distracted before he could find out by a sluggish rolling and slapping of liquid. He turned and regarded the water, if it *was* water. Its surface now swayed from side to side in wave-like motions, and yet there was no froth, no splashing; it was thick and viscous, almost like glue. Then he was distracted by something else, something deep below it.

The glowing blue object had broken apart into myriad glinting particles, which now began slowly to swirl upward like miniature stars in a spiral galaxy.

'Pavlos?' Anton breathed. *'Pavlos, look at this …'*

But Pavlos was nowhere near. He had retreated across the dock, pulling the notebook from his pocket and now flicked frenziedly through its pages.

Anton could only peer at the pool, entranced. It continued to roll and undulate, yet even now there was no break in its membrane surface. The multiple glowing particles were still ascending, still spiralling outward; soon they would encompass the entire breadth of the pool. They appeared orb-like in shape, and while most were blue, others were purple or indigo, their 'deep ocean' light running in fluid patterns across the cavern roof and walls, across Anton's wondering face.

He was vaguely aware of two new presences. His men, unable to hold back any longer, had advanced to either side of him, and now stood transfixed. Only Pavlos was uninterested. He had found a cubbyhole in the rock wall, crouched and inserted himself. Having settled on a page in his book, he now incanted words – words with no meaning to Anton. Not that this mattered. The vision in the pool was all; it was astonishing, mesmerising. Searing light poured up from it. The orbs, of which there were literally thousands, were almost at the surface. Anton's men gazed down blankly. Anton himself wanted to cry out with awe, but also with an intangible sense of fear.

What they were witnessing here was impossible; it could not be. His hair prickled …

The girl was the most astounding thing Dimitri had ever seen. She wore a sleeveless, white shift, bound at the waist with a length of vine and so filmy that he could see the naked body beneath. Her hair was lustrous and black; at full length it would hang in twisting, raven coils, but now was fixed high on her head, which was somehow even more captivating. Her face, throat and arms had been painted white – unnaturally white, corpse-white – but there was a deep purple brocade around her glittering blue eyes, and blood-red staining on her lips. She was barefoot, and had been prancing around a low fire, playing a pan flute, when he'd first spotted her, emitting the mysterious tune that had drawn him here.

Now she put the instrument aside, but continued to skip around the flames, her curved hips and high breasts swaying beneath her flimsy garb. Dimitri stumbled forward, allowing his rifle to drop to the woodland floor. What was he seeing here? Some priestess of the old religion, some forest nymph, a dryad?

Closer up, he observed that her eyes shone like glowing blue crystals because they were actually closed, and their lids had been painted. She had a pouch at her waist, from which she cast pinches of powder into the crackling flames. Each one elicited a different coloured plume of smoke: orange, violet, yellow, green. She murmured to herself in a chant that was low but intense, like the drone of a hornet. It was the same tune she had been playing on the pan flute, only now with words.

Dimitri couldn't make them out but was hardly concerned. His mouth watered as he feasted his eyes on the sensual form.

When she abruptly ceased her otherworldly caterwaul and swung around to face him, a sweat of desire stippled his brow. Her painted eyelids snapped open to reveal an alluring, brown-eyed gaze. They stared at each other for long, taut seconds, before the priestess lowered the shoulder-straps of her shift and let it rustle to her feet.

This was all the invitation Dimitri needed. He blundered forward, fiddling at the buttons on his trousers, glancing up again eagerly as he reached her. Straight into the muzzle of a Mauser 9mm.

Dimitri's mouth dropped open.

The priestess regarded him with a cold and terrible indifference.

One by one, the orbs broke the surface of the pool, and bobbed there like buoys on the sea. The air quickly became rank with a stench like rotting fish. Though they glowed with an intense internal radiance, they were ugly to look upon: hard, fist-sized lumps of rubbery gelatin. In addition, they were alive, for each one abruptly swivelled and turned – until they had all focussed on Anton and his men.

Yes, *focussed* …

Because Anton knew without doubt that what he was seeing here were eyes, as attested to by the pupil in the centre of each one, the hideous, black, malignant pupil.

The trooper to his right gave a shout that quickly rose into a piercing scream, and then the middle of the pool surged upward in a great glistening dome, as though lifted by some vast force below, and hung there in stasis, the ghastly eyes speckled all over it, yet mostly congregated at its front so to fix on those who had disturbed its slumber.

The Battalion trio turned and fled, shrieking, foam spraying from their lips.

'I thought you were our next hero!' Pavlos called raucously. 'You should be braver than this, Anton … this creature is a mere servant, a mindless slave! Nothing like the real thing …' But as the vast being flowed over the dock in a mountainous, glutinous wave, he watched it with awe. 'Mind you, it is ancient and powerful … so powerful.' His voice rose again. 'The last time it was woken, it took a *real* hero of the Greeks to confront it. In those days we called it the 'Hydra' …'

The colossal beast was now changing form, translucent tentacles writhing forth like a nest of snakes, the tip of each one swollen and globular, roughly the shape of a human head, and all clustered with those piercing blue eyes. When seven such tentacles thrashed across the paving stones towards him, Pavlos incanted again, pouring out the verses he had copied from those crumbling parchments.

A sweat of terror streamed from his brow as seven horrific visages pored over him. Human yet gelatinous, their liquid features shaping and reshaping, portraying the countless tortured faces of victims past. Pavlos intoned feverishly.

'*Noord kisqa oiiih waskew ... Aforgomon ... Tekeli-li ... Castifriiidez Yog-Sothoth ... uaaaah faithrodog ... Yog-Sothoth! Noord kisqa oiiih waskew ... Aforgomon ... Tekeli-li ... Castifriiidez Yog-Sothoth ... uaaaah faithrodog ... Yog-Sothoth!*'

Of course, he didn't really know what these words meant, any more than the Mycenaean priests who'd carved them on the lintels of the Hellenic temple's inner sanctum. But in the same way that words, or the forms of words, or the vibrations that words and certain strains of music create in the air, the ocean and the deep rocks of the Earth, have often served as summoning knells, they could also offer protection – and they did so now.

The seven monstrous heads scrutinised him but did naught else. And all the while, from the cave's roof and walls, the rainbow-hued moisture – which of course was not moisture at all – extruded down in thick, gooey rivulets, spilling across the paved floor to merge with the main bulk of the abomination, which suddenly surged away from Pavlos, briefly breaking itself apart to ooze through the row of pillars, only to re-meld on the other side, slide to the foot of the marble stair, and swiftly ascend.

The Battalion trio sweated and swore and frothed at the mouth as they staggered up the tower of steps. Initially, sheer horror gave them strength and energy. But all knew that this would not last. Several times they turned and fired. Every slug smashed an unguent head to a cascade of quivering gobbets. The eyes would drop out of them like golf balls, bouncing on the marble treads, yet were always re-absorbed as another tentacle squirmed up from behind. When he saw this plan was a failure, Anton sacrificed his underlings. On the basis that one evades a ravening wolf by throwing him fresh meat, he fired two shots into each when their backs were turned.

But unintentionally, this proved a form of kindness.

The odious heads on their squid-like tentacles ignored the corpses as they threshed their way past. It was true that when the main bulk surged over the bodies, it crushed them to a porridge of blood, bone and meat, and sucked them in through suppurating vents to ingest at its leisure, but by then their pain was over.

Further up, Anton, exhausted and tottering, already knew that his life could be counted in minutes – and he marvelled that he accepted this so calmly. Perhaps it was the effect of the war? He had witnessed so many innocent souls sent without warning to their maker; he had arranged it more times than he could remember. Had life really become so cheap so quickly that he held his own in such little regard?

On all sides now, protoplasmic tendrils were extending outward from what he'd once thought were damp patches on the stairwell walls, or descending from the ceiling, hanging jellylike excrescences, pulsating and twisting as they searched for him. It continued even when he reached the top of the stair and the short tunnel to the excavation hall. Undulant horrors writhed towards him from all sides. When, midway along the passage he saw the upright figure of Sergeant Mateus, he was briefly hopeful; Mateus was a rugged customer who could fight. But then Anton realised that this was not Sergeant Mateus so much as what remained of him. He had been swallowed by a vitreous mass, which no doubt had seeped down on him from above. By his straining bug-eyes and yawning mouth, there was life in Mateus yet, even though his clothes were disintegrating, his flesh and muscle melting in the monster's acid interior.

Anton halted as the amoeboid blob in which Mateus was encased slid towards him, filling the passage. From behind came more slitherings as the main monstrosity flowed up the stairwell. He glanced at the Luger in his hand. There was no option but to end it quickly. True, this would be the coward's way, but he was certain the Lord would understand. Anton had fought hard for his homeland and his beliefs. What more could any god ask? He spun around to the rock wall on his left, hoping to secure one of the golden crucifixes for his final act. But all he saw there was a triangle of cross-shaped niches. It was the same on his right.

He glanced accusingly at the bones and liquefied flesh of Sergeant Mateus, still conscious, still suffering. Located at various points around the tortured figure, but tantalizingly out of reach, were the holy items he had sought to steal.

Mateus wouldn't even have the consolation of the Lord in his dying moments. And neither, it seemed, would Anton.

The commandant put the pistol to his temple anyway.

'I care not!' he screamed hoarsely. 'I knew my duty and I performed it! What I did, I did for Greece … but,' and his lips trembled, dribbling with saliva, 'but God … *God forgive me* …'

The gun was snatched from his grasp.

Anton looked wildly around. A tendril from the ceiling had taken it, and now wrapped it in a worm-like embrace, yanking it out of his reach as he lunged.

Anton howled as the Hydra engulfed him.

Thea scrubbed the makeup from her face, neck and arms, climbed into a pair of trousers and boots, then pulled on a heavy overcoat and buttoned it.

She kicked dust over the fire and slid the Mauser beneath the dead trooper's sheepskin doublet. The gun didn't belong to her anyway. Several weeks ago, Giorgos had insisted she take it in case she'd have need to defend herself. She'd always hoped the moment would never arise, and even on this occasion didn't consider that what she'd just done had been an act of self defence – more of revenge. Her father had only told her the previous night that one of the two men hanged at Messia had been her beau. The horror that she hadn't recognised him herself thanks to the savage beating he'd suffered only added to her anguish.

How swiftly a world at war could change a person: this time yesterday she would never have believed she could derive so much pleasure from killing.

She took the trooper's corpse by his feet and lugged him through the cypress trees and blackberry tangles. It was awkward, tiring work. The May sun beat down, the body was heavy, and its clothes continually snagged, but at last she got it to the excavation entrance, where she waited nervously, glancing over her shoulder. There was no movement in the silent groves around her. No-one knew they'd come to this place, though the truck was sitting out in the open no more than a few hundred yards away; at some point somebody would spot it, even if only by accident.

She jumped when she heard scraping and grunting from the tunnel below, and a clumping of feet on the duckboards. But the sight of her father, grimy with dirt and sweat as he stumbled up into view, drew a huge sigh of relief from her.

'Did … did it work?' she asked.

Pavlos panted for breath as he brushed dust from his hair and jammed his cap back into place. 'It worked.'

'Where … where is it?'

'Back in the depths. Even that brute must take time to digest its meals. But it will return now that it's awake. Here, help me.'

He grabbed one of the corpse's legs and backtracked down through the entrance. Thea took the other. With two of them, it was easier. They stopped alongside the timber hoardings. Here, Pavlos shooed his daughter back to the surface, waiting several minutes until her footfalls had receded. Then he took the two stick-grenades from the trooper's webbing, pulled their cords and tossed them behind him, as he too scrambled up the tunnel. Half a minute later, the explosives detonated simultaneously, searing flashes bursting apart the recent woodwork and the older, age-blackened timbers behind it. An avalanche of liquid soil poured through …

On the surface this manifested as a distant rumble, but very quickly afterwards there was an exhalation of rank underground air, and a great wave of oozing mud and filth erupted into the daylight, burying not just the access tunnel but the entire excavation mouth, fanning out for dozens of yards through the lush, marshland foliage.

Pavlos and Thea were already several hundred yards away under blossom-filled trees, moving at a fast walk along what had once been the lake's eastern shore. They would make their way back to Messia on foot, but only by the most circuitous route.

A metallic clanking drew Thea's attention to a leather satchel by her father's side. In it, she saw a glint of grimy gold. With a gasp, she recognised the six Byzantine crucifixes that had once occupied the tunnel above the stairwell.

'They were just lying there,' Pavlos said defensively. 'Should I have left them? To be buried for all eternity?'

'Of … of course not.'

'Besides, if things don't go to plan, we may need a form of wealth that we can take with us easily.' He buckled the satchel closed as they hurried on, the trees ahead giving way to dry, sloping pasture covered with scrub-thorn.

'Father,' Thea said. 'Father … what if they dig down there?'

'Who? That bunch of drunken, whoring hogs? Well, suppose they do … it would take another ten millennia to uncover those vaults. And even in his wildest boasts, Hitler only gave his reign of hell one millennium.' Pavlos smiled grimly. 'Me, I give it two years.'

IN HUMAN GUISE

Every type of monstrous horror has bestridden the distant past of the Mediterranean. The Chimera for instance was so hideous to behold – it was literally a hotchpotch of different animal parts, all attached to the immensely powerful body of a fire-breathing lion – that it became another word for a confusion of things that have no business together. Geryon was one of Hercules's most horrific opponents, a blood-crazed ogre possessed of three heads, three bodies and six hands, each one expert in the use of some specific lethal weapon. The Gigantes were an army of towering hoplites made from the very rocks and stones of the Earth; again, it took the mightiest protagonist of all, Zeus himself, to fell them with his lightning. Talos, the bronze colossus, would lie in a fire until he was red-hot, and then embrace any ships that came to his island so they would burst into flame. The sphinx was another patchwork of animal parts, but it had the head of a beautiful woman, and would prolong its victims' torture by giving them false hope, only feasting on their flesh if they failed to answer its ultimately impossible-to-solve riddles.

And yet it's a sad and frightening reality of this beautiful region, as with so many other places on Earth, that there are no monsters of myth here nearly so cruel as those that have roamed it in human guise. The lands that adjoin the Mediterranean Sea are no different from any other in that they have given birth throughout their history to strange and terrible individuals, who have sought and found satisfaction in the callous destruction of their fellow men. Yes, even here, in the Cradle of Western Civilisation, where some of the most ancient and artistic cultures once flourished, in a realm that David Attenborough called the 'First Eden,' serial killers have made their mark, human fiends who would go on to terrorise their homelands as gleefully as any giant or dragon or titan, the main difference in this case, of course, that the screams of their victims were real.

In truth, there are far too many Mediterranean-based killers to list here, but some of them are more bizarre than others. In fact, there are few worse tales of horror anywhere to be found than that of Leonarda Cianciulli, also known as 'the Soap-Maker of Correggio'.

In appearance an everyday housewife and a popular figure in Correggio, northern Italy, Leonarda never achieved a high body-count, but what she did to her victims defies all understanding – though it seems likely that insanity lay at the root of it.

She had certainly known difficult days. By the commencement of World War Two, when she'd been married for over 20 years, she'd endured 17 pregnancies, but only four of her children had survived. This seemed to tie in with a deep worry from her early life, when she'd visited a gypsy palm-reader, who'd told her that few of her children would live (for the record, another gypsy had told her that her future lay either in prison or a lunatic asylum). When in 1939, Leonarda's eldest son, Giuseppe, announced plans to join the Royal Italian Army, she became convinced that he'd be killed in combat. The only solution, she felt, was to send others in his place (i.e. perform human sacrifices). Thus, over the following year, she lured three neighbouring women into her home, and hacked them to death with an axe. The bodies she dismembered and, using caustic soda, broke them down into 'mush' – to use her own word – some of which she mixed with chocolate, milk and flour to make teacakes, which she served to her other neighbours, though the last victim she made into a range of pretty soap bars, and these again were distributed among friends.

Leonarda was brought to book in 1946, when relatives of the missing reported their suspicions to the police. She was spared the firing squad on the grounds of mental instability, spending the rest of her life in custody, and as that fortune teller had prophesied all those years earlier, dying in the lunatic asylum at Pozzuoli in 1970.

Equally eerie is the case of Spain's first ever recorded serial killer, Manuel Blanco Romasanta, later known as the 'Werewolf of Allariz'.

This is a story filled with twists and turns, but in a nutshell, Manuel, a man of small stature and 'effeminate' mannerisms (according to other men at the time), first arrived in Rebordechao, in Galicia, in 1845, while wanted for the murder of a government official. In terms of his appearance alone, Manuel seemed incapable of violence, and indeed, though he set himself up under a false name, Antonio Gómez, he proved an industrious member of his community, working hard at a number of jobs, from cook to field-hand. However, his main *profession seemed to be as a mountain guide; he would show travellers, mainly women, the way through many of Spain's most famous ranges, always returning home and cheerfully informing their friends and loved ones that they had reached their destinations safely. Despite this, it wasn't long before sharp-eyed observers noted that Antonio Gómez was selling soap and items of second-hand clothing in local markets. The soap could have had innocent origins (though it probably didn't), but the clothing seemed suspect.*

Under questioning, he admitted 13 deaths but denied murder because, he said, on each occasion he had uncontrollably transformed into a wolf and then torn the women apart with his claws and teeth, cannibalising the remains.

Even in the mid-19th century this was viewed as an attempt to plead insanity (the last actual werewolf trial in Europe had been held in 1624, some 229 years earlier). Manuel was thus found guilty and sentenced to die by garotte. However, the intercession of the celebrated French physician, Joseph-Pierre Durand de Gros, a forerunner of Freud and Jung, who claimed that the killer, while not a werewolf, was suffering from a state of delusion called lycanthropy, led to Queen Isabella commuting his death penalty to life imprisonment, though Manuel still left this world within a decade, possibly murdered in jail, but maintaining right to the end that he was a genuine shapeshifter.

If both the killers so far appearing on this roster were treated with surprising leniency by the authorities, that is distinctly not the way it went for the next murderous duo, though only after they'd been given one remarkably even-handed opportunity to mend their ways.

It's a difficult thing to imagine today, when we know Greece as a sun-kissed holiday idyll, and the Greeks as the perfect hosts, but this venerable, culturally rich land was once, and in relatively recent times, something of a lawless hell.

One of the worst periods in Greece's recent past came immediately after World War One, when there was political instability and rampant crime. The brothers Giannis and Thymios Retzos completely embodied this era. Country boys by origin, but militarily trained, they'd been raised in the rugged, mountainous region of Epirus, where respect for the law was non-existent and the vendetta commonplace, an atmosphere that led to their creation of a small-time rural mafia. Almost all the crimes that followed are connected to this lifestyle, but it's the sheer preponderance of them that is so jaw-dropping.

In 1917, after avenging the death of their father by killing his assailants, Giannis and Thymios rounded up their own gang of desperadoes, made camp in the mountains, and commenced a robbery and kidnapping spree that would lead, in police estimates at least, to an incredible 82 murders. Many of these were robbery victims, shot down without mercy, or captives held for ransom but killed rather than being released, or the members of rival clans who met their bloody end because the hills of Epirus could only house so many brigands at one time.

If this makes the northwest region of Greece in the early 1920s sound like the Wild West, that would be an appropriate comparison because in 1924, with the emergence of the Second Hellenic Republic, and in an effort to end the chaos, a general amnesty was granted to outlaws.

Taking advantage of this controversial ruling, Giannis and Thymios handed themselves in and, to the fury of the bereaved, were immediately released, going on to celebrate loudly and arrogantly all that first night in the town of Ionnina. But leopards don't change their spots, because their worst offence was yet to come.

In 1926, the brothers, with a new gang in tow, carried out the infamous Petra Robbery, bushwhacking a truck from the National Bank carrying 15,000,000 drachmas. Again, it was the kind of thing that wouldn't be out of place in the Old West, but the violence used was excessive even by those standards, the bandits killing a total of eight bank employees.

If the ease with which they'd evaded prosecution previously had encouraged this act of criminal barbarity, it was a mistake that wouldn't be made again. Heavy reprisals were taken against the communities that had previously shielded them, while the gang themselves were hunted wherever they fled, even overseas, and finally arrested in 1928 in Bulgaria.

Their story ends in 1930, when Giannis and Thymios and three accomplices were stood against a wall outside the old fortress in Corfu, and a line of 30 police riflemen fired on them continuously until they were all dead.

If the full weight of the law finally fell harshly on the Retzoz brothers, then our final entrant in this hall of infamy illustrates that *sometimes the law itself may know no limits.*

The case of Hadj Mohammed Mesfewi, the so-called 'Beast of Morocco', is one of the most horrifying ever recorded, though in many ways Mesfewi was perhaps the most common type of predatory sex-killer.

A seemingly harmless shoemaker and public writer (which means that he took dictation from illiterate people wishing to send letters), he ran a shop in Marrakesh in the early 1900s. With the assistance of an elderly woman known only as Annah, he advertised his services all around the streets and markets of that bustling town, mainly with the aim of attracting young women to his premises. Any who went were literally dicing with death, because once Mesfewi had established that they were alone, he would offer them refreshments. Some no doubt refused. How many of these left his shop alive we can never be sure. Probably hundreds, but at least 36 didn't, because those who accepted a drink from Mesfewi were ingesting a drug that would knock them insensible, at which point he would drag them to a closed-off section of the building, where he would molest and behead them.

In so many ways, it's a story reminiscent of serial killers the world over, though unlike most of those, the law here responded in exceptionally brutal fashion. It was 1906 when it became apparent that young women were disappearing, and enquiries with other tradesmen soon led to Mesfewi's door. His premises were searched, and 20 headless corpses found in a pit in the cellar, another 16 in a similar pit in the garden.

Mesfewi and Annah were interrogated so severely that Annah expired during the course of it and Mesfewi confessed. This was the 20th century and civilisation as we would understand it today had arrived in the Mediterranean, but such was the public outcry that Mesfewi was sentenced to death by crucifixion. When foreign officials complained, the Sultan of Morocco commuted the penalty to decapitation, but in response to this, angry mobs gathered in Marrakesh. Many had lost female relatives and demanded retribution. Finally, the authorities settled on having Mesfewi flogged daily for four weeks (with spiny acacia rods!), at the end of which they chained him into a coffin-sized recess cut into the wall of the bazaar, where they bricked him up.

Death by immurement usually resulted from suffocation or thirst and could be a lengthy ordeal, but the crowd, who had pelted Mesfewi with stones, offal and excrement before the bricks were set in place, still weren't happy. They waited around for two days until his muffled screams ceased, many still expressing dissatisfaction that he had not suffered adequately.

The laws of man can be harsh. Sometimes so harsh that one wonders what inner demons might drive anyone to risk breaking them.

MISTRAL
Mark Morris

'I think this must be it,' Lucy says.

The house is built into the side of the valley, so from the dust track that serves as a country road, it appears to be sinking into the earth. Above the scrubby verge peeks a pan-tiled roof and a pair of white chimneys. To the right of these, stone gateposts stand sentinel, the black iron gates attached to them yawning invitingly open.

Ross brings their hired Citroën to a halt, a cloud of white dust rising in the wake of the car, and dispersing against a backdrop of sky so vividly blue that it hurts his eyes. In the back of the car, Poppy shifts restlessly.

'I don't feel well, Mummy.'

'We're here now, poppet,' Ross says, 'just in time for lunch.'

'I feel sick,' Poppy groans.

'You're just hungry,' says Lucy. 'Come on, unclip yourself, and let's check we're in the right place.'

Ross can see a black plaque affixed to one of the gateposts, but as the posts are set back from the verge, over a hump of weathered tarmac, he can't make out the words from here. He watches as his wife and daughter get out of the car, Lucy stretching, and then reaching out her hand for Poppy to take.

Not for the first time, he feels a wave of wonder and gratitude wash over him. To him, his girls are flawless. Lucy is slim, graceful as a dancer, her auburn hair shimmering like polished oak in the sunlight. And Poppy, their miracle child, is all big blue eyes, rosy cheeks and blonde ringlets.

Lucy's sleeveless summer dress slides back and forth across her body in the late summer breeze, hugging its delectable contours, as she bends to read the plaque. After a moment, she half-turns and gives him a thumbs up.

'Mas de Pierre Blanche,' she calls. 'There's a paved road down to the house. Pops doesn't want to get back in the car, so I'll walk down with her.'

He nods, and the girls set off, hand in hand, their flip-flops slapping the ground. More distantly, but no less sharply, come occasional cracks of gunfire from the clumps of woodland that adorn the hinterland south of Avignon.

Manoeuvring the car through the double-gates, he passes the girls halfway down the curving road to the house. Poppy, revived by the fresh air, waves as he crawls by. At the bottom of the hill is a large paved area ending in a low wall, which he remembers from the online instructions is where he should park the car. There is already a battered 4x4 there, its olive-green paintwork dulled by a layer of fine white dust, but there's still plenty of room for the Citroën, and probably a couple of other vehicles too. Easing into the far left-hand space, he switches off the engine and opens the driver's door, just as a man appears around the side of the house.

He's tall and big-bellied, his bushy red beard streaked with grey. He's wearing sandals, a baggy linen suit the colour of curdled cream, and a white straw trilby with a bright blue hatband.

'*Bonjour! Bonjour!*' he bellows, holding out a hand the size of a leg of lamb. As Ross's own hand is enveloped by the man's thick, meaty fingers, the girls come into view.

'Monsieur Barnes?' the man enquires, then gestures expansively at Lucy and Poppy. '*Et Madame Barnes? Et qui est cette belle fille?*' He reverts to heavily-accented English as he leans down to address Poppy. 'What is your name, *mon petit?*'

Poppy stares wide-eyed at him, too intimidated to answer, so Lucy says, 'This is Poppy. And I'm Lucy. You are Monsieur Blanchet?'

'*Oui, oui! Monsieur Blanchet!*' He takes Lucy's hand and plants a kiss on the back of it. '*Bienvenue!* Welcome! Welcome! I show you *appartement, oui?*'

Ross nods. 'Yes. Thank you. *Merci.* I'll get ... er ... *la luggage.*'

He makes a half-move towards the car, but Monsieur Blanchet wafts a dismissive hand.

'*Non, non. Plus tard!* Later! I show you first!'

Because of their IVF schedule – 'a final try' Lucy called it – they didn't book the holiday until the end of June, so Ross is amazed at how beautiful the place is. Their accommodation encompasses around a third of the old farmhouse – so big and grand it has its own central courtyard, open to the sky, like a Roman villa – and is a beautiful conversion, elegant and spacious, and with every modern appliance you could wish for. The wooden furniture and stone floors look expensive, the wall-mounted plasma widescreen TV is bigger than Poppy's bed back home, and the marble kitchen surfaces gleam like polished mirrors.

When Monsieur Blanchet has shown them around and taken his leave, Ross and Lucy grin at each other.

'Have we landed on our feet or what?' Ross says.

But a moment later Lucy's smile slips, and her eyes brim with tears. 'We deserve it after the year we've had.'

Ross crosses the tiled floor and hugs her. 'It'll be okay. *We're* okay. Poppy's enough for us. More than enough. We're blessed to have her.'

As if speaking her name has conjured her, Poppy is suddenly at the door to their room, having finished exploring hers.

'Is Mummy okay?'

Lucy breaks away from Ross's embrace, swiping at her eyes, offering a shaky grin. 'I'm fine, sweetie. Just tired after the long journey. And very hungry. Shall we have lunch outside?'

She gestures towards the French windows at the foot of the king-sized bed, through which can be seen a balcony overlooking a blue swimming pool glittering with sunlight, and the rolling French countryside beyond. On the balcony is a wooden table and four chairs. Poppy nods eagerly.

'Can we have crusty bread, and cheese, and olives?'

'*Mais, oui!*' cries Ross, kissing his fingers, then throwing his arm up in the air like a comedy chef. 'What else?'

'Then can we swim?'

'When your food has settled,' says Lucy.

They unpack. Eat. Swim. As Ross and Poppy splash in the pool, Poppy shrieking with laughter as Ross pretends to be a shark and ducks under the inflatable crocodile she's lying on, Lucy sprawls on a sun lounger.

It's not easy to relax, though. Her head is still cluttered with the stress of the past few months, with the giddy hope and the plunging disappointment, and the tension in between.

Poppy had been conceived after their first round of IVF eight years ago, and Lucy's subsequent pregnancy had been textbook, problem-free. As if to punish them for their complacency, their attempts since – five in all, twice as many as is generally recommended – have ended in failure. Now both Ross and Lucy have decided that enough is enough, that the process is taking too much out of them (and Lucy in particular), both physically and emotionally.

Financially too, though Ross has always asserted that the money doesn't matter, that they'll find it somehow. It can't be denied, though, that they're in more debt than they care to think about, not only to the bank, but to both sets of their parents, and to Ross's sister. In truth, they shouldn't have come on this holiday, but they needed it. They *really* needed it.

She closes her eyes, and slowly feels her muscles start to relax. She's drifting off to sleep, despite the splashing and yelling from the pool, when a chilly breeze that raises goosebumps on her bare arms plucks her back into wakefulness. She sits up and shivers.

'It is the Mistral,' says a voice beside her.

Lucy's shoulders jerk in shock, and she looks round. The woman standing beside the lounger is beautiful but severe-looking, her eyes cat-like above high, jutting cheekbones. Her greying hair, pulled back from her tanned face, snakes across her left shoulder in a long plait. She wears a caftan with a brown and blue design that makes Lucy think of Aztec art, and she is barefoot, her toenails painted yellow.

'What?' Lucy says, trying to pull her thoughts together.

'The Mistral.' The woman's voice is smoke-roughened, heavily accented. 'The wind. It is common at this time. Very cold. Very strong. But not today. Today only ...' She cups a hand in front of her face and blows on it.

'Soft,' Lucy says.

'Soft, yes. Gentle.' Abruptly she extends the same hand, wooden bangles sliding along her wrist with a clatter. 'I am Madame Blanchet. You meet my husband.'

Lucy shakes the woman's hand, which feels as scrawny as a chicken's foot.

'Yes, we did. He showed us round. I'm Lucy. That's my husband Ross, and my daughter Poppy.'

Ross waves from the pool.

'I have daughter also. Marcelle. But not here. In Toulouse. Son also. Laurent. He is chef. For ...' she struggles for the word and eventually says '... famoose?'

'Famous?' suggests Lucy. 'Like celebrities?'

Madame Blanchet jabs her finger at Lucy, her bangles rattling like bones. 'Yes, yes! But in two day he come home. He cook for you.'

'Oh,' says Lucy, unsure how to respond. 'He doesn't have to do that.'

'Yes, yes, he cook. He love to cook. He is beautiful cook. He come, we all eat together, yes.'

'That sounds great,' says Ross, emerging from the pool. He grabs a towel and starts to dry himself. 'But are you sure he won't mind?'

'No, no, he love to cook,' Madame Blanchet says again, and gestures expansively, describing a circle with her hand. 'You all come. Eat with us.'

'We'd love to. Thank you,' says Ross.

Madame Blanchet nods, deep creases carving through her thin cheeks when she smiles. Far away, carried on the breeze, come a series of irregular pops, like firecrackers.

'Hunters,' Madame Blanchet explains as Ross turns towards the sound. 'Is season. Not good to walk in field and trees. If hunters see you, they think you wild pig. Bang! Bang!' She laughs.

Ross laughs too, albeit uneasily. 'Thanks for the advice. We definitely won't go out walking.'

'No, no walking. You go in car. Many pretty places, all around. Very close.' She smiles again, and wiggles her fingers in a girlish wave at Poppy, who is still in the pool. 'I see you later, yes. You have fun.'

Poppy doesn't climb out of the pool until Madame Blanchet has gone. As Lucy wraps a towel around her, she asks, 'Was that lady a witch, Mummy?'

'Poppy!' Lucy exclaims, but Ross laughs.

'I don't think so,' he says, winking at his wife. 'Although she does look like a vampire from an old movie, doesn't she? Beautiful and aristocratic, but with a kind of … hunger about her.'

Lucy slaps the side of his bare thigh. 'Shush. You're as bad as your daughter.'

Ross grins at Poppy. 'Your Mum's right, Pops. Don't listen to me. I'm sure Madame Blanchet is very nice.'

The sun has disappeared behind a cloud now, and as another cold breeze wafts over them, Lucy shudders. 'Can we go in now, please? It's getting chilly.'

They return to the apartment, and while Lucy unpacks their cases and puts their clothes away, Ross and Poppy play a noisy game of Snap. Afterwards, Ross heads off to the bedroom for a read, while Lucy works out how to get the oven up to temperature after filling a casserole dish with ingredients they bought in a supermarket earlier that day – chicken breasts, shallots, carrots, garlic, fresh herbs, stock, tomatoes.

She's crouching in front of the oven doors, leafing through the instruction manual, when Poppy appears behind her.

'There's a funny spider in my room.'

Lucy turns. 'What do you mean a funny spider?'

'Come and see.'

Poppy skips away. Lucy shudders as she rises. She might be a strong, independent woman, but she bloody hates spiders. Catching them is Ross's job. She yells his name as she grabs a pint glass from the wall cupboard above the kitchen counter.

He appears, groggy and yawning, as she steps out of the kitchen. 'What's up?'

'Spider alert.' She hands him the glass. 'Poppy's bedroom. Deal with it.'

He takes the glass with a sigh. 'I was having such a lovely dream.'

'My heart bleeds.'

Lucy follows him across the lounge, both wanting and not wanting to know what is so 'funny' about the spider in Poppy's room. Their daughter is waiting for them in the doorway, and raises an arm to point as they approach.

'It's there, Daddy, above the bed.'

Ross steps into the room and looks at where Poppy is pointing. Lucy sees his eyes widen. 'Holy shit!'

'What is it?' she says, her flesh tightening. But she doesn't wait for his reply. Stepping past Poppy, into the room, she follows her husband's gaze.

Perched above Poppy's headboard, like an ugly blemish on the white wall, is a shiny black scorpion. It's eight inches long, its fat-pincered forelegs splayed in front of it, like arms open for a hug. Its tail, ending in a hook-like stinger, is curved up over its body, as if sensing the threat from the three people in the doorway.

Lucy gasps, and takes such a sharp step backwards that she has to grab the door handle to stop herself from falling. To her, the scorpion looks utterly evil. She hates spiders, but this is like a spider with added attachments, all of them capable of harm. As Ross moves towards it, glass held out, she impulsively makes a grab for him, but misses.

'Don't go near it!'

'How can I get rid of it if I don't go near it?'

'I'll get Monsieur Blanchet.'

'Don't be daft. He'll think I'm a wuss.'

'Well, be careful then. Don't let it sting you. If it stings you …'

Then she realises Poppy is looking at her wide-eyed.

'What will the funny spider do if it stings Daddy, Mummy?'

But Lucy doesn't know. Just *how* dangerous is a scorpion's sting? Before she can come up with an answer, Ross says, 'It's not a spider, Pops, it's a scorpion. And it's not going to sting me.'

As if to prove his point, he walks right up to it and places the glass over it. Immediately the scorpion, motionless until now, drops from the wall and scuttles up the inside of the glass, towards Ross's fingers. Lucy knows that if that had been her, she would have instinctively snatched her hand away, dropping the glass, letting the scorpion loose. She shudders at the thought of it falling on to Poppy's bed, burying itself among the bedclothes.

'Can someone get me a postcard or something?' Ross says, still holding the glass pressed firmly to the wall. Lucy darts out, looking around frantically, as if she's afraid the scorpion will somehow escape if she's not quick. Spotting a laminated card welcoming them to their holiday home, she grabs it and races back into the bedroom. Ross slides it between wall and glass, then tilts the glass upright, the scorpion sliding to the bottom. Springing immediately to its feet, it raises its pincers and tail aggressively, but it's trapped now. It can't scale the slippery glass wall.

Triumphantly, Ross crosses the room towards them, holding the glass. Lucy backs away, unwilling to get too close.

Poppy, though, is fascinated. 'Can I see it, Daddy?'

Ross holds the glass out towards her at face level. 'Isn't it a beauty?'

Lucy stifles an urge to warn her daughter to be careful as Poppy places a finger on the glass, a few millimetres from one of the scorpion's upraised pincers.

'He looks very angry,' she says.

'He does, doesn't he?' says Ross.

'If you see another one, you're not to go near it, Pops, you understand?' Lucy says. 'They're dangerous. They can give you a nasty sting.'

'Can they kill you?' Poppy asks.

'I ... don't know.' Lucy looks at her husband. 'Can they?'

He shakes his head. 'I don't think so. I think it's like being stung by a wasp.'

'Perhaps we should ask Monsieur Blanchet.' Almost angrily Lucy adds, 'I didn't know they had those things here. I wasn't expecting them.'

There is a hint of dusk in the air as they exit the apartment, trudge along the side of the house, and duck through an arch fragrant with late-blooming bougainvillea. On the other side of the arch is the main part of the house, where the Blanchets live. They cross a stone patio towards the large back door, but before they can reach it, a voice hails them.

'*Bonjour!*'

Beyond a set of steps leading off from the patio is an orchard, a hammock slung between two of its trees. Further back, they spot Monsieur Blanchard, holding a wooden box full of apples. Carrying the box in one hand, he raises the other as he trudges towards them.

They show him the scorpion, and he peers at it as if he's not sure why they've brought it to him.

'It was in our daughter's room,' Lucy says, trying not to sound accusatory.

Monsieur Blanchet shrugs. 'It is the Mistral. They are cold, so come inside.'

'Like spiders in the autumn back home,' Ross says to Lucy.

She shivers. 'Will there be more of them?'

Their host shrugs. 'Perhaps. Perhaps not.'

'But are they dangerous?'

His response is amused, dismissive. 'No, no. Only small sting.' He pinches the back of his hand to demonstrate. 'Many stings, very bad. But one sting only ...' He gives a classic Gallic shrug, fleshy lips pursed through the thicket of his beard.

They take the scorpion to the far end of the field behind the house and let it go. Then they trudge back, Lucy jittery despite Monsieur Blanchet's words, imagining movement in the grass all around them. That night she sleeps badly, picturing black, chitinous bodies scurrying up the white sheets towards the exposed flesh of their arms and faces as they sleep. Next morning she's washed out, exhausted, snappy.

'Shall we head out for lunch today?' Ross says. 'It looks too windy to sit by the pool.'

Lucy shrugs. 'Fine by me.'

Ross brandishes a leaflet he's been looking at. 'There's a village seven or eight miles up the road. Very picturesque. Lovely architecture, lots of little shops and cafes ...'

Lucy scowls. 'I've already said yes, haven't I?'

They set off after breakfast, following the French-speaking sat nav, though it's a pretty direct route. It's a warm day, but they keep the car windows closed as a strong breeze is blowing dust across the road, whipping it into spirals.

They're three miles out, fields to their left, woodland to their right, when they hear a commotion. From the trees, which are throwing dark, twisted shadows across the road, comes the high-pitched squealing of an animal in distress. Ross taps the brake, slowing the car, and next moment a small, dark shape bursts from the foliage ten metres in front of them.

'A piggy!' Poppy cries delightedly, as it careers across the road. Ross has barely registered that it's a very young boar, coated in a layer of soft reddish fur, with brown and cream stripes running down its back, when there's a sharp crack, and the animal flips into the air, then crashes to the ground at the far side of the road like a heavy sack.

Acting on instinct, Ross slams his foot down on the brake, bringing the car to a screeching halt. Beside him, Lucy, who has been silent and sullen up to now, yells, 'Oh my God!' In the back, Poppy screams, then dissolves into a wrenching flood of tears.

Dust rises around the car, as if to screen the horrific sight of the young boar's back hoofs twitching and kicking, while blood pours from a ragged hole in its side. Ross sits stunned, barely able to comprehend what he has just seen.

As Lucy turns towards him, Ross registers the rage on her face. She is *glaring* at him, and for a moment he assumes she thinks *he's* done this, that he hit the animal with the car.

'I didn't –' he begins, but she cuts across him scathingly.

'Why did you stop? Get us away from here. Poppy doesn't need to see this.'

He gapes at her, then nods. 'Yes, of course. I ... I will.'

He tries to calm himself, to shut out Poppy's wailing and go through the procedure of re-starting the car. But as the engine rumbles into life, two men step out of the trees at roughly the same spot where the boar emerged.

Both are carrying shotguns, and both turn to look at them. One of the men is short and stocky, with a black beard that looks painted on, and a shiny bald head that reflects the sunlight. The other is taller, rangy, unshaven. A brown baseball cap with a ragged rim is perched on his head, and his eyes are hidden behind aviator shades. The men are wearing what Ross thinks of as hunting gear – heavy-duty, drab-coloured jackets and trousers with plenty of bulging pockets.

The men regard them steadily for several seconds, during which Ross's hands tighten on the wheel. Ridiculously, he feels as though he and his family are in the wrong place at the wrong time, like witnesses to a gangland shooting.

Then the bearded man nods, turns away, and trudges towards the dying boar. The other grins and raises a hand. '*Bonjour*,' he calls. And then, glancing at their kill, '*Pardon*.'

'Get us out of here, Ross. Now,' Lucy mutters through gritted teeth.

Ross nods, and next moment they are driving away. Glancing in his rear-view mirror, he sees the two hunters staring after them, their faces blank.

By the time they reach their destination, Poppy is calmer, but still upset by what she's seen. She hardly touches her lunch-time pizza, and keeps her head mostly down as they trudge through the quaint, narrow streets of the village, clinging tightly to Lucy's hand.

Although the village is beautiful, none of them can raise much enthusiasm for sight-seeing, and so they cut their afternoon short, arriving back at the farmhouse around 3pm. Once inside, Lucy says to Poppy, 'Why don't you get your book and bring it to Mummy and Daddy's bed, and we'll all have a read?'

This is a weekend treat that Poppy has enjoyed since she was little, but it's never happened on a weekday afternoon before. Warily she says, 'But it's not Sunday.'

'So? We're on holiday. We can do whatever we want.'

Poppy goes to fetch her book, and when she's out of earshot, Lucy says, 'Do you think she'll be okay?'

'Course,' says Ross. 'Kids are resilient. She'll bounce back.'

'That was a horrible thing to see.'

'It was. And those guys shouldn't have been shooting towards a main road.'

'We should report them.'

'I'll have a word with Monsieur Blanchet.' He takes her hand. 'But how about you? Are you okay?'

She sighs. 'Yeah, I'm fine. Just tired and … you know.'

'I know,' he says and kisses her forehead.

Poppy cuddles up between her parents, and is soon engrossed in her book – one of a series that she loves about a Victorian adventuress called Maisie Hitchins. Ross picks up a doorstop of a book he's been reading for weeks, but which he's determined to finish this holiday, and Lucy, who is not much of a reader, flicks through the internet on her tablet, a small frown furrowing her brow.

Within minutes Lucy's eyes drift closed, and seconds later she's snoring softly. Ross and Poppy continue reading for several more minutes, but then Poppy lays her book aside and says, 'Why did those men hurt that piggy, Daddy?'

Ross closes his book and leans over to kiss the top of her head. 'They were hunters, honey. It's what they do. They hunt animals.'

She scowls. 'But that piggy was a baby. Those men are just mean bullies. Why did they hurt it?'

'Well, I suppose they would say they did it for a reason.'

'What reason?'

'Well, you eat sausages and bacon, don't you?'

'Ye-es,' she says guardedly.

'And you know sausages and bacon come from pigs, don't you?'

'Yes, but only dead ones who've fallen asleep like granny did. Not little baby ones.'

Ross experiences a pang of sorrow. He's aware there are moments in every child's life where hard truths have to be faced, and he knows that for Poppy this is one of them. He could lie to her, of course, but he and Lucy have always vowed that when the difficult questions arise, they will endeavour to answer them truthfully.

'I'm afraid it doesn't quite work like that,' he says.

'What do you mean?'

'Well, if they made sausages and bacon from old pigs it would be tough and fatty, and it wouldn't taste very nice. The best meat always comes from young animals. It's just the way it is, Pops. It's what they're bred for.'

She looks up at him, and he sees tears shining in her eyes. 'No, that's not true!'

'I'm afraid it is. But the animals are well looked after while they're alive. And if we didn't eat them, they wouldn't have a life at all. So really –'

But she's crying now, not listening to him. Squirming in the bed, she pummels his chest with her little fists. 'No, it's not true, it's not! Shut up, Daddy! Shut up!'

For the second time that day, she bursts into tears, and Ross, feeling terrible, wraps his arms around her, gathers her in, hugs her tight.

'Hey, hey,' he says gently. 'Hey, it's okay, it's okay, I'm sorry.'

Amazingly, Lucy sleeps through her daughter's wrenching sobs. Poppy continues to cry for a little while longer, but eventually her tears subside, and Ross feels her body soften and relax in his arms.

'Pops?' he murmurs, but there's no response. Exhausted by her own distress, she has fallen asleep too.

Gently he lowers her to the duvet, and plumps a cushion up behind her head. He's too wound up now to read, so he decides to get some air. Ideally, he'd like to go for a walk around the local area, but he doesn't want to encounter the hunters again, and he certainly doesn't want to get shot accidentally. He contents himself, therefore, with a stroll around the grounds, which are fairly extensive. The Blanchets own several fields and a sizeable orchard, which, in the holiday literature, they invite their guests to explore. He strolls through a wildflower meadow, enjoying the sighing of the wind and the chirruping of insects, and when he arrives back at the farmhouse, Madam Blanchet is sweeping up the leaves that have blown on to the swimming pool's tiled surround.

'You have good day?' she asks.

He hesitates, wondering whether to tell her about the hunters, but in the end decides he can't be bothered to explain. Instead he says, 'Yes thank you. The girls are sleeping, so I decided to have a walk.'

Madame Blanchet nods and then, to his surprise, clutches his arm. 'Laurent, he come tomorrow. You eat with us, *oui?* You all three. Tomorrow night?'

Ross is a little unnerved by her intensity, but he nods. 'Sure. That'll be great. What time? Er … *quelle heure?*'

'You come at six, yes? We have drink?'

'Six. Great. We'll see you then.'

That evening the girls are subdued, and don't seem too enthused by Madame Blanchet's invitation.

'Do we have to go?' says Lucy. 'It'll just be embarrassing. You know how terrible I am at languages.'

'They won't expect you to speak French,' Ross says. 'Their English is pretty good.'

Lucy looks dubious.

'Anyway, I've said yes now. I'm sure we'll have a great time. Their son is apparently a top chef.'

'So his mum says.'

'Will there be any other kids there?' Poppy asks.

'I don't know. Does it matter?'

'I'll be bored,' she whines.

'No you won't,' says Ross. 'It'll be an experience. And it's very kind of them to ask us.'

They eat, then start to play a board game, but no one's really enjoying it, so they abandon it halfway through. When Poppy slopes off to bed around nine, Ross pours Lucy and himself a nightcap, which they take out on to the balcony. They sit and watch the moths flutter around the outside lights.

Ross sighs. 'Not exactly turning out to be a dream holiday, is it?'

Lucy is silent for a moment, then says, 'It's not your fault. It's just ... circumstances.'

'Maybe we ought to pack up and go home.'

'Now you're being silly.'

'Am I? If we're all going to be miserable, I'd rather be miserable at home. At least there won't be any scorpions there.'

'We're not leaving early, Ross. We'll stick it out.'

'It's not supposed to be an endurance test.'

'I didn't mean that. I meant ... it's just the scorpion, and then the boar getting shot right in front of us – right in front of Poppy. It's not been the best start, has it? But I'm sure it'll get better.'

He laughs humourlessly. 'Once we've got the ordeal of dinner with the Blanchets out of the way, you mean?'

Sighing, she says, 'Like you say, I'm sure it'll be fine. We'll probably end up having a great time.' She knocks back her drink. 'Come on, let's go to bed. I'm knackered after last night.'

She insists he check the bedding before she's willing to climb in. She lies with her back to him, so he snuggles up to her, his left arm draped across her hip, his hand resting on her belly.

'We probably won't see another scorpion the rest of the time we're here,' he says.

'Don't talk about it,' she replies testily. 'Don't tempt fate.'

'Sorry.'

He strokes her stomach, his hand moving in a gentle circle over the soft fabric of her nightshirt. Then he slips his hand lower, between her legs.

She gives a discouraging moan. 'I'm too tired, Ross.'

'Okay,' he says softly. He kisses her shoulder, and rolls over on to his back. For a long time, he stares at the ceiling, telling himself the dark shapes he can see crawling on it are only in his imagination. Just as he's beginning to think he'll lie awake all night, sleep claims him.

When he wakes with a start, he feels sure he's only been asleep for minutes, but the room is bright with early morning sunshine. He grabs his mobile, unplugs it from the charger, and stares blearily at the screen. It's 6:52am.

He's fumbling the phone back on to the bedside table when he sees something out of the corner of his eye – a dark shape on the pale-wood floor he instinctively knows shouldn't be there. Blinking the blur of sleep away, he turns to focus on it.

It's another scorpion. It's standing motionless between the bed and the open door into the living room, its pincers and tail raised high as if challenging him.

Fuck. A thrill of fear runs through him. They really are vicious looking things. And if Lucy should see this one. In their *bedroom*, for God's sake …

Glancing at her to check she's still asleep, he lifts the edge of the duvet and swings his legs out of bed. He's fearful not only of waking Lucy, but also of startling the scorpion into scuttling life. He doesn't know how fast they can move, but the last thing he wants is for it to disappear under the bed or behind a piece of furniture. He looks for a glass, or anything to place over the creature, but there isn't one. He's going to have to go to the kitchen – which means stepping over the scorpion to get out of the door.

Sliding his feet carefully into the flip-flops which he left by the side of the bed (they don't offer much protection, but it's the best he's got), he stands up. The scorpion seems to be quivering slightly, as if preparing to leap, or is that his imagination? He takes a couple of steps towards it, careful not to tread too heavily, not to create any sort of vibration; the scorpion doesn't move. He breathes in, then lunges forward, a huge step, almost a leap, which takes him over the top of the creature and through the door. Landing on the other side, he stumbles a little, the bottom of his flip-flop hitting the floor with a slap. Clenching his teeth, he looks back, and is relieved to see the scorpion still standing there, motionless.

Getting a glass from the kitchen means taking his eyes off the thing for fifteen, maybe twenty seconds. He feels sure that when he returns, it will be gone – but it isn't, it's still there. He creeps towards it, then places the glass over it. Easy! He slides the same laminated card he used last time under the glass, and then, with another glance at Lucy, who remains blissfully unaware, he lifts glass and card up together and carries the scorpion into the kitchen.

Placing it carefully on the counter – it's active now, agitated, its sting curved high over its back and wavering in the air – Ross creeps back into the bedroom and grabs the shorts and T-shirt he was wearing last night. He dresses quickly in the living room, then fetches his trainers from beside the door. Wary, a little paranoid, he upends them before pulling them on, to check they're empty. Once he's dressed, he retrieves the trapped scorpion from the kitchen and sneaks out of the house.

The air is fresh this morning, the breeze gentle and warm. After yesterday, a lazy day is probably what they need, a day by the pool, so they'll be nice and relaxed by the time they have dinner with the Blanchets tonight. He strolls past their hire car, past the swimming pool, and through the little gate at the end of the narrow path that leads into the field where they let the first scorpion go. He wonders idly whether this is, in fact, the same scorpion they saw in Poppy's bedroom; whether, once they had released it, it simply made its way back through the field to the house. It looks the same, but it can't be, can it? Scorpions aren't that smart. They don't have homing instincts, like pigeons.

What's more likely is that there are thousands of scorpions around here. There are probably hundreds in this very field. But immediately the thought enters his head, he wishes it hadn't. His ankles are exposed, and the grass is long enough to tickle his calves and shins.

Checking where he's putting his feet, he walks to the end of the field. Before releasing the scorpion, he looks up. The sky is a brilliant blue already, completely cloudless. He tips the scorpion out of the glass on to the ground, and watches it scurry away. It doesn't head back towards the house, which is a good sign. He fills his lungs with fresh air, revelling in the fact that not a single person in the world knows he's here. Then he turns to retrace his steps.

But instead of heading towards the gate directly ahead of him, he decides to cut across the field on a right diagonal, aiming for the gate that leads into the back of the orchard. The idea of walking across the sun-dappled ground, early morning light winking and flashing through the branches overhead, appeals to him.

And it's every bit as idyllic as he imagined. The apples look so shiny and appealing that he's unable to resist picking one and biting into it. He doesn't think the Blanchets would mind, though he knows he'll feel guilty if he's spotted. The apple is crunchy and juicy and sweet, just as he likes them. He's almost finished it when he hears the murmur of voices.

Instantly he drops the core on the ground and hastily swallows what's in his mouth. He's immediately wary, though he doesn't know why. Perhaps because it's early; perhaps because the exchange sounds furtive; perhaps because he simply can't be bothered to explain himself.

He edges forward, trying to keep his footsteps light, and through the trees he sees the back of the Blanchets' farmhouse, the big patio area outside their back door, where various herbs grow in pots. Three figures are standing there, talking, their heads close together. One of them is Monsieur Blanchet. And he's unsettled to see that the other two are the hunters they encountered on the road yesterday, the ones who shot the young boar.

At first he wonders whether the hunters are bringing meat for the Blanchets – perhaps for tonight's meal. But then he sees one of the hunters, the short, stocky one, reach into the hip pocket of his jacket and pull out a wad of what can only be money, rolled up tight and secured with an elastic band. The man hands the roll to Monsieur Blanchet, who shoves it into his trouser pocket. '*Au revoir*,' the men mutter to one another, then the two hunters slope away. Monsieur Blanchet watches them go, his face unreadable, then he goes back into his house and closes the door.

Ross remains where he is for several minutes. His heart is thumping hard; he can't shake off the feeling he's seen something underhand take place. Could the hunters be paying Monsieur Blanchet for the privilege of hunting on his land, in his woods? If so, is that legal, or does it circumvent certain rules and regulations?

Deciding it's not his business, he turns and heads back the way he's come. He was going to cross the Blanchets' patio, on the far side of which is the arch separating the two halves of the property, but on reflection he thinks it best he not be seen right now. He hurries back through the orchard and cuts across to the gate he originally came through. By the time he re-enters the apartment, he's sweating.

The girls are still sleeping, and they remain so until he starts cooking bacon, whereupon Poppy emerges from her room, rubbing her eyes.

'Is that the little piggy?' she says in a shocked voice.

Immediately Ross realises how tactless he's been. What does it say about him that he threw the rashers in the pan without even giving yesterday's incident a moment's thought?

'Course not,' he says, trying to make light of the situation. 'This is the bacon we bought in the market on the way here, remember?'

'But is it from another little piggy?' Poppy asks.

'I don't know. Maybe it's from an older one.'

Poppy, who has always loved bacon, shakes her head in disgust. 'I don't want any.'

'Well, that's fine,' he says. 'There's cereal and toast. You have whatever you want, sweetheart.'

He puts the bacon on a low heat while he wakes Lucy with a mug of tea and a kiss.

'I think our daughter's about to become a vegetarian,' he says.

She sips her tea and looks at him groggily. 'What?'

'She won't eat bacon after what happened yesterday.'

Lucy shrugs. 'She'll get over it – or she won't.'

'I just hope they don't serve suckling pig at the meal tonight,' Ross says.

It's a hot day, the hottest since they arrived in France, the Mistral no more than a gentle, not unwelcome breeze that provides them with the occasional momentary respite from the merciless eye of the sun. They slather themselves with Factor 50 and spend most of the day dozing beneath parasols. Even Poppy is listless, taking dips in the pool only when she wants a break from the sun, but otherwise burying herself in her book.

They don't talk much. Ross ploughs doggedly through his own book, not enjoying it much but determined to finish it. At lunchtime they graze on cheese and olives and crackers.

It's mid-afternoon, and he's drifting, when he becomes aware of a tapping sound that it takes him a moment to recognise as approaching footsteps. He opens his eyes, squinting against the sun until two figures blot it out. At first he's sure it's the hunters, here to demand why he was spying on them that morning. Then he realises it's Madame Blanchet and a younger man, good-looking, tanned, wavy black hair.

The man smiles warmly as Madame Blanchet proudly introduces him as her son, Laurent. He's dressed simply, in a crisp white polo shirt and blue board shorts, yet there's an aura about him, a sense of cosmopolitan coolness.

Laurent continues to smile as he shakes Ross's hand. His hands are big, his nails well-manicured, his grip firm but not crushing. He wears an expensive watch on one wrist, a cheap, braided bracelet – something he might have bought from a beach trader – on the other.

'Tonight I cook for you, yes?' he says. The sentence is framed like a question, but Ross gets the sense there's no debating the fact.

'We're really looking forward to it,' Lucy says gushingly. She's smiling more than Ross has seen her smile in weeks.

'And this is the little *mademoiselle*,' Laurent says, crouching and offering his hand to Poppy, as if inviting her to dance. Poppy, as if mesmerised, slips her small hand into Laurent's much larger one, whereupon, to Ross's mild consternation, the young man tenderly kisses the back of it.

'I will see you later,' he says. 'Yes?'

Poppy nods bashfully.

Laurent stands up. 'Tonight we feast,' he declares. Madame Blanchet giggles and nods.

When mother and son have gone, Lucy says, 'Well, he was rather nice.'

'You think so?' says Ross.

Lucy smirks. 'Didn't *you* think so? Or do I detect a little jealousy?'

She's teasing him, and it's true that Ross did feel paunchy and pale and drab next to the younger man, but that isn't it – or not entirely.

'I dunno,' he says. 'It's just...' he drops his voice '...well, kissing Poppy's hand like that. She's only eight, for God's sake. Didn't you think it was a bit creepy?'

Lucy laughs. 'It's just his Gallic charm.'

'Is that what you call it?'

'I do, yes. Come on, Ross. You don't honestly think there was anything sinister in it?'

He shrugs. 'I just didn't like it, that's all.'

Suddenly Lucy is looking forward to that night's meal more than he is. That night she wears her sexiest summer dress and no bra, which Ross snidely comments on.

She rolls her eyes. 'Oh, don't be a boring old fart. This is a backless dress. If I wore a bra with it, it'd look awful.'

'You seem to be making an awful lot of effort for an informal dinner, that's all.'

'The French are classy people, and Laurent's a professional chef. It's kind of the Blanchets to invite us. *I'm* not going to let the side down.'

Ross is inclined to wear an old T-shirt and shorts out of spite, but in the end he puts on one of the new short-sleeved shirts he bought especially for their holiday. As he examines himself side on in the bedroom mirror to check his belly isn't sticking out too much, Lucy sidles up to him and kisses him on the cheek.

'You look very nice,' she says. 'You're the only one for me, you know.'

'I hope so,' he says. 'I really love you, Luce.'

'I love you too,' she says, and her sudden smile is dazzling. 'Sorry for being a bit out of sorts lately. We're incredibly lucky really, aren't we?'

'We are,' he says.

When Poppy too is ready, wearing her favourite yellow party dress, and her mermaid necklace that her granny and grandad bought her, they walk round to the Blanchets' part of the house. Ducking through the heavily-perfumed bougainvillea arch, they see that a long wooden dining table has been set up on the patio, a row of tall candles arranged down the centre, the light from them gleaming on wine glasses and silver cutlery.

Monsieur Blanchet greets them like long-lost friends and plies them with aperitifs. Tonight he's wearing a powder-blue suit and a grey tie, and Madame Blanchet looks elegant in a long black dress, her hair pinned up to expose her long but scrawny neck.

'And for you to drink, little princess?' he asks, planting his spade-like hands on his knees and leaning forward to address Poppy.

Poppy glances at her mother and says shyly, 'May I please have a lemonade?'

'But of course!' exclaims Monsieur Blanchet. 'You are Guest of Honour!'

As he enters the house, another woman emerges from it, causing Ross to do a double take. This new arrival, who he has never seen before, is a much younger, more stunningly beautiful version of Madame Blanchet. She wears an emerald green dress, cut low at the front, and her hair is so dazzlingly blonde he has to fight the urge to squint.

Her smile is dazzling too. 'Hallo,' she says, her voice soft and husky, 'I am Marcelle. You are having a nice time, yes?'

'Er ... yes,' says Ross. Suddenly he feels oafish and clumsy. 'You're Monsieur and Madame Blanchet's daughter. I ... I thought you were in Toulouse?'

'Yes. But I come home. To surprise my brother.'

'Well, it's ... very nice to meet you,' Ross says, shaking her slim, fine-boned hand, and hoping his own isn't too clammy. He catches Lucy's eye, and she smirks at him.

They have more drinks, and by the time they sit down to eat, Ross is feeling a little light-headed. He sits on one side of the table between Madame Blanchet and Marcelle, and Lucy sits facing him, between Monsieur Blanchet and an empty chair that he assumes will be occupied by Laurent, who is currently in the kitchen, plating up the starters.

Poppy has been placed at the head of the table, which does indeed make her look like the Guest of Honour, though Ross supposes it's just so that she doesn't feel intimidated being flanked by adults.

Monsieur Blanchet pours them all wine, and then Laurent appears brandishing a large tray of starters.

'*Tartlettes balsamiques et oignons rouge au fromage de chèvres,*' he announces.

Ross tries to translate Laurent's words in his head.

'Balsamic red onion tartlets with cheese of ... horses?' he ventures.

The Blanchets all laugh.

'It is goat, not horse,' says Marcelle. 'But the rest, yes!'

'Oh yeah, goats' cheese. That makes more sense.' Ross grins, his face flushed with drink.

Laurent distributes all the starters to the adults, then moves round to Poppy's chair.

'And for you, *mademoiselle*, something very special. These are cheese ... er, *tourbillons?*' He looks at Lucy and makes a spiralling motion with his finger.

'Swirls?' hazards Lucy.

'Oui. Cheese swirls with ... er, *crisp de carottes.*'

'Carrot crisps,' says Ross, and leans forward. 'They look delicious, don't they, Pops?'

Poppy nods.

'What do you say to Laurent?' Lucy prompts.

'Thank you, Laurent,' Poppy says.

Laurent laughs and throws his hands in the air. *'Très bien!* Now eat! Eat!'

They tuck in with relish, and for the next few moments there are exclamations of delight and appreciation.

'Delicious,' says Ross, but behind the creamy tanginess of the cheese and the sweetness of the balsamic, he detects something bitter, an odd and not altogether pleasant aftertaste – some type of herb maybe? He glances at Lucy to see if she's tasted it too, but if she has it doesn't show on her face. He glances at Poppy, who is devouring her own, child-friendly starter.

'Is that nice?' he asks.

She nods vigorously. 'Yummy!'

He grins at her, but as he does so he becomes aware that his lips feel… odd. Numb and fat, like they sometimes do after an injection at the dentist's. He places his knife beside his plate, and lifts a hand towards his mouth. But his arm feels tingly, heavy, and when he rubs his fingertips together he can't feel them.

Then he gasps and jerks forward at a sudden sharp, stabbing pain in his stomach. He wraps arms that feel heavy as lead around his guts, as if to contain them.

'Ross? What …' Lucy says, but then, after a moment's pause, she says 'oh' very quietly.

His stomach is on fire now, and he's sweating, and he's losing all sensation in his limbs, but he manages to raise his head. Across from him, Lucy's eyes are unfocused, and she's swaying in her seat. Her mouth opens and closes, as if she can't breathe, while her face grows increasingly redder.

Food poisoning, he thinks, his guts roiling, spasming with pain. *We've all got food poisoning.*

But next to him, on his right, Marcelle Blanchet seems fine. Indeed, she's sitting calm and upright in her seat, and she's regarding him not with alarm, but with a calm and curious patience, which doesn't seem right.

He expects her to ask him if he's okay, but instead she lays down her cutlery, then her napkin, before rising to her feet. She walks over to Poppy at the head of the table, who is staring with alarm at her stricken parents, and she crouches down beside her, so that their heads are on the same level, and she talks quietly, soothingly, to their little girl.

Ross doesn't hear what she's saying, because his blood is rushing in his ears, his heartbeat booming, as he struggles for breath. But he hears Poppy cry out, 'What's wrong with my mummy and daddy?' And then, distorted and faint, he hears Marcelle say, 'They will be fine. We will get help for them. Come with me.'

The beautiful, dazzling woman holds out a hand, and Poppy takes it, and is led away. Ross wants to call out, wants to see where Marcelle is taking their daughter, but the numbness, the heaviness is like a pressure crushing him down, and he can't turn his head quickly enough.

Opposite him, there is a strangled cry, followed by a slithering crash and the tinkle of breaking crockery, and although he hasn't seen it, Ross is sure it's the sound of Lucy tipping from her chair, falling to the ground.

His body racked with both pain and numbness, Ross half-turns as he tumbles forward, his left shoulder thudding against the edge of the table. Now he sees Madame Blanchet on his left, her husband sitting across from her. Monsieur Blanchet is watching him without expression, sipping wine. His wife has a slight smile on her wizened, once-beautiful face. She looks more like a witch than ever.

Although his vision is fading, darkening around the edges, Ross senses movement behind Monsieur Blanchet, and suddenly two figures step out from between the trees in the orchard. They are the hunters who were here this morning, and who he and his family encountered on the road yesterday. Now, they are dressed for dinner, wearing baggy, wrinkled suits. Monsieur Blanchet greets them effusively, and pours wine for them as they pull up chairs and sit down.

The hunters no more than glance at Ross's slumped form at the other end of the table, before chinking glasses with the Blanchets and knocking back their wine.

Ross's senses are growing increasingly fuzzy now. His vision blackens, blurs. The conversation around the table becomes distorted. He no longer has any sensation in his arms or legs.

Just before slipping into unconsciousness, though, he smells something, and involuntarily his mouth begins to water.

It's the exquisite aroma of roasting meat.

GHOSTS OF MALTA

Malta, an archipelago of sun-scorched islands in the centre of the Mediterranean Sea, is one of the world's most fascinating countries. The tenth smallest on Earth and yet the fourth most densely inhabited, it sits in close proximity to Sicily, Libya and Tunisia, is literally a stepping stone between Europe and Africa, and for this reason has a dramatic history traceable virtually to the dawn of mankind.

Its prehistoric temples, dated to 3600 BC, are some of the oldest free-standing structures in the world, though human occupation of Malta has been traced back as far as 5900 BC. Since then, in roughly this order, it has belonged to or been occupied by the Phoenicians, the Carthaginians, the Romans, the Greeks, the Arabs, the Normans, the Aragonese, the Knights Hospitaller, the Napoleonic French, and the British. It was also the location of two of the greatest battles ever fought. The now near-mythical siege of Malta (1565) saw the 7,000-strong forces of the Knights Hospitaller stand off Sultan Sulieman the Magnificent's grand invasion fleet, the total manpower of which numbered half a million. The battles in the harbours and around the walls and towers of what is now Malta's capital city, Valletta (named after Jean de Valette, the island's Knight-Commander), became the stuff of legend, but the next great power to launch itself at Malta was even more formidable. This attack lasted three years during World War Two, when the Axis powers continuously carpet-bombed the island, by then a British colony, in an attempt to destroy the Allied air and naval forces based there. The courage of the Maltese people, who withstood some of the heaviest bombardments the world had ever seen, was later rewarded by George VI, when he awarded the entire population the George Cross.

With a violent past like this, it's probably no surprise that Malta boasts an absolute plethora of ghost stories. However, one of the scariest is relatively recent and comes to us from Senglea, in the southeast corner of the main island. It concerns a very devout housewife, named Mrs Mangion, who attended the early Mass at St

Philip's Church every day. When we say early, we mean very early, because the Mass usually commenced at 5am. However, Mrs Mangion was so strong in her faith that she one morning arrived at around 4.30am, half-expecting the church still to be closed, but in fact finding it open. She saw two candles lit on the altar but was the only person in the congregation. This wasn't perhaps unusual at such an hour, though she was surprised to see a service already underway.

She took her usual place in a pew while the priest, wearing a hooded cassock, stood with his back to her and proceeded with the Mass. It is not clear at which stage Mrs Mangion started suspecting that something was wrong. The two candles were smoky and burned with dull red flames, which gave off little light. She also struggled to hear the priest's voice, so much so that she was unsure what language he was speaking, though it didn't sound like Latin or Greek.

The service then finished abruptly, at which point the priest turned to look at her.

She gazed in horror at the bare, rotted skull under his hood.

Fleeing, Mrs Mangion found the main entrance door locked, and collapsed against it, sobbing, expecting the apparition to approach her from behind. This didn't happen and a minute later the door was unlocked from the other side. It was the sacristan, opening the church so that the real priest could prepare for the real Mass. When the small group went back into the main body of the church, it was dark and cold. No candles had been lit.

St Philip's had no reputation for being haunted and nothing similar was reported again, though local folklorists cite a connection to the severe outbreak of plague that ravaged Senglea in 1676, killing thousands, huge numbers taken from that very parish.

An equally unnerving story, again from well within the last century, concerns a sizeable townhouse, its exact location unspecified though it stands on Gozo, the northernmost island in the Maltese archipelago.

The tale tells how two local brothers inherited this valuable property and though they weren't the best of friends, agreed to share it. Their cohabitation initially went well, but a problem arose when the younger brother became involved with a beautiful young woman, who agreed to be his wife. Insane with jealousy, the older brother hatched a villainous plan. One night, he drugged his sibling and while he was unconscious, hacked off his hands before tossing him into a deep well, from which, with only stumps for wrists, he could never climb out. The bereaved fiancée, who thought she had simply been abandoned, was heartbroken and yet in due course became close to the surviving brother, eventually marrying him. However, an eerie presence in the house soon began to oppress her. Several times, she thought she heard a scuttling sound behind bookcases or along the high shelves. Often, the pair would come home to find a terrible mess, as though someone had broken in and done damage. And still the wife heard those bizarre scuttling / scampering sounds, up and down the stairs and along the passageways, usually at night. Exterminators were brought in but discovered no trace of vermin.

Then, one terrible morning, the young wife awoke and found her husband dead alongside her, his face twisted with horror. Investigating police decided that he had been strangled. The wife was an obvious suspect, but the extreme bruising on his neck was deemed incompatible with her dainty hands. Whoever had been breaking in previously – for the police now suddenly took that part of the story seriously – had clearly done so again, this time with deadly intent.

The building was left empty and turned derelict. Stories circulated that it was haunted, but when a new-arrival in the district, a forthright man who brooked no nonsense, overheard, he scoffed and said that he would stay overnight in the house and prove that it was safe. However, the following morning, he came out a gibbering wreck, insisting that he had slept in one of the many empty rooms, only to be disturbed in the early hours by a choking sound. He followed it to another room, to see that what had earlier been an empty shell was now richly furnished, and that two people lay in the bed: a young woman who was deeply asleep, and a young man, the latter writhing and goggle-eyed as a pair of severed hands, having fastened to his throat, slowly throttled him to death.

This tale must rate as one of the most Gothic horror story-like legends associated with Malta, but many of the lesser tales are quirky and unnerving.

Consider, for example, the thoroughly unpleasant events concerning the murdered brides of Malta. In the 1780s, a young lady was imprisoned by an unsuitable suitor in an upper room of the Verdala Palace. Attempting to climb free, she fell to her death.

Wearing a blue dress at the time, she is now known as the Blue Lady, her sad phantom often seen in mirrors in the palace, standing on high balconies or even falling, her blue dress billowing in the wind. Another tragic tale tells how in medieval times in the city of Mdina, a woman called Katrina strongly resisted the advances of an amorous knight, but in so doing accidentally killed him. For this crime she was sentenced to death. Married shortly before she went to the block, her decapitated form is now said to walk the nighttime streets in her bloodstained bridal gown, approaching the lovelorn and advising them to give up on love and join her in death.

Malta even has its own unique version of the Phantom Hitchhiker. Two young men were driving one night from St Paul's Bay to Mosta, when the figure of an elderly man came into the road, trying to flag them down. The driver swerved around him and kept driving. The passenger was concerned. It was late, and he felt they should have offered the old man a ride. But the driver now seemed frightened and accelerated all the way to Mosta. When they arrived safely, the driver explained that he hadn't needed to pick the old man up, because as soon as they'd passed him, he materialised in the backseat and stared intently through the rearview mirror for the whole journey.

For all this, and countless other stories like it, Malta remains a splendid, welcoming location, unfailingly friendly and vibrant with Mediterranean culture. Its astonishing history is soaked into every inch of it, relics of the turbulent past visible on all sides, yet the Maltese live there contentedly. For this reason if no other, it's probably one of the less terrifying locations on our tour.

MAMMONE
Carly Holmes

The dining room of the hotel looked identical to every other hotel dining room they'd eaten in over the last fortnight, or maybe it was just Billie's tired, jaded perspective. The bedroom, with its narrow twin beds and brittle plastic chairs angled towards each other under the window, had looked drearily familiar as well. Her mother, Vi, had emerged from the small ensuite bathroom when they'd arrived, and moved Billie's case briskly from one bed to the other. 'I always sleep in the bed nearest to the door,' she'd said. 'You know that. If there's a fire then I've got a clear escape route.' Billie hadn't asked whether her mother would even pause to wake her up as she beetled to safety, hadn't wanted to know the answer.

They took their seats at the large round table and greeted their dining companions. *I wonder why*, Billie thought as she glanced down at the laminated menu, speckled with a season's worth of dinners, *we instinctively cleave to the familiar even when we're in a foreign country, presumably there to experience the unfamiliar.* They'd seated themselves with this group of people on the very first night of the trip, over two weeks ago, and so they must now all sit together every evening. *And we don't even have anything in common, beyond all being here in Italy, whirlwinding our way from city to town to resort.*

There had been a full day in Rome, – 'Not ancient enough for *me*' her mother had said – two days in Florence, – 'Ugh, too many people, how am I expected to see *anything* when there's such a scrum of tourists?' – a blur of other cities that might have been Siena, Perugia, Teramo, Naples… Billie was pretty sure she remembered a dusty afternoon in a beautiful medieval walled town, the hysterical urge to hide inside the cool café that served peach bellinis thick with ice when the coach arrived to sweep them up and transport them onto the next place, the next hotel. Her kidneys had started aching after the first week, her long legs swollen and throbbing at the knee joints from the hours of sitting in a cramped coach seat day after day. And at all times having to broadcast the gratitude that was expected of her for this treat, this mother/daughter adventure.

A waiter appeared at their table with a bottle of wine. He offered it to guest after guest, filling glasses with a steady and serene smile despite the lack of thanks. Billie turned from her mother's disapproving monologue on the menu choices – 'I don't know if I *dare* risk the fish after last night. And the pasta is *bound* to be so oversalted as to be inedible' – and nodded gratefully when he reached her, said *Grazie*. His smile widened into one of genuine pleasure and he filled her glass to the brim and then turned to her mother. 'And for your sister?' he said with a pat flourish of chivalry. 'Would you like wine, Signorina?'

Her mother tittered with scandalised delight. 'I'm not her *sister!*' she said. 'Oh dear, Billie, what does that say about *you*, if people think you're my *sister*?' She looked around the table, inviting the other diners to share in her mock horror. The waiter gave Billie a tiny shrug of apology, dropped one eyelid in a half-wink. She responded with a thin smile and a curt nod, hating the mortified flood of scarlet beating across her cheeks. She didn't try to smooth things over, make things a little easier for him, when her mother sipped the wine and then winced with distaste and called him back. 'Too sharp,' she said. 'My grandmother was French, you know. It gave me the palate for only the very best red wines. I'll have a rosé instead.' She'd done this at every hotel on the trip, and had also sent most of her meals back, waving her hands above the plates in a very 'French' way to indicate that she shared continental blood with these Italians; she was more discerning and somehow *better* than the other British tourists who shovelled up whatever was put in front of them without complaining.

Just five more days. And all of them to be spent here, in this hotel in a quiet village on the outskirts of Salerno. No more early mornings, racing to the coach at 6am with a dry roll swiped from the breakfast buffet and hastily wrapped in a paper napkin; no more anxious negotiation between drinking enough water to fend off the inevitable dehydration headache and not so much as to need the toilet when there were still three hours of travel left before reaching that day's destination. There were going to be excursions organised around Salerno, but Billie was determined that she wouldn't be on them. She was going to get up late, nap in the afternoon, wander around the streets and squares, eat lunch whenever and wherever she wanted. And if possible, she was going to do all this alone.

People faded away after the meal, heading for the bar or their bedrooms, forming little gossipy groups in the lobby where shiny sofas looked out on the twilit hotel grounds. There wasn't much in the way of greenery, the rutted carpark with its dusty row of parked coaches dominated, and Billie felt a sudden pang – more than that, a sharp and desolate longing – for the damp, muddy leafiness of home. It was bound to be raining there, it was August after all. Her cat, Teal, was probably crouched on the kitchen windowsill right now, glowering at the weather, cursing her for the abandonment.

Vi, popping up suddenly at her shoulder, made Billie startle and then strive to conceal the spike of alarm. She moved away before the stuttering of her breath, the jittery way she cupped her own elbows and pulled them into her waist in an awkward hug, could springboard another lecture on pulling herself together and toughening up. Once she'd seen the blister pack of tablets in Billie's washbag, had learnt what they were for, her mother's disapproval had been vast. She was resolved to take Billie's anxiety as a personal affront to her mothering, while at the same time distancing herself from its probable cause by giving regular pep talks on how much tougher *she'd* had it in her life and just look how resilient and without self-pity *she* was.

'Up the wooden hill?' she said now, following her daughter to the glass doors that opened onto the carpark. Her cheeks were blotched from the humidity and the wine, her lipstick clotted like scabs in the corners of her mouth. She looked old, small and frail, peering hopefully into Billie's face. She wouldn't admit that she was tired, that this holiday with its early starts and late finishes, with its ceaseless parade of new experiences and new places – and the heat! God, the heat – was more exhausting than staying at home would have been.

Love for her unfolded grudgingly through Billie, burnt a path down through her chest and settled like indigestion in her stomach. She knew once they were in their room her mother would perk up, insisting on a herbal tea and a vicious dismantling of their fellow guests' characters before they turned in. She'd probably send Billie back downstairs to the lobby desk for extra pillows, or with a request to swap the kettle for one without limescale. She'd probably chatter on even after the lamp was switched off, her high voice reaching her daughter in trilling spurts through the dark pockets of night that separated the beds, keeping her awake when all she wanted to do was sleep.

'Yes,' Billie said. 'Let's go. It's been a long day.' She linked arms with her mother and led her towards the slippery marble staircase whose treads chilled the balls of her feet through the thin soles of her sandals.

The window that Billie had opened the night before was closed now, the heat in the room dense and stifling. She opened her eyes just enough to see the clock on her bedside table – 8.40am – and kicked off the sheet that covered her, rolled onto her back. She tried again to open her eyes, managed to crawl onto an elbow and look around at the familiar/unfamiliar room.

'Finally!' her mother said. 'I thought you were going to

sleep all day.'

She was perched high on her bed, propped up by pillows and sipping a coffee. 'The coach is leaving at ten so we need to hurry if we want breakfast.'

Billie dragged herself to the window and pushed it wide. Traffic rumbled in the distance and people called out to each other on the street below, voices raised and gunshot quick. She couldn't tell if they were excited or argumentative. She raised herself onto tiptoes and peered down curiously, ignoring her mother's shrill warning not to show too much skin to the locals. A scent heavy and sweet drifted in on the warm breeze. Some kind of jasmine? There was a plant creeping up the trellis of the outside wall of the hotel; worn, scorched fronds curling into the hinge of the window as if they wanted to find a way inside and shelter from the sun.

'Why did you close it?' she asked. 'It's hell in here now.'

'You sleep like you're dead,' her mother said. 'I watched you for ages earlier this morning; you were lying stretched on your back with your arms crossed on your chest. Like a saint or a statue or something. You didn't move at all. You were barely breathing.'

'I'm not going anywhere today,' Billie said, staggering across the room to the bathroom. 'I've had a lot of emails come through from work and I have to deal with them. But you go. There's no point in you staying behind; I'll be no company at all.'

She closed the door and sat on the toilet. She could hear her mother shifting from the bed and moving across the room, was glad she'd slid the bolt home.

'You can't just stay behind!' Vi wailed, rattling the door handle. 'What will everyone say? What will I tell them? They'll think we've argued.'

Billie turned the shower on and stepped into the tub. The cool water sliding down her back was delicious. She bowed her head and let it wash over her, goose bumps trailing in its wake.

'Of course they won't,' she called. 'Just tell them I'm busy.

We're not all blissfully retired, you know.' If she had to resort to faking a broken leg she was staying behind today, and if she had to resort to breaking her mother's neck and concealing her in the wardrobe, she was staying behind alone.

When she got out of the shower, she saw Vi's washbag sagging open on the shelf. Her bottle of perfume – 'My signature scent. I wouldn't use *anything* else!' – poked from the pile of pots and jars. Billie looked at it for a moment, hesitating, then lifted it out and pushed it carefully into the middle of the folded pile of towels, tugging their edges down to conceal the tiny bulge. It was spiteful, petty revenge for the night before and it made her feel instantly better.

Vi was subdued, reproachful, when Billie emerged from the bathroom with a dressing gown wrapped around her. She'd gathered the usual necessities into her huge cloth day bag and was standing by the window looking out, sunglasses on and lips a slick of purple. 'It's gone nine,' she said shortly. 'Breakfast will be finished soon and I'm hungry. I was waiting for you, otherwise I'd have gone down hours ago.'

'You look very chic,' Billie told her. 'What colour is that one?' She pressed her lips together and opened them with a little *pop*, a blown kiss.

'Oh, really?' Her mother smiled and hunted through her bag. 'Plum Diva. You can use it if you like. I'll leave it here.'

'Thank you.' Billie took the lipstick and leaned in gently to kiss the older woman's thin, dry cheek. 'Now go and get some breakfast and have a lovely day. I'll see you this evening and you can tell me all about where you went.'

She watched Vi fuss around the room, straightening bed sheets and checking she had her purse, checking again before finally leaving. The tap of her heeled sandals beat a severe tattoo on the landing outside before fading to silence.

When she was sure that her mother wasn't going to return, Billie locked the door and flung the gown across the bottom of the bed, walked naked to the window to lean there a while and sniff the scented breeze.

The street the hotel was on curved downhill to the centre of the village. Billie could see the cluster of orange tiled roofs ahead of her as she trod slowly along the narrow pavement, keeping as close to the shadowed treeline as she could. She'd been too late for breakfast and was starving. Was it too early for a peach bellini with her lunch? She dropped the lipstick into a bin, heard the hollow rattle as it plunged through the sticky layers of cans and bottles. Irretrievable now.

She passed a row of other hotels, almost identical to her own with their rutted car parks and twists of dusty shrubs beside the doors. There were a couple of cafés, smiling waitresses guarding the entrances and gesturing to her with menus, but she didn't stop. A bar further down the street was already serving a group of loud, sunburnt tourists who clashed glasses and roared at each other as they emerged into the bright courtyard.

Billie quickened her pace, desperate to find somewhere quiet and secluded, away from the throngs of holiday makers. She turned off the road into a small side street, took another turn into a lane that meandered towards a little fenced park or garden at its end. Through the iron railings she could see benches, swollen clusters of rose bushes in rich pinks and reds. The urge to be completely alone for the first time in over a fortnight, to sit on the warm grass under a tree and take her sandals off, push her toes into the earth, overwhelmed her.

Tucked into the entrance to the park, beneath the thick branches of a hazelnut tree, a tiny stone building stood. It was low, more a shed or a refurbished animal pen than a house, with a glossy red tin roof and a narrow doorway you'd have to duck to pass through. The door stood open, and the smell of coffee drifted out. There were neat circles of tables and chairs lined either side of the doorway.

On one of the tables a black cat sprawled, front paws crossed and tail hanging heavy, swinging lightly. Its eyes were the same blueish green as Teal's and it watched Billie impassively as she stopped and reached out a hand to stroke the rough fur along its spine.

'Hello, darling,' she said. 'Aren't you a handsome boy.'

The cat murmured its pleasure and rolled onto its back, offering its belly. Its claws peeped from their furred sheaths and Billie laughed softly. 'I'm not falling for that,' she told it.

'Mammone.'

The voice made her jump, her hand leaping to her chest. A man stood in the gloom of the building, just inside the door. It was difficult to make out his features until he stepped forward into the sunlight, and then she saw that he was short, a little more than middle-aged, attractively crinkled around the eyes.

'His name is Mammone,' he said, ruffling the cat's neck fur briskly. 'He likes you. He doesn't normally let strangers touch him.'

'He's gorgeous.' Billie smiled at the man. 'I have one called Teal; he reminds me of your Mammone.'

He began to flick at the tables with a cloth he had draped over his shoulder. 'He is named after the folk legend of Il Gato Mammone. Have you heard of it? No? Sit.' He swept one of the chairs out from under its table and gestured to it. 'I'll tell you all about it now, but you will need refreshments. One moment.'

He disappeared inside the shop and Billie perched on the chair reluctantly, eyeing the park over her shoulder. Was that an invitation or was she expected to pay? This must be a café of sorts but there was no menu. She felt the tourist's momentary spike of resentment that she had been so cavalierly manipulated into being this man's customer, her politeness a disadvantage to be trampled over and abused. But then Mammone stepped delicately from his table to hers and butted her hand with his sharp cheekbone, foraging for a fuss, and a warm, herby smell of bread or biscuit wafted through the door, making her stomach lurch with hunger. She'd stay for a while and eat, and she'd pay whatever exorbitant bill she was given.

'Here.' The man reappeared carrying a tray which he set down on the table Mammone had vacated, transferring plates and glasses deftly over and laying them in front of Billie. The cat shimmied onto her lap, and she shuffled back in her chair to accommodate him.

'My focaccia is famous around here,' the man said with a humorous wink. 'And the olive oil is from the hills above Salerno. Those little cakes are stuffed with almonds, and the wine,' he filled her glass, 'is practically nectar. Believe me. Try it.'

Billie tried it, closing her eyes for a moment as the lightly fizzing liquid played across her tongue. 'It really is,' she said, laughing and taking another gulp. The man nodded approvingly and took a seat beside hers, legs splayed across the gap between them. His feet were tucked beneath her chair with an easy intimacy that made Billie hot and self-conscious.

'Eat,' he commanded, 'and I will tell you about Il Gato Mammone.'

His long hair, swept back into a loose ponytail at his nape, glinted indigo in the sunlight, iridescent as a magpie's wing feathers. Threads of silver sparked among the shifting black. He tipped his head to the sky and dropped a speared olive into his mouth, his prickly throat working as he chewed and swallowed. His physicality, the rawness of his pleasure in the food, were mesmerising; Billie gulped the rest of her wine and looked away, looked back.

'There was once a lady,' the man began, 'with two daughters. One was beautiful,' he tipped his head gallantly towards Billie, 'and the other was ugly. Do you have a sister? Is she ugly? And your mother, is she a bad woman?'

Billie spluttered and put her glass down on the table, watched as he refilled it. 'No sister, and I wouldn't go as far as to say my mother is *bad* exactly…'

He grinned. 'But not a good woman? No? Let us say she is a difficult woman. This woman in the legend, she loved her ugly daughter and she hated her beautiful daughter. Jealous, of course. She sent the beauty to ask for a favour from the fairies who live in a castle in the woods just a few miles from here,' he waved his hand vaguely behind him, 'thinking she would fall foul of their games and never return. But Mammone, the demon cat, he rules the understairs of the castle with his legions of cat helpers, and the beautiful girl, like you, loves cats.'

He paused to take a drink and stuff a piece of the focaccia into his mouth. 'Have you tried this?' he asked. 'You must eat too. Just wine in this heat is not wise. Well, the beautiful girl helped the cats with their tasks and was very happy to do so. Mammone saw how pure and kind she was and made sure she was rewarded and sent safely home. There was something about a donkey and a rooster as well, I don't remember exactly.' He shrugged charmingly. 'The ugly daughter thought she could do the same and return with riches as her sister had, but she didn't like cats and wouldn't help them with their tasks and Mammone saw this. He chose not to keep her safe and she died. Or she went home with a donkey's tail on her head. It was one or the other.'

'A donkey's tail?' Billie stroked the purring cat on her lap and frowned curiously at the man. 'He doesn't sound very demonic for a demon.'

'Sshhh.' The man covered her lips lightly with his finger and then touched his own mouth. 'He might hear you. Would *you* like to walk around for the rest of your life with a donkey's tail swinging from your forehead? And that was just one of the versions of the legend. The nicest version. As I said, in other versions Mammone followed the beautiful girl home and killed the ugly sister, and her mother too. In dreadful ways.'

He shuddered dramatically and refilled her glass again, gestured to her to drink. 'My Mammone,' he said, 'has the demon inside him as well, though you wouldn't know it because he likes you. He bit one of my customers on the hand last year, right down to the bone, after the man tried to move him from his seat.'

He lowered his voice and leaned close to Billie. 'And only a few weeks ago he scratched an old lady who lived in one of the cottages behind here, took exception to her ushering him from her garden with a broom, and she died the next day. The very next day.' He tapped her arm meaningfully. 'It is said that she'd once had an evil mother and a beautiful sister who she hated with a fierce spite.'

Billie looked down at the cat, now curled into a tight ball across her thighs. His paws kneaded the air and the tip of his tongue lolled scarlet from his mouth. He looked adorable. 'Well,' she said, 'I'll make sure I don't upset Mammone in that case. Or stray near the fairy castle in the woods. Thank you for the warning, and for the lunch.'

She stooped to fish her purse from her bag, being careful not to disturb the sleeping cat, but the man waved her attempt at payment aside.

'It was my pleasure,' he said. 'And now I will lift him so that you can continue with your day. It is better that he feels cross with me rather than with you.' He grinned at her, holding her gaze for a long moment. 'And you won't do anything to harm the difficult mother?' he teased. 'Leave that to this one, eh?'

He slid a hand beneath Mammone's body and swept him deftly up, cradled him for a moment against his chest before setting him down on the ground. There had been a second as his fingers had rested on her thigh, before he scooped the weight of the cat up, when Billie had wanted to lay her hand on his wrist to trap him there. *I'm so lonely*, she'd wanted to say. *I can't find anyone who'll love me. I have to go on holiday with my fucking mother.* She raised the glass to her lips and tipped it up, emptying the last inch of wine into her mouth. 'Of course not,' she said. 'I promise.'

Behind them on the lane a straggle of people approached, with another straggle close behind them, and the man called out in Italian, waving his cloth above his head. 'My customers,' he told Billie. 'The staff from the local hotels, the cleaners and waiters on their breaks.'

She stood up and watched the group as they drew near, feeling embarrassed by their sweat-stained blouses and red faces, signs of the work they'd had to do on her behalf so that she could enjoy her holiday without the inconvenience of emptying her own bathroom bin or picking up her own towel. She was envious, too, of the way they interacted with each other, the linked arms and laughing exchanges in a language she didn't understand. They nodded when they reached her, polite but disinterested, eager to sit down for a while in the shade and eat lunch.

'*Grazie*,' she said to the café owner, and he smiled at her quickly before leaning down to clear the plates from her table. '*Prego, cara*,' he said. 'Come back again. And tell your friends.'

He had already disengaged from her, speaking in quick questioning sentences to the people who stood and sat around him, weaving between the tables and then disappearing inside the little building.

Billie hovered for a moment, feeling suddenly bereft, then followed Mammone in through the gates of the park. Almost immediately the cheerful chatter faded to silence behind her, swallowed by the thick myrtle shrubbery. She wandered to the farthest corner and settled down on the grass beside a tangle of rose bushes, to while away the afternoon dozing with the cat.

She was back at the hotel later than she would have liked. She'd fallen properly asleep and had woken with a start in the late afternoon, floundering around on the grass in a panic. It was as if someone had shaken her roughly or shouted in her face but there was nobody around; even Mammone had deserted her. The sun had sunk behind the village rooftops, the park sliced into wedges of deep shadow and a rich honeyed light.

Feeling light-headed and slightly hungover, Billie had staggered across the park to the lane, pausing briefly to run her fingers through her short hair – she regretted the decision to chop the dark length of it more than she'd ever let her mother know – and rub at the creases in her dress before stepping through the gate to walk past the little café. But she needn't have worried about her appearance: it was closed for the evening, the wooden shutters unfolded at the window and the door shut. A small brown bird hopped below the tables, pecking up crumbs. She thought the man and Mammone must live somewhere else – there was surely no room inside the building for a proper home – and the bird knew that he was safe.

The walk back up the hill to the hotel was long and hot. Twice as long as the walk down this morning had been. Billie's throat was parched, her mouth tasted bitter, and she had a rash across both arms. It itched and stung; her upper arms livid with huge bumps that she couldn't stop herself from scratching.

Vi, when she saw her, let out a scream. 'I was about to phone down to the reception desk to ask them to send the police,' she said. 'I've been worried sick. Where have you *been*? What's wrong with your arms, you look *dreadful*.' She laid aside her magazine and leapt up from the bed.

Billie pushed past her and into the bathroom, turned the taps on full. 'I need a bath,' she said. 'I'm fine, Mum, I just wandered around the village for a while and had lunch in a lovely little café with a cat on my lap, then I fell asleep. I think some insect bit me.'

'Fell asleep *where*? In the café? Were you *drunk*?'

The tub was filling with cool, cloudy water. Billie squirted shampoo into it to raise some bubbles and began to strip. Her mother, as she'd hoped, retreated quickly as the clothes began to come off. 'For God's sake,' she hissed through a crack in the door, 'have some modesty!'

As she lay in the bath, half listening to her mother clucking and tutting in the bedroom, Billie held the flesh around her hips and haunches in loose fists, weighing them in her hands, squeezing at them. When had she stopped caring about her figure? When had she morphed from a slender, long-haired young woman into this solid, lumpy, middle-aged creature? There must have been an hour, a day, when she'd simply stopped looking in the mirror, or looking after herself, but she couldn't remember the moment of transition from that to this. *I was once the beautiful daughter from the legend*, she thought as she rubbed shampoo over her shorn scalp, *and now I'm the ugly daughter. With my difficult mother. This is my life now.*

Vi was waiting, lips pursed, when Billie emerged from the bathroom. 'Come here,' she said briskly, 'let me put something on those blisters.' She turned her daughter and tugged the towel down so that it drooped at the base of her spine, dabbing the milky calamine lotion gently over her arms and back. The smell of it brought memories of chickenpox, days off school, lying on the sofa with a mug of hot chocolate and a book.

'There.' Vi snapped the lid back onto the bottle and patted her shoulder softly. 'That ought to do it. Try not to scratch and I'll put some more on before bed. Have you seen my perfume? I can't find it anywhere.'

Billie had forgotten how well her mother responded to physical illness, how a revealed weakness in others tugged a pocket of maternal warmth up from the depths of her. But not mental illness, not the kind of emotional fragility that might open the door to judgement and blame; to – God forbid – talking about the past.

'Thanks, Mum,' she said. 'It feels better already.'

'I've got a good mind to speak to the owners of that café,' Vi said. 'Show them what their manky, flea-ridden cat did to you. We'll go there tomorrow morning after breakfast.'

'It wasn't Mammone.' Billie turned away and groped in her suitcase for clean underwear. 'I told you, there were lots of midges around and they always go for me.' Her voice was sharper than she'd intended, the almost teary affection she'd felt for her mother a moment ago now buried beneath the reflexive, ever-constant impatience. She saw the older woman flinch and then gather herself, fussing loudly with her bed, undoing its neat lines and remaking it. *I'm too hard on her*, she thought as she tugged a fresh dress over her head. *I never give her credit for being anything more than just a very silly, very irritating person.*

They looped the straps of their handbags over their shoulders and left the bedroom together. Vi darted quick glances at her daughter as they made their way through the hotel to the dining room. There was something vulnerable about the steady tick of her head, swinging up and down as she sought to divine Billie's mood, and about the way she chattered incessantly as they moved along the corridors, not seeking a response but rather just pouring words into the space between them, clogging it with an attempt to connect, to fill the cavity that always seemed to be there.

There was entertainment after the meal tonight: a troupe of folk dancers performed the tarantella while the hotel guests ate dessert and clapped along. Billie tried to focus on the graceful movements, the vivid faces and swirling skirts. The dancers looked like they were enjoying themselves, their smiles huge and unforced as they swept around the floor, but she supposed they were skilled at masking any boredom or frustration they might feel at being trundled from hotel to hotel, night after night, to give tourists a taste of the 'authentic' Italy. She was desperate to scratch at her insect bites through the thin cotton of her cardigan, her hands forming claws on the tablecloth.

Vi nudged her and beamed over her empty bowl of gelato. She was loving the display, jiggling around on her seat in clumsy, jerky response to the music. Billie remembered a trip to Ireland some years ago – remembered also vowing she'd never take a holiday with her mother again after bearing cringing witness to a couple of haughty tantrums at the hotel – and Vi's insistence on seeing 'proper Irish folk dancing'. They'd taken a taxi to a nearby town and ended up in the draughty function room of a pub, huddled over gritty tables with their glasses of warm wine while a line of plump schoolchildren dressed in a shade of green so bright it was almost fluorescent had kicked and scampered their way up and down the stage. Billie had leaned over to her mother, half smirk half grimace on her face – *God, isn't this dreadful!* – but Vi, when she'd turned to meet her daughter's stare, had been beaming as widely, as joyfully, as she was now. She seemed to have a personality totally devoid of irony or cynicism, and that lack lent her an innocence, an ability to experience pleasure, that Billie rather envied.

Billie had fallen asleep quickly despite the afternoon's long nap, and she slept heavily, waking in slow and dense inches to a room that was still thick with night. Her mother was whimpering and gurgling beside her, her breath tearing in her chest as though teetering on the verge of a snore. Billie raised herself up in a daze of exhaustion and slumped back down, murmured *Sshh* and turned over, folding her pillow over her head to block out the sound. She drifted back to sleep, woke again seconds or hours later when her mother screamed and something crashed over on the bedside table that separated the beds.

'Jesus Christ, Mum, what's wrong?' Billie was across the narrow space and on her mother's bed before her eyes were fully open, not even aware of having moved. It was as if she had awoken already there, and the swift leap over the gap between them hadn't happened. She clutched at Vi's arms as she slapped and yelled, her hands slipping on the older woman's damp shoulders and sliding down her neck, fingers meeting in clenched, tight curls. She tried to reach out for the lamp but couldn't find it, jumped up instead and switched the ceiling light on.

They both reeled and flinched beneath the cruel press of harsh white light. Billie groaned and pushed her palms against her eyes. She shuffled blindly back to her mother's bed, lowering her hands gingerly when her shins bumped up against something solid, squinting as she edged along the mattress and sat down. Vi was crouched in the corner, hands also over her eyes, and she mewled and wailed as Billie tried to tug at her wrists. 'Has it gone?' she asked frantically. 'Has it gone?'

'Has what gone?' Billie's voice was shriller than she'd

intended, her heart bulging in her throat, choking her. She drew her feet up with a child's instinctive terror of what might lurk under a bed, then lowered them again and took a long breath to calm herself. 'There's nothing here,' she said. 'You were dreaming. I imagine you've woken the entire hotel with your shrieking.' She was trying for a wry, quiet tone of humour, and failing. She could see that from her mother's crumpled face, the red cheeks damp with tears or sweat and the expression guarded, even a little cowed.

'What do you think was here?' she asked more gently, stroking wet strands of hair from Vi's forehead. 'Because there's nothing to be scared of. It's just us, I promise.'

'I don't know … yes, maybe it *was* a dream.' Vi pulled back a little from Billie's touch and sat propped against her pillows. 'But I was sure there was someone, something, on my chest. I couldn't breathe properly; it felt like it was crushing my windpipe.' Her eyes flicked around the room, paused at the open window. 'Could you shut that, please?' she whispered.

Billie switched the lamp on and the ceiling light off. Shadows immediately rose from every corner of the room, flowed out from behind the half-open bathroom door. She had to force herself not to drop to her knees and peer under the brittle metal bedframes, fling the wardrobe doors wide. *Just in case*.

She walked over to the window and stood there for a moment, looking down at the street below. It was deserted. As she turned back into the room the trellis that climbed the exterior wall up past the window shivered slightly. She spun back and leaned over the sill to peer down.

A long way below her something leapt from the trellis to the ground. Something small and dark, that slunk quickly past the glow of the streetlamps and disappeared into the hedge.

Billie shut the window and faced her mother. 'There's nothing there,' she said. 'Nothing to worry about. Do you think you'll be able to go back to sleep?'

She climbed into her own bed and reached over the space to pat Vi's hand. 'Shall I leave the lamp on?'

Vi shuffled down on her mattress and smiled weakly. 'No, switch it off. I'm fine now. Thank you, darling.' Her voice was hoarse, and her fingers massaged her throat. 'I won't be able to sleep but I'll just lie here and rest until it's time to get up.'

The room was stifling within minutes of the window being closed. Billie kicked her sheet off and turned onto her side. She lay as still as possible, listening to her mother snoring lightly, and watched the darkness at the window grey and lighten, become rosy. She twitched and jerked at every sound, her breath stalling and restarting as she strained to decipher the tiny alien sounds and fathom their danger. A muffled cough from a nearby room; the sudden surge of power through the boiler that serviced the building's hot water system; the far-off machinery of the hotel's new day. Many floors beneath her bed, men and women right now would be firing up ovens and wheeling laden trolleys across rooms, smoothing crisp unstained cloths over tables. Paving the way for her, in a couple of hours, to make a choice between eight different kinds of breakfast and then eat what was on her plate as messily as she liked. She could even serve herself far too much and leave half of it for some nameless person to clear away, as so many guests did. As she had done at times.

She wondered if she'd met any of the staff who currently toiled below her, if they'd been part of the group who'd gathered at the little café by the park the day before. She doubted she'd recognise them again.

'Look at me! Look at my neck!'

Vi was dancing furiously in front of the mirror, stamping from foot to foot and pulling at the collar of her dressing gown. 'Just look at the state of it!'

Billie groaned and staggered up. 'Let me see.'

Her mother's neck and chest were etched with the same raw lumps as Billie's. They traced a livid path down her flesh and disappeared beneath her gown.

'Insect bites,' Billie told her. 'They look sore, Mum. Stop

scratching. Where's the calamine?'

'Bedbugs!' Vi shrieked. 'Or fleas! I caught them from *you*!'

It wasn't that irrational an accusation given her own identical rash, Billie supposed, despite its vicious delivery. Maybe she had picked up a few fleas from Mammone and brought them back with her. She rooted through her mother's washbag for the lotion and told her to sit down, started to dab at the marks.

'They're clustered all over your chest,' she said. 'Maybe it's a heat rash; it is really hot in here.'

'It's that cat,' Vi hissed. 'You just couldn't help yourself, grabbing at it and bringing its germs back here when you know I'm allergic.'

They had versions of this conversation every time Vi visited Billie's home; her visceral dislike for Teal – for cats in general – masqueraded as an allergy that meant he had to be shut away in a different room, or else risk her mother's insistence that she'd be ill for days after. The hostility had always felt as though it were less about Teal and more about Billie, about the wholehearted way she loved him compared to the miserly, brittle affection she doled out to Vi.

As she examined the lumps, Billie remembered last night's drama and its aftermath, the creature she'd seen drop from the bottom of the trellis when she'd got up to close the window. But it was highly unlikely that a cat would have scaled three storeys to climb into their hotel room and make itself comfortable on her mother's chest. Had she mentioned it to her? No, she was sure she hadn't.

'How are you feeling now?' she asked tentatively. 'After last night.'

Vi twitched away and marched across to the bathroom. 'What do you *mean* how am I feeling? I'm tired and itchy, that's how I'm feeling.'

Even through the closed door, Billie could hear her mother uttering little screams and wails as she examined herself in the bathroom mirror. She grinned with sudden amusement and then felt immediately guilty. For Vi, a person's appearance was the most important thing about them, attractiveness a virtue that she grimly clung to despite her old age. The colour of her shoes always matched the delicate scarves she tied around her neck, her nails matched her lipstick, and her repulsion for any woman who 'let herself go' was visceral. This rash, which was a slightly unpleasant inconvenience for Billie, was positively traumatic for her.

Vi emerged from the bathroom buttoned into a long-sleeved blouse and swathed in a bandage of silk scarves from her jawbone to her collarbone. She could barely move her head, swivelling her eyes angrily as she passed her daughter, sweat already shiny on her forehead. Billie wanted to tell her to unknot the scarves, let the rash breathe fresh air and give it a chance to dry up, but she didn't.

'I still can't find my perfume,' Vi said. 'I think the maid's had it. And I want my lipstick back.'

'I gave it back yesterday,' Billie told her. 'Don't you remember?' She turned away to hide the sudden twitch of guilt and horror, sidled into the bathroom to retrieve the perfume bottle from the pile of towels and slip it back into her mother's washbag.

A trip into Salerno was planned for the day. Billie had already offered excuses and was looking forward to another joyful stack of hours alone but as she watched the careful, wary way her mother interacted with the other hotel guests at breakfast – tapping at her neck every few seconds to make sure her scarves were still in place, ducking her head when someone spoke directly to her, as if they might be about to point a finger and pull a face of disgust – she felt a hot surge of protectiveness and pity. It wouldn't hurt to give up her time and show some support, distract Vi from her present misery.

There was a trip to a museum, and then shopping in the afternoon. Billie carried her mother's bags as they trotted from shop to shop. She nodded enthusiastically as Vi held up hats and earrings, smeared lotions onto the back of her hand, tutted over the cost of everything. Her head and jaws ached with the pressure of smiling. At times she felt the urge to drop her plastic-clad bundles of expensive goods and simply walk away, push her arm out into the crowds lining the street and summon a taxi to take her to the nearest airport: go home to Teal, and clouds, and rain. But her passport was back at the hotel, along with the rest of her money. *Only three more days*, she chanted to herself. *And then I'll be back at my little flat with all my things around me, my routines. And I won't have to answer the door if Mum comes by, I'll pretend to be out or asleep.*

They waited for the coach in a bar on the sea front, sipping thirstily at huge glasses of wine and watching the sleek, shiny boats flow past. Vi was cheerful now, crowing jubilantly over her purchases. The silk scarves had twisted themselves into a damp knot at her throat, the revealed skin blotched crimson and raw. When she got back to the hotel and realised how she looked she would be furious with Billie for not telling her, for exposing her to the stares of others. But for now she was oblivious, and she interpreted her daughter's wide smile as simply being the result of a pleasant day.

Mammone was draped over a chair outside the dining room that evening when they went downstairs for dinner. Billie stumbled to a halt, crying out with pleasure and causing a pileup of bodies as the people walking behind collided with her. She stepped to the wall and looked around for him, crooning his name, but he'd disappeared.

'What on earth are you doing?' Vi asked crossly. 'Everyone's looking.' She clung to Billie's arm and tugged her through the doors towards their table. She was wearing new lipstick, a fleshy-pale coral applied too thickly. It had clumped across her teeth and gathered in the corners of her mouth like scraps of skin.

'Nothing,' Billie replied. 'I tripped.' The scene, if her mother knew there was a cat inside the hotel, would be excruciating.

He appeared again briefly during dinner, slinking beneath the tables near to them. Billie was sure it was Mammone: he had the same blue-grey eyes, the same long tail, and when he sat down for a wash and peeked at her from beneath his raised rear leg those eyes softened with recognition and affection. She glanced quickly at her mother to make sure she wasn't watching then blinked slowly back at him, pursed her lips into a kiss.

By the end of the meal she'd collected a nice parcel of fish in her napkin, secreted on her lap under the cover of the tablecloth. She urged Vi towards the bar for a nightcap and then followed the flick of Mammone's tail out into the corridor and down to the swinging double doors that gave onto the kitchen. The space behind the doors crashed and bellowed, a legion of men and women dealing frantically with the aftermath of their guests' evening meal.

Billie paused a few feet away and called Mammone to her, crouching to lay the spread napkin on the floor. His nose twitched and he began to tread delicately towards her, then the doors swung wide behind him and he turned and slipped quickly through. Billie waited for a shout, the unceremonious ejection of an unwelcome animal, but the minutes passed and nothing happened. People passed her, stepping over the napkin and looking at her curiously, and she eventually picked it up to take back to the dining room and leave on a table.

She felt embarrassed and oddly rejected as she made her way to the bar; she could barely focus on Vi's chatter as they sat and played a game of dominoes. When she stood up to get them both more wine she caught a glimpse of herself in the smoky mirrored wall above their seat and reeled for a second, frozen in horror. She could have been looking at her mother. There were the thinned lips, the harsh lines fanning out from eyes narrowed with dissatisfaction. There was the tightly impatient expression. Shock – worse than that, grief – took the breath from Billie's chest and squeezed it hard, released it in a sudden rattling sob. She fumbled euros from her pockets to pay for the drinks and made her way back to her seat with her eyes averted from the sight of herself.

Vi, returning from a trip to the toilet, waved at her across the room. She was teetering on the edge of being properly drunk, swinging her hips as she weaved between the tables and stopped to speak to those they knew. People grinned as she passed them, covering their mouths and leaning over to whisper to their partners behind splayed hands. As Vi twirled towards her then turned away to tap someone's shoulder and hold up her new handbag – 'Italian leather. Only the *very* best!' – Billie saw that her mother's dress was tucked into the elastic of her knickers. The veined length of her thighs, the crumpled flesh of her buttocks, were displayed to the room.

'Mum!' Billie stood up and gestured to Vi, patting her own rear. Vi glanced at her and flapped a hand in dismissal, continued her circuit of the bar. Billie edged out from behind the table and stood there with her arms half raised, fingertips twitching. Then she edged back in and sat heavily down. She looked around her, caught the eye of a couple at the next table and grimaced, shrugging and sniggering as they clutched each other and giggled. Something dripped icy cold down her chest and settled in her stomach. A cruel, sickly satisfaction. A victory.

She smiled when Vi finally returned and sat beside her. She smoothed the fabric of her mother's shawl away from her shoulder and nudged her glass towards her. 'There you are, Mum. Shall we go up after this one?'

'Thank you, darling.' Vi gave her a crooked, hazy grin and raised the glass. 'Bottoms up!'

She would go back to the café tomorrow, Billie decided. She'd never even asked the man's name and now she dearly wanted to know it. She would take him a bottle of wine to thank him for the free lunch, maybe a treat for Mammone. As she folded the sheet over her hips, kicked out her legs to find a cool spot on the mattress, she allowed her thoughts to stray in a careful, sensible way towards the idea of spending a couple of hours with him before his lunchtime customers arrived. She would be less shy, more forthcoming; she would return his gallantry with compliments of her own so that he knew she was happy to flirt with him.

Vi snored and snuffled beside her, uttering little cries every few minutes. Billie was used to it now, though she hadn't realised until this holiday just how much being asleep seemed to torment her mother. Every night seemed to bring a fresh nightmare, if the small sounds of distress she made were anything to go by. But she woke every morning seemingly refreshed and serene. 'I don't dream,' she'd proudly announced last week. 'Never have.'

The window was open and a slight breeze flowed over Billie's shoulders. She rolled onto her back and closed her eyes, willing herself to relax into sleep. The queasy, spiteful pleasure she'd felt at Vi's humiliation down in the bar still thrilled through her in spurts of adrenaline. She'd tugged the dress down only when they got to their room as Vi, distracted, bent over her handbag and fumbled for the key. She'd let her mother walk through the hotel and up three flights of stairs with her buttocks on display. It was as though the cruelty of what she'd allowed had released something in Billie and she felt strong, untethered.

The breeze lifted a little more, picking up pockets of rich scent and bringing them into the room, along with vague sounds from the street below – the gunning of a car engine and the metallic crash of a bin lid, laughing voices calling out to each other. Billie pushed the sheet from her body completely, paddling it into a heap at the bottom of the mattress, and let her thoughts drift.

It was the sound of purring that woke her. Or it was the sound of Vi breathing in ripped moans, as though she were having the breath squeezed from her. Billie rocked onto her front and pushed her face into the pillow. 'Teal?' she murmured. 'Mammone? Go to sleep now.'

The cotton cover smelled different, perfumed, and there was something spread across it, finer than cat fur. It spilled into Billie's mouth, coating her tongue. She choked and coughed, trying to scrabble at her mouth to get it out, but her hands were frozen, locked into claws and she couldn't lift them. Beside her ear, much louder now, Vi whimpered and snorted, the sound clicking wetly in her throat. There was a weight on Billie's back, the steady rhythm of kneading paws.

She tried to buck her body to lift the cat, brought a knee up beneath her to raise herself, but it wedged against something solid, warm, twitching, and she collapsed forward, mouth filling again with that wispy substance. It was brittle, familiar. Hair. It was her mother's hair in her mouth, and her mother's body fluttering and jerking beneath her.

The weight lifted suddenly, and there was a thud on the floor of the bedroom, a sound at the window. Billie could raise herself now, swing back on her mother's bed so that she was no longer crushing her. She could loosen her grip now, release her mother's throat. This could be another nocturnal disturbance, another nightmare to be forgotten about when the sun rose and the room was light again. Another thing they would never talk about.

She opened her eyes for a second, saw through the thick darkness the damp gleam of Vi's gazing eyes, wide and round and strangely calm beneath her. They flickered, eyelashes whirring, and then closed. And Billie closed hers. She kept squeezing.

EXTINCTOR DRACONIS

The mythology of the Mediterranean is rich in dragonlore. In his quest to establish an oracle at Delphi, the sun god, Apollo, had first to destroy the most dreaded dragon of all, Python, while the Golden Fleece, hanging in a sacred grove in the land of Colchis, was protected day and night by a dragon so ferocious that even the hero, Jason, was unable to defeat it, calling instead on the beautiful witch, Medea, to lull the beast with her magical potions.

Dragons also abound in Mediterranean folk tales related to Judeo-Christian beliefs. The 'Book of Job' described a dragon called Behemoth so huge and powerful that it turned all the lands east of the Garden of Eden into a desert, while in 'Revelation', Satan himself is referred to as a towering Red Dragon. These latter examples may be stretching our Mediterranean boundaries a little, but most famously of all, Saint George, in reality a Christian Roman officer who was martyred by Emperor Diocletian for refusing to recant his faith, became in medieval legend a knight in shining armour, who slew a dragon in the land of Cappadocia, which is part of modern-day Turkey.

Of course, fights between heroes and dragons were recorded all across Europe, from the pagan era, when Norse and Germanic warriors like Sigurd and Beowulf battled dragons like Fafnir and the Firedrake, through to Christian times, when the warrior-bishop Romanus slew a dragon called La Gargouille that had swum up the Seine, and the Northumbrian knight, John Conyers, fought and killed the fearsome Sockburn Worm, the half-melted falchion he used still in the safekeeping of Durham Cathedral.

But for all the anecdotal evidence we have that some of these tales might be based on real events, the one that most undeniably possesses much more than a grain of truth comes to us from the Mediterranean. It is the story of the Dragon of Rhodes.

In the 14th century, the Knights Hospitaller, a military religious order first formed in Jerusalem some 200 years earlier to provide a warrior arm for the St John the Baptist Hospital, had a fortified base on the island of Rhodes, which they were determined to hold, firstly against the Byzantines, who had originally controlled the island and now wanted it back, but mainly against the Ottoman Turks, who by this time were preeminent in the Middle East. Rhodes, one of the last Latin strongholds in that region, had long been seen as a springboard for crusader armies entering the Levant, and so it was considered vitally important for strategic reasons as well as cultural.

It was during the 1330s, a period when Helion de Villeneuve was Grand Master of the Hospitallers, when a ferocious dragon was said to have been terrorising the dense pine and cypress forests on the outskirts of the city of Rhodes, eating both people and livestock and then always retreating into a murky swamp where it couldn't easily be cornered. Thus far, the tale sounds like every other dragon-slayer myth, except that in this case, Helion de Villeneuve, a real person with a proven historical identity, is named as having participated, though not in a particularly heroic way … because, though he initially sent soldiers and dogs against the beast, all were slain, and in due course he issued orders that the people must look out for themselves. However, one of his knights, another real personality from history, Dieudonné de Gozon, considered such inaction dishonourable and vowed to kill the monster.

He undertook the quest alone, finally tracking it to a flooded underground cavern, which, apart from providing the dragon with its lair, was also the main water-supply for the city. This created the additional problem of the drinking water being polluted by the rotted remains of the creature's victims, many still floating there, and the added threat that it posed to anyone who actually came down to collect water in a vessel (apparently, several of these people, mostly servants, had also been reported missing).

Gozon, fully armed and armoured, thus entered the cavern and battle was joined.

The full details of what happened were not written down, but though Gozon suffered severe wounds, he ultimately triumphed, severing the dragon's head with several strokes of his longsword. As proof of his victory, he brought this grisly trophy back into the city to the amazement and jubilation of the population, who hung it over the main entrance gate. Gozon, lauded for the rest of his days, recovered from his wounds and later became Grand Master himself, and in 1347, now known as 'Extinctor Draconis', bravely marched his army in defence of Constantine V of Armenia against the Sultan of Egypt.

The story of his battle with the dragon passed down through the generations, and yet, in 1837, a British traveller who was fascinated by the natural world and something of an accomplished sketch artist, was astonished to arrive on Rhodes and at the main gateway to the city, behold a gigantic saurian-like skull suspended overhead.

He made a detailed drawing and on his return to England, took it to the Natural History Museum, and showed it to their resident experts, who congratulated him on his find. In their opinion, he had sketched the larger-than-usual skull of a Nile crocodile.

For the record, the Nile crocodile is one of the biggest species of reptile in the modern world. Some specimens have been known to reach 30 feet in length. Moreover, they are a breed that can tolerate salt water. It is 400 nautical miles from the Nile delta to the island of Rhodes. A huge distance to travel even for one of these majestic beasts. But it is only 25 miles from Rhodes to what then was Western Anatolia. It doesn't seem too improbable that a crocodile, maybe held in a menagerie on the Turkish mainland, had somehow got loose and crossed the narrow sea to a new home.

Could this be the explanation behind many of Christendom's so-called dragon encounters? Was it a simple case of misidentification? Well, as a question, it's purely academic. Highly likely, it made no difference to those they were devouring.

VROMOLIMNI
David J Howe

Toby pulled back his arm and threw the small stone as far as he could.

In the heat, the object turned and glittered as it arced towards the water.

The surface was glassy, mirrorlike, and reflected the even blue of the sky. The stone broke the surface, sending perfect circles rippling away from the point of impact.

Toby could see the stone for a few seconds as it sunk into the clear water, and then was swallowed by the depth.

The ripples continued to grow until they gently lapped against the edge of the pool.

Then the surface grew still once more, the lake returning to a quiet, silent reflection of the sky.

Toby looked around. The heat was starting to prickle against his back again. At this time of the day, the Cretan Sun was hot. So hot that you really couldn't stay out in it very long.

Sally, Toby's wife, was lounging in a nearby chair, shaded by an awning, and eating an ice cream that she had bought from one of the vendors dotted around the massive pool in the middle of the town.

Toby headed over to her, keen to get out of the sun. It was around forty degrees, hot for the area and the time of year, but for Toby and Sally, who hailed from the north of England, it was way too toasty.

'You okay?' Toby asked, smiling at his wife.

'Sure,' she said. 'Did you want an ice cream?'

Toby nodded and headed over to the vendor.

The one good thing about Agios Nikolaos was that all the

vendors pretty much sold the same fare. So, the ice cream was all fresh and flavoursome. He chose a chocolate and toffee mix, and headed back to where Sally was finishing her own.

'It's a bit warm,' she said, waving herself with her hand to try and create a breeze.

Toby nodded, enjoying the cold ice cream on his tongue.

When they had set off that morning, leaving their hotel for an exploratory walk around the town, it had already been thirty degrees, and the temperature had steadily climbed as the sun rose higher and higher in the sky.

Now just venturing into the sun was like stepping into a baking oven. The shade provided a little respite, and so Toby and Sally had taken to scuttling like crabs from one piece of shade to another ... and then having to buy drinks and ice creams at regular intervals, attempting to stay cool and hydrated.

Sally gestured at a stray cat, which was wandering across the small plaza. 'Heat doesn't seem to affect it at all.'

The cat stopped at a plastic ice cream tub which had been left on the ground and filled with clean water. It lapped for a few moments, and then scurried off across the scorched concrete towards some nearby trees.

Toby lifted his hand. 'Look at that.' His hand had a frosting of white across the back of it. He lifted it to his nose and sniffed, and then dabbed at it with his tongue. 'Salt!' he said. 'It's salt.'

'It's that hot,' said Sally. 'Even our sweat is evaporating in seconds!'

Toby nodded, finishing off his ice cream with a couple of bites. His teeth crunching into the last point of the wafer cone.

'Come on,' he said. 'Let's head up there ...'

He gestured to the small hill on the other side of the lake. There was a path and roadway, which circled the area and led up to a viewpoint on the top. Toby loved exploring and finding new places to go, whereas Sally would have been perfectly happy just sitting by the hotel pool, under a parasol, and drinking margaritas all day.

They stood and walked across the plaza area towards the roadway. The heat sizzled off the concrete around them, making the air shimmer.

Everything was so still and quiet, thought Sally, looking around her. Anyone with even an ounce of sense was staying at home, in the shade. Only mad dogs and Englishmen went out in the midday sun!

They picked their way across to the road, and walked uphill, ducking in and out of the shade in the form of numerous trees planted along the roadside. Beyond the trees they could see the lake and the small selection of boats bobbing on the still water on the far side.

As the road rose, so the view started to open up, and they could see down onto the pool, with the Aghios Nikolaos bridge and marina beyond it ... and beyond that the sea and the small island of Agioi Pantes. The name meant 'All Saints', typical of Crete where the locals still seemed very superstitious.

As they walked, their speed slowing all the while as the road grew steeper, they saw that they were approaching one of the oddities about the island: something they had assumed was a death board.

Toby felt that there was probably a better name for it, but that was what it seemed to be: a noticeboard erected by the side of the road, onto which were pinned various sheets and cards, each with a photograph, the name of the person, and a date. It seemed that this was the date the people had died. The sun had quickly bleached the images and yellowed the paper, but these small memorials to unknown people were dotted around the town.

As they approached, a very old man, his face lined and grooved with time and age, stepped out from behind a tree, and stood inspecting the board.

Toby and Sally came closer and stopped just behind him.

'Good afternoon,' said Toby politely.

The man glanced at them, his eyes black and impenetrable. He nodded sharply and returned to his inspection of the board.

As the couple watched, the man pinned a new card to the board. He crossed himself a couple of times, and then stepped away once more behind the board. Toby stepped forward but the man was already lost to view.

Toby was puzzled as to where this person could possibly have gone in so short a time. *Very strange.*

His thoughts were broken by Sally. 'Toby? Come look at this.'

She was staring at the small card that the man had just placed on the board. There was a photograph of a woman on it, and a floral border.

'Isn't that the woman from the hotel two nights back?' said Sally.

Toby looked closer, remembering the lady who had loudly asked one of the waiters for a double scotch on the rocks. Later they'd seen her, drunk as a skunk, trying to dance. If it wasn't her, then she looked very similar.

'What does it mean?' asked Sally, almost to herself.

Toby straightened. His shirt was sticking to him, and the heat was so uncomfortable he could barely think.

'No idea,' he said.

There was still no sign of the man who had placed the card, and no movement in the air. Even the ever-present crickets were silent as though they too didn't have the strength to sing in the oppressive temperature.

'Come on,' he said, trudging up the hill again. 'Maybe there's somewhere to get a drink at the top.'

Sally took a final look at the card. It *was* the woman from the hotel. She knew it. But she wasn't sure what the relevance of her picture being placed on this board was.

She stepped away and started up the hill, following Toby. The view was really starting to open up now, and as they progressed a little higher, so the air seemed to become a little fresher, with a slight breeze moving past them, cooling their skin and bringing much needed relief.

Whose idea was this to come somewhere so oppressive on

holiday? She blinked as sweat trickled into her eye, and she tasted salt on her tongue. Sally was fast losing her will to keep climbing. *There had better be a taverna at the top!*

The lager was ice cold, and as soon as the waiter set the two glasses down in front of them, condensation sprung forth.

Toby and Sally sat with a panoramic view down over the centre of Agios Nikolaos. The pool, a supposedly bottomless salt lake called Voulismeni, was below them. To the horizon, the Mediterranean could be seen along with the bay of Mirabello in the distance. Set in the sea was the island of Agioi Pantes, shimmering slightly in the heat haze. It was beautiful and almost made the painful climb in the heat worthwhile.

Sally picked up her lager, her fingers prickling on the coolness of the glass, and took a large gulp of the chilled liquid.

She swallowed another draft.

'That hits the spot,' she said, smiling.

Toby followed her lead and savoured the cold drink as it went down his throat and cooled his core. 'I like that they chilled the glasses,' he commented, studying the glass in his hand and turning it to look at the condensation pooled all over it.

The waiter stepped over. He was presumably also the owner of the taverna, a weathered, lined man, with calloused hands and an all-year tan. He had a patterned scarf around his neck and a stained, once-white pinafore around his waist.

'Another?' he asked.

Toby smiled and downed the rest of his pint. 'Please,' he said.

Sally smiled. 'Thank you,' she said. 'You have a beautiful town.'

The man smiled, showing a row of teeth like aged kerbstones. 'We like it,' he said.

'The lake,' said Toby. 'What's it called? Voulismeni?'

The man again smiled. 'Ah,' he said. 'Yes. We call it Vromolimni ... it means ... the lake of ... the lake of smells!' He chuckled. 'My English is not so good.'

'Lake of smells,' said Sally. 'Lovely! Well, I can't smell anything ...'

Toby nodded, 'Except for your food!' he said, smiling at the taverna owner.

'Can I ask,' said Sally, 'On the way up here we passed a noticeboard by the road. Lots of pictures of people on it. What is it?'

The man's smile flickered, and he crossed himself quickly. 'Here in Agios Nikolaos we celebrate the dead.'

'Celebrate?' echoed Sally.

The man nodded. 'The dead are still with us. It is only their physical presence which leaves. Their body. Otherwise, they remain ... and they ... look over us. It is right that we celebrate them for they bring great harvest and sunshine and rain and all that makes our town so prosperous.'

Sally took this in. She had heard of other pagan beliefs over the years, and of course it was widespread in the past that the farmers prayed – and even sacrificed – for good weather and for spring to follow winter. Strange to hear similar here in this modern age though.

'And you,' said the man. 'Are you passing through? Here on holiday?'

Sally nodded. 'Yes, we're just here for a couple of weeks, and then back home to the normal grind.'

The man nodded thoughtfully.

'We saw an old man pinning a picture to the board? He vanished before we could speak to him.'

The taverna owner shook his head. 'You saw ... no ...'

Sally looked at Toby. 'We did see. A man ...'

The owner narrowed his eyes and looked at the tourists carefully.

'It has been very hot this year,' he said carefully. 'We hope this breaks soon or the fruit crop will spoil.'

'Well, yes,' said Toby. 'It could do with being a bit cooler.'

The owner blinked and seemed to emerge from his thoughts. 'Another drink?' he asked cheerfully.

Sally felt a shudder pass through her. A goose walking over her grave, her mother used to say.

'Yes, please,' said Toby. 'Another two.'

The owner nodded with a strange little bow and backed away.

'What was that all about,' asked Sally. 'Very strange.'

Toby nodded. 'I know … shhh, he's coming back.'

The man reappeared with two more chilled glasses filled with clear, frigid amber lager. He placed them on the table in front of them.

'Compliments of the town,' he said with another wide smile.

Adam grinned back. 'That's very kind,' he said and picked up his glass. 'Here's to the town!'

Sally picked up her glass and they clinked them together.

The man backed away, still smiling.

Sally turned her attention back to the view, her gaze drifting down to the large, still pool beneath them. She could see that the colour started with a paler blue around the edge, which then rapidly faded to a deeper blue and then almost black towards the centre. It looked a little like an eye, she thought. A massive eye looking up out of the earth and into the sky.

The afternoon drifted on, and with three more lagers placed in front of them, Toby and Sally were feeling quite mellow by the time the sun started to descend. The place was renowned for its sunsets, and the evening looked like developing into one of the best yet, as the sky started to tinge with pinks and reds as the sun sank towards the sea.

Toby roused himself. 'We need to get back,' he said.

Sally looked at the last inch or so of lager in her most recent glass and nodded.

They pushed themselves from the table, and looked around for the owner, so that they could settle up. He was nowhere to be seen. In addition, they noticed that they were now the only people in the taverna.

When they had first arrived, there were about three other

couples sitting and enjoying the view, but as the afternoon had progressed, they had drifted away.

'Oh well,' said Toby. 'We can always come back tomorrow and pay then.'

They headed for the exit to the taverna, and made their way down the road again, back the way they had originally come.

As they passed the houses on the left, they could see slight movements as windows closed, shutters gently eased together and curtains twitched. It seemed that their progress was being watched.

'I don't like this,' said Sally, holding onto Toby's arm. 'It's only early, so why are they all inside and shutting up?'

'No idea,' said Toby. 'Let's get a move on.'

A hundred yards or so farther on, and there was a sharp hissing noise from the left. Toby shot a look to see a local woman standing in the doorway of her house. The woman shook her head and said, 'Hurry!'

Sally and Toby stopped walking and looked across at her. 'Hello?' Sally said. 'What was that?'

The woman took a hesitant step forward.

'We can't stop it,' she said. 'It's coming. *Grigora, ela, tora!* Quick ... come now!'

Sally looked at Toby. 'What's coming? What are you talking about?'

There was a flurry of movement behind the woman, and a man appeared. He shouted something unintelligible in Greek and grabbed the woman's arm, pulling her back into the house. The door shut with a slam which echoed around the two people on the road.

Toby and Sally looked at each other, and then around them.

There was no sign of anyone else, and everything was still.

To their right was the escarpment leading down to the pool, and the water was still and calm. The sun was dipping lower and lower, the light taking on a scarlet tinge, which lit everything with red and black shadows, picking out the textures in the tree trunks, rocks and house walls.

Sally crossed her arms and shivered. It was still very warm, and there was no breeze.

'I … I think we need to get back to the hotel,' she said. 'I don't like this.'

Toby nodded and strode down the road towards the plaza.

Sally followed, looking around herself and wondering why she was feeling so on edge.

There was a movement out of the corner of her eye, and she looked across the road to where the strange, ancient man had once again appeared. He stepped towards the display board and pinned something to it, before once more going around it and disappearing into the undergrowth on the other side.

Sally walked across to the board.

'Toby! Look at this …'

She pointed at the piece of paper that the man had just pinned to the board.

It was a photograph of her and Toby. Blurry but obviously them and taken the previous day at the hotel. Sally was sitting on the sun lounger applying lotion, and Toby was standing beside her, drying himself off as he had just emerged from the pool.

'What the fuck …' muttered Toby. 'Where did that man go?'

He looked around the board and into the tree and bushes lining the side of the road. There was nothing there. Five feet farther and the edge fell away towards the walkway around the pool. There seemed nowhere for anyone to go.

Toby checked the photo again. It was definitely him and Sally … but who took it? And why was some stranger pinning it to this board?

'I think we need to go,' said Sally, looking around again. 'I really don't like this.'

Toby nodded and set off down the hill once more. Sally followed, the only sound the flapping of her heel-less shoes against the tarmac.

As they approached the bottom of the hill and the plaza which bordered the lake, there was a splashing sound.

Sally looked around, trying to find the source, but all she could see was a growing circle of ripples on the top of the water. As though a rock had been thrown into the lake.

She stopped and watched as the ripples raced each other wider and wider.

The air was oppressive and clammy, and the light had dulled to a red glow which illuminated everything around them as though it was washed in blood.

There was another sound, a strange sucking noise, that of a thick drink being siphoned up through a straw. Sally looked at the water and saw a dark shape emerging in the centre.

She sniffed as the most stomach-wrenching smell came to her. It was like the worst septic tank, a stench of old effluent and decay.

She looked over at Toby and saw that he too had stopped and was watching as something slowly rose from the lake surface.

At first, Sally wasn't sure there was anything there. The light was fading and the red glow suffused everything, but the surface of the water was undulating and moving, sending ripples out towards the edges of the pool while the centre seemed to rise up.

With a sucking noise, a form crested above the water, a red-black sheen of liquid spilling off it as it rose. The lake splashed and cascaded around it, while smaller objects emerged all around the central mass, cutting through the surface smoothly as though they were somehow designed to flow with the lake rather than against it.

The smell intensified as it moved, and Sally gagged. She covered her mouth and nose, but the stench still broke through and filled her nostrils.

The water bulged. Something vast was coming up from deep below, and the sound was that of a wellington boot being slowly lifted from a pool of thick, gelatinous mud.

The lake sloshed around the edges as the thing heaved itself out, and when it fell back, the water level dropped by at least a foot, the space that the object emerging had taken was now being filled with water.

Sally took a step back, her eyes not quite comprehending

what was in front of her.

It was dark and seemed to suck the light into it. The redness from the lowering sun cast shadows over the creature, and it glistened as the water fell from it in sheets.

It was a central mass, from which numerous arms, or tentacles emerged, each moving independently from the others in a slow dance. Some of these arms had something like crab or lobster claws on the end, which opened and closed slowly, as if the creature was stretching.

It continued to rise from the pool, impossibly large, and blocked out the remaining light from the sky.

As Sally watched, a tentacle emerged onto the land, and slithered across the paving slabs of the poolside atrium. She was rivetted by the spectacle and unable to move. The appendage appeared to be seeking something, and touched the ice cream seller's hut, which was all closed up for the night. It gently caressed the wall of the hut before moving on.

Something touched Sally's leg and the spell she was under broke as she jumped back with a squeal.

Another of the tentacles moved around behind her. She jumped over it and looked around for somewhere to run. There was nowhere.

Toby hurried to her. 'What is that smell,' he said. 'And that … thing!'

The number of tentacles and limbs now exploring the dry ground had grown, and the splashing intensified as the creature shifted itself closer and closer to the edge of the pool.

They looked up at the being as it towered over them. They could see it was supporting itself on larger tentacles, or arms, and that they had embedded themselves into the sides of the cliff around the back of the pool.

'We have to …' began Toby, but he was knocked off his feet by one of the questing limbs of the creature. Immediately, the appendage returned to explore what it had touched, and Toby shrieked as he was whacked across the plaza.

The creature moved forward relentlessly. And the smell roiled around them like poison gas.

Sally found herself trapped in a closing nest of writhing, suckered arms, and she span from side to side as she realised that she could not get away.

The creature swept both Toby and Sally up, nestled in a cradle of wet, slimy flesh, and tipped them screaming into the centre of its body where a dark cave opened up.

The sounds of their cries abruptly stopped as they vanished inside the glistening, black and red tinged maw of the creature.

There were further splashing sounds, and a slithering, sucking noise, as the creature returned to the water. Foot by foot it sank back down into the black pool, its tentacles returning with it, making one final sweep of the plaza, as if seeking whatever sustenance might remain.

As the sun dipped below the horizon, the thing slipped beneath the murky depths. The surface heaved gently in its wake, ripples chasing each other to the rim of the pond, the water level again returning to its normal height.

The smell slowly dissipated, growing weaker.

A slow dripping noise was all that could be heard as the last remnants of water ran to the ground from the ice cream hut and the edges of the pool.

Then there was silence.

Morning broke, and on top of the hill above the pool of Agios Nikolaos, the owner of the taverna, Demitrious Doukas, opened up the shutters.

The sun was already above the horizon and peeking over the hill behind him, and the insects were chittering and buzzing in the nearby olive groves and hedgerows.

Demitrious pulled a damp cleaning cloth from his belt and wiped over the tables, cleaning them of the morning dew and of any debris which had fallen overnight.

The intense heat from the last few weeks had broken, and the morning was fresh and beautiful.

He looked down the road and saw the back of the display board which celebrated those who had died. He crossed himself.

That last couple seemed nice. But nice wasn't something he was prepared to think too hard about. In this town, it was important that the traditions were upheld, and, again, Nikolaos had fulfilled the bargain. Sacrifice for continued good health, good weather, and good fortune for the town. It had worked for his father and for his father's father, and as far back as the family oral history would go.

Those who tried to change the system ... bad luck befell them. And those who tried to escape, well, Nikolaos had a way of finding them.

A small yellow bird flew down and perched on the back of a nearby chair, eyeing Demitrious with a twitchy head.

A squirrel ran across the courtyard of the taverna and foraged in one of the flower beds for seeds or other foodstuffs which might have ended up there.

Demitrious smiled and looked over the horizon at the small island of Agioi Pantes, and at the cerulean blue sky.

Life would go on. It would always go on.

He looked down at the pool, quiet and still and serene. Vromolimni – the stinky lake – and sometimes it really lived up to its local name. The surface was like a mirror this morning, reflecting the azure of the cloudless sky. A perfect summer day.

He turned and entered the taverna ... there would be guests soon. People to serve cold beer to, and to enjoy his dolmades, tiropita and saganaki.

Life was good. And, with Agios Nikolaos' help, it would stay good.

THE OTHER DEVILS

In 1971, Ken Russell's historical horror movie, **The Devils,** *caused controversy wherever it was screened. It told the tale of the alleged possessions at Loudun in central France in 1634, a real-life incident, which culminated in the burning at the stake of Father Urbain Grandier for witchcraft and sorcery. Russell being Russell, the movie was filled with sacrilegious dreams, graphic torture and wild histrionics. But it served to bring a genuine witch trial of the 17th century, little known by the 20th, back to public consciousness. However, what might surprise the average person is that the case of the Devils of Loudun was neither the first nor the most sensational scandal involving demonic possession in a French nunnery. This honour goes to a similar incident at the Ursuline convent at Aix-en-Provence over 20 years earlier, without which a whole series of 'nun possession' outrages, including Loudun, would likely never have occurred.*

It is easy for modern people to sneer at these events and dismiss them as tragedies caused by gullible fools who did terrible things because they were too uneducated to know better or because they were being steered by a sinister autocratic institution, i.e. the Catholic Church. But that would be too simplistic an approach. There were many complex social and cultural reasons why the horrors at Aix-en-Provence were allowed to happen, not least the absolute faith that many had in the Divine at a time when life for most was shorter, uglier, and more filled with chaos and suffering than many today could ever imagine.

That said, it is certainly true that the Catholic Church in France, which, as well as being a influential force, had also done good things in terms of charitable work, but was now under increasing pressure to get tough. The Wars of Religion were not completely settled, and in the minds of many, Roman Catholicism was no longer Christendom's dominant religion. In fact, among certain European rivals, such as England, Catholics had been actively suppressed. The time was probably right for the French Catholic Church to demonstrate its supreme authority by striking some spectacular blows against the Evil One.

The problems began at Aix-en-Provence in 1609 when a young novice in the Ursuline convent, Sister Madeleine de Demandolx de la Palud, was sent home to recover from various neuroses. Here, she was counselled by a handsome and capable priest, Father Louis Gaufridi. When rumours circulated that Madeleine and Gaufridi had commenced a sexual relationship, Mother Catherine de Gaumer, head of the Ursuline order, summoned her back to the convent, where she could be isolated from Gaufridi, whom the abbess considered a dissolute nuisance but no more than that.

Normality returned to Madeleine's life until 1610, when she began having fits and complained of terrible dreams in which demons visited her bedchamber. The convent's spiritual director, Father Romillon, attempted an exorcism but failed, and now other nuns in the convent, particularly a certain Louise Capeau, demonstrated similar symptoms.

When Madeleine claimed that Gaufridi had ensnared her for Satan by use of blasphemous sexual ceremonies and had given her a green imp as her familiar, Father Romillon contacted Sebastian Michaelis, the terrifying Grand Inquisitor of Avignon, who tried to exorcise Madeleine and Louise himself in a public ritual, which drew a large crowd but was unsuccessful. At the end of it, another inquisitor, Francois Domptius, concluded that Madeleine was possessed by a range of powerful demons, including the Princes of Hell themselves, Beelzebub, Leviathan, Baalberith, Asmodeus and Astaroth. Amid all this lurid theatricality, Louise also named Father Gaufridi as the warlock responsible for her condition, accusing him of numerous sexual crimes against young nuns.

Gaufridi was arrested and imprisoned but made scornful denials and no physical evidence was located on his property. The accused priest had powerful friends, and so he was released, but Michaelis was convinced of his guilt.

Meanwhile, Madeleine's deranged state worsened. She is said to have danced wildly, sung obscene songs, whinnied like a horse, vomited continually and given lurid accounts of Black Masses she attended with Gaufridi, at which kidnapped infants were killed and eaten. Whether the girl was 'performing to order', so to speak, is open to question, but Michaelis made good use of it, putting her and Louise in front of the Parliament of Aix, the local civil power. The demoniacs didn't disappoint, astonishing the audience with their sordid antics, though there were occasions when Madeline appeared to relent, claiming that she'd made it all up because Gaufridi had been her lover and she wanted him back; this might have put doubt into the court's mind, had she not been physically examined and 'witch marks' found.

While all this was going on, Gaufridi had been arrested again, and though spared torture, was kept shaven headed, chained and underfed in a filthy dungeon, where he was subjected to constant, aggressive interrogations, which left him exhausted and dispirited. Unable to take much more, he finally confessed, though in no detail. When Michaelis insisted he sign a document listing 52 different Satanic crimes, he refused, instead making a statement that he'd only admitted his guilt because he was coerced into it.

The court was unimpressed by that, and Gaufridi was still convicted of sorcery, magic, idolatry and fornication. Brutal attempts were then made to locate his accomplices, because he doubtless had them. This time, the priest, who had now been defrocked, was tortured by strappado, which broke and dislocated many of his bones. He named no names but confessed more vociferously in order to end the pain, his final words on the matter that, 'yes, he had roasted and eaten human babies ... why not, seeing as the truth didn't matter anymore'.

This was unsatisfying for inquisitors like Sebastian Michaelis, who always preferred to be completely vindicated, but he still considered that he'd won a victory over the Dark One.

On April 30, 1611, Louis Gaufridi was dragged on a hurdle around Aix, so the population could mock and decry him, and then was tied to a stake and piled with bushels. Only the intervention of the Bishop of Marseille prevented the ultimate horror. Possibly as a final indication that Gaufridi still had friends, the senior cleric instructed the executioner to strangle him before lighting the fire.

It was all over for Gaufridi, but horrific repercussions followed. Louise Capeau continued to claim that she was possessed, one accusation leading directly to the burning of a blind woman a couple of months later, while near-identical outbreaks of supposed possession occurred at several other convents: St Claire's in Aix later that same year, St Bridget's at Lille in 1613, and the most infamous of all,

Loudun in 1634. However, none of the one-sided prosecutions that resulted from most of these cases would have been possible had it not been for the precedent set at Aix-en-Provence, wherein the testimony of a supposed demoniac was deemed permissible. Up until then, given that Satan was the Father of Lies, no person claiming to be possessed was considered reliable as a witness.

A terrible door had been opened, not least because the victims of these possessions, who were mostly young women forced to live in the sexually repressed, intellectually deprived confines of austere convents, were suddenly allowed to give full rein to their tortured fantasies, which would then be taken as fact. It's notable that most of the nun possession cases in 17th century France appeared to focus on sexual deviance, which speaks volumes about the psychology of the sufferers (and probably the interrogators).

The cause of the mayhem, Madeleine de Demandolx de la Palud, lived to the ripe old age of 77, though was constantly hounded by accusations of witchcraft, and regularly needed to pay fines and serve prison sentences. She could count herself fortunate. For someone who'd admitted roasting and eating babies, such penalties seem lenient.

GERASSIMOS FLAMOTAS:
A DAY IN THE LIFE
Simon Clark

When Gerassimos Flamotas set off on his moped – an ancient machine pitted with rust – to cross the island's mountains he had hope. Or at least he clung to hope as a man ruptured by tumors clings to the dream of a miracle cure.

He had set out early. Partly to beat the fierce Greek sun and partly so he could pause at each roadside shrine to piously cross himself and whisper a prayer in a way that, to him, seemed completely sincere. It was still dark enough to marvel at how the oil lamps filled the glass-walled shrines with a soft amber light. The glow winked from the gilded icons and crucifixes. The portraits of his namesake, Saint Gerassimos, gazed back with the gentle eyes of the martyred. Somewhere He sat, thought Gerassimos the mortal, and He gazed down upon the tortured Earth. Once the torture had been famine, earthquakes, epidemics, the rusty nails of bandits hammered into flesh, or Nazi bayonets disemboweling his countrymen. Now the tortures were more subtle, and infinitely prolonged. The unpaid land taxes, the overdue mortgage payments for his farm: he'd accumulated a heap of debt as high as Mount Ainos itself, rising up before him to punch solid rock through the dawn mists.

Still Gerassimos Flamotas carried hope.

He arrived in Argostoli by ten.

By eleven he sat on the marble steps of the bank. Hope gone.

Worse. What hope he had possessed had been broken, mashed, splintered. That and his spirit, too. Spirit and hope. Shattered. Gone forever.

The sun burnt his balding head. Why hadn't he brought his

hat?

Why hadn't he hair?

He recalled himself twenty years ago. Confident, handsome; returning home from the Greek army a sergeant major; a fortune in his pocket. He remembered the evening strolls in Argostoli's town square, enjoying the admiring glances of the prettiest girls.

Oh, and the plans he had.

Now bitterness filled him. It spiked his tongue; his eyes watered and he never even noticed the tourists he hated so much wandering aimlessly up and down the road. He climbed onto the moped for the long ride home.

Twenty years ago, he had told himself, he would be a millionaire by the time he was forty. Now he fifty-one. A sun-shriveled little man. Poor, poor, poor.

When he was two kilometres from home, he stopped at the roadside. In the distance he could see his peasant's house, which hung lopsidedly on the hill. There he was going to cultivate grapes, make wine, be the biggest wine producer in the whole of Kefalonia.

Now it was Calliga. *Drink Calliga Wines* announced roadside hoardings by the dozen. *Calliga Wines Maintaining The 3000-Year-Old Wine Making Tradition.*

'Calliga, Calliga, Galliga. Ach ...' he spat. His wines would have been sweeter, the reds darker, and the rosé? Ah, the rosé would have had the faintest blush of pink like a spring rose.

Even from here, he could see his thistle-choked vines. One hundred acres of grief. Pure undiluted grief.

His wife's brother had been an imbecile. Normal vines would not grow on this soil. Everywhere else on Kefalonia, yes. But not here. Not here!

He cursed. Bitterness threatened to wash away his reason. For a moment, he wanted to kick over his moped, tear at his clothes, and run screaming and blaspheming down to the sea. To end, once for all, his miserable life in its salty waters.

Across the road, Saint Gerassimos stood in his glass box shrine, watching him with those big cow eyes. Those ridiculous, dopey eyes. A thousand, two thousand times he had prayed there.

For what?

For nothing, Gerassimos. For nothing. What was that phrase he had heard from the lips of a drunken Englishman? *For bugger all.*

Reaching down, he picked up a stone the size of a tennis ball. His arm whipped forward, the stone left his fingers. The glass exploded into splinters that flashed in the sun. Feeling hollow, emotionally flat, Gerassimos walked across to the shrine. Saint Gerassimos had fallen into the dust; his pitiful martyr's face split in two.

'I am dead,' Gerassimos Flamotas told his wife.

She was chopping at the dull earth with a pick where they grew garlic and onions. She did not look up.

'I am dead,' he repeated in a flat voice. 'The bank will repossess the farm. We have nothing, no living. I am dead.'

His wife stopped hacking the concrete-hard ground and looked up. 'We knew this would happen.' There was no surprise; her tone matter-of-fact.

'Banks!' he spat.

'The banks have been good to us. They've reduced payments; they've given us more time. We couldn't ask for anything more. Now …' – she clapped the dust from her hands – '… are you going to accept the job my brother offered you?'

'Waiting tables for tourists!' He swore and stomped his way down through the olive grove to the beach. As always, it was deserted. No tourists came here to this rocky shore.

His only daughter, Rose, had followed him. Nineteen, lumpy in her black dress, loose mouthed – and dumb. She had never uttered a word. Not so much as a single 'Mamma'.

She followed him like a shadow.

Gerassimos disliked her.

She would never marry. Never earn a living. Useless. Dead. Like him.

A dead man with his dead family on their dead farm.

He walked along the beach, kicking stones at the sea. Then, sitting on a rock, he lit a cigarette.

His daughter came to sit next to him and put her hand on his forearm. A mute gesture of affection. Gerassimos shrugged the hand away as if it had been an insect. Irritating, but unimportant amongst all his other worries.

The sun pressed on his hairless head like hot metal. He should have brought his hat. Ah, twenty years ago he had hair. Thick, jet black ...

'How much for the girl?'

The voice startled him. He looked around. Behind him, the beach was empty. To his left sat Rose, picking dry eelgrass from her bare feet.

'How much for the girl?'

Almost dazed, Gerassimos Flamotas squinted up against the sun.

A shape moved. A man certainly. Foreign, perhaps. Gerassimos shielded his eyes against the glare. The man was tall, thin. Still, he couldn't see the face. But he got the impression of wealth. Great wealth. Gentility almost.

'How much for the girl?' repeated the man.

Gerassimos struggled to his feet, struggling also to assume parental outrage. 'My daughter is no whore. Clear off before I beat you into the ground!'

The tall man did not flinch.

'Don't you need the money?' asked the man smoothly. 'Everyone needs money, I would have thought.'

Suddenly, it occurred to Gerassimos that perhaps the man was a tourist who needed a maid. Yes, that was it. He had misunderstood. A sane man would never try and purchase sexual favours of a girl from her father.

'Sir ...' said Gerassimos thinking quickly, 'my daughter is mute, she's not intelligent, but she can scrub floors, cook a little...'

The man held up his hand. 'No. Nothing like that. All I want is her ... company. Just for a few hours. Until five o'clock, to be precise.'

Gerassimos was bewildered. 'Sorry, sir, I do not understand you.' At least he pretended to sound bewildered. He'd been in the army long enough to know what men really meant when they said that they wanted the *company* of a girl.

The man nodded out to sea where a yacht lay moored in the bay. Gerassimos squinted against the dazzling glare of the sun. The boat was large, a millionaire's vessel – it may have been the angle, but the boat looked black.

'I just want her to stay with me for the afternoon.'

Gerassimos nearly asked why, but he was a shrewder man than that. 'Eh, you said you, eh …' Gerassimos plunged in: 'How much? You said you'd pay?'

'Indeed, yes.' The elegant gentleman held a parcel wrapped in brown paper. It was the size of a small pillow. 'One million euros.'

The blood thudded in Gerassimos's ears. 'One million?' That was more money than he'd ever seen in his life before.

'So …' The stranger nodded at the girl who sat dumbly on the beach watching the pair of them. 'My man will take us to the yacht in the dinghy. There we will spend the afternoon. Don't worry, I'll return your daughter in one piece. What's her name?'

'Rose,' muttered Gerassimos as if only half awake. Suddenly the father in him tried to assert itself. 'You won't hurt her?'

'Perish the thought.'

Gerassimos now became hesitant. Rose was ugly, stupid – but she relied on him for protection. He didn't want her hurt or frightened or … or violated. 'I don't know. I … I …' He shook his bald head.

The stranger held out the package. 'One million euros. Tax free. No questions. All yours.'

Gerassimos almost snatched the package from the man and tore away the paper at the corner. Inside, tightly packed, were wads of banks notes. They smelt so good.

'All right,' Gerassimos said quickly. 'Take the girl. But return her by five.'

'In one piece,' purred the man. 'In one piece.'

Gerassimos ordered Rose to go with the man. Obediently, she followed the stranger with the shadow face, down to the dinghy. The oarsman had hunched shoulders, giving him the appearance of having no head. Gerassimos Flamotas shivered.

Then the headless oarsman, the faceless gentleman, and Rose looking trustingly back at her father, slowly floated out to the black yacht.

She'll be all right, he reassured himself. She won't be hurt. In five hours, she would be back in one piece. Besides, whatever happened she would never be able to tell anyone anyway, she could neither speak nor write.

Gerassimos walked up the beach to where the gnarled trunk of a tree protruded from the stones and dirt. He lay down in the shade it offered and made himself comfortable, the packet of money resting on his stomach. There he planned his future, a warm glow rising through his body. With this money, he could hire a team of workers to strip the weeds from the fields and plant more vines; specially cultivated ones that would thrive in his gravel soil. In a dizzying rush he saw it all: a new car; a fine villa; supermarkets stocking his wine with labels that bore a photograph of his face. Here is a rich and happy man, envious people would say. And first of all, the very first thing, he would repair the shrine of Saint Gerassimos that he had smashed; he'd gladly replace the glass and buy a new icon of the blessed saint. Yes, he would restore it. Make the shrine a monument to his good fortune.

One minute after five he awoke.

The dinghy with the headless oarsman was already leaving the beach for the black yacht.

Where was Rose?

Then he saw her. She lay on the beach.

Bastards!

They had killed her.

No. No. They wouldn't have done that, surely? Probably drunk or drugged – some men like their women like that.

Holding the packet of money tightly, he hurried down the

beach.

If they've hurt her, he thought, panicking, what will I tell my wife?

But as he approached his daughter, he slowed.

She did not look right.

Rose lay naked. But it was more than an absence of clothes. Somehow, she had altered. There was still a good fifty metres between them so he could not be sure, but …

Then he saw what they had done to his poor, mute girl. He froze.

'I will return her in one piece,' the man had said.

Oh, they had done that all right. In one piece. His stomach pumped a foul taste into his mouth. He needed a cigarette.

'In one piece.'

She was in one piece. Only they had… he shook his bald head in disbelief… they had changed her around.

His eyes absorbed their handiwork. She was dead. Cold, stone dead – thank God for that mercy.

In five hours, they had hacked her to pieces. Then that sick, sick man had stitched the pieces together. The head, severed at the shoulders, had been stitched to her flabby belly. As he slid his feet nearer, he could see the hundreds of neat stitches, which sealed every cut. The face had a bruised, swollen appearance. Horrified, he looked closer still. Her eyelids were stitched together. What had they done with her eyes? The sockets were empty behind the closed skin shutters.

Her limbs had been amputated, then re-attached to the body. The arms to the hips; the legs to the shoulders. It gave Rose the appearance of being transformed into a four-legged spider. A big white spider, belly up on the pebble beach with a head jutting out from its stomach.

He couldn't take his eyes away from the only person left in the world who shared his blood. Tortured. Violated.

Softly, he whispered, 'My daughter.'

Then she moved.

Uncertainly at first, then it lifted and turned its face toward him. Like a blind person on hearing their name being called.

The sight knocked the breath from him. He stumbled back with a warbling cry. 'No …'

How they'd created this thing he didn't know. The limbs began to move. In a shaking, uncoordinated way at first, then they found their balance. They lifted the girl's torso into the air, two arms, two legs working together.

Like a bloated white spider, she began to move toward him, the bare palms of her hands and feet slapping rhythmically down onto the pebbles.

'No … No … Please …' Turning, he ran, holding the precious money packet to his chest. Behind him, he heard the rapid slap, slap, slap of the hands and feet.

Good God. She could run; she could run.

Gerassimos ran along the water's edge, the pebbles rolling, slipping, grating beneath his sandals.

Once he paused to glance back. The flesh wobbled, the sightless head set on the torso, like a turret on a tank, twisting left and right. Dear God. It listened for him – maybe it even smelt him?

Its breath came in ragged, farting crackles from its anus. There the tissue was red as tomato skin as the blood vessels strained to accommodate the rush of oxygenated blood. The now-blotching torso trembled. And, as he watched, his daughter pissed. The new internal arrangement of organs forced the urine outward and upward under tremendous pressure. It burst up into the air like breath from a whale's blow-hole; the misty spray the same golden yellow as beer in the evening sunshine.

Gerassimos Flamotas turned and ran again, his feet slipping over the loose stones. He could no longer get a proper grip. Yet, somehow, he managed to scramble away, not daring to pause again.

If that thing caught him. If it touched him …

Oh, sweet Saint Gerassimos. Save me … save me …

And as he ran, he remembered the shrine. That morning – the stone … his fury. The broken glass and the portrait of Saint Gerassimos lying in the dirt. Those dark, spiritual eyes gazing through Gerassimos Flamotas, gazing up towards heaven, as if this small, balding man was as transparent as the glass that had once enclosed the shrine.

He ran.

Until he could run no more. Collapsing, he huddled into a ball on the beach, eyes tightly shut, clasping the money to him, and begging the monster to leave him alone.

He heard the hands and feet approach. But slowly now. There was something thoughtful in the step. Then he felt a hand (or was it a foot?) gently stroke his back. At last, he had to look.

He opened his eyes and turned his face toward his daughter.

The hole left by the neck had been stitched together to form a tightly stretched rump-shaped thing. The eyeless face looked impassive – almost doll-like. From behind the creature, the rasping breathing continued louder than ever.

Where were her eyes, her pretty eyes?

Then he saw them.

Wave upon wave of revulsion battered him. Whoever had done this must despise humanity more than God loved it.

The eyes.

The breasts had been split at the nipples. A single split in each one, large enough to accommodate one eye. The breasts hung down like slack udders from where they had been stitched onto the body. The white spider had to lift the torso up so the moist, brown eyes could see Gerassimos's tormented face.

The eye-nipples blinked slowly. A single tear fell from an eye to splash on the beach.

The mute Rosa spoke for the first time in her nineteen years of life, 'Papa. I love you.' The voice was a little girl's voice.

Gerassimos rolled face down on the stones.

The little girl's voice came again, 'Papa. Why did you let them do this to me? Why?'

Gerassimos Flamotas wept. He would hear those words forever.

LORD OF THE UNDEAD

It's a curious fact that one of the oldest recorded cases of vampire-like activity in Europe comes to us from a country where vampires are mostly absent from folklore. We often associate stories about vampirism with Eastern Europe, and the Balkans in particular. In the west, there are occasional written references to vampire scourges in Britain, France and the Germanic countries, but these legendary blood-drinkers are almost never mentioned in Spanish mythology ... with the exception of Guifredo Estruch, whose tale dates as far back as the 12th century.

During the reign of Alfonso II of Aragon, a kingdom stretching from Valencia to the Pyrenees, there was much concern among the Christian nobility, and in the royal family particularly, about an unspecified pagan presence in the Emporda region of Catalonia. The written history is not informative about who these pagans were. Some kind of cult? Worshippers of the elder gods? It might have referred to the presence of Muslim settlers, who of course had populated much of southern Spain, though in that era it would have been unusual for that particular racial group not to be described as 'Moors' or 'Saracens'. More likely, it referred to Cathars or Albigensians as they became known later, a Christian sect deemed heretical by the papacy for their belief in dualism. Whoever these designated enemies of the state were, Alfonso chose to correct the problem by sending one of his favourite knights, Guifredo Estruch, to wrest the region back for God.

Estruch is referred to several times as a heroic warrior, but there is no historical record of his achievements on military campaigns. What there is evidence for, and lots of it, is his willingness to use violence. A reign of terror is said to have followed in Emporda.

Estruch, who made his base in the awesome Llers Castle, perched high on a Pyrenean crag, took fire and sword all across his new realm. Suspect villages were burned, suspect villagers massacred, and local nobles slain in battle, imprisoned or executed, their own strongholds captured or destroyed. Whether Estruch focussed his efforts purely on

313

those wrongdoers whom King Alfonso had instructed him to target is unclear, but everyone was soon terrified of him. Anyone deemed to have information, whether they themselves were under suspicion or not, were tortured, often to the point of death. There were also reputed to have been mass burnings of witches, whole fields of human beings on upright stakes set fiercely ablaze.

This latter detail perhaps puts question-marks against the factual nature of the tale. In no other country in Europe were witches burned at this time. Wholesale witch-hunting was not an aspect of life in Christendom until the 15th century, mainly as a result of Heinrich Kramer's 'Malleus Maleficarum' (the 'Hammer of the Witches'), first published in 1486. However, it was a witch who was said to have caused Estruch's downfall, cursing him as she was bound to the stake, a curse which, within days, had brought about his death. (For the record, another possible cause of his unexpectedly early demise was said to be a fellow knight called Benach, who, weary of his comrade's cruelties, murdered him with poison).

But in the inimitable fashion of all great vampire stories, the death of the monstrous antagonist at the heart of it was only the start of the terror.

Within days, the few servants remaining in Llers Castle, now a brooding half-empty monument to the wickedness of its former owner, reported seeing him, or some hideous demonic version of him, stalking the corridors at night. A few days later cattle on the estate were found to have been killed and mutilated, their hearts and entrails torn out. These could have been acts of vengeance perpetrated by the families of those Estruch had brutalised, but then there was a series of murders in the surrounding villages. For the most part, the victims were young men or boys, their bodies often found in roadside ditches, their throats cut or torn, all the blood drained out.

There wasn't a word for vampire in Europe at this time, but everyone now feared they were dealing with a member of the undead, the ghoulish relic of a creature so evil in life that Satan had sent him back to wreak further havoc in death.

Thus far to a modern eye, everything is explicable.

Perhaps a serial killer, now feeling freer to act after the departure of the ultra-ruthless lawmaker, was sating his lust in the nearby towns. Maybe the pagans whom Estruch had so ruthlessly persecuted were

Devil-worshippers themselves and now seeking vengeance against his people. Perhaps bandits or other general-purpose criminals were feeling more emboldened. But it is only now that the really inexplicable part of the story commences.

Whoever the fiend in Emporda was, he suddenly switched his attention to girls and young women, a number of whom were abducted with great violence, and only released days later. Those who survived were half-deranged and told terrible tales of their vampire-like former master holding them in the empty shell that was Llers Castle, drinking their blood, and raping them repeatedly. Almost as proof of this, each one was found to be pregnant, and yet when they gave birth, their children were invariably dead or grotesquely deformed.

You'd have thought that, by now, King Alfonso, as the root cause of all this, might have sought to put it right himself, but his name is never mentioned again in the story. In fact, according to folklorists, two different individuals are credited with destroying the monster. The first was a rabbi whose Jewish family had been decimated by the beastly noble while he was in mortal form. He, it is said, used magic from the ancient Kabbalah to dispel the malignant entity back to Hell, though perhaps because in a good Christian land it was deemed undesirable for the demon to be dispelled by a Jew, later tales insist that it was actually a fearless nun, the sole survivor of an order also ravaged by Estruch, who entered the castle during daylight, located his body in its coffin, uttered prayers over it, then staked it down and cut off its head. This second version sounds suspiciously like every other vampire story we've ever heard, all of which date from the following centuries, so it's probable that this version was added later as a form of Christian propaganda.

Remnants of Llers Castle remain today, though the vast bulk of it was shattered during the Spanish Civil War. Those who've visited the site insist that it possesses the most malevolent atmosphere they've ever known.

SHOULD NOT BE
Gary McMahon

What the fuck am I doing here? she thought, and not for the first time, as the battered old Jeep chugged up yet another narrow mountainside road. The sun was not yet at its peak but it was already a hot day. Sally was beginning to suspect that it was *always* a hot day here. The road, as much as it could be called a road, was dry and dusty and strewn with sharp stones; its ragged nearside edge dropped off a non-existent verge in a sheer fall to even sharper rocks below.

The Jeep's driver, Simon, was one of those ageing hippy types she encountered a lot on her travels: long, thin bedraggled hair tied up in a loose ponytail under his wide-brimmed hat, faded geometrical-pattern tattoos on his neck and arms. He wore shorts that were so old and washed-out the colour and type of material was no longer discernible, and she'd not heard of the band whose name adorned his equally faded t-shirt.

'Nearly there!' he kept his eyes on the road as he shouted. Hands firm on the steering wheel.

He slowed the vehicle to allow a herd of small, dirty goats to clear out of the way. A tall, stern-looking man who was standing at the side of the road raised his hand. Simon slapped the horn by way of greeting.

They continued their ascent. Below them and to the west was Lake Köyceğiz. It was a beautiful sight, shimmering like liquid mercury in the sunshine, and she wished that Harry could have been here to see it.

The Jeep rounded a bend at too high a speed, causing her to grab the edge of the door, and then it swerved onto a dry track between two high rocks, where it continued for a hundred metres before skidding to a halt.

'We walk from here. It's a short hike to the top.' His smile made the corners of his eyes crinkle; when they smoothed out again, there were lighter tracks in the dust of his face. Sally decided that he had kind features. 'Do you have a hat? This sun … it's ridiculously hot.'

Nodding, she reached into her pack and took out Harry's old Nike baseball cap, its peak bent just so and the Velcro fastener frayed where it connected at the back. 'I'm good,' she said, raking back her sweaty hair and sliding the cap in place.

'Okay. Let's go.'

Sally had flown in late last night to Dalaman Airport. The Turkish authorities had rushed through a visa so she could be here as soon as possible. A private taxi brought her to the quiet, out-of-season riverside resort of Koyuluk – a mere thirty-minute drive from the airport – where she'd grabbed a few hours sleep in a clean, well-furnished little apartment behind a cheap barbeque restaurant. Simon picked her up just after 9am. It was the first time they'd met after speaking twice on the phone and exchanging a series of terse, business-like emails.

It had all happened so fast. Everything converging towards a point at the top of this mountain somewhere on Turkey's Turquoise Coast.

She followed Simon's thin but muscular figure up the narrow mountain trail, breathing heavily, trying not to think of the extra pounds she'd gained since Harry's death. Weren't grieving widows meant to starve themselves skinny? Instead, she'd been cursed with an appetite that had her waking up at three in the morning to eat a packet of ready-salted crisps or a cold hot dog, even after consuming three large meals a day.

Grief wasn't starving her; it was feeding her. Filling the gaps created by Harry's absence with all the worst kinds of junk.

Up ahead, the rocks opened out into a wider area. The grass and shrubs here were parched from the sun. The sky looked huge, and was a light shade of blue that seemed to represent the forever she'd missed out on because of the cancer that had taken her husband away.

'A couple of shepherds found it.' Simon spoke without

turning around, but he slowed his step as they came to the clearing. 'They said it looked as if the rock had erupted from within, opened up a hole in the mountain. When they looked inside, they saw the box on the ground.'

'Did they touch it at all?'

Simon came to a halt. He turned to face her. 'Nobody has. The shepherds were too afraid – they said the air in the cave was wrong, a bad atmosphere, so they got the hell out of there and sent for the local gendarme.' He wiped his brow. It was even hotter up here, as if they'd climbed closer to the sun.

'So … nobody has handled the box?' She looked into his eyes – a shade of blue that reflected the sky, forming tiny clouds – and saw fear there of a type she couldn't interpret.

'Nobody. They were all too scared. They're all pretty superstitious around here, despite it being a tourist spot in the summer months. The old ways never die, I suppose. They cling on like barnacles to a ship's hull.' He smiled, showing crooked but white teeth. 'Listen … I have to tell you something.' He shrugged off his rucksack, took out a vape, and started puffing on it as if his life depended upon the quick inhalations. His sudden desperation was off-putting. Sally tried not to turn away from the sickly-sweet smell.

'I've been to every kind of disaster,' he said, pausing in his consumption of the vapour. 'Every kind of site you could imagine. Tsunami. Terrorist attacks. Unimaginable fires that devastated the landscape. I've seen it all – *felt* it all. Or so I thought. Until I came here.'

He sucked again on the vape.

Blinking into the sun, he continued: 'It's just a small cave in a mountainside; a hole that's opened up inexplicably. And in that cave is a small lacquered box. But you know it shouldn't be there. Once you go inside and see it – once you experience the off-kilter atmosphere – you know, somewhere deep down inside of you, that there's nothing natural about any of this. It simply … Should. Not. Be.'

Harry standing beside her, holding her hand and telling her not to be afraid. To walk on, into the darkness, and embrace whatever she found there. Use her scientific detachment to investigate, evaluate and document. Leave her emotions outside, in the dust.

She stared at Simon, trying to exert some kind of authority. 'I don't believe in ghosts or curses or religious bullshit. I'm a scientist. I believe in what I can see and touch and pull apart. Empirical data that can be logged and examined.'

Simon smiled. 'Me too. Until now.' He slipped the Vape into his back pocket, hoisted his rucksack, and walked on, expecting her to follow.

Sally walked behind him, wishing all of a sudden that she could run the other way. All the way down the mountain, to the small apartment, and then to the airport. Return home, to where her heart was. But where nothing else was, now that Harry was gone.

Two uniformed men with holstered firearms stood nearby, passing a cigarette between them. They both nodded a greeting to Simon but ignored her – standard behaviour: to some Turkish men, she'd discovered, women were second-class citizens, even educated foreign women armed with a PHD and a research grant.

Simon approached the two men and leaned in close, speaking to them in Turkish. One of them laughed and glanced at her. She had the feeling Simon had made a joke at her expense, perhaps to ingratiate himself with the guards, or maybe just to keep them onside. Whatever the reason, it galled her, and she made a mental note to pay him back somehow for the insult.

The opening in the rock face was tall enough that an average sized person could step inside without having to stoop. It was narrow, though, so they had to turn to one side and squeeze their way in past the zig-zagged edges of the fissure. As soon as she was inside, Sally felt the drop in temperature. It wasn't exactly what she'd call a cold spot; it was less conspicuous than that. Just a few degrees. Enough to notice but not to disturb or be particularly uncomfortable.

Someone – possibly the guards posted outside – had been thoughtful enough to position a few battery-powered lights on a natural rock shelf so the darkness was pushed back against the rear of the shallow cave. It was a small space – a long fissure more than an actual cave – so she caught sight of what she'd come for almost immediately.

It was on the floor. In the reddish dust. A black lacquered box that seemed to absorb the illumination cast by the lamps rather than reflect it, as if it was eating the light. She knew the box was six inches wide by six inches long by six inches deep. Once it was measured, the dimensions would match exactly: a mathematically perfect cube. There was a black clasp on the front but otherwise the surface of the box was so smooth and regular that no join was visible to evidence a lid. There were no markings on the exterior: just that lacquered effect, as if the box had been dipped into liquid darkness and then left to harden.

Harry at her side again. Silent. Grim-faced. Gripping her hand so tightly. This time she had no idea what he was telling her, but she knew he would want her to stay, to look, to cast her eyes upon this small wonder. What had Simon called it? Something that Should Not Be.

'So here it is.' Simon's voice sounded strange inside the cave, lacking in depth or inflection. A dead voice. A dead language. Words that were insufficient to express the importance of what had been revealed by the hot Turkish landscape.

'Do you think this is really it?'

He stepped forward, stopping a few yards away from the box. 'Honestly? Yes, I do. I think this is the Box of Yabbel. The artefact barely written about, hardly ever spoken of. The box that, if the legend is true, is meant to contain the end of the world.'

Sally remembered scouring ancient texts in forgotten library vaults in search of even a single mention of this box. It had taken her months to find anything: a single line in a thin volume written by a Turkish warrior two thousand years ago, a brief mention of the box in what was probably a fictional anecdote about an Ottoman prince who fell in love with the wrong woman and caused the fall of a great city.

Simon's voice was no more than a soft whisper in the poorly

lit cavern: 'I never really believed it existed.'

She looked over at Simon. On his face was an expression she could only have described as rapture.

'The atmosphere,' she said. 'You were right.' She felt cold from the waist down, warm above the belt line. There was a sound in her head like the distant droning of flies. Her lips were dry; her eyes were damp. She kept remembering small, insignificant things from her past: the taste of a particular ice cream cone when she was eleven years old; a small cut on Harry's hand caused by a knife slipping when he was peeling an apple; a blues song she'd once loved so much that she played it non-stop for an entire month; a novel that had made her cry; a small terror in the night when she'd experienced her first period.

Harry cleared his throat before speaking again. 'I... I remember the tiny things, the minute details. Things I thought I'd forgotten. How about you?' It was as if he were reading her mind.

'Is the box doing this?'

He nodded. 'I think so. Other people who've looked at it, or been it its presence, have reported similar experiences. It seems to be looking for something... sifting through our memories, like a panhandler sifting for gold.'

She shook her head. 'No. It's just a box. I can't... I can't believe this, even for a second.'

Simon laughed but it sounded sad rather than an expression of happiness or amusement. 'Just give it a few minutes. Once you've been in here for a little while, it all starts to seem incredibly real. You'll start to believe it's true. Even though it can't possibly be. After all, isn't the truth simply a myth that stops being a lie?'

'Oh, how profound. Did you find that one inside a fortune cookie?'

Simon did not reply.

She stared at the box. It did indeed look unreal... no, that wasn't quite the right word. It wasn't strong enough to express what she felt. The box looked *unearthly*.

It wasn't just the fact that the rock had opened up, or that the box should really be crushed or at least damaged, or even simply dirty. It was more the fact that it was starting to look less like wood and more like something organic. Flesh, perhaps. A box formed of smooth, charred and black-stained flesh.

It was rumoured that the artist and supposed necromancer who'd made the box – a man named only Yabbel, and about which little else was known – had stumbled upon the thing that would eventually end the world and crafted this container to hold it.

During some archaic ritual or pseudo-scientific process, he had conjured or summoned or perhaps even created the compound or object that he believed would destroy the entire universe. Then he'd done the only thing he could think of: put it in a box and buried it in a mountainside.

None of this had ever been written down; it was only ever spoken of in certain esoteric circles of academia, usually in the late hours and after too many drinks. It was considered a myth, a story that had been created from nothing, possibly by a group of bored ancient scholars trying to outdo each other with creepy tales, but one whose theme had persisted to this day.

The Box of Yabbel.

A nonsense. A joke to be brought out and dusted down after long dinners enjoyed by pissed-up archaeologists and hopped-up physics professors. But Harry – *her* Harry – had always believed that within the story was buried some kernel of a greater truth. He'd always hoped that some physical evidence of its existence would appear in his lifetime. He'd almost made it.

What should I do? How the hell should I approach this?

But Harry wasn't speaking to her; his ghost was no longer here, at her side. Perhaps it had slipped outside to share a cigarette with the guards.

'I never got to tell Harry, but I found mention of the box somewhere else last year.' Simon sounded sleepy. His voice was soft and quiet, as if he were talking to himself and didn't care if she was there or not to hear.

'I was attending a dig on a hillside near the Syrian border. Some small temple long-buried by ground heaves and movements in the substrata. A new chamber had been exposed. Scratched in ancient Orkhon Turkic symbols on the chamber wall was a sentence that translated as: 'Yabbel's Box must never be opened.' It's the only instance of it ever being mentioned outside of loose talk and chit-chat. It seems odd now that I should find it just after Harry's death, and twelve months before we find this here. As if it were … preordained.'

Sally stepped forward, moving towards the box. She knelt down before it and reached out a hand, not quite touching it but placing her fingertips so close that, if she allowed her imagination to run free, she could say that she detected a subtle vibration in the air around the box. Something like the delicate beating of a hummingbird's wings, or the thrum of an electrical charge in the air.

'I don't believe in ghosts,' she said again. 'Or magic, or devils, or God.'

Harry drifted back into the cave behind her. She could smell his aftershave, feel the air movements caused by his passing. He leaned down and told her – as he always had – that it didn't matter if she believed in them or not. What mattered was if they believed in her.

She closed her eyes, leaving her hand where it was. The vibration intensified. She wished that Harry would remain here, with her, but before she'd opened her eyes again, he was gone. He was never really there in the first place.

Softly, Sally began to cry.

Later that night, as she strolled along the dusty main street in Koyuluk, she thought, with amusement, how this was the first time she'd even been to a tourist destination. Everywhere she'd visited, whatever country in which she stayed, she had been there on a field trip or doing research funded by a grant, and it was usually in somewhere obscure and inhospitable.

This was the first time she'd ever stayed in a place where

people – normal people – went to take a holiday. It seemed ironic to her that such a great and important historical discovery should be made a few miles from here, just a relatively short drive up the hillside. Harry would have found it hilarious.

Koyuluk was a low-key resort; the whole area in which it was nestled was a conservation area, mainly because of the turtles that laid their eggs every year on nearby Iztuzu beach. The town itself – a former fishing village and still the site of a traditional market – was situated on the delta of the River Koyu, from which it took its name. It had a laid-back vibe. There were no Bodrum fun-seekers here, just Turkish families on a weekend get-away or Europeans on a quiet vacation.

The bars along the short main strip, of course, all boasted the usual cliched names: Rumours, Rodeo, M&M Rock Bar. She chose the latter for a drink because Pearl Jam videos were playing quietly on a loop on a wall-mounted television beneath the awning above the main entrance.

As she sipped a strong Mochito, an elderly man with his long grey hair tied up in a manbun paused at her table and started up a conversation.

'Are you English? On holiday?'

'Yes, I'm English. I'm here for work.'

'Nice. What kind of work you do?' He placed the tray he was carrying on the table but thankfully made no move to sit down.

'I'm … I'm an archaeologist. A professor. We've found something interesting up in the mountains.'

He nodded sagely; part of the act. 'There are many interesting things in the mountains around here. Lots of history – myths and stories. Some of them are even true.' He smiled, nodded again. 'My grandfather, he was a shepherd. He told me lots of scary stories. Ghosts and spirits in the caves, *kallikantzaroi* hiding deep under the earth. Many strange things in the dark, running in the night.'

Sally smiled and took another sip of her drink.

'Even the name of this place: Koyuluk. You know what that means in English?'

'I'm sorry, my Turkish isn't very good. I'm afraid I have no idea.'

'Ah,' he said. 'Denseness, or darkness. It means darkness.' Then he picked up his tray and sauntered towards the bar, dodging tables and pausing only to stroke a one-eyed cat perched on a stool.

Sally finished her cocktail and left a large tip. If nothing else, the owner, or whoever he was, had kept her amused so she didn't have to drink alone. As she re-joined the main street, the smells of cooking meats filled her nostrils; different songs from cheap speakers competed for customers in the bars; smartly dressed young men tried to lure her into restaurants to sample their food. She wasn't hungry. She was too tired to eat. Her stomach felt like a void; whatever was inside that box in the mountain cave had sucked her dry.

Several times she caught a glimpse of Harry – or, more truthfully, she imaged his pale, almost transparent ghost – walking through the thin crowds, leaving a bar, entering a restaurant, or sitting on the prow of a tiny boat down on the river.

On the way to her apartment she ordered *pide* from a street vendor. She still wasn't hungry, but the Turkish flatbread pizza looked tasty and she probably needed the calories if she was to put in a full working day tomorrow. She took the food back to her room on the ground floor and ate only one slice. It had gone cold. The cheese was like rubber. The void bloomed like a dark flower within her, trying to turn her inside out. Harry's presence, for now, remained agonisingly out of reach.

Sleep did not come easily that night. It was too hot and the air-conditioning unit was far too noisy. She got up several times, and finally surrendered to insomnia and sat outside on the narrow balcony, gazing up at the stars and the mountains and the daunting entrances to the Lycian tombs carved into the rocks above the river. A long-dead civilisation had created those tombs, cutting them out of the rockface and forming tunnels within the side of the mountain. Malaria and warfare had killed them off; as it had done so with many other ancient civilisations before them, death had claimed them when they were at their most arrogant.

Our turn now, she thought. *But only if we open Yabbel's Box.*

When the sun rose, she was still sitting there, a cup of cold coffee on the table before her. She'd managed to scribble down some notes on a pad. These would form the basis of her report, but she was unsure of exactly what was happening here, and even more uncertain regarding the foundation of her own beliefs.

Listening to the morning *adhan* – the beautiful and somehow frightening call to prayer emanating from a nearby mosque – she stood and stretched, then went back inside to perform some yoga poses on the apartment floor in the hope that the exercise might help wake her up. The morning heat cut her exertion short. It was cloying, even now; by midday it would be unbearable.

Her mobile rang. The screen displayed Simon's number. Pausing only for a second or two, she picked up the phone.

'Hello.'

'Good morning. Shall I pick you up in an hour?'

'Yes. I just need to shower and change. It won't take long.'

'We'll get you up there before the sun is at its peak and it all gets too uncomfortable. I'm sorry about yesterday – my rambling monologues. It's just… this thing. It's an affirmation of what Harry and I always believed. This is like a Catholic seeing Christ's face upon the waters.'

'Or in a piece of toast, or the foam in a coffee cup,' she said, unable to help herself.

He sighed. 'You still don't believe, then?'

She didn't know what to say. How to answer his direct question. A lie or another cynical quip would have been too easy and she owed him – and Harry's memory – so much more than that.

'Not yet,' she finally said. It was at least a form of truth.

She was outside waiting for him when Simon pulled up in the Jeep. His greeting was silent but affable. Halfway up the mountain, they hit a snag. A dilapidated minibus had broken down on an acute bend, its rear wheels perilously close to the drop.

'Shit,' said Simon. 'I'd better see if I can help.' He got out of the Jeep and strolled over to where the driver was standing outside the open bus doors, yelling into his phone. The two men exchanged a few words, shook hands, and Simon stuck his head under the yawning bonnet to inspect the smoking engine.

In another world, another life, she would have found Simon attractive. He was smart, funny and capable. A lot like Harry, in fact, but that was the problem: there had only ever been one Harry. In all the history of the universe there had only ever been one of him and he had taken away her heart when he died. This man was a poor copy of the real thing, a shadow of the man she had loved, and they both knew it.

Half an hour later, the bus was moving again, engine straining against the incline. Simon backed up the Jeep as they watched the bus driver manoeuvre the vehicle around the tight bend and on its way. He gave two hoots of the horn and Simon raised a hand in farewell. They waited a few minutes in silence, just to let the bus get ahead, and then carried on up the mountain road.

The armed guards were at their posts again. Sally wondered if there'd been a shift change or if those same two men had stood up here all night protecting something that did not need the protection of humans, watching something that she was beginning to suspect was in fact watching over them all.

Again, they failed to acknowledge her but they greeted Simon like an old friend.

'Don't be offended,' he said as they stood outside the opening to the cave. 'It isn't personal. It's just the way they are here.'

'Fuck them.' The words felt and sounded good coming out of her mouth; they tasted like something she thought might have been lost when Harry died but was still there, inside her. 'Fuck them all.'

The heat of the sun felt like a laser burning through the top of her head, carving a tube through her brain, down into her body, to meet the ever-present void at her centre. She felt empty yet filled at the same time with something indefinable. The closest she could come to describing it, if asked, would have been to say that she was filled to the brim with an empty light.

Then the moment passed and she felt normal again. At least, whatever passed for normal in her loss-stained world.

They entered the cave. Nothing had changed. Everything had changed. The box was in exactly the same position on the rock floor, but to Sally it seemed as if the location in time and space had altered. A temporal shift had occurred. By entering the cave, they had travelled miles – or perhaps light years – and were standing somewhere else entirely, but still surrounded by the same cold, hard rock as before.

She understood entirely why the locals were too afraid to come here, and why nobody had even tried to open the box.

Harry at her side. Touching the back of her hand. Telling her that everything would be okay. Whatever happened next, whatever went down in this lonely place, it would be all right. She would be fine.

Simon's voice interrupted the visitation, causing Harry's form to fade and disappear; a small light going out in the big world.

'I have to open the box. I have to see what's inside.'

Sally turned to look at him. There was a knife in his hand. His knuckles showed white in the gloom. 'Don't try to stop me.'

A single gunshot from outside, and then one of the guards forced himself sideways through the opening and into the cave, his rifle scraping against the rock wall. It was a tight squeeze; he was a bigger unit by far than either Simon or Sally.

The guard said something, softly and in Turkish. Simon replied, not taking his eyes from Sally's face.

'He says we should kill you. As an offering to the box, to make it serve us.'

Sally backed away, moving closer to the back of the cave, and to the box. She turned to look at it. Harry was standing there, behind the box, smiling and nodding. His face was radiant. The air was cold. Sally could smell something that reminded her of long-empty houses, of neglect and the absence of love.

In that moment everything changed, and she knew exactly what it was she had been brought here to do. In a heartbeat, she dropped down into a low squat, reached forward, and clasped the box in both hands. It felt like cold, moist flesh – the flesh of a cadaver kept cool in a morgue.

Tears in Harry's eyes. His face diminishing as he stepped back into an enveloping darkness.

'No.' It was all that Simon could say. He said it again, louder this time. 'Not you ...'

'Yes,' she replied. 'It's why I'm here. I understand that now. I understand ... everything.'

The guard raised his weapon, fingers tight around the handle. He pulled the trigger but there was no sound of detonation. It all slowed down. Everything. As if they were moving underwater. The bullet left the rifle barrel. Vapour trailed and rippled behind. Cutting through the butter-thick air. The bullet's trajectory changed: it bent at ninety degrees, turning a corner. Then it did the same again.

The guard's mouth hung open.

The bullet smashed, slo-mo, into the front of his face. Sally thought it was like watching footage of a watermelon explode, but with the film slowed right down. His face came apart in a slow flower of red. Gobbets of blood moving through the air like bubbles of fluid in an anti-gravity chamber. Chunks of bone and brain matter. Mucus spatters.

Then normal time resumed, and the body fell heavily, with a sound like meat hitting a slaughterhouse floor.

Sally's fingers had already found the invisible joints in Yabbel's Box. Her hand twitched once, and then the box opened, as if it had been waiting for the right moment to do so. So easy ... it had been waiting centuries for her touch.

Harry's face, smiling. His arms around her shoulders.

Simon standing before her, pushing something sharp into the soft meat of her lower belly and then pulling it upwards. She felt nothing. Heard nothing. Smelled and tasted nothing.

Then the world went black.

Not the cave.

The whole world.

The mournful voice of a muezzin wailing the adhan to summon the followers to prayer. The image of a small man with large hands, his body bent in labour, carefully constructing a box to contain the end of all things, to hide away the specific moment that would herald the extinction of everything.

Sally stepped forward into the waiting darkness, knowing that Harry was out there somewhere. He always had been. Waiting for her.

Something made her look down at her stomach but the blackness was by now so absolute that she could not even see herself. She felt around with her fingers and discovered a wound. A split from sternum to crotch. Smooth and curiously painless. If it were visible, she knew what she would see: the void inside her had hatched, splitting her open from the inside so that it might emerge and join with the matching void that she had let out of the box.

Then came one final thought before her mind became as dark as the place where the world used to exist/no longer existed. One sweet revelation to carry her across the threshold of nothingness:

I'm free.

SOURCES

All stories in *Terror Tales of the Mediterranean* are original to this anthology, with the exception of *The Catacomb* by Peter Shilston, which was first published in *More Ghosts & Scholars* in 1980, *The Wretched Thicket of Thorn* by Don Tumasonis, which was first published in *All Hallows #29* in 2002, *Reign of Hell* by Paul Finch, which was first published in *World War Cthulhu* in 2013, and *Gerassimos Flamotas: A Day in the Life* by Simon Clark, which was first published in *Dark Voices 5: The Pan Book of Horror* in 1993.

OTHER TELOS TITLES
YOU MAY LIKE

PAUL FINCH
Cape Wrath & The Hellion
Terror Tales of Cornwall
Terror Tales of Northwest England
Terror Tales of the Home Counties
Terror Tales of the Scottish Lowlands
Terror Tales of the West Country

MAXIM JAKUBOWSKI
The Piper's Dance
Fantasy novel

Just a Girl with a Gun
Crime novel

RAVEN DANE
THE MISADVENTURES OF CYRUS DARIAN
Steampunk Adventure Series
1: Cyrus Darian and the Technomicron
2: Cyrus Darian and the Ghastly Horde
3: Cyrus Darian and the Wicked Wraith

Death's Dark Wings
Standalone alternative history novel

Absinthe and Arsenic
Horror and fantasy short story collection

FREDA WARRINGTON
Nights of Blood Wine
Vampire horror short story collection